COOPERSTOWN

EUGENA PILEK

A Touchstone Book
Published by Simon and Schuster
New York   London   Toronto   Sydney

TOUCHSTONE
Rockefeller Center
1230 Avenue of the Americas
New York, NY 10020

TOUCHSTONE and colophon are registered trademarks
of Simon & Schuster, Inc.

For information regarding special discounts for bulk purchases,
please contact Simon & Schuster Special Sales at 1-800-456-6798
or business@simonandschuster.com

Designed by Jamie Kerner-Scott

Manufactured in the United States of America

1   3   5   7   9   10   8   6   4   2

Library of Congress Cataloging-in-Publication Data
Pilek, Eugena.
Coopersown: a novel / Eugena Pilek.
p.   cm.
"A Touchstone book."
1. Cooperstown (N.Y.)—Fiction. 2. Eccentrics and eccentricities—Fiction.
3. National Baseball Hall of Fame and Museum—Fiction. I. Title.
PS3616.I44C66   2005
813'.6—dc22   2005045168

ISBN-13: 978-0-7432-6694-9

ISBN-10: 0-7432-6694-3

Map of Cooperstown, 1788 by Daniel Smith, courtesy of The Paul F. Cooper, Jr.
Archives, Hartwick College, Oneonta, NY.

In memory of
Nick Alicino & Kitty Hamilton

Baseball is a game but it's more than a game. Baseball is people, and if you are around people, you can't help but get involved in their lives and care about them. And then you don't know how to talk to them or tell them how much you care and how come we know so much about pitching and we don't know squat about how to communicate? I guess that is the question.

GARRISON KEILLOR

SECOND

STREET

William Coop...

X HERE THAR BE BASEBALL

FAIR STREE

Andrew Craig

Gardens

COOPERSTOWN

BATTING PRACTICE

It is a haunted game, in which every player is measured against the
ghosts of all who have gone before.
—GEOFFREY C. WARD, *BASEBALL*

The psychiatric ward of the Selma Wellmix Sanitarium in
Cooperstown, New York, sits back on a hill on a cozy street
called Fair. Its windows, though barred, grant an inspiring view of
the Susquehanna River as it flees the confining womb of Lake Otsego. The river runs south over four hundred miles, through dairy
farms and woodlands, to Pennsylvania. There, east and west
branch merge, rushing onward toward Havre de Grace, Maryland,
where the river flings itself hopelessly into the Chesapeake Bay.

It is on the banks of the Susquehanna, on a June morning in
1957, that a stocky thirty-nine-year-old man called Francis (Frank,
if you know him well) stands with a group of tourists, swatting
mayflies from his neck with a battered baseball cap. He has been
explaining to these city folk that the river is prone to flooding but
that when she behaves, the Susquehanna is a wonderful source of
recreation for swimmers, canoers, and fishermen in search of
bass and muskellunge. At this exact moment—Frank has it timed
to a T—they coo, delighted to witness the reconstruction of history: the General James Clinton Canoe Regatta. The canoers paddle seventy miles from Cooperstown to Bainbridge, the same
journey made by Clinton in 1779.

The tourists have come to Cooperstown to escape the trials
of city life, to ingest some clean country air and a good old-
fashioned dose of Americana. "For this," says Frank proudly

with arms open wide, "is where the national pastime was born." He says it with grand authority, as though he had invented baseball himself. It makes the tour seem more authentic, which means more money for Frank. Not that he is in it solely for the cash. To him, baseball is the reason for everything. It's the reason he has the kind of job that allows him to work outdoors in comfortable clothing. It's the reason he thanks God each morning that he abandoned a brief attempt at city life to take up roots once more in his hometown: here, where he belongs with his friends, his woman, and his history. It's the reason for his audience, and they play their part, oohing and aahing as he explains that baseball wouldn't exist were it not for good old Cooperstown.

The tourists feel their guide is special, unexpected. It hasn't occurred to them before now that of course people *live* in Cooperstown, a place as magical as Disneyland. They are here because their heroes are here, the spirits of ballplayers past, to bring their children, or because they came here with their own parents when they were kids. The men throw their arms lovingly around their wives, who smile contentedly, having read about this pristine country town in the pages of some stylish magazine. They request photos of Frank, who charges a buck for headshots, and two for full-body poses. He looks just like they imagined a Cooperstonian would: weathered, elfin, with a mischievous twinkle in his eye and a thick gray beard. The beard is actually the victim of a bad frost job, an accident that occurred when Frank's wife attempted to enhance his appearance, but they don't need to know this. It's good enough for them that their puckish guide wears saddle shoes and a funny tie portraying Roy Rogers, whose TV show Frank is sad to lose to "all those *Wagon Train*–type westerns." He sports one of those fancy electric watches and little pea-green woolen shorts that look out of place in small-town America, but the tourists don't mind, because they are not yet sure what is and isn't part of the show. The reality is simply that pants annoy Frank; they're hot and they itch. He bought the shorts years ago at the garage sale of a German neighbor and has been wearing them ever since. He dons a baseball cap that's one size too small and thus seems to perch on top of his balding head. The cap is pointed on top from being pulled by its wearer, which only serves to make the elfin effect more pronounced. The tourists take snapshots of the canoe race, quickly, for Frank says there is plenty more to see. They haven't even gotten to the best part, the foremost sports museum in the world: the National Baseball Hall of Fame!

Frank takes advantage of the photo op to nibble the sandwich his wife packed for him. It is smothered with margarine; he's about to ask if the newly popular sandwich spread is big in the city as well, but before he can open his mouth he is interrupted by a tap on the shoulder and a gruff voice saying, "Hey there, tour guide." This annoys Frank, because he prefers the title "historian," one he intends to win fair and square from his friend Charles, who runs the local history museums and who Frank thinks is more of a "curator." And it is Charles who addresses him now, his young son in tow. One might assume they've appeared innocently out of the blue, but Frank knows *nothing* is spontaneous with Charles, who is somewhat of a control freak. He hands Frank a note, crushing it against his chest with an urgency that makes Frank uneasy. He's about to shove it back when he sees Charles's boy handing out brochures to the Farm Stead museum. Frank isn't falling for it, no way. He shoves the note in his pocket, motioning for the intruders to "git," because he isn't being paid to pass notes on the street like a little girl.

He opts for the scenic route, guiding his guests down River Street, which slopes gently toward Lake Otsego, known locally as Glimmerglass. Frank says the name comes from a book by James Fenimore Cooper, "America's foremost frontier author whose father established this very town." He says the book is *The Last of the Mohicans,* although he is not sure that is true. He has told these stories so many times that everything, fact and fiction, gets muddled together, and the more he muddles them the better they sound. He knows from a display at one of Charles's museums that that book is 131 years old and still selling, so it seems as good a source as any.

He shepherds the tourists down a stone staircase that leads to the shore, gesturing for them to stop when they reach a granite veranda imbedded with a white arrow that indicates north. They take pictures of the Sleeping Lion, Cooperstown's modest mountain, and of Kingfisher Tower, a local landmark teeming with gulls.

Frank speaks quickly, mumbling a myth about an unflappable missionary who lay beneath a rock in the water during a game of Test Your Faith with some Indians. "'My god is bigger than your god,' each claimed. Whoever lay under the rock and was rescued, won." The tourists want to know who won, they always do, and Frank says the Indians, because he hates this part of the tour. He hates the dinky little boulder, Council Rock, that lies at the end of his prompter, because only someone who is soft in the head would believe a whole tribe of Indians once sat on it or that a grown man got stuck beneath it, unless they were all midgets. He can tell these are not the type of people to fall for it anyway. They're clever people. City slickers.

He takes them upriver and is about to point out his home, which he is proud to claim is among the oldest buildings in town, evidenced by the fact that the front is painted one color and the sides another, an old Cooperstown tradition. But his wife pokes her head out the kitchen window just then, and Frank fears she will come out and start interrogating people, which she does sometimes, being a curious and friendly person. He needs her to stay inside today, for she has a puke-green beauty mask slopped all over her face, which she made out of bad oatmeal, and it looks like she has dyed her hair again, this time the color of apricots. He shakes his finger—no, no—in her direction, softening the command by blowing her a kiss, which she snatches from the air, smiling a smile that sends Frank's stomach down around his knees. He thinks about how lucky he is to have a gal like her, how pretty she looks even with a puke-green face and orange hair. She is his girl. His beautiful girl.

He gestures with his prompter toward a row of old stone mansions that line River Street and begins to talk about ghosts. As if on cue, blind old Dr. Buckner, with his uncanny sixth sense for fresh blood, toddles out of his Victorian Gothic-style house and ushers the tour right out from under Frank's nose. He takes the tourists inside, where for a buck-fifty a head they behold a portrait of Judge William Cooper, the town founder, whose eyes follow wherever they move. They do *seem* to, the tourists think before stepping back outside. A pack of kids fly down the street on their bicycles, nearly knocking one or two of them over. When the kids reach the wall that lines Dr. Buckner's front lawn, they peddle faster and avert their eyes. Frank says this is because beneath that wall more Indians are buried upright. He says to "watch your step now," because if a stone comes unfettered and falls into the street, "you can bet your great aunt Martha it's a peeved native eager to stand." The tourists seem nervous until Frank explains, "This is a town built upon myths." His voice is full of confidence and showmanship, a pride in all things Cooperstown: "A place where spirits—the ghosts of farmers, warriors, pioneers, and ballplayers—share farmhouses and pastures, shoreline and barrooms with the living. And leading the way are the Holy Trinity: Judge William Cooper, James Fenimore Cooper, his son, and Abner Doubleday, who invented the sport that embodies our nation." He says the controversial Judge Cooper founded the town in 1786 and then clod-hopped his way toward early capitalism, surviving everything from a stint in the U.S. Congress (and, subsequently, a near impeachment) to the death of his beloved daughter. He also raises the question of whether all the land the judge doled out so eagerly along the way belonged to him in the first place. He calls Cooper "an old sugar-pusher," touting the tastiness of New England's maple products to the likes of George Washington and Thomas Jefferson: "From land to maple sugar, and from potash to politics, Cooper took full advantage of the new American republic." A republic that, according to Frank, meant land was a free-for-all, and "too bad for you if you if you didn't step up to the plate and grab some for your-self."

He asks the tourists to close their eyes, to imagine the draw of this little village nestled between the Catskill and the Adirondack mountains, to early settlers who poured in from throughout New England and New York: Puritans, Yanks, farmers and surveyors, the ambitious and escapists, all manner of migrants seeking a place to call home. The tourists do as they're asked, closing their eyes to welcome the spirits of those early arrivals, exhausted and elated, by wagon or on foot in time for what Frank calls Open-ing Day. They view this Eden through pioneer eyes, a land of rolling hills where a great gushing river spills from a crystalline lake surrounded by miles of green. They see it like Frank calls it: Indians packing up to leave the field, white folks gearing up for their own at bat, and a state road built to increase attendance. They see churches springing up, just a few, because "Judge Cooper was a rainy-day Quaker at best." They see settlers, one by one taking their place in "the great green ballpark of independ-ence." They see houses and shops—Cooperstown a tight-knit, compact community where neighbor lives on top of neighbor to ensure everyone gets along, that they play nice. Frank explains that back in the day, if your house was brick you batted for team Genteel. And if you squatted in a wood hutch and let your ani-mals run amok? Well, then you were more or less a loser.

The tourists open their eyes as Frank concludes his history les-son with a line about the final score: Pioneers thirty-five, Natives zip. He says, to soothe any critics in the crowd, that of course Cooperstown still proudly upholds certain native traditions, like the annual Tots Turkey Trot, the Singles Snowshoe Slog, and, a plug for Charles's sake, "there's also plenty of basket weaving and loom tinkering to be done at the Farm Stead if you're not one for stimulation." He says the horses that used to race across the frozen Glimmerglass during winter Frost Fest are now pickup trucks and that the birch canoes once used in the regatta are now fiberglass, but the tourists get the idea. One of them remarks that

Cooperstown seems to do a lot of racing, which annoys Frank, because anyone can see if you want to sit back and enjoy life, *this* is the place to do it. A man can watch his life go by and not feel sore about it in a town like Cooperstown; watch it like a motion picture and, if he's smart, take notes along the way. Frank won't explain this to outsiders, though. Nor will he answer offensive questions about why the lake is such an "unripe color," which is thanks to another dye job (the current mayor's bright idea to make aerial shots on travel brochures more enticing).

Frank excuses himself, stepping briefly beneath an elm tree to read Charles's note. Find out what's so damned important that it can't wait until the end of the workday. The note turns out to be from Amos, Cooperstown's wannabe mayor and another of Frank's pals, one he hates to admit is the leader of their posse. The note says to meet him, Charles, and their buddy Duke Cartwright, who coaches ball at the school, in Duke's office in thirty minutes. Frank crumples the note, refusing to end his tour before he is good and ready, even though he can tell from the way Amos has written in large capital letters that the meeting is important. As a compromise, he shuffles his herd a little quicker down Main Street to a footbridge spanning the river. The kids are back, looking smug in the illusion that they're riding on water, like a gang of Jesuses on banana-seat bikes. When they reach the other side of the bridge they slow. The pavement turns to gravel, which means inching their bikes through an iron gate to a narrow path in the woods. "To the left," Frank says, "is Indian Mound." More natives entombed upright. One of the kids tells the tourists that Cooperstown's elementary school teachers bring their classes to the mound each year during Local History Month. The tourists smile, envisioning these little Cooperstown cherubs consuming baloney and Chex Mix on top of the dead. It is an oddly wholesome image at once shattered by a loudmouthed boy with a duck's-ass hairdo who points out the Louse House, a small shack on the riverbank where he claims half the town's youth forfeit their virginity.

Frank tries to shoo the kid away with his cap, but the kid starts hassling him, begging for a part-time job at the baseball museum, where Frank is chief security guard. Frank is about to rip into this young smart aleck when he recalls something his wife said: the kid's ma ran off with a tourist. He holds his tongue, but only until the kid starts poking fun at his beard, asking the tourists if they've seen that new fright film *I Was a Teenage Werewolf.* The tourists laugh and Frank shakes his stick at the boy, turning red as a beet. The tourists sigh, disappointed, because they liked where this was going. The children pedal off, disappearing into the woods. They leave behind a toy that looks like a plastic pie plate to Frank, who tosses it into the river so it will float down to meet them. He knows they have gone to swim by the old stone bridge. The bridge is where Cooperstown's youth go when contemplation becomes involuntary, to skip school, to lament broken homes or broken hearts. Mostly they go there to get into trouble, and Frank knows this because he used to hang out there too. He steers the tour in the opposite direction, figuring Cooperstown deserves to keep one or two things for itself.

As they walk up Main Street, Frank takes advantage of the lull in conversation to reflect on a bright summer day just like this in '39. He and the guys had rigged a rope around a tree overlooking the Susquehanna and had swung from the bridge to the shore, making bets as to who would fall. Frank had gone first and he remembers being scared, not trusting the rope to keep him suspended above the water, where the snapping turtles supposedly lurked. It's a summer he will never forget. The summer of the baseball centennial—two members of each of the sixteen major-league ball clubs were in Cooperstown for an all-star game. The centennial lasted all summer, including a couple of exhibition games: Yanks versus Bears and the Philadelphia Athletics versus the Penn Athletic Club. He and the boys were lucky enough to witness the actual induction of eleven out of some twenty greats initially elected into the Hall of Fame who were still living, including four of the inaugural five: Ty Cobb, Babe Ruth, Honus

Wagner, and Walter "Big Train" Johnson. Christy Mathewson had passed away. They got autographs from Ruth and they got to meet Cobb, who signed balls for them and gave Amos the idea about keeping a diary, especially to record his finances, no matter how "willy-nilly" things got. In 1940, they got to witness the first Hall of Fame Game, Chicago versus Boston (Cubs 10–9 over Red Sox), and the museum's first exhibit, the Doubleday Baseball. They watched postwar interest in baseball grow and with it many legends develop. In Frank's mind, they were their own inaugural club, the real McCoys, the last of the Mohicans: Amos, ever waging an eternal war against the Coopers, determined to one day run the town; Duke, with his incredible gift of gab; Charles, insisting he be called Chuck, because his father was called Charles and he comes from a long line of sons who butt heads with their old men; and Frank, who would rather be here with them than anywhere else in this world. Soon they'll induct a fifth member into their club, just like Ruth and Cobb. But Frank doesn't know that yet. Nor does he know that it will happen without their permission on this very day. For now he is content with yesteryear, with the image of Cartwright shouting, "Your mama's a Commie!" as he jumps from the old stone bridge, that architectural acknowledgment of their coming of age.

He moves the tour toward Doubleday Field, abridging the tale of its namesake, Abner Doubleday, who he says attended school in Cooperstown before going to West Point, and took it upon himself one day in 1839 to turn the game of town ball into something more substantial, more sophisticated. "Doubleday took a stick, drew a diamond in the dirt, threw some bases around it, and the Lord shone down upon it," Frank says. He says a foolish few may contest this, but a special panel, at the behest of one Albert Goodwill Spalding, proved it so in 1907. "The miracle," he says, was reconfirmed twenty-six years later when a dingy, old cloth-stuffed ball belonging to an acquaintance of Doubleday (one Abner Graves, a Colorado mining engineer who claimed in a letter to the editor of the *Akron Beacon Journal* in

1905 to have been present when Doubleday invented the game) was found in a farmhouse three miles from town. "A local philanthropist bought it for five bucks, people paid to see it, a museum was built around it, and the rest?" Frank smiles, sensing their anticipation. "Well, I guess you'll just have to follow me to find out!"

The tourists trail behind him like obedient ducklings, stopping for another photo op when they reach the Baseball Hall of Fame. A few break off from the group to enter the museum, while others disappear into the bookstore, which Frank thinks should be a part of Amos's mayoral campaign strategy: they should sell less wild beatnik *On the Road* stuff and more books about staying put, more books about baseball. He considers it a disgrace to display peculiar titles like *The Cat in the Hat* beside Max Shulman's *Rally 'Round the Flag, Boys!* and John F. Kennedy's *Profiles in Courage.* He's even working on his own book about Cooperstown's local legends and haunts, *Don't Bump into Bumppo!*

He loses a few people temporarily to the Doubleday Deli, where Amos sits tapping his foot against a barstool to the beat of the Everly Brothers' "Wake Up Little Suzie." Amos is drinking O'Mihops, the local brew, and when he sees Frank he barks, "Don't you have someplace else you're supposed to be?" He doesn't look like he is enjoying his beer—more like he's drowning in it—and Frank realizes that whatever this meeting is about, it isn't going to be fun. He reminds Amos that cirrhosis of the liver killed Senator Joe McCarthy, and that if he wants to be around for *manager* Joe McCarthy's induction into the Hall of Fame, he had best lay off the booze. Amos responds with a curt "Be at the school in ten minutes."

Frank exits the deli, ushering his followers through a parking lot to the ballpark that squats just off Main Street. An uncanny gargoyle, a statue called the *Sandlot Kid,* stands guard at the gate; a barefoot boy with a bat slung casually over one shoulder in a manner that reminds passersby what it means to be young and play ball. The tourists know that Doubleday Field lures people like them each summer in droves. They can almost taste the hot dogs sold in the stands, hear the cheers of the crowd rooting for their team. What they don't know is that to locals, when it's not being used for ball games, the field is a rendezvous point, for teens a make-out joint, or a stead to get sated on bourbon or beer. It's enveloped by houses on three sides, on the north end by the parking lot, which any Cooperstonian knows has only one entrance and one way out. For Cooperstown's youth, a stroll through that lot means a straight shot "downtown."

Frank loses a few followers to the nearby batting cages, where they indoctrinate their swings. A few more step inside a small shop to have bats turned on a lathe, engraved with the initials of beloved ball fans back home to whom they'll be presented as gifts like no other.

Back on Main Street, Frank points out the movie theater, now playing *The Bridge on the River Kwai,* and blushes when a female tourist says he looks a little bit like Alec Guinness. He points out Sal's Pizzeria, gathering place for Cooperstown's youth. It's there that all young decisions are made: where the party is, Run-Down Hill or the Brushback Forest; who will go skinny-dipping at Three Mile Point; and who will take whom to the annual cotillion. "Ballroom dancing is mandatory for our children, Cooperstown being a place of tradition," Frank says.

A flagpole is stationed in the middle of Main Street. Frank stops the tour there. He gestures quickly left toward the lakefront, where a bronze sculpture of the *Indian Hunter* and his dog stands on top of a large boulder, safeguarding the boats. He gestures right to Pioneer Street, which means the way to school or the way out. A tourist asks which is north and which is south, and Frank says, "In Cooperstown, if you know which hand to place over your heart during the Pledge of Allegiance, you have every sense of direction you'll ever need, and then some." He feels blue as the tour draws to a close, aware, as he stands in the middle of Main Street, that every restaurant, every store, is gradually being consumed by souvenir shops. He fears that eventually there will be no more favorites. No one to say "My god is bigger than yours." No testing of faiths. He consoles himself with the idea that Coopers-town might one day become a dominion worthy of ancient Greece: a god for everyone, be it the Mick or the Say Hey Kid. He knows people don't have to love baseball to live in Cooperstown, but he feels they had better respect it, that it gets in the pores. It flows from the taps of the bars and from the mouths of the men and women who bond over beers at the Slugger Saloon. The tourists, too, sense this, licking their lips as though they can taste it, a time when a man could feel baseball in his blood. They smell it in the air, an inveterate history that means, at this moment, they belong—that they are more American than any other Americans. And Frank leaves them there just like that, in the middle of Main Street, licking their chops clean of time.

Duke pulls up in his truck and leans on the horn. He's been sent to ensure that Frank gets to the school on time. Frank jumps onto the truck, standing on the step below the cab, and, as Duke drives away, he waves his cap at the tourists, who wave back until he's gone. The moment Frank climbs inside and buckles in, he regrets it, because Duke starts chattering away, always the coach, unable to keep still. He talks about the upcoming Hall of Fame Game, St. Louis Cardinals versus Chicago White Sox, Jimmy Hoffa and the Teamsters, the odds that the Russians will launch a dog into space, "and what's Eisenhower gonna do, send a monkey?" He wonders aloud about how long Liz Taylor can stay married to one man and about the impending destruction of Ebbets Field. He says Jimmy Dorsey's death marks the end of an era, but that Lawrence Welk, "his show ain't so bad." He is talking even more than usual and Frank realizes it is because he's nervous. He can smell it on Duke the way he smelled it on Amos, on his boozy breath. And for a minute he wants to jump out of the truck, to run back to his flock, back in time. He wants to turn off the moment, to drown out Duke, who's now doing his best Buddy Holly imitation and fudging the words to "Not Fade Away," which seems like a portent, but he stays put.

When they arrive at the school, Frank follows Cartwright through the gymnasium to his office. Amos is there. The lights are off. Charles is there too, sitting with his head in his hands like he's hearing for the first time that his beloved wife is dead. He has a heart murmur, and Frank thanks God that someone invented the pacemaker. Chuck looks like he is going to need one.

Frank won't cross the threshold. He's nervous and is about to insist that someone tell him just exactly what the hell is going on when Duke hands him a flashlight. He wishes, for the first time in a long time, that he was wearing pants. He feels suddenly cold. But he doesn't have time to say so, or to say much at all, because it is right there in front of him—the reason—on the paper Chuck hands him, his eyes averted. Frank does not want to read it. He knows he won't like what it has to say. But he accepts it anyway, shining the flashlight upon the paper, because Amos says to. And before he has time to comment, to take a seat, or shout, or faint, there is a gasp—someone is behind him, behind the door, breathing much too fast. Frank shines the flashlight through the crack and Amos flings the door open. Then they see him, a teenager standing in the dark corner with a bag of base-balls in one hand and a bat in the other. He's been reading over Frank's shoulder.

For a minute Frank wonders if the kid is going to use the bat, but he looks too scared. He looks like Frank feels, like he just got smacked in the gut with a stove poker. Frank tries to place him. He's a friend of Chuck's son, Immanuel somebody—*Immanuel, God with us!* And suddenly it becomes painfully clear. The boy is glaring back at them, his fear turned to anger, and Frank feels like he's been rammed in the chest with a rifle butt as two genera-tions, two versions of the same tour, collide right there in the room. He squeezes the pocket Bible he keeps in his shorts, re-calling Isaiah 7:16: *Before the boy knows enough to reject the wrong and choose the right, the land of the two kings you dread will be laid to waste.* He watches helplessly, everything moving in slow motion as the kid runs out of the room. Amos chases him. The paper in

Frank's hand feels like it's burning right through his flesh. He drops the flashlight, and the room goes dark. And their worlds, all five, are forever changed.

Standing in the blackness, Frank wonders what he would do if he had a choice: Would he freeze right there, hold his breath, and lick his lips clean of time? Or would he break his own rules, flash forward twenty-some years to see how it all plays out? Because the truth is he can't stand it. He can't stand missing history.

FIRST INNING

When you enter a ball park your sole duty is to umpire a ball game.... You no doubt are going to make mistakes, but never attempt to "even up" after having made one. Make all decisions as you see them and forget which is the home or visiting club.... "BE IN POSITION TO SEE EVERY PLAY."

—Baseball-almanac.com,
General Instructions to Umpire

Traditionally the term career *has been reserved for those who expect to enjoy the rises laid out within a respectable profession. The term is coming to be used, however, in a broadened sense to refer to any social strand of any person's course through life. The perspective of natural history is taken: unique outcomes are neglected in favor of such changes over time as are basic and common to the members of a social category, although occurring independently to each of them. Such a career is not a thing that can be brilliant or disappointing; it can no more be a success than a failure. In this light, I want to consider the mental patient.*

This from Erving Goffman's *Asylums: Essays on the Social Situation of Mental Patients and Other Inmates,* which is what Dr. Kerwin Chylak had been reading before his next patient entered the room. Citing outside sources saved him the patience and time to solve the problems of people in a town where the people's problems seemed suspiciously linked. It was the summer of '79 and Chylak found himself to be an impartial spectator in a town partial to speculation. The people in his new town were proof that the human brain hid ninety percent of its functioning capabilities from an amenable ten. The same ten percent that allowed said people to exist in la-la land, poking out, on occasion, into the world of reason only to be faced with a prescription. Meanwhile, that elusive ninety percent kept human beings from communicating telepathically; from remembering birthdays and wedding anniversaries or to file their tax returns; from knowing what they wanted, or, *worse,* from knowing better than to try and figure out what *other* people wanted. Why not sit back and save energy, stealing the words of the more experienced, instead of overextending oneself amid such odds? Chylak felt he had no advice to *give.* He was certain, however, that he could get away with citations if he avoided that universal gesture—winking pointer and index fingers on both hands—implying a quote had been committed.

Chylak fancied the word *committed.* He was the only psychiatrist in Cooperstown, population 2,032. Potential patients: 2,031. Chylak: 1. His was a dangerous profession, the study of psychosis, as it made one vulnerable to certain psychotic ideas. It seemed best to remain aloof when playing therapist in a town whose former inhabitants were buried prostrate ("Indian style") in the hope they'd be comfortable while their land was pillaged, ploughed, and planed into a baseball diamond. Cooperstown was a town stuck deep in the thick of denial. A town where baseball was thicker than blood, and where blood was an arbitrary thing, so what had you?

Chylak stared at his sleeve, wondering whether his shirt was brown or maroon and hoping it matched his slacks. He wanted to look presentable in his new position, and being color-blind was a bit of a hindrance. He wore his sideburns long and his beard trimmed short. He was bespectacled twenty-four hours a day, even while he bathed and even while he slept, hesitant to forgo vision during the most vulnerable third of his life. His glasses had thick Coke-bottle lenses that granted him a look of perpetual astonishment. They had been dropped once too often and were held together at the bridge with duct tape.

Chylak had completed his medical training at a prominent psychiatric facility in Lebanon, Indiana. But, as he told his lovely wife, Babe, the position he accepted thereafter had been rather limiting, and he'd always longed for the chance to play good country doc. Thus, the Chylaks moved to Cooperstown some three months ago with their children: thirteen-year-old Alice and nine-year-old Elliott, an aspiring whiz kid imprisoned in that awkward stage of development when one's body has yet to proportion itself to one's head.

Chylak put aside his book and glanced out the window toward his home across the street. Living so close to a psych ward didn't sit well with Babe, but for Chylak it was quite convenient. A dark truck was parked down the street, the engine idling. Chylak hoped it didn't belong to a deliveryman from whom Babe had ordered more furniture they couldn't possibly afford. Alice was playing a game on the lawn with the neighbor girls. Elliott—who wore shorts pulled clear up to his middle and sandals despite his white tube socks (an indication, to Chylak, that he was resigned to a lifetime of inactive observing, or playing with girls)—sat on the curb and watched. Chylak didn't blame him. It was a ludicrous game the others played. Aside from a bat his children had received from a Bronx relative—Mickey Mantle's John Hancock forged onto its barrel by Chylak, who had been given a wood-burning pen for Father's Day and who knew of only one ballplayer, Mantle—there were no props. In Chylak's experience, children *required* props. Alice disappeared briefly behind a bush, returning to brandish an invisible object, which she shouted had been hit "Foul!" It was clear these children, at the height of summer, on June 21, were conducting a virtual ball game—virtual in that the house was too close to the street to allow for an actual ball. Alice was the victor and was presented with a trophy: a new candy bar called the Twix Caramel Cookie, which when squished in a ball was rendered *almost* unrecognizable by parents. Children, in Chylak's experience, were also prone to presenting each other with trophies. He marveled at Alice's agility as she ran a victory lap around the bases, despite the clunky constraints of her Doc Martens boots.

Chylak retrieved a baseball from his desk drawer, one given to him as a welcome gift by his secretary, Mrs. Gibs, on his first day at work. To him, this particular prize appeared as a corklike cerebral cortex wound in sinewy string, a cowhide-covered cerebrum, a little white bauble of a brain at once malleable and invincible. If he was resigned to working out the inner mechanisms of the mind defunct in a town centered around baseball, a sport he thought redundant at best, he hoped to benefit from such analogies. Chylak had never picked up a ball in his life. He wasn't interested in sports, and even if he had been, a fierce lack of coordination and an unfortunate astigmatism were against it. To him baseball was a dated theory, a pointless physics equation, a cuckoo form of camaraderie that offered no insight whatsoever into the greater context of things. He was confident that the moment his children consumed the chocolate, they would forget about the game—the hits, the runs, and keeping score—and resort to a more practical form of leisure: a reenactment of *The Bionic Woman* with Alice as Jaime Sommers and Elliott, conical cranium a character plus, as Callahan the Fembot. The Chylaks' new home came equipped with an odd little kennel in the backyard, which the self-professed dog-deprived Chylak children used during reenactments that required a jail. Chylak enjoyed watching the children lock one another in its stalls, alternating villains and good guys, while waiting for that special bionic someone to set them free. He often rooted for Elliott to play that part. For that was the beauty of childhood: even the runt is bionic.

Just as the good doctor withdrew his eyes from the game, the girls disappeared into the house, leaving Elliott, a miniature Chylak-in-the-making (he could name all known neurotransmitters by age six) alone on the lawn. He picked up the bat, swung, and hit a virtual home run. Had Chylak been watching, he might have seen his son look up from home plate (his missing copy of Lewis R. Wolberg's *Medical Hypnosis: Volume II*) to see if his father had witnessed the feat. He may also have noticed that after the boy completed the run from home around the bases and back, he then repeated the motion backward while hopping on one foot and reciting, at the top of his lungs, a dirty limerick, which got him snatched inside the house by his mother. But Chylak was thinking about his next patient, one who would no doubt be late and no doubt troubled by *feelings*. Chylak was paid rather well to discuss feelings. Feelings gave him the creeps. He was happy to discuss the emotional framework of others—except his wife, and preferably not his children, or neighbors prone to awkward chats on the lawn—but he was not much for discussing his own. He was a man of the desk, the Couch; the more dignified sit down and give it a go *singuralis*. He preferred his role as it was: the objective objector—no favoring of teams; call 'em like you see 'em; who's to say what's fair and what's foul (besides Chylak); and all that. Chylak—reader of dated psychology books just to make things more interesting (for the patients!), believer that aliens had long ago arrived on earth in the form of streptococci, interpreter of enigmas—was an enigma himself, if you asked his wife.

Chylak had met Babe while waiting for a bus in Plainfield, Indiana, years ago when it was still possible to be caught up in the moment. It annoyed him how one never knew when a significant moment was about to occur, not until hindsight caught up with foresight, giving one a good hard kick in the ass and implying, "*That* was a moment." It had been a wintry day—shards of snow and loose pages from the *Lebanon Times* spiraling in a draft above the depot. A scrap of the crossword page landed on Babe, on the soft shoulders of her camel coat, "the Turkish word for fate," she would later recall. She stood there, a young redheaded beauty from Noblesville awaiting the bus, smiling despite the cold, clutching a Bible between two petal-pink hands raw with cold. It had all been too much. Chylak had been smitten. He had *felt*. And this feeling translated into his handing her his muffler, a concise courtship, a swift wedding ceremony, and years later two kids— and a promising life in the country. It had taken Chylak years to realize that book Babe had been clutching so carefully may as well have been subtitled *How to Convert Unsuspecting Suckers You Might Meet on a Bus Bound for Lebanon,* and that she had been trying to save him for the entire ride. In a way, she had.

Over the years, the atmosphere of that inclement day had worked its way into thoughts, feelings, and more feelings. It had even worked its way into the bedroom, where Babe now refused Chylak's advances. This began when they arrived in Cooperstown in late February, Babe preferring instead to confer with the Lord while Chylak struggled to sleep, shimmying and shivering away in their god-awful Hammacher Schlemmer water bed. Babe wanted to sleep with the windows open despite the frigid air, claiming to love a good draft, an airing-out, which Chylak pegged to be a form of subconscious *mentalation;* Babe had been acting rather chilly since, and it was Chylak's intent to diagnose why. If only he could find the time between Babe's increase in church activities and his sudden increase in patients. Virtually no one had come to see him during his first month in town, so he was suspicious of his sudden popularity. Perhaps the townsfolk viewed him as some kind of sideshow freak. After all, nothing of significance ever occurred in a place like Cooperstown. Or so he'd been told.

He tapped his pen against a legal pad, wondering what he was up against for the afternoon. His next patient was a man who required patience. And one who might very well confirm his belief that the entire township was going kookadoodledoo. It was a good season for psychiatry and, if you cared about that sort of thing, a good season for baseball.

Chylak flipped forward through his desk calendar, dismayed to find his secretary had circled Thursday, August 3, and written "Hall of Fame Induction Ceremony" beside it with a smiley face for emphasis. He suspected the induction ceremony would come and go, and with it the people's relentless preparations for an onslaught of tourists—where to house them, how to feed them, and what to charge when they parked on your lawn—to soon be replaced by the *moment*. A dilemma had been plaguing the township for months: the threat of a baseball theme park.

Could it be true? Could Cooperstown, home of baseball, mecca to sports fans, have finally had enough? That one lived there did not mean one slept clad in a glove and cuddling a bat, or watched the games on television, or had ever played the game oneself, or cared to know who did. At least this was Chylak's opinion. As for the rest of the townsfolk, despite an increase in grumblings over the park, they couldn't wait for Hall of Fame weekend to arrive. Chylak was certain they would forget about the inductees and the tourists alike—as they had many others before—the day after the ceremony, when Cooperstown molted and returned to its preferred form: past perfect. The form of assuming the *moment* had already arrived.

In the interim, he would let the people have their day, lose their minds, and face their demons and he would be there to clean up the mess in the morning. The mess that is inevitable when mankind attempts to distinguish myth from reality, never mind to reconcile the two. In the end it was about what one chose to believe. What one needed to worship and for how long, what one required be *real*. And reality, this psychiatrist knew, was a big fat arbitrary thing.

SECOND INNING

During practice a catcher begins his field leadership. That means no fooling around and constant learning. . . . Being a field leader means that others will automatically look to you to find out what should be done. That means the catcher must know the correct answer.

—CHUCK ROSCIAM, *ENCYCLOPEDIA OF BASEBALL CATCHERS*

Amos Fusselback was well aware that he'd been dubbed Amos the Fuss. He was used to the title, which did not grant people license to use it in his presence. He was a plump, old "reformed" drunk, and it was a rare day that he shaved. His hair was white and stood in tufts on top of his head. He had a pinched, triangular nose and severely arched brows that lent him an air of permanent befuddlement. He felt best when wearing a leisure suit and he never buttoned his shirts above the navel.

Amos kept a diary—a small notebook containing insights, memories, things to remember, and letters. He wrote many letters, but he never mailed them and he never dated them. Unconcerned with dates (he couldn't remember them), he was a meticulous calculator of time. He sat in an overstuffed chair on his porch, across from the Pit Stop, the bar's wooden sign swinging back and forth in the wind like a relentless metronome. It was enough to drive anyone mad, especially the town mayor. He wrote.

> 3:00 pm. I was standing in front of the Hall of Fame this morning and a tourist gave me a dollar. I'm the MAYOR! Over the years, people have tried to hurt me, emotionally or spiritually. It started when I was a boy. I believe in my life there

is a pattern: a HURT pattern. I no longer care what others
do with their time: ME, Amos Fusselback, FIRST.

Amos always began his entries with the exact time and he always emphasized his point with capital letters. He rubbed his
barrel belly with a knotted, arthritic hand and continued.

I was born in Cooperstown on November eighteenth, 1914 if
one wants to go back. I for one DON'T. I have noticed the
aging process is not the same for everyone. Some wear out.
Some burn out in their teens. How SLOW. I have memories
of a farmhouse, FOLKLORE, a milkman delivering milk. I can
take myself back to age seventeen, thirty-seven, forty-
three . . . It's not a good idea for me to stay there too long.

He jotted down a brief, half-assed chronology.

1957:	THE KID. Frank dies. Martha leaves. Alcoholics Anonymous.
1960s:	PRETTY GOOD!
1967:	Kid cracks. SOBER.
1973:	Kid back. Last drink.
1978:	January, "Marse Joe" McCarthy dies. July 4th parade: Dusty P. wears red dress. Dreamt of Charo ("coochie-coochie").
1979:	Feb.? Shrink comes. March: Chuck's ticker stops. Reporter returns. Theme park!!! ONE drink.
May 1:	First session with doc. LAST drink.
June 11:	Dreamt of wife and Johnny (wife said, "Diet").
June 16:	Dreamt of dogs, DEATH, shoveling snow.
June 18:	Saw undertaker.
June 19:	Dreamt of rubber waders??
June 21:	Now. I mean it: LAST DRINK!

It was becoming a theme: the last drink, the last time. It was
a theme of sour breath, god-awful hangovers, and perpetual
THIRST.

Amos put down the pen, stretched, and stepped off his porch, careful not to place too much weight on his bad knee. He slipped his diary in a breast pocket, and then headed for his golf cart. He drove that cart everywhere, Cooperstown being small enough (and his license having been revoked often enough) to permit such a vehicle. It was only a matter of three or four blocks to the sanitarium, but his joints had been giving him trouble, he was late, and it was a nice day for a ride.

He headed up Pioneer Street, turning left on Main toward River, avoiding the shortcut to the sanitarium through Cooper Park on Fair Street. The statue of James Fenimore Cooper that squatted there made Amos nervous. He was in no mood for young Cooper, who sat, day after day, looking smug with his cane and his top hat, a reminder that his father had established, had *run,* the town people said Amos was now running straight into the ground. He made a mental note to have the statue replaced with a large boxwood shrub. He dreaded that a similar statue of his own son, Johnny, might one day be erected just seventy miles away in the city of Albany, where Johnny was currently an assemblyman en route to the Senate. Amos hadn't spoken to Johnny above a grunt in years. Johnny managed to avoid seeing his father whenever he visited his home district office in Cooperstown. After Amos's wife left and his pals started dropping like flies, everything went to piss in a pot and his son went too. He had never understood why. Johnny loved Cooperstown! He shared his old man's pride in its history, and he had been a decent ballplayer too. True, he was no Manny Barrett, Cooperstown's finest; used to be anyway. Like Amos always said, when it came to Manny, a person could go soft in the head living too long in the middle of nowhere. The proof was right before him.

At the intersection of River and Main, a man stood in the center of the street straddling a bicycle between two bandy legs. He startled Amos, who mistook him for an apparition—River Street was famed for its haunts. It could be argued that the man before him *was* a specter of sorts, a self and a former self, the latter making rare appearances when in a certain mood. "Electroshock my keester," Amos murmured, annoyed at the way Duke Cartwright had tourists and townsfolk alike eating out of the palm of his hand, riding his bike around town like a one-man carnival show performing tricks, which were liable to land his ancient ass in the hospital. To Amos, Cartwright was a shyster and a smart aleck, a man who was more coherent than he let on. The two of them went way back.

Duke had been the baseball coach at Cooperstown High and, before that, had had a shot at the big leagues. Now he was groundskeeper at Doubleday Field, a ball field built to major-league standards, which Amos was proud to tell anyone who asked and had done so since '39. Duke was responsible for maintaining the field—raking, watering, mowing, seeding, and resodding. That is, when he was not mucking it up with his bicycle, riding around the bases like a loon. If you were a kid in Cooperstown with a dream, or even an inkling of a dream that included a ball and bat in the equation, you knew Duke. He had coached Manny Barrett, who was once bound for the minors.

Duke stopped in the middle of the street to recite his ridiculous list of retired uniform numbers and was showing off for a group of tourists who had read about him in an unauthorized (by Amos) brochure. He was on the Cleveland Indians, mumbling numbers through the mouth guard he wore, which reminded Amos of a large pacifier.

"Nineteen. Five. Three . . ."

When Amos idled his cart closer to break up the show, Duke pointed at him and began shouting, "Sixty-five! Sixty-five! Sixty-five!"

"Hush up!" growled Amos, who didn't need reminding that he had reached retirement age. He spat, in no mood for a duel. When the tourists were distracted by Duke's geriatric attempt to pop a wheelie, Amos reached quickly for the bottle of Geritol he kept in his sock, which contained just enough alcohol to sate him, undetected, and he took a swig. "All right, now," he said, "party's over."

Once the crowd dispersed, Amos, who was now *very* late for his appointment, attempted to drive past Duke, but each time he drove to the right, Duke rode his bike in that direction. And each time he rode to the left it was the same.

"A balk, a ball, a base, a batter—fly ball, foul, grand slam!" Duke yelled.

Amos turned off the ignition.

"That's enough now," he hissed. "They're gone and I'm late for an appointment! Let me by!"

"Single, steal, strike!" And with that, Duke the determined kook began riding his bicycle around Amos's cart, chuckling so hard that Amos feared he would fall off and croak right there on Main Street.

"I mean it, Cartwright. Don't pull this crap with me!"

Amos considered turning around to swing by the ballpark. Perhaps the kids he had shooed from the dugout last night had left behind that bottle of strawberry wine.

"Foul ball!" Duke continued, cutting too close and accidentally ramming Amos's vehicle. He hit it hard enough that Amos feared it would tip, and in a rush to escape, Amos pressed the gas pedal, causing the cart to lurch forward uncontrollably and hit the curb.

"Look, I know what's eating you," Amos said. "I have to clear out Chuck's place. I will! His son's back and he's wanting to move in."

Duke opened his mouth, about to reply, when a dark blue pickup truck whizzed down River Street, turning a sharp right over the footbridge in the direction of East Lake Road.

"Interference! Interference!" yelled Duke, and Amos, struck by the change in sporting terms, tensed, knowing exactly what he meant.

The truck screeched to a halt. Duke gasped and hopped on his bike, pedaling quickly toward the curb. Amos held his breath as the truck began heading backward toward him, gradually gaining speed. Before it reached the bridge, however, the driver seemed to change his mind, hitting the gas and disappearing toward the lake in a cloud of dust.

"Jesus," Amos said, exhaling, his hand over his heart. He reached for the bottle in his sock and swigged it. Duke had a smirk on his face. "I'll handle it!" Amos hissed. "I'll handle everything."

Ignoring the pain in his knee, the pounding in his chest, and the desire for something stronger than Geritol, Amos climbed in his cart and sped off toward the sanitarium.

T HE PATIENT APOLOGIZED FOR being tardy. He gave Chylak a knickknack he claimed to have bought at the Hall of Fame gift shop. It was a freebie, however, and Chylak knew this, because they were also giving these trinkets away at the bank. It was a plastic paperweight, a little snow dome that when shaken, coated the miniature Cooperstown inside it with tiny white flakes, as though the town had been overcome by a terrible snowstorm. The patient settled himself on the couch across from the doctor's desk and opened his diary.

Chylak congratulated the mayor on the courage to read aloud from something so private, something so full of secrets. "Secrets," he said, "are sometimes necessary." Secrets, he felt, were sometimes good. So good that he pitied himself for not being able to share more of them, bound by the Hippocratic oath and all that. He thanked the mayor for the bauble and put it in his pocket. Later he would show it to Babe as evidence the move had been smart, that all the long hours he was away from her and the children would be worth it—at least his patients appreciated it. He remembered his Goffman, a passage he had been practicing for just this patient. Taking his citation addiction to extremes, he quoted Goffman quoting Melville. Mayor Fusselback had been a navy man in his youth, and Chylak hoped to appeal to his well-publicized sense of nostalgia.

"'In the American Navy the law allows one gill of spirits per day to every seaman.' If you feel your resolve weakening, try to minimize yourself to one gill."

"What's a gill?" asked Fusselback.

"Something like a shot," replied Chylak, who began writing out a prescription for Librium, his drug of choice that month. He had been sampling the pills himself and had to admit they had quite an effect on one's spirit.

The mayor interrupted to say sobriety was killing him. "I'm losing time!" Time sifting through his fingers like so many grains of uncountable sand. Time in which to make his mark, and to record his personal history lest it be forgotten before it was ever really known. He was threatening to write his memoirs when Chylak crossed out "Librium" and changed it to "lithium." The mayor continued, preferring to read his thoughts aloud rather than express them directly. In this the two men were alike, though Chylak kept his own "notes" logged safe in his brain, and thus out of Babe's reach, as he suspected she would holler "Aha!" if she read them.

The mayor cleared his throat and read aloud from his diary.

> 3:00 pm. I've been thinking of my life experiences. Perhaps I am too STUBBORN, too SENSITIVE, or too SLOW to learn from them. I found a wallet down by the lake. An eighteen-year-old lad (another KID) left it. I took it to the police. HONESTY. Life goes on for Amos Fusselback. Some time I may surprise myself.

Chylak wondered if he had ever surprised *himself*. When was the last time he had caught himself off guard? The concept was disconcerting. He supposed it was when he had withheld from Babe the truth behind their move, which he was still doing, which meant he was still surprising himself—*fascinating!* He had never lied to Babe before and marveled at how easy it was, how effortlessly it all poured out once he began. Before he could stop himself it was too late: voilà! They were in a new town starting a new life. Now, if he could just keep it together and not spend the rest of his days self-medicating with all manner of iffy FDA-approved pick-me-ups—the guilt was becoming too much.

He followed the mayor's gaze out the window and across the street to where Elliott ran around a tree with a paper bag from the local grocery store, Save, America!, on his head.

"I met Stanley Auffswich last night," the mayor said. Stanley Auffswich was the undertaker.

Chylak sighed. Amos the mayor had been meeting Stanley the undertaker to discuss his "looming demise" for a month. "It might do you some good to get away this summer," he said. "Take a vacation."

"Impossible! I'm the may-or," said Fusselback, who was prone to enunciating his title as though it were an eggy sandwich spread. "The people need me! There's the induction ceremony, the Hall of Fame Game, and let's not forget the goddamned theme park!" He rubbed the back of his head, frowning. "It keeps me up at night, Doc."

Chylak suspected that the only thing keeping Amos Fusselback up was Jim Beam, that bourbon-breathed buddy who had been known to whisper into his ear late at night such profound revelations as the idea to move the town sewage plant to the soccer field behind the junior high school. Chylak was concerned that the mayor's sobriety was slipping.

"You've already protested the park," he said. "It's time to let go."

The issue of plans for a baseball amusement park to be built in a town already mired deep in baseball amusement was a prominent one of late. This and the fact that it was a particularly hot month. In Chylak's experience, extreme fluctuations in temperature did not bode well for community mentality. He expected someone, somewhere between Main Street and Route 166, to snap. Perhaps it would be the mayor.

He followed the man's gaze out the window to where Dusty

Paquette, the local cosmetics lady, stood in front of his house pushing Home-Run High and Tight Instant Face Lift serum on his wife. When Babe politely dismissed her, Paquette waddled across the street to "inspect the flower boxes" outside Chylak's window, as was her willful little habit. Chylak planned to speak to her about the perils of eavesdropping, once he was through avoiding her.

The mayor made a pretense of rolling his eyes. Secretly he found Mrs. Paquette quite charming.

Chylak drew the shades.

The mayor went over his to-do list aloud: Doubleday Field needed watering; he needed at least forty ticket takers for the Hall of Fame Game and a head count on ushers. Not to mention the baseball museum: the brick needed cleaning, the floors waxing, and certain displays were in dire need of some oomph. In August, Willie Mays, Warren Giles, and Hack Wilson were being inducted. The latter two were dead, Giles recently. Amos had admired him as a fine fellow leader, a soldier, no less. And he identified with Wilson, who grew distant from his own son following a divorce from his wife and who also had a liking for liquor. At least he would get to meet Mays. He told Chylak he had been thirty-seven when Bobby Thomson hit his pennant-winning "shot heard round the world." Johnny was eight. Mays was the on-deck batter. He also confided his secret desire to have Johnny be at the induction ceremony when he introduced Mays—though that would mean speaking to Johnny, which would require a miracle, and miracles required energy. Amos had none, though fortunately, his was a kingdom that defied progression: no fast food, no fast cars, and no goddamned modern amusements! He was certain his town would never change. As certain as he was that it was going to rain—he could feel it in his knees, in the way his bones ached with that cold metallic tingling indicative of age—and as certain as he was that in certain civilized regions of the world, it was cocktail hour.

"May I have something to drink?"

Chylak gestured toward the water tank, where the mayor helped himself to a cup of orange liquid, compliments of Chylak's secretary, who had replaced the water that came in the tank with the powdered concoction Tang.

"I'm going to protest again," said the mayor.

"What?" said Chylak.

"The park! I'm going to protest again, with pizzazz!"

Chylak shook his head. The mayor's last attempt to protest with pizzazz included having Terry Daulton, the local journalist, print WE DON'T WANT IT on the front page of *The Journal* when a local philanthropist threatened to build a statue of Cooper just two blocks from his porch. The headline was printed above a close-up of Fusselback chewing what Chylak assumed was the symbolic key to the city. It hung from a shoestring around his neck, and he had a bad habit of chewing it in situations where tastier liquid alternatives were not permissible. It looked like an ordinary house key.

The philanthropist had ignored the mayor's plea, and Chylak was trying to prepare him for the fact that the state would probably ignore him as well. According to a recent article in *The Journal,* Cooperstown, home of baseball or not, had little say in a matter that could bring millions of dollars into an area of New York State that had long been dependent on cattle and tourists for income. The idea, they said, was to build a theme park that would bring a new sentiment to the sport, something to attract larger crowds and to provide entertainment for those who sought variety, something beyond the baseball and museum. The truth, everyone knew, was that it was all about cash.

"Perhaps you *should* protest," said Chylak, humoring the mayor, though he wished the poor man would retire and spare himself the headache of losing a battle against the state, regardless of what the people desired. The people, he hoped, would get over it.

"How?"

"A petition."

"What good's a petition going to do?"

"Well, if handled properly it could be taken quite seriously."

"If you mean to imply—"

"I'm a doctor. I never imply. I simply *re*ply and you asked for my advice."

"Theoretically."

Chylak perked—theoretical advice was his specialty. "Draw up a petition, get as many townsfolk as you can to sign it, and let fate take its course."

The mayor frowned, smacking his lips. He wondered if there was a policy against sipping Geritol in the presence of a shrink. "What are my alternatives?" He twisted the key around his neck so tightly that he began to choke. Noticing Chylak's concern, he attempted to tuck the key inside his shirt, forgetting it was unbuttoned.

The doctor's voice was gentler now. "I'm concerned that you view preventing this park as a game. But have you considered that it might be a game you can't possibly win? Perhaps we should focus on keeping you healthy once it's *built*."

"It *is* a game!" Fusselback growled. "And it *won't* be built!" It was a game of David (Cooperstown) against Goliath (the state), and Goliath came armed with the ability to withdraw aid for the new gymnasium the townsfolk were demanding, the old one having been annexed to the ever-expanding Hall of Fame. Amos Fusselback, loser of time, was determined to find a solution. He knew if the theme park came, the people would blame him, and on this, his last year as mayor of the village of Cooperstown, he would not go down without a fight. Abner Doubleday had entered this town and given it baseball! Amos Fusselback would exit defending it—*from itself?*

Fusselback twisted the key. "I have to get back to work," he said, rising quickly from his seat.

"We haven't finished the session."

"I don't have time!"

Amos had more important things on his mind than his mind.

Tonight, he wouldn't sit on his porch, envying those who stumbled in and out of the bar across the street while he recorded regrets in his diary. Instead he would come up with a plan to save Cooperstown. He would take Chylak's prescription, his theoretical advice, and shove it in a drawer. The one in the table beside his bed, in which he kept letters, mementos, and lists—the reminders of everything he had never done—and this time he would *do* something. And afterward, after a quiet dinner of sausage and applesauce on the good china his wife, Martha, had left behind, he would remove the flask of bourbon tucked in that drawer and dare it to defeat him. He would let the warm familiar serum burn its way down his throat to the place where he needed it most: the place of forgetting, the place, sixty-five or no sixty-five, interference or no interference, of beginning anew.

He drove home slowly, enjoying the ride, and even took the shortcut through Cooper Park, hardly aware of the statue of Cooper that sat in the middle.

It had been a long day. There was the school board luncheon, the Venerable Veterans' Powwow, the Ladies Auxiliary for the Beautification of Main Street lobbying for more potted geraniums, and the question, at the town meeting, of why the Baseball Library did not contain more books on Ty Cobb.

"You can read his diary at the Hall of Fame!" Amos had said.

Tonight, he would savor the tranquil slumber of one who is sure he will not remember his dreams.

THIRD INNING

*A replaced Designated Hitter shall not re-enter
the game in any capacity.*
—*MLB MISCELLANY: RULES, REGULATIONS AND STATISTICS*

There was nothing wrong with Terry Daulton. That was his problem. He did feel at times as though he were losing his mind—that he had become detached from himself and the world—but it usually passed with a hot cup of coffee and a swift panic attack. He was working on a feature about Cooperstown's residential gardens. The focus was on Mrs. Coxey's ability to prune juniper bushes into the shape of baseball bats, despite suffering from benign essential tremor. Mrs. Paquette had pitched him the story and he decided, against his better judgment, to run it. Daulton was a local reporter, a benign but essential post. He was generally addressed by his surname because folks had admired his father. Or perhaps there was just something about small towns: calling people by their last names created the illusion that there was more distance between you and them.

Daulton had abandoned his former aspirations to become a baseball writer. He left Manhattan, returning to "the Coop," where he now worked for *The Journal,* a paper with a history that, he cringed to recall, began with a published memo from Jesus "found" tucked beneath third base on Doubleday Field. Daulton's father, Chuck, displayed the memo for years in a case at the Fenimore Funhouse, insisting until his dying day that it was legitimate. Because it claimed Cooperstown was "Paradise on earth," no one seemed to mind that it was written on the back of a Breck Shampoo ad. No one but Daulton.

His beat included the war memorial parades, the annual Frost Fest ice sculpture contest, the cotillion, and whatever minor misdemeanors occurred in the wee hours of the night, in a town where beer was as plentiful as lake water. What he did *not* want to write about was baseball. Little League and high school home games maybe. But the thought of covering the Hall of Fame Game—two major-league teams going head-to-head on Doubleday Field, a tradition since 1940—*that* was another story. Daulton was done with sports writing before his career had ever begun, perhaps because it hadn't been his idea to begin with. "You haven't got the balls to play ball," his father had said, more times than Daulton cared to remember. In high school, Chuck constantly compared him to the kids who *could* play, kids like Manny Barrett. "If you can't join 'em, write about 'em," was Chuck's attitude. And it was just that attitude that convinced Daulton to leave town after he graduated from high school and never look back.

He spent the summer of '57 helping Chuck out at the museums; come fall, he left with only a small duffel bag, a typewriter, and a copy of *The Last of the Mohicans,* a rare edition Chuck gave him as a going-away present. It was the last thing Chuck would ever give him, aside from a relentless stream of unwanted advice, and Daulton was ashamed to admit that he had never read it. He had idolized James Fenimore Cooper as a boy, but now that he was thirty-nine? Reading Cooper in Cooperstown, much like playing baseball, seemed rather akin to eating where you shat. Besides, Chuck's inscription (DON'T READ THIS!!!) was hardly encouraging. Assuming it one of Chuck's manipulation tactics— get the kid to read it, then quiz him on it later to see who knew his Cooperstown history best—Daulton opted to take the inscription literally, deriving a perverse pleasure from having the last word when he buried the book with Chuck. He regretted it now that he was a parentless prodigal son, returning home too late to say good-bye to his father, and too soon for anyone else to notice he had ever left in the first place. The old folks in town still treated him like he was a kid, and the women? They were as interested in him now as they'd been when he was an awkward seventeen.

Daulton was extremely interested in local politics: rising tensions between the town and the state of New York over plans to build a theme park. He eyed the crumpled draft of his latest article, which lay in the wastebasket on top of yesterday's *New York Times*. He kicked the basket away from his desk. Seeing *The Times* brought to mind all those rejection letters he had received from big-city editors who were not interested in hiring some small-town hick to cover sports. They criticized him for being subjective to a fault and for an inability to distance himself from his subjects. "You are *not* Reggie Jackson," one editor wrote.

Daulton had a different take on things. He viewed things from afar. So far that he could not always tell if people were who they were supposed to be, including himself. Ever since the summer he first left town, it was like he had been demoted to the role of a minor character in his own motion picture: a man confined to running without actually moving until whatever it was he was running from caught up and bit him in the ass. He had a tendency to forget who he was around people. Not in the usual way people forget themselves, wanting to impress, to be something they're not. He really had no idea sometimes if he was himself or the person he was talking to. He was like a jigsaw puzzle scattered across a table: all the pieces were there, but there were too many of them and they were too jumbled up for anyone to give a damn about what their sum portrayed. "You *cannot* write interviews entirely in the first person," another editor wrote, "what about the other guy? Are you *both* of you?" That editor had also written, "Seek counseling."

Such feedback only made Daulton more determined to excel. The trouble was, at what? He wanted to be a journalist, not a mere beat writer. At *The Journal,* they cut him a lot of slack, but he covered what they said to cover. He desired a position that would allow him to use his unique, if faulty, perspective to an advantage. The trouble was, baseball was in his blood. He hated to admit it, but in Manhattan he had felt a surge of pride whenever someone asked where he was from. The response to his "Cooperstown" was always the same: "Baseball Hall of Fame! My dad took me there when I was a kid!" He wouldn't have left the city if Chuck hadn't died. Nor would he have stayed in Cooperstown now if Chuck hadn't made it so easy by telling everyone he was some big-time writer, building him up until the editors at *The Journal* practically begged him to stay. That was the other thing about small towns: the slightest fact got blown out of proportion; if you returned home for a reality check, you discovered what you'd gone off and become behind your own back.

Chuck had been the curator at the Farm Stead and the Fenimore Funhouse, the local nonbaseball history museums. Both his time and his loyalties were often divided; the museums were run by the state historical society. He lived alone in the end in the same stone cottage near the museums on West Lake Road that Daulton had grown up in. Chuck was a local icon, a staple. Everyone knew him and everyone respected him. He was the keeper of the town's history, along with the mayor, Duke Cartwright, and Frank Paquette before he died. They were the last of a breed, a species that seemed to fade more and more each year as the town's quaint, old-fashioned charm succumbed to the crunch of commercialism, baseball museums, and memorabilia shops replacing a previously more subtle appreciation of the sport. Daulton couldn't believe how much Cooperstown had changed. It was like returning from abroad to find your boyhood home smack dab in the middle of Disneyland. His last article predicted that the movie theater would eventually be replaced with one that only showed baseball films.

It seemed fitting, somehow, to have buried *The Last of the Mohicans* with one of Cooperstown's last true natives.

Daulton picked up the pocket watch he had inherited from Chuck, which ticked so loudly that he often expected it to explode. Its original owner had been loud too.

"It's your dad," is what Manny had said when he called Daulton in the city a few months ago with the news about Chuck's decline. "He's not doing too good." It was the first he and Manny had spoken since they graduated from high school, though Daulton had heard more than enough about Cooperstown's former Golden Glove from Chuck in his letters. Chuck had been battling high blood pressure and heart palpitations for months. Whenever Daulton vowed to come home, Chuck refused, saying, "Absolutely not! Having you here will just make me feel guilty when we find out it's nothing." Manny said Chuck was being admitted into the Selma Wellmix Sanatarium. The doctors wanted to run some tests to be sure it was what Chuck claimed, mere indigestion and stress. He just needed rest, Manny said, to unwind and get his blood pressure down. And the next thing Daulton knew, he was dead.

Manny was with him when he died. He called Daulton a second time to say Chuck had suffered a sudden massive heart attack after barking out two orders, the first (and loudest) being that under no circumstances should they notify his son that he was in the hospital. Manny confessed to having already defied that order, and said Chuck went ballistic. Daulton rushed home, but a blizzard stopped him in his tracks. By the time he arrived, Chuck was gone. And if there was one reason that he now wished he and Manny were on speaking terms, it was to find out what Chuck's final words, what that second order, had been. Was he alert? *Afraid?*

The coroner's report stated the heart attack was shock induced. But Chuck had been surrounded by calm professionals, soothing friends, and nurses in cute white uniforms. That's how Daulton liked to imagine it anyway. Why the sudden distress? He had asked Manny about it the moment he arrived in Cooperstown. Manny skirted the issue, assuring Daulton that it was best he wasn't there when Chuck died because it would have broken Chuck's heart for him to see his tough old man so "weak." That sounded like Chuck to Daulton, who had never doubted Chuck loved him. The problem had always been that Chuck loved him *too* much. He had been downright smothering ever since Daulton's mom died of cancer when he was just a kid.

Daulton had met Manny and the mayor at the morgue. Fusselback was standing beside the cold steel table on which Chuck's body lay covered in a white sheet, shaking him and shouting, "Wake up! Wake up! I need you!" Amos and Chuck had been competitive for so long that Daulton figured they had probably even argued about who would die first. He expected Cooperstown to wither up and die along with Chuck, but Fusselback had kept it going, and, in the back of his mind, Daulton supposed he was grateful. He moved back "temporarily" to arrange the funeral and await the burial, which was postponed until spring, when the ground thawed. Spring came and he was taken aback by how beautiful Cooperstown was. He had been urban for so long that he had forgotten about the barn swallows diving so gracefully from the cottage roof, the yellow daffodils lining the Funhouse walk, and all of the beautiful butterflies. It had been a long time since he felt so inspired. He decided to take advantage of it while he could, taking a freelance gig at the paper. He even fantasized about writing a book to see if, like his old hero Cooper, he had any talent in that direction.

His fantasies were cut short, however, when the mayor insisted he leave town. Fusselback played the guilt card, saying Chuck wouldn't have wanted his son to forfeit his future in order to sit around grieving. "Don't worry about a thing," he had said, promising to pack up Chuck's belongings and ship them to the city. He made quite a show of wanting to spare

Daulton more pain, saying that it was too much for a man to have to ransack his own childhood home. It was an odd choice of words, *ransack,* but Daulton let it slide; the mayor was grieving too. But the more frequently people told him what to do, to *leave,* the more it reminded him of Chuck, and the more determined he became to stick around and find out why. His article about Manny's defecation on the courthouse steps sealed his decision. It was his "big break" at the paper. It was also what finally broke their friendship.

The "Barrett Suspected of Bowel Play" story got Daulton promoted to a full-time position at *The Journal.* He knew that in his own misguided way Manny had simply been making a statement, taking a proverbial dump on the law because he had lost custody of his kids and his wife, Ruby, wanted a divorce. Whatever the reason, it was too good not to write about when the only alternative was a Girl Scout Jamboree. And it could be argued, if Manny even cared, that the story made him even more of a myth than he already was. It made people wary of him, which he seemed to crave: to be the guy who gave up his shot at "the Show" to fight for his country, then mysteriously abandoned his family to live alone in the woods. People questioned his stability. Manny had lost the right to raise his sons after a long, drawn-out, and very public court battle for which Ruby blamed Vietnam. The whole town did, in fact, except Daulton, who had known Manny long enough ago to know that whatever demons he catered to, they were bred much closer to home. He was certain they were traceable to the day Manny up and quit baseball for no good reason.

It was the summer of '57. Daulton had been writing in his journal in the woods one afternoon, needing some space from Chuck. He was at his and Manny's secret place near Lot's Tower off Raccoon Road. Manny came crashing through the woods on his bike. He was wearing a baseball uniform, so Daulton assumed he'd been working late, helping Cartwright coach the Little Leaguers down at the school. He looked frazzled, however. His shirt was torn, and he was missing one cleat. He stood there not uttering a word, and Daulton began to suspect that he too needed some space. "What is it? What's wrong?" he had yelled, tripping over a tree stump to get to his friend. Something had scared the shit out of Manny that day, something potent enough to prevent him from confiding in Daulton, or anyone else, that day or any day since. Daulton figured Manny had heard from the Yankees and they didn't want him. But that wasn't the case. They did.

Shockingly, Manny passed up his chance at the minors, quit his assistant coaching job, and took night classes to become bailiff at the county courthouse. Daulton could see he was miserable. He married Ruby, had a baby, and buried his head in domesticity. Everyone knew he would marry Ruby, but no one—least of all Ruby, who had planned to attend State College before she got pregnant—expected it to be so soon. Manny spent the rest of that summer telling people how pleased he was with his decision. Yet he was restless, like a stopwatch, a time bomb waiting to explode. Daulton stood beside him one last time at his wedding, as his best man, before their friendship began to wane.

Manny grew distant, no explanation, no good-bye when Daulton left for school that fall. He rarely came by the cottage, and when he did, he acted like it was *Chuck* he was afraid of. Until Chuck practically adopted him, taking him under his wing—the two of them tight as peas in a pod. Manny cut off whatever friends he had his own age, buddying up with Chuck and his pack of geezers, who treated him like the Second Coming even though he was a quitter. Daulton supposed Manny had no choice, since all his real friends were heading out to seek their fortunes elsewhere. He had *chosen* to stay behind. Maybe it was Manny's way of coping with the loss of his childhood pals. His new pals paid for his wedding and even helped him buy a house. Daulton asked Chuck how the hell they had the money to contribute to what he facetiously termed the Golden Boy Fund when he was hitching a ride to college because Chuck was too damned busy to drive him and couldn't afford a second vehicle. Chuck never answered, but he was happy to report on Manny over the years: how he had gotten a raise at the courthouse, that Ruby was pregnant again, or how Manny was "truly one of a kind." It was like Chuck *wanted* Daulton to be jealous, to stop talking to Manny. Then one day Manny enlisted in the U.S. Army, and he was gone. And Chuck rarely mentioned him again.

Daulton picked up the paper, proofreading his piece on the Farm Stead, an actual farm-turned-museum that had belonged to James Fenimore Cooper in the 1800s. The museum seemed to shrink down in size each year due to a lawsuit that involved the question of whether it had been partially built on what was once Sam Bunting's lawn. It crept forward toward the road and away from Bunting, a few yards each year, along with its general store, schoolhouse, and sheep. Daulton had publicly posed the question of what the 1980s would bring to the Farm Stead: whether the state historical society would sell it to Bunting—a wealthy "clubby," as the summer folk were called, who planned to turn it into a resort—in favor of increasingly insatiable consumerism, or find a compromise between its pastoral roots and the village's desire to keep the sport it had birthed in the spotlight. Daulton was jotting down notes for a follow-up article when he heard a commotion outside.

His office had a decent view of the courthouse and the jail, which looked like any other jail aside from the lavender curtains that hung in each cell, compliments of the Ladies Auxiliary for the Beautification of Main Street. Cooperstown was lucky if it saw ten criminals per year, and they were generally imported from neighboring towns, rural communities where borrowing a neighbor's plough without asking was as felonious as it got. Daulton got a rare sighting of one now. A young man in a bright orange jumpsuit was being forcefully escorted to the jail by the police chief, Tony Bear, to whom he was handcuffed. The prisoner grinned fiendishly as he passed Daulton's window, just a young punk shouting a rock song at the top of his lungs: "Lie lie lie lie liar you lie! Lie lie lie lie tell me why, tell me why!" The kid reminded him of Manny, running naked onto Doubleday Field during Hall of Fame Game '57: St. Louis Cardinals versus Chicago White Sox. "Lies!" Manny had shouted. "It's all lies!" Ruby, his then fiancée, Daulton, and half the township, not to mention thousands of tourists, had watched in horror as he broke down in the middle of center field and cried.

Daulton slammed the window shut.

He had wanted so badly to help Manny that day. But Chuck was determined to handle it his way. And whatever Chuck said to Manny had worked. He, Duke Cartwright, and Frank Paquette dragged Manny, defeated, from the field, and to Daulton's knowledge, Manny never set foot in a ballpark again. People said he was on drugs. Manny had never been into that sort of thing, however. He was a serious athlete. Nor, Daulton thought, was it a coincidence that Manny's coach, Cartwright, was struck mute as a lamppost around the same time. At least, mute in the sense that he ceased speaking in a manner that encouraged actual conversation. Cartwright quit coaching too, as though there were no prospects worth bothering with, now that Manny was out of the game. He became groundskeeper at Doubleday Field, dragging dirt and building and rebuilding the mound over and over just for the hell of it, like some kind of misplaced Sisyphus, for the next two decades.

After "the naked incident," Manny managed to live a carefree life for a decade, until '67, when the war ripped it away from him. He actually *enlisted*, leaving behind a seven-year-old son and a pregnant wife. When he returned four years later, he was damaged beyond recognition. In her letters, Ruby said everyone was talking about Manny and Daulton had felt sorry for her, but mostly he wondered why no one was talking *to*

Manny. Perhaps the myth had finally overcome the man. There had always been a lot of pressure on Manny to play ball, to be the local hero. Daulton was surprised to learn from Ruby that he had holed up at Chuck's place upon his return from combat. Ruby was unable to make payments on her car, couldn't depend on Manny, and didn't *want* to depend on the generosity of the mayor and Chuck, as she often did, so Cartwright had loaned her his truck. And Aidan, Manny's eldest, gave Cartwright Manny's old Schwinn bike in return. It was a sweet gesture, and Cartwright must have thought so too, because he had been riding it in circles ever since.

Daulton had interrogated Chuck about why he was enabling Manny, letting him live at the cottage instead of sending him home to his wife. Chuck claimed that Manny was psychotic, that he wasn't to be trusted, that he was a danger to himself and to others. Then he turned around and kicked that "psycho" out, sending him back to Ruby, who took him back like a fool, and allowed herself to get pregnant again.

Daulton was sure that whatever the reason behind Manny's discharge—or his going AWOL, if you were of that camp—it was honorable, and that Manny was then and now perfectly sane. Daulton was of the discharge camp—it was perfectly reasonable that Manny would be discharged, psychotic break or not, after four years of service as an enlistee. In fact, he suspected that Manny should have been back in three. Perhaps Manny had milked the war for another year to make his homecoming that much sweeter, or to hide. Maybe he equated being discharged with failing. Maybe it reminded him what everyone else already knew: that he had already failed himself by giving up his one true love. Baseball. Manny was like a character out of a Cooper novel, Natty Bumppo: a man living alone in the woods, getting by on solitude and stocking feet. Daulton called him that behind his back sometimes, Bumppo. Or whenever Mrs. Paquette was within earshot, knowing she was bound to deliver the taunt, in person, to Manny later. It was childish, of course, picking fights with Manny like they were still kids. It seemed like Daulton was right back where he had started, and perhaps the key to survival was pretending he had never been there at all.

He left his office, crossing the parking lot toward the white Mustang convertible that had once belonged to Chuck. He loved the smell of the leather interior and the way the hubcaps gleamed in the sun. Other than that it was a piece of shit. The passenger door was rusted shut. He climbed in and revved the engine, listening to it sputter and growl.

"Wait!"

The Journal receptionist ran across the parking lot toward him, waving a piece of paper.

"You just missed a phone call! I wrote the guy's number down. He said it's important!"

She paused when she reached him, and looked slightly embarrassed.

Daulton took the paper. "That it?"

"No, sorry, but I've been asked to remind you that you're on deadline."

"Thanks, Sal," he said facetiously, reading the message. His mood brightened and he gave her his best city smile. "Do me a favor? Tell the higher-ups I'll be back in a jiff!"

"I think they meant *now.*"

Daulton shook the note triumphantly. "This is good news, Sal, real good! Tell 'em it will be worth the wait!" He sped off down Main Street, humming along with the radio.

I said, young man, pick yourself off the ground. I said, young man, 'cause you're in a new town.

Soon, he was having the dreaded daydream. The one where some generic Hall of Fame committee, led by Chuck, insisted that he get his shit together by the end of the year, or else; the dream, more of a fugue really, featured Daulton looming far

above the earth, peering down at its antlike inhabitants while trying to figure out what they were and who he was among them. It
always ended the same way: with him asking the committee just
what the hell he was designated to do.

Young man, there's a place you can go . . .

He popped a tranquilizer in his mouth and checked his watch.
It was time for a session.

In the park on Fair Street was a circular road, a lazy sort of
traffic rotary, in the middle of which Daulton's childhood hero
James Fenimore Cooper sat on an oval of grass guarding the quiet
street. The lights from the Baseball Library cast a shadow over the
statue's face, distorting it. Daulton's headlights flickered against
Cooper's legs and made it appear as if the statue were moving:
Cooper tapping his foot and Daulton his fingers to the beat of the
Village People. Daulton slammed on the brakes, panicked, and
momentarily forgot who he was: the statue or the man—the cow-
boy, the policeman, or the Indian chief.

*No man does it all by himself. I said, young man, put your pride on the
shelf.*

He slowed as he passed the library, nearly flooring the brake.
The shapely silhouette of Bobby Reboulet was visible in the
window. He jumped when it moved, then struggled to envision
his own silhouette, which seemed rather amoebic. When Bobby
stepped outside for a smoke, he turned his gaze toward the
river.

*That's when someone came up to me, and said young man, take a walk
up the street.*

He thought about the old stone bridge that spanned the
Susquehanna. Some of his best memories were of hanging out
there with Manny during high school. They often *skipped* school,
in fact, with Johnny Fusselback and Honus Cronin, to drink and
spy on Bobby and her friends, who skipped school to drink and
spy right back on them: radios blasting pubescent angst in the
guise of "Chances Are," "All Shook Up," or "Something's Gotta

Give." Daulton had a crush on Bobby back then, though he never had the gumption to admit it. And from what Honus said, these days Bobby wasn't interested in romancing.

He pulled into the Chylaks' driveway. The doctor's kids were sitting on the lawn, legs outstretched, feet touching. They were playing the Game of Life. Daulton approached them just as the boy spun the fated wheel and hit "Bankrupt: Retire to the country and become a philosopher." He wanted to tell the child to stay there. *Stay right there.*

A pickup truck peeled off down Fair Street, too fast for Daulton to get a read on the license plate. The children looked up, startled. "Probably just some crazy tourist," Daulton told them, glad traffic violations were not his beat.

Dr. Chylak greeted him on the steps with a Tupperware cup full of scotch. Daulton followed him inside and waited in the living room while the doctor made a phone call. He admired the Chylaks' utilitarian style. There were no curtains in the windows, bare wooden floors, and a sofa covered in plastic, beneath which was a set of worn bedsheets peppered with characters from *Battlestar Galactica.* It was a comforting aesthetic, a temporary veneer that assured Daulton he wasn't the only person in town who had yet to fully commit to being a resident.

He had felt indebted to Chylak ever since Chuck's funeral. The doc had moved to Cooperstown just weeks before Chuck died and was apologetic about overstepping his bounds as both a physician and a newcomer. But Daulton had assured him that he was welcome. He knew from Chuck's letters that Chylak had made quite an impression on him. "I just let out steam," Chuck wrote, "and he absorbs it." Chuck had apparently been quick to welcome the doctor during his first week in town, *and* to become a patient. Daulton didn't know why Chuck, who was always so in control, needed a shrink, but he was grateful for anything Chylak had done to make his dad's final days easier, even if neither of them knew the end was near. Or did they?

Daulton had stopped by Chylak's house after Chuck's funeral, hoping Chylak would tell him something about his father, or his death, that he didn't already know. Before Chylak arrived, Chuck's letters had gone from "Health is fair. How's the writing?" to desperate pleas that Daulton not return home under any circumstances, even for Christmas, but that if he had to, to travel light. "Leave your stuff, *all* of it, in the city," he wrote. "I've got plenty of your old stuff here." It was an odd request, but Daulton dismissed it because old people did strange things sometimes. When Daulton's mom died, Chuck had splurged at Christmas, trying to fill the void by buying his son an endless supply of new toys. He figured Chuck wanted to do that again, for old time's sake, get him a bunch of new clothes or whatever for that hot job he was supposed to land in the city, not that Chuck could afford it.

Daulton stared at a crayon sketch of what he assumed was a brain, which hung on the wall of the Chylaks' living room. Or was it a piece of fruit? It reminded him of the drawings he had made for Chuck. He felt like he was letting Chuck down, having returned to town against his wishes. He expected Chylak to analyze that, initially, to give him advice on mourning—not his father, but his lost youth or some such malarkey. But during their first session the two of them simply sat on the doc's back porch, drinking—Chylak hardly saying a word. It was as if Chylak were waiting for him to extract himself, like an old banged-up turtle from its shell. To reveal the real reason behind his visit when he was good and ready, which Daulton appreciated. He had enjoyed the company. Chylak knew little about his past and did not judge his future. They had been meeting regularly since.

Chylak escorted Daulton to his "after-hours office," his back porch, where a set of plastic lawn furniture sat facing a miniature stable. Daulton took a seat, blaming his late arrival on a deadline. He decided not to mention the phone message he'd received from *The Journal*'s receptionist.

Chylak asked what he was working on.

Daulton said *The Journal* had finally granted him permission to write an experimental piece: an essay from the perspective of *Uncle Charlie,* regarding the question of whether or not he was being exploited. Charlie was Cooperstown's own special curve ball of sorts, a two-ton block of gypsum carved in the shape of a man that, according to legend, a nineteenth-century farmer had discovered while digging a privy. The farmer claimed it was the petrified remains of the first-ever ballplayer, the people claimed to believe it, and they'd been charging tourists anywhere from fifty cents to five bucks a head to view it ever since. It had even once aroused the attention of P. T. Barnum. It toured the country before it came to rest at the Farm Stead in the late 1940s, further cementing the nation's faith in Cooperstown as the true home of baseball. Now Charlie lay on the ground beneath a tent at the museum, outside with the goats and the sheep, his giant jowls grinning at the tourists that gawked back at him.

Daulton heard the doctor's kids arguing inside. Mrs. Chylak yelled for them to do something productive, like "Read Revelation!" She was a strange woman, Barbara Chylak, though not as strange as Bobby. Bobby Reboulet was one of the few people in town he had looked forward to seeing again, though she hadn't seemed to share the sentiment. Perhaps that was *why* he liked her. He was sure Chylak would have a theory about that and was about to ask him when Chylak excused himself and stepped inside. Daulton tried to drown out the sound of the doctor arguing with his wife. His mom died before he was old enough to start analyzing his own parents' relationship, and he figured that was probably a good thing. Marriage had never been a priority for him, but he was open to it, if the right gal came along, and at the right time. That time was not now.

He closed his eyes and thought about Bobby. She always had that look in her eye—one that said her mind was elsewhere, though her body resided in Cooperstown, must be four decades now. He didn't believe she had stayed in town all these years to nurture a wounded heart like Mrs. Paquette claimed. Nor did he believe she didn't *have* a heart, which is what Honus said. Surely Bobby, who looked as good now as she had at sixteen, with a brain and a sharp wit to boot, was a catch for any man. It wasn't surprising that Honus, who had always had an ego, thought *he* was that man. Daulton had run into his old pal recently at the Hall of Fame while checking out the Scribes and Mikemen exhibit. Included in the display was sportswriter John Kieran's typewriter, from which he had foolishly convinced himself he could garner good luck or at least a second chance. As if he could channel Kieran to clank out his fate on the keys: "You tried, now get a desk job." Grantland Rice's typewriter was there too, and Daulton noted, with interest, that Rice had coined the phrase "It's not whether you win or lose, it's how you play the game." He got lost in the museum, accidentally entering the employees' lavatory, where Honus stood before a mirror, admiring himself. He hadn't changed.

Chylak returned, apologizing profusely, and pulled up a chair, facing it toward the old kennel that stood at the edge of his lawn. It looked like it had once housed miniature ponies or very large dogs. Daulton seemed to recall it was the latter, remembering the delightful Indian family, the Bhavanadhans, who had lived there when he was a kid. There was something eerie about the structure now that it was empty, and he began to feel as though he weren't present. Like he was looking at a photograph of himself, contemplating a cage. He was startled back to reality when the doctor's daughter slammed the screen door, shouting over her Walkman—"*Oh, didn't I, didn't I, didn't I see you cryin'?*"

Chylak asked if he was covering the theme park saga.

"Looks that way. There's no one else to do it and it's newsworthy, around here anyway. Got any opinions on the matter, Doc? Anything you want to share as the town head-shrinker?"

Chylak rubbed the tape on the bridge of his nose and smiled. "My opinions cost seventy-five bucks an hour. You?"

"I have one or two left." Daulton sipped his drink. He was debating whether to confide his suspicions about Chuck's death: that the mayor and Manny knew more than they let on. He decided against it for now. He was probably being paranoid. "I found a place over on Mill Street," he said. "It's just a rental."

"So I heard."

Daulton cocked his brow.

"Mrs. Paquette told the mayor and—"

"I get the picture."

Daulton knew Chylak wanted him to move into Chuck's cottage or to at least clear it out for closure. It would be a great place to write. The lease was technically still in his family's name, despite what the mayor claimed. The building was officially property of the Funhouse, which was managed by the state historical society, and it wasn't like Fusselback was in a hurry to find a new curator. The last time Daulton inquired about it, the mayor said the lock on the front door was busted and that until he got someone over there to replace it, the key was useless. He said he was busy with the induction ceremony but promised to take care of it the second summer was over.

Daulton changed his mind and asked the doc if he was being paranoid. Perhaps the mayor was simply procrastinating, not wanting to erase the last visible signs of Chuck by opening his home so Daulton could clear it out. Chylak suggested that Daulton and Fusselback had an unconscious arrangement: as long as neither of them discarded Chuck's belongings, neither one would have to face the fact that they would never see him again. "Codependent denial," he called it. He said he shared a similar dynamic with his wife.

Daulton had to wonder, *was* he in denial? Because now that he thought about it, other than having arrived smack-dab in the middle of yesterday and demoting himself to a small-town gossip columnist, after Chuck died he *had* no real reason to stay.

He just did.

◆ ◆ ◆

C HYLAK NOTICED THAT WHENEVER his patient spoke about anything remotely serious he stared straight ahead as though reading from a prompter. Terry Daulton looked uncannily like his father—the dark hair peppered gray, the ruddy complexion and Romanesque nose. Chylak missed Chuck. Was it possible to miss someone you had only begun to know? When he first arrived in Cooperstown he found, to his horror, that not only was he the lone psychiatrist but there were no *psychologists* either, not even a social worker to buff him from the dirty details of his patients' psyches while he stuck to doing what he did best, doling out meds. It was as though nothing had ever gone wrong in Cooperstown; no one had issues to iron out or required any outside assistance. And that would have been fine, had the hospital director not asked him to play every role, "just in case." He had been tricked, misled about the position, and was certain he was the wrong man for the job. When an actual *patient* showed up, Chuck, he wasn't sure which one of them to medicate first, Chuck or himself. But Chuck took pity on him, insisting on daily sessions every day for a week. Their sessions often ran over and Chylak was surprised to find he actually enjoyed them. Chuck, a jocular fellow, had been about the only person in town who could say "Call me crazy" without basis.

Chylak asked Daulton whether he was on speaking terms yet with Mr. Barrett. "You two go way back. My mother used to say, 'Choose your friends. Don't let them choose you.' Did you choose him or was it the other way around?" Daulton replied that they went so far back he had forgotten who chose whom.

Chylak thought about Babe. He supposed they had chosen each other. He gazed at the kennel wondering which ate more: a small Boston terrier or a large Tibetan spaniel? He was trying not to listen. Chylak felt like the odd man out in Cooperstown. Listening to Daulton could lead to a diagnosis, a diagnosis could lead to a cure, and a cure could rob him of the one shot he had at making an actual friend. A friend who suffered from an identity disorder with symptoms of depersonalization, sure, but one could argue that such conditions were triggered by trauma and the only thing distressing Daulton was his location. He constantly sought reassurance that it was all right for him to *be* in Cooperstown.

Chylak decided to test a new theory he'd read about the intestines, the gut, as a "second brain." It meant urging his patient to trust a brain prone to gas, but whatever. He steered the conversation toward a topic he hoped would sway Daulton to remain in town.

"I saw Ms. Reboulet this morning."

Daulton perked, then panicked. "Is she a patient?"

Chylak hardly knew the baseball librarian, though he had run into her at the nursing home where she had volunteered to read to patients. Her choice of reading material, a personal abridgment of Eliot's *The Waste Land,* caused one elderly woman to hyperventilate. Ms. Reboulet apparently had a way of telling it like she saw it, and telling it to children and the infirm was no exception. Chylak was curious about her, this female who was fodder for so much local gossip. She fascinated Babe, which made him nervous. She was probably a vegetarian. All he needed was some militant, vegetarian feminist librarian whisking Babe off to join some all-chick commune, along with the children, who would eventually succumb to being raised by so many "mommies" they would inevitably forget about dear old Papa. A trip to the Baseball Library was in order; he could kill two cuckoo birds with one stone: quench his curiosity about Reboulet and seek answers, amid the library's endless shelves, about the sport that made his new town tick. He was about to suggest that Daulton ask the librarian for a date, but that meant breaking his rule about not getting personal amid depersonalization. Besides, he was no authority on women. At breakfast, Alice had asked for a childish show of hands as to who in the family resented the move. Chylak had not expected *Babe* to raise her hand as well, as though she had simply been asked whether she wanted a new dishwasher.

Daulton swatted a mosquito from his ankle. Chylak took advantage of the distraction to peruse the book he had tucked beneath the plastic Diazepam cushion beneath him, which he had obtained from a pharmaceutical rep. He plucked a fresh quote from *Going Crazy: The Radical Therapy of R. D. Laing and Others,* edited by Dr. Henrik M. Ruitenbeek and reprinted for a second run in '72, a delightful seven years behind the game. The first page said "*Going Crazy* offers a different kind of radical relief," but he feared such a comment would encourage his patient. The book contained several baseball analogies, which might be just the remedy for a baseball writer, particularly one who claimed to no longer care about baseball. At worst, it might light a fire under Daulton's indecisive derriere, forcing him out from under his father's shadow and onto his own path. Daulton stared at the kennel, now completely preoccupied, so Chylak quickly read aloud.

> *The realization of the nonsubstantiality of the self is at the base of what is probably the most radical and transforming experience in "therapy."* ... *The problem has to be seen, but inextricably wound up with the seeing of the problem is the seeing through of the self. And so one laughs and laughs with the other who sees through one's self and sees through one's seeing through of one's self. The pain remains totally real but can now become the ball of a joyous ball game without loss of its value as pain.*

"What?" said Daulton, snapping to attention somewhere between "the other who sees" and "seeing through of one's self."

"Never mind." Chylak sighed. He was beginning to feel not unlike a child who desperately wanted another child to like him. He returned to a more productive topic: Chuck. He hadn't always listened to Chuck's confessions either, because he liked him. However, he recalled that some possession of Chuck's had been plaguing him, something that seemed irrelevant at the time. Whatever it was, it might be of use to his son. It was as though

Daulton the younger had forgotten, in the truest sense, *who* he was—that, or he simply didn't want to face it, a feeling Chylak related to. After breakfast, as a gesture of good faith, he had inquired about Babe's plans for the day. She grabbed a pen from his briefcase, and scrawled on her napkin that it was "silent week at church." "We're not *at* church!" Chylak snapped, which led to her storming off to the kitchen.

He decided urging Daulton to clear out his father's so-called dirty laundry was just the psychological enema Daulton needed. "I think it's time for you to sort through your father's things. Perhaps he left valuables behind. Something that could wind up in the wrong hands? He would have appreciated your looking after his things."

"There really isn't much there, Doc," said Daulton. "Chuck got rid of all the good stuff, jewelry and antiques and such, when Mom died, and that was decades ago. Since then, the two of us led a pretty simple life. I don't imagine he owned much of importance, aside from some old baseball cards."

Chylak supposed it had been the cards. "They could be worth something. You could sell them, donate them to the Hall of Fame."

"I guess. Listen, Doc, I promise I'll get over there as soon as the induction ceremony is over."

From what Chylak understood, the induction ceremony was *never* over. It came around each year like an indomitable horsefly. The next time it came, he just hoped he'd be quick enough to move out of the way before it stung him too.

D AULTON WAITED FOR THE doctor to refill his drink, feeling a twinge of irresponsibility at having withheld something from his therapist that might impede his progress. He had changed his mind about covering the Hall of Fame Game, and he had done so *because* of Chylak. It was that metaphor for pain as a baseball. He knew what Chylak would say if he covered the game: that he was struggling to prove something to Chuck, who was dead and thus had no expectations. He even agreed with Chylak, in part. But if he stuck around to cover the game, it *might* be the answer to all his problems. It would allow him to write about baseball, to interview some big players, without the pressure of worrying that what he wrote would be rejected; he was on staff at *The Journal* and they always covered the game. They were *begging* him to cover it. He could be, just once, what Chuck had wanted him to be, a baseball writer, and then he could move on, having satisfied them both. It was convenient closure: surely Chylak would agree. Besides, Daulton thought, thrilled with the phone message he'd received earlier, the more research he did on the theme park, the more eagerly he anticipated its arrival. The townsfolk knew they didn't want it. Daulton knew they had no choice.

Cooperstown's economy had been declining steadily since the mid-1960s; the townsfolk had taken their wallets to the nearby cities—Oneonta, Utica, and Albany—to do their more serious shopping, leaving Cooperstown's mom-and-pop shops dependent on tourists who flocked to town primarily in the summertime. Gearing merchandise strictly toward tourists was becoming a problem, because it meant *not* catering it to locals, who had more baseball key chains, pins, pendants, pencils, Doubleday refrigerator magnets, and Hall of Fame hand towels than they needed. Soon there would be nothing left to *buy* in Cooperstown, aside from counseling, groceries, and, Daulton hoped, the paper. The ball game would provide an excuse to stick around and see the theme park saga through. This was a temporary gig, he assured himself, a mere pit stop in his plans, and if he played his cards right, the game could mean his ticket out. He grew more excited by the minute, determined to come up with an angle that would give the annual Hall of Fame Game a fresh spin. Perhaps tie it into his final piece on the park. *The Journal* was paying him to report, so the townsfolk would have to understand that even though he was technically one of them, he *had* to be objective while digging up dirt, even if that dirt lay close to home. The question was, *could* he be objective? He was anxious to return that phone call.

"You still with me?" Chylak said, rattling his cup in Daulton's face.

"Yeah, Doc, but I gotta take off." Daulton downed his drink and stood, thanking Chylak as he reached for his wallet.

"Don't be crazy," Chylak said, refusing the cash. Daulton was doing him a favor—he enjoyed these little cocktail chats. Besides, he wasn't sure how it would look to his new employers, inviting his patients home for drinks, and he couldn't afford to find out.

"I'll try, Doc, thanks," Daulton said.

He made a lame excuse about needing to call Judge Yëld for a quote on the theme park, then shook the doctor's hand and walked briskly toward his car. He was rounding the corner of Chylak's house when it occurred to him that he wasn't sure which side of the theme park saga Chylak was on. It was smart to gather a variety of perspectives.

"Hey!" he called. "You sign the petition?"

Chylak shook his head. "I'm not at liberty to say!"

"Suit yourself," Daulton said, laughing. "But if the mayor finds out, he'll have your hide!"

"You're the one who's going to Albany to interview his son!"

Daulton halted in his tracks, his hands on his hips. "Now who said *that?*" he demanded.

"Well, my wife heard it from Mrs. Paq—"

"Uh-huh," Daulton said, disappearing around the corner with a brief wave over his shoulder to signal the session was over.

He drove through Cooper Park toward Main Street. Bobby stood on the library steps, smoking. She seemed mesmerized by Duke Cartwright, who circled the statue of Cooper, riding his bike with no hands. Mrs. Paquette sauntered by, makeup bag in tow. Daulton saw her before Bobby did—poor Bobby had no idea what, or *who*, was about to hit her. Daulton honked to warn her, laughing when Paquette began extracting items from her old kit bag to present to a visibly peeved Bobby. He sped away, smiling smugly. He had news for old tittle-tattle Paquette. He eyed the phone message on the seat beside him. He wasn't going to Albany.

Johnny Fusselback was coming to town.

FOURTH INNING

Progress always involves risk; you can't steal second base and keep your foot on first.

—FREDERICK WILCOX

The museum was sweltering, thanks to President Carter's national energy shortage solution involving temperature restrictions on public buildings. Fortunately for Honus Cronin, the National Baseball Hall of Fame wasn't open to the public after five o'clock, which gave the security guard total run of the place.

Honus loved the museum, which he thought of as a shrine to the memory of his beloved predecessor, Frank Paquette. Sometimes he even imagined himself an honorary Hall of Fame inductee, a fantasy that included a hug from the mayor, who said, "Honus? You're like the son I had, only better!"

Honus's job description included patrolling each room in the museum to be sure the exhibits, and the tourists, were safe during the day, and locking the museum up each night after the maintenance crew had finished cleaning. This allowed him the luxury of examining exhibits with neither curator nor tourists around there to bug him. Sometimes he manhandled the artifacts, though not without returning them to their proper places afterward. Today he was wedged inside Joe DiMaggio's old locker, and sat on the bottom shelf to take a light reading break. Honus was a small guy, but his looks made up for it.

He squeezed his bony rump out of the locker and stretched, fanning himself with the latest issue of *Sports Illustrated*. The cover story read "Nolan Ryan just misses a record fifth no-hitter." Hoping to find a switch that controlled the central air, he searched the wall for the fuse box. It hung next to a display entitled *70 Nights in a Ballpark,* a guide from the late fifties meant to increase ballpark attendance. Honus ran a plump hand through his hair—the same dapper duck's-ass coif he had donned for decades. He admired his reflection in the glass.

The display read THIS OR THIS? and was accompanied by two illustrations, one of a vacant ballpark and one that was packed full. They seemed to pose the question "Baseball or baseball?" He began to wonder if the theme park would pay better than the museum. Not that he'd ever work at a theme park. Frank wouldn't have approved. Nor would the mayor, for whom Honus would do just about anything. The mayor said the Hall of Fame was in danger of being eliminated, replaced by some kind of ride, its precious artifacts strung out on a long conveyor belt, like so many cheap carnival trinkets for all the world to see. They *had* to fight the park.

He swung a flashlight back and forth across the exhibit. If he swung quickly enough, the illustrations came to life, miniature ballparks with Honus's handsome head looming center field. He flicked the flashlight on and off, enjoying the effect. Then he inserted a key attached to his belt into the lock on a shadow box. It contained a battered baseball made by Babe Ruth while Ruth was a boy at St. Mary's Industrial School for Boys, an orphanage and reformatory. The museum also housed a bat carved by an anonymous Ruth fan that was bedecked with beads and looked like a tiny totem pole with a little voodoo Ruth god on top. Honus loved Babe Ruth, for he too was an orphan. Of course, neither of them was *really* an orphan: Ruth's father sent him to St. Mary's for disciplinary reasons and Honus's ma ran off with a tourist when he was a kid. He had never known his dad, and his therapist suggested that was the reason for his constant hankering to please people like the mayor. Lately Honus was experiencing a pang for *maternal* love, one that flat-out plunked when it came to Bobby. Because of her, the Baseball Library was off-limits to Honus until

Dr. Chylak said he could go there without giving her a second thought. It had been much easier to see Bobby when she worked at Town Library, which was down the street from the Hall of Fame. But Mrs. Paquette had caught her smoking in a room full of rare Cooper first editions, and Bobby had been fired.

Honus listened for signs of life in the museum. He wanted to be sure that Walker Peabody, the janitor, hadn't left without him. Peabody was upstairs, vacuuming. Honus breathed a sigh of relief. He loved the museum, but that did not mean he liked being alone in it. It helped that Frank's spirit was all around him. Frank had left countless personal items behind when he died, tucked inside exhibits. He was quite the hoarder—like one of those Egyptians who stashed things they might need in the afterlife within their tombs. It was like a part of him, his soul, still watched over the museum. Once, Honus had found Frank's shaving kit inside an old box of "Babe Ruth Underwear." Another time, he found a pair of Frank's saddle shoes inside Babe Ruth's locker. They reminded him of a fairy tale his ma used to read about kids lost in a forest who leave bread crumbs behind in order to find their way home. He had tried to get Mrs. Paquette to claim Frank's stuff, but she had refused, saying it was too painful.

Peabody was making a racket upstairs, cranking the gramophone they were under strict orders not to touch, the one that featured Teresa Brewer and Mickey Mantle singing *I Love Mickey! Mickey who? Mickey you!* Honus tapped his feet to the rhythm.

He shined his light on the ten-foot-tall scoreboard that had once hung from the balcony of the Blair Hotel in Waynesburg, Pennsylvania, so fans could track the World Series in the mid to late 1920s. He took the dry mop Peabody had left leaning against the wall and reached up to dust cobwebs from the top of the board, running the mop back and forth over the words "hit" and "error." The scoreboard began to sway. "Shit!" Honus yelled, stabilizing it before it could come crashing down upon him. Something fell out from behind it and landed at his feet with a sharp smack—another random item that didn't belong in the museum.

It was a book, *The Last of the Mohicans*. The elevator hissed to a standstill, signaling that Peabody was about to exit the building. Honus figured Frank wouldn't mind if he borrowed the book. He knew just what to do with it. He tucked it under his arm and ran up the stairs—any second now the lights would go out and the Hall of Fame, so pleasant in daylight, would become ominous, a dark cavern of colorful spirits, ballplayers and curators, lingering, lonesome, in its hallowed halls.

CHYLAK WAS HOME IN his study, wondering how he had already misplaced the copy of Freud's *A General Introduction to Psycho-Analysis* he had plucked just that morning from the fifty-cent bin at Town Library. He wanted to finish that chapter on narcissism before his next session with Honus Cronin. Freud said one thing, Kernberg another—he decided to mix them together and sprinkle a little Chylak on top.

"Make me happy," Cronin had demanded during their last session. Chylak had clarified that he did not get paid to make people happy, but rather to make them realize they were *not*. He considered the object of Cronin's affection: the mysterious Ms. Reboulet. "Reboulet," Mrs. Paquette had told Babe, was a bastardization of the French *rebuter* (to put off), *rebrousser* (to turn back), and *poulet* (chicken). Chylak had warned Cronin about bothering her at work. But Alice had seen him at the Baseball Library last night. She had no idea Honus was one of her father's patients, of course. The idea of his patients consorting with his children made Chylak uneasy. He had drilled Alice about the interaction, not because he feared Honus would harm her—his condition was nonviolent—but because he was afraid Honus would tell Alice something about *him* (for instance, that he was an inadequate therapist). Alice said the security guard had hung around the circulation desk and was pestering the librarian to come over after work and look at their high school yearbook over beers. Ms. Reboulet had shooed him out, though not before

Honus gave Alice a suggestion for her summer reading list. Alice had a rather intensive reading list, initiated by Babe to ensure she was in sync with her fellow schoolmates come fall. Babe's syllabus focused on local history texts, and Chylak was sorry he hadn't scoured it for books about baseball. *Baseball* wouldn't get Alice into college. He decided to chaperone her next visit to the Baseball Library and, while he was at it, take Elliott to the Hall of Fame to warn him about the perils of fanaticism when combined with the wielding of wooden instruments.

Cronin's obsession with the librarian intrigued Chylak. She was quite the local beauty, though Cronin was clearly the local narcissist. He had exchanged a brief smooch with Ms. Reboulet in junior high school and seemed determined to hold on to what might have been. Longing for a woman, his Echo, who defied all semblance of mythology by refusing to love him back. He had recently asked Chylak if it was possible for a person to love you and not *like* you. Chylak said they would address that next time. He had several theories on the matter, culled from personal experience. "It's impossible," Cronin insisted, but Chylak disagreed. Then again, he generally disagreed with patients on principle, because it seemed pointless for them to pay to hear what they had already told themselves.

Chylak had pondered this question of like versus love just this morning, when he discovered a plastic crucifix that Babe had hung above the toilet off his study. He told her it made relieving oneself an unnecessarily pious experience. He then suggested that perhaps even Christ had occasionally enjoyed a good ham for supper. Perhaps they could have one tonight with a nice honey glaze? Babe simply snapped, "You don't *get* it, do you?" Chylak got it, all right, and he told her so: he was onto her with the incessant vegetable consumption, and if she was punishing him, or his stomach, for something, she ought to come out and say so; the children shouldn't have to pay for it too. It was a low blow, but not as low as Babe bellowing, "They already are!" then slamming the door in his face. Chylak had marched off to work, determined to bury himself in paperwork until lunch, when guilt overcame him. He trudged back home to his study to make a show of being present while continuing to work. In his opinion, Babe should admit to a few things herself, such as why she, the oh-so-virtuous vixen from Noblesville, had *married* him if she was so diametrically opposed to his beliefs or lack thereof. He, after all, remembered their wedding night, and the "Jesus! Yes! Yes!"es and the sex toys had *both* come from her.

Elliott was chattering away to himself upstairs, his high-pitched voice wafting through the floorboards and into Chylak's study, which meant he was in Alice's room and probably uninvited. Chylak listened.

"Asteroids are better than Space Invaders."

"What's your problem?"

"I hate it here."

"You're nutso."

Chylak had caught him playing the same game earlier in the week, Elliott addressing the poster of Leif Garrett that hung beside Alice's bed as though Garrett were a therapist (as though, Chylak supposed, Garrett were *he*). Elliott had a bad habit of snooping in his sister's room; he had been flipping through the pamphlet that Alice hid beneath her mattress. Babe had given it to her one night during dinner after announcing, to Alice's dismay, that Alice was becoming a woman. *Natural Me,* it was called, and, if one subscribed to Elliott's interpretation of it, it contained "dirty pictures" and warnings about "what happens when you kiss people with sores." Chylak had also caught him nonchalantly nibbling the tip off Alice's Bonnie Bell bubble gum lip gloss. Elliott claimed there was nothing better to do in "the Coop," a nickname for his new town that he had acquired from the neighbors.

Chylak smacked a palm across his forehead: he had forgotten to inquire whether it was too late for Elliott to join Little League! Babe was bound to find out from their neighbor, Mrs. Olsen. She thought playing ball would help Elliott acclimate, but Chylak was wary of the idea, as was Elliott, who argued that he could contract athlete's foot from unsanitary gym showers and those stuffy little cleats. Babe said Elliott's new pal Joey Olsen had joined and loved it. Elliott replied that Joey was only his pal because when two kids were new, their moms *made* them become friends so their moms could be friends. The Olsens had moved to Cooperstown from Cincinnati a week before the Chylaks, and Babe had been on Chylak's case to introduce himself to Dr. Olsen and to invite them over for dinner. Chylak had refused, having immediately pegged Olsen as an overeducated social worker apt to analyze him in front of the children.

He could hear the pitter-patter of Elliott's feet descending the stairs. The boy was singing in a silly, nasally Kermit the Frog voice, which seemed a positive sign until Chylak listened closely to the lyrics. *"Have you been half asleep? And have you heard voices? I've heard them calling my naaaaame . . ."*

He held his breath, expecting Elliott to march into his study and inquire about schizophrenia, having forgotten their pact: whenever Elliott felt compelled to ask a health question, he was to sing a song instead. If he could go an entire week without pestering Chylak for some preposterous diagnosis, the two of them would go see *Star Trek: The Motion Picture.*

Elliott entered the study and, sure enough, went straight for the step stool below Chylak's towering shelves. He climbed to the upper rung, groping around for the *American Psychiatric Association's Diagnostic and Statistical Manual of Mental Disorders* in search of a suitable ailment to bring to the dinner table. Chylak had hidden the book. He and Babe were onto Elliott's naughty new attention-seeking ploy. Elliott was becoming a small hypochondriac, or, more to the point: a rather big faker. It began on the long drive from Lebanon. They were playing Mad Libs in the car, Elliott inserting all manner of miserable mental afflictions in the fill-in-the-blanks game where more upbeat adjectives should've been. Chylak felt unable to mollify his son's fears about the move. It was much easier to tell adults when they were being irrational, but children? Their entire world struck him as irrational: they talked to themselves (they talked to *everything*), pitched hypomanic hissy fits whenever the slightest thing, a shoelace or a belt buckle, was uncooperative, and were known to pick chewing gum off the ground at a moment's notice and, sometimes, to *eat* it.

Babe was in the kitchen humming along to a gospel tune, "Why Me?" Why indeed, thought Chylak, wishing Alice would lend her mother a pop record. If Babe continued resorting to religion at this rapid rate, soon they would all be wearing loincloths, and the children would forget about puppies and demand a crabby little baby camel for a pet.

Elliott asked if what Alice said was true: Did Chylak work in a laboratory where they performed "gross experiments on people's heads"? Alice had made up a song about it, to the tune of "Le Freak," by Chic. It was a tune that got her grounded for the weekend. Chylak plucked his son off the ladder and set him on the floor. He handed Elliott a copy of *The Dancing Wu Li Masters: An Overview of the New Physics,* by Gary Zukav, which claimed to take readers from quantum mechanics "beyond to the Einstein-Podolsky-Rosen effect and Bell's theorem." *So* far beyond that not even Chylak could say where. He intended to bore Elliott straight out of scientific texts altogether and reintroduce him to something more practical for his age, like Pooh. Elliott flipped through the text like a fiend, seizing on several passages that Chylak had forgotten he'd highlighted. Elliott read them aloud, doing his best to sound out what he called "the biggies." The words he didn't understand.

"'The common denominator of all experiences is the "I" that does the experiencing.'" "'What is nonsense and what is not, then, may be merely a matter of perspective.'" He asked what "perspective" meant, and before Chylak could respond, Babe appeared in the doorway, hands on her hips, replying with a curt "Nonsense! The common denominator of all experiences is the Savior Christ Jesus. Dinner in five." She turned on her heels and disappeared, leaving the Chylak men to point at each other as if to say "It's your fault we're in trouble." Elliott giggled.

Chylak went to help Babe with dinner. If working from home earned him brownie points, contributing unasked to meal preparation was bound to get him a gold star, perhaps in the bedroom, where he most wanted it. Babe stood by the stove, tracing a recipe in the *Better Homes and Gardens Cookbook* with one hand and stirring a pot of turnip stew in the other. She was newly a vegetarian and determined to take the rest of the family down with her. She looked rather pretty—face flushed pink from the steam and strawberry blond hair arranged into two loose ponytails that made her appear, at thirty-five, just as she had the day they met. Chylak recalled the way he'd brushed snow from her coat at that bus stop so long ago. He was about to free a strand of sweat-soaked hair that clung to her swanlike neck, but he retracted his hand when she turned around to shout in his face for Alice to come to dinner.

"I'll get her," said Chylak. He was about to ask where Alice was when he heard her in the backyard. Once more, at the sound of his child singing, his spirits rose.

"Once I had a looove! It was a gas. Soon turned out to be a pain in the—"

Babe slammed the door closed, drowning out Alice, and called Elliott to come wash up for supper. The boy appeared holding a pair of surgical gloves that Chylak had stolen from the sanitarium. Elliott liked to blow them up into balloon roosters. Chylak shook his head to imply this was not a good time for such shenanigans, and picked him up, holding him over the kitchen sink to ensure he washed his hands.

"Where's Alice?" Elliott asked.

"In the backyard," replied Babe. Alice was apparently heartbroken at Chylak's recent suggestion that her beloved Freddie Mercury might not like girls. "Kerwin!" she scolded. "How could you? Go talk her out of her funk."

Chylak did as he was asked, crossing the yard with Elliott in tow. In the moonlight the boy's oblong head threw a strange shadow across the lawn, making it look as though he had arrived on the other side long before he actually had. Elliott noticed too and seemed to like this about himself. They stooped to examine the remains of a box of Boo Berry cereal scattered at the base of a tree. Elliott found a stray Susan B. Anthony coin as well and pocketed it without asking to whom it belonged. Chylak despised the coins, certain they were created to annoy adults who confused them with quarters and to make children rich off that confusion. Something fell on his head. He looked up to where Alice was perched in the tree. She was puffing on a candy cigarette and had just chucked the cereal box down at them. Elliott remarked that with headphones on, Alice's head looked "big like an alien." Chylak had to agree. He wondered if he had lost his daughter forever to the wearisome Walkman.

"What are you listening to?" he yelled to her, silencing Elliott—who was chanting "You're iiin troooouble!"—with a pat on the head. He motioned for Alice to turn off the Walkman. He was unsure how to approach matters of the heart where his newly teenage daughter was concerned, particularly now that she was becoming a woman, a state that came equipped with a gamut of moods as foreign to him as holistic therapy, if Babe was any example.

A scowling Alice replied, "The Logical Song."

Elliott asked what "logical" meant.

"It means you're retarded," said Alice.

"You are!"

"No, *you* are!"

"Children, please!" Chylak reproached.

"Fine!" said Alice, pouting. "It means what makes sense."

Elliott declared with a stomp of his sandaled foot that *nothing* made sense. Why was his dad always late for dinner when he worked right across the street? How could his mommy be a bride of Christ if she was married to his dad? Did his new school have a jungle gym? Chylak scooped him up and said these were all very good questions, best addressed at a more appropriate time. He gave Elliott the can of Mello Yello with which he had hoped to entice Alice inside, where there was ice to go with it.

"What do you guys want?" Alice demanded.

"Mommy says it's time to eat!"

Elliott attempted to leap from Chylak's arms and into the tree, but Chylak gently removed him by the seat of his pants. The boy had inherited his poor vision and thus, tree climbing was best left to daylight.

"I'm not hungry," Alice said.

"Tough. It's your turn to set the table," said Chylak.

"*So?*"

Chylak's jaw dropped. This back-talking business was new and seemed to come with the territory. Lately, when it was not his children, it was his patients.

"*Laverne and Shirley*'s on after!" Elliott cried.

"Okay, I'm comin'," said Alice.

Inside, they took their places around the dinner table, Alice shouting "Liar, liar, pants on fire" at Elliott when she found turnips on her plate where he swore a hamburger would be. There was shin-kicking under the table.

"If everyone will kindly bow their heads, I'll say grace," said Babe. "Tonight's prayer is a passage from Romans 14:2. 'One man's faith allows him to eat everything, but another man, whose faith is weak, eats only vegetables.'"

This vegetarian vengefulness was exactly as Chylak had thought, an underhanded opportunity for Babe to make a totally unrelated point. But what was it? He was being punished, that was certain. Midway through the prayer he opened his eyes and looked at his wife as he did every night; it was the only opportunity he had anymore to observe her without inviting the third degree. Her head was bowed, her blond bangs hanging before her pert little nose, her pink lips mouthing the prayer, the *plea,* it seemed, the response to which he was certain she alone could hear. He reached across the table to stop Alice, who was slipping turnips casually into her napkin. Elliott had a noodle dangling from his upper lip like a mustache. Chylak shook his finger at him, and then winked. Unable to wink, Elliott blinked back, over and over until Chylak realized he had left his manual on motor ticks in the bathroom and that the boy was now using it against him. He cleared his throat, "A-hem," interrupting the remainder of Babe's recitation to discuss a new theory he had read regarding the social habits of orangutans. "If you think about nonhuman primates," he said, stuffing a fat turnip into his mouth and then, aghast at its bitterness, gesturing for Alice to quickly pass him the milk.

"First of all, I wasn't done saying grace. Secondly, why must you always say things like 'nonhuman primates'?" Babe bristled. "Why can't you just say what you mean? What's wrong with 'orangutans'?" She had apparently seen the same episode of Mutual of Omaha's *Wild Kingdom* and was in no mood to converse with the primate she'd married.

"What's an oran-goo-tang? Why can't you just say *monkeys?*" asked Alice.

"I want a monkey, Dad!" said Elliott, raising his hand as though he had been given a choice.

Chylak took a moment to restrategize, determined to instigate a proper flow of spontaneous, familial communication. "I have an idea! Let's go around the table like we did in Lebanon and tell one another about our day. Elliott? You first."

Alice rolled her eyes.

Elliott had spent the afternoon at Joey's house playing video games and had been traded a Bobblehead Joe Morgan figurine for his Stretch Armstrong, a rubber fellow with gelatinous innards that Chylak, for one, was glad to be rid of. It was a disturbing toy: a man stretched to his limits and exposed like a defenseless infant in tiny little underpants. It was clear that Elliott's new acquaintance—who had a baseball cap, a Little League team, and a bobblehead ball player collection—was adapting quite well to Cooperstown. Meanwhile, Elliott had resigned himself to simply surviving it sans recurring *E. coli* enteritis, which he was proud to announce in the middle of dinner was "a fancy word for diarrhea," the sort that occurs when one spends too much time in a place one is not used to. Babe looked at Chylak. "Alice? Your turn," he said.

Alice seemed to miss the point entirely; she confessed a burning desire for a curling iron so powerful it would allow her to feather her hair into a perfectly symmetrical tube all the way around her head. She then went on about a Coke commercial she had seen in which Mean Joe Green gives an admiring young fan his jersey. "'Hey, kid!' he yells."

Elliott interrupted to say he had seen a better commercial, one for a Jawa Droid Factory.

A frustrated Chylak told the children that if they were done eating, they were excused from the table. They were happy to oblige, leaving their plates half full of turnip stew. Elliott flew upstairs and Alice into the den to watch television.

Chylak decided that tonight, he would do the dishes, run a bath for Babe, and then watch television with Alice, just as soon as he finished prepping for tomorrow morning's session. Babe sat across from him. They eyed each other in an unspoken duel, both eager, anxious, hopeful that the other would draw first to break the tension. Chylak opened his mouth and then closed it immediately. He had not prepared anything to say. Though it was clear from the expression on Babe's face—her brows were raised expectantly—that winging it might do. Partial to well-rehearsed dialogue, he did his best, testing her with a topic that seemed safe: controversial new theories in the psychiatric community about borderline personalities. As though regular, run-of-the-mill personalities weren't problem enough.

Babe exhaled slowly, shoving her chair from the table, and said she had to call her mother, leaving Chylak to review his own day in his head. He didn't bother. He knew how it ended: him alone at the dinner table before a plate of cold vegetables, wondering what went wrong. He retired to his study, and by the time he finished his notes, Babe had run her own bath, Elliott was in bed, and Alice was in her room blasting "Do Ya Think I'm Sexy" at unbearable decibels from her Cher Sing-Along Phono Turntable.

Chylak ascended the stairs, hands over his ears, wondering if there was indeed some merit to Elliott's claim that teenagers sometimes played records backward "to hear a special message from the devil." He rapped on Alice's door, gesturing for her to turn down the music, and then entered the pink-wallpapered room. Alice was on her bed with her feet up on the wall, reading *Teen Beat*. He motioned for her to remove her shoes, said goodnight, and gave her a kiss on the cheek. On his way out the door he hesitated and said, "I'm sorry for what I said about your friend."

Alice looked at him.

"Freddie Methyl?"

She rolled her eyes.

"He's not my *friend,* dad. It's Mercury and he's a rock star."

"I see," said Chylak, nostalgic for a time when *he* was the star of his daughter's universe, versus the guy she asked for advice when Babe wasn't available, like some second-rate parental understudy. He apologized again and Alice softened, telling him not to worry: she was over that fellow and had developed a new crush on one Officer Frank Poncherello. Chylak implored her to say she meant the character from *CHiPs* and not another older man whom she had met at the library. Alice looked at him—a quicksilver flash of braces as she smiled—and he relaxed. Somewhere in there, below the tough attitude, puffy hair, and Andy Gibb T-shirt, she was still his little girl.

Elliott was in his room debating aloud with some unseen deity as to whether it was necessary to pray before meals *and* at bedtime. "Mommy says yes, and Daddy" (who had forgotten he said this and regretted it now, as it was bound to later make its way to Babe out of context) "says it's optional, depending on 'if you believe God hates people because of fruit.'" Chylak flinched. Elliott then vowed aloud to save his allowance for a bus ticket back to Lebanon. Chylak's heart sank. He was debating whether to enter or call it a night when Elliott made the decision for him.

"I'm a one-eyed, one-horned flying purple people eater! A one-eyed, one-horned—"

"Settle down now. It's time for bed," Chylak said, entering the room. Elliott was clad in Incredible Hulk footsy pajamas despite the heat and was jumping up and down on the bed.

"Alice. Is. Playing. Music." He protested as he bounced.

"I've asked her to turn it down."

Chylak snatched Elliott from the air midbounce and laid him on the bed, peeling away the scotch tape Elliott had stuck to the bridge of his glasses. Elliott introduced his father to Joe, the bobblehead figurine tucked beneath his arm where Pooh Bear used to be. Chylak had a sudden overwhelming desire to find that old bear and coddle it. Elliott was growing bigger every day. He had a rather grown-up-looking book on his bed as well, one that was worse for wear. There was a mustiness to it.

"I can't sleep," Elliott said.

"Count sheep."

"Sheep have rabies and rabies make you insaaaane—yayayaya," Elliott replied, mimicking Paul Lynde from *Hollywood Squares*. When he asked to be checked for agoraphobia, Chylak sighed and acquiesced, humoring him with a quick lymph check, though not before explaining that agoraphobia is a fear of being in public, and everyone knew Elliott had spent the day at Joey's. Elliott giggled, guilty though pleased to have earned the spotlight.

"Try to think about something pleasant," Chylak told him.

"Like Lebanon?"

"No. Like Princess Leia, or Fluffernutters."

"I'm allergic to marshmallow." Elliott clutched his chest, his tongue hanging from the side of his mouth as he feigned death by fluffernutter. "Read to me!" he demanded.

Chylak used to read Elliott psychiatric manuals; at one time they induced him to sleep. Now the tactic was coming back to haunt him. He snatched the book on Elliott's bed. It looked as if it had been pulled from the trash. "Where did you get this?" he said, flipping it over to examine the cover. "It smells terrible."

Elliott looked guilty, mumbling that the book belonged to Alice.

"Did you *ask* to borrow it?"

Elliott shook his head. Chylak said he would return the book for him, but to ask next time. *The Last of the Mohicans,* it was called, and he hoped the Mohicans wasn't a baseball team. "I have a better idea," he said. "You tell *me* a story. Tell me what you've been reading."

Elliott made room for him on the edge of the bed, explaining that he had only read one page, in which a group of people, including a girl called Alice, were hiding in a cavern and heard a spooky noise; the girl shrieked, at which point, Elliott said, *he* heard a spooky noise. He told Chylak that Alice's new friend, Judy White, had a ghost in her attic and that he and Joey had each paid a quarter to see the noose with which she had hung herself. Apparently, it looked suspiciously like a macramé plant hanger.

"Ghosts are not a suitable topic for bedtime. Please finish the story."

"I can't."

"Why not?"

"Something ate the middle."

"I don't suppose that something was the flying purple people eater?" Chylak said. He knew this scenario well: next Elliott would demand that his *Happy Days* night-light be left on all night and that Chylak check beneath his bed for boogeymen.

"Read to me!"

"All right, all right. What about *The Cat in the Hat?*"

"Nooooo! A big one!"

"The 'big ones' are off limits."

"Pleeeeease!"

"Fine," Chylak sighed. "But if you tell your mother, I won't bring you any more gifts from the sanitarium."

"I want a plastic brain!"

"Don't we all," murmured Chylak, exiting the room.

In his bedroom he grabbed a book off his nightstand. He planned to bore Elliott to sleep. He paused outside the master bath listening to the soft splash of his wife in the tub, and debated whether to join her. It had been ages since they had bathed together, limbs wrapped around each other, struggling to keep the suds from each other's admiring eyes as they dreamed of the future. He heard a faint cry, a single heave, and panicked—perhaps she wanted to be alone. He grabbed a bottle of lithium from his briefcase and returned to Elliott's room. Elliott wasn't the only one having trouble sleeping.

He popped a tablet in his mouth, regretting it when the pill lodged in his throat and dissolved painfully slowly—a burning reminder about the no-no's of self-medicating. It was a bad habit, but not a new one. It began a month before they left Lebanon. Chylak justified it by telling himself it was unethical to prescribe medication to patients that he had not already tested on himself. He justified avoiding Babe's bubble-bath blues with the idea that reading to Elliott was important—children in the midst of transition needed to recognize patterns of their former routine.

As he drew Elliott's blinds, he spotted a pickup truck parked down the street. The engine was running, but he couldn't see who was inside.

"I'm ready!" Elliott sang, propping his bobbleheaded friend on the pillow beside him.

Chylak sat on the edge of the bed, dismayed by the notion that the little ballplayer would also be listening. The figurine grinned facetiously as though to scoff at his parenting skills. He turned its head toward the wall and opened *Going Crazy*.

If one sees one's life as a linear trajectory—out of some past, through the present, heading toward a future—one may be deluded (a normal delusion that madmen are deprived of) into conceiving that there is a goal at some ultimate point on this line that gives the trajectory a topographical definition amongst other "life lines" or social "world lines," and thus gives meaning to our lives.

He paused to show a diagram to Elliott and, at Elliott's insistence, to Bobblehead Joe.

Person ⟶ Future Nothing
The Goal

He continued.

> *What we do is to seize on a piece of the nothingness of our future and convert it into a quasi-concrete goal object lying on the trajectory of our life, thus effectively blocking our vision by our very desperation to see. We then live by this reified, hypostasized false end and, insofar as we live by it, we die of it.*

Elliott seized on the mention of death. Most children asked for a hug when in need of attention. Elliott asked for a diagnosis. Chylak obliged him for the last time with a quick prod behind the ears, causing Elliott to giggle uncontrollably between yawns.

"Are you tired? Should I stop reading?"

Elliott shook his head.

"Any questions, Joe?"

This made Elliott giggle louder, resulting in a "Shut it!" from Alice down the hall.

Chylak continued quietly.

> *Perhaps we have then to settle for meaning as being, quite simply, nothing but the nothingness of the geometric point on our life trajectory where we are at this moment. Maybe God has enough problems on his hands without taking on ours . . . in fact, God's biggest problem, if we can be compassionate enough to entertain the possibility, might be his problem about not being God.*

"What's God's problem?" Elliott asked, as though it were a suspense novel and God had just been caught, red-handed, with the stolen loot.

"Ask your mother," said Chylak, skimming down the page, inspired by the idea that people were like pebbles: each one appeared the same from a distance, but if you got close enough, it was clear that some were special. For example, he told Elliott, the "pebble" that discovered positron emission tomography, which could take a picture inside a person's head, or the pebbles so nobly attempting to rid the world of smallpox, or those that had enabled *Voyager 1* to photograph Jupiter. "And especially," he said, pulling the blankets snug around his sleepy son, "those brave little pebbles who find themselves in a strange new place and feel out of sorts, but who only need to give it a chance and they'll be the most special pebbles of all." Unsure that Elliott got the moral of his story, he clarified, "I'm talking about the *individual* at a pivotal moment in history." He pressed Elliott's button nose. "You never know who that individual is going to be."

Elliott stared at him blankly.

"Good night," said Chylak, leaning down to kiss him on the forehead. Elliott cried out when something tumbled from Chylak's breast pocket and onto his head. It was the plastic snow dome the mayor had given him, with the tiny Cooperstown inside. Elliott held it up toward the light, pleased when he turned it upside down and the snow went to the top. "I'll leave it downstairs in my study. Then you can play with it whenever you wish," said Chylak.

"It's not Lebanon," Elliott said, scrutinizing the miniature town inside.

Chylak pretended not to notice, peering through the opposite side of the dome at his son. "No, it's not," he sighed. "Is it?"

He promised to bring Elliott some nice "stationery" from the sanitarium tomorrow and said there was a big celebration coming to town. They would go to the baseball museum and spend the whole day together, just the two of them! He kissed Elliott good night, frowning when he realized Bobblehead Joe also expected a kiss. Elliott held the rubbery fellow up to his face and he obliged, planting a quick, begrudging smack on Joe's unsteady skull. Since Joe wasn't plush enough to sleep with, Chylak agreed to watch over him until morning. He turned off the light.

"Dad?" Elliott asked when he had reached the door.

"Yes?"

"What's hy-po-sta-sized?"

Chylak gazed into the darkness at his son, so small, so innocent in his footsy pajamas.

"It means 'to assume the reality of.' Now go to sleep."

In the master bedroom, Babe reclined on the waterbed, reading, Chylak was pleased to see, a newspaper. In his opinion, proselytizing, like sugar, ought not to be ingested at bedtime.

"I read an interesting story about Molly-Sue Coxey's garden today," she said. "Did you know there's a plant called the weeping cedar of Lebanon?"

Chylak did not know this. However, he suspected what she really meant was, "Why did we move here, schmuck?" "We don't have to stay here forever, you know," he replied with a sigh, about to crack open Elliott's book so he could monitor the boy's reading material.

"I know that," Babe said, rustling the pages of her paper. "What I want to know is *how* we arrived here in the first place."

"We drove."

"Don't be smart."

Chylak humored her. "All right. I assume you don't like it here either?"

"Wait, *you* don't?"

Babe perked at the possibility, tucking her knees into her chest and fluffing the pillow behind her, eager to hear more. Chylak couldn't tell if she was excited by the prospect that he might admit the move was a mistake, that it was his fault the cogs of the marital wheel were well out of whack, or if she anticipated an opportunity to open a dialogue beyond arguments and prayers. He wanted the same, but he couldn't help himself. "I love it here," he lied. He *did* like Cooperstown, but that wasn't the same as feeling well liked *in* it, which was important to his self-esteem, more than ever. The people were friendly, but the only ones he really knew were patients, and it wasn't the same when your "friends" were paying you, and you in turn were plying them with drugs. "By 'either' I meant the *children*," he said. "They're not adjusting as rapidly as I'd hoped."

"They're children, not houseplants, Kerwin," Babe said, placing a sympathetic hand briefly on his arm. Long enough to encourage Chylak to inch closer beneath the covers. He removed his glasses, prepared for a bout of lovemaking.

"One second," he said, taking a swig from the glass of water on his night table—he had forgotten to brush his teeth and had been overenthusiastic with garlic powder at dinner, hoping to drown out the taste of turnips. He slid out of his slacks and unbuttoned his shirt, then turned toward his wife. Babe was waiting with her hand outstretched. He took it and she looked at him like he'd lost his mind, snapping her fingers to signal that she wanted him to pass her jar of night cream. Chylak sighed, handing her a white plastic container labeled COLD CREAM in black block letters. He knew better, at this point, than to assume they were getting kinky with lubricant. Babe began slathering the cream across her face and neck, as she had done every night for as long as he could remember. Her brand had changed—they were sticking to the generic aisle at Save, America! until funds improved—but the ritual was the same.

"The children will adjust," Babe assured him.

"Yes," he sighed, "they will."

But could he say the same about himself? He took solace in the fact that at least Babe was maintaining her own former routines. Tough new exterior aside, she was still his soft-skinned beauty. He was glad she hadn't been suckered into buying any of Mrs. Paquette's pricey cosmetics. They were on a tight budget until his patient load increased, tighter than Babe knew. Chylak had been out of work that last month in Lebanon. For four weeks he had only pretended to go, instead spending his days on a bench in the park near their home, feeding pigeons. But there was no point in telling her this now. It would only make matters worse. He watched Babe grease her elbows and knees, thinking it would be nice if he weren't always the one to make an effort. She could, for example, come to bed in something more appealing, *revealing,* and with a less virtuous vibe than her oversized BIBLE CAMP '78! T-shirt. He tried to recall the last time he had had a real peek at what lay beneath it, eyeing the freckles that ran down Babe's neck to her milky white shoulders. He was about to go for it, sliding closer to her, when she began smacking her hands, like a self-flogging martyr, across her dewy fresh face.

"What on earth are you *doing?*" Chylak said.

"Mrs. Paquette recommended it as a cheap beauty ritual. It gets the blood flowing."

Chylak's blood was flowing as well, but not to where he wanted it to be flowing. It was coming to a rapid boil, in fact, and he was about to ask what Babe's problem was and what, as Elliott so eloquently put it, was God's problem too, since the two of them seemed to be in cahoots. Perhaps the three of them should have it out once and for all. He cringed when Babe opened her Bible. Why couldn't she read bodice rippers at bedtime? Why was she always *denying* him things? Why all the new dietary regulations, the passive-aggressive punishments? There was no way she knew what had happened in Lebanon! How could she? He had kept her away from the gossiping doctors' wives those last few weeks, even sending her and the children on vacation to her mother's house in Florida (one he was *still* paying for). Babe stared at him incredulously. Or was it the look of a *temptress?* It had been so long since they were intimate that he no longer recognized her moves. He put on his spectacles and stared back, giving her his sexiest smile.

Nope. She was peeved.

"*Now* what have I done?"

"Is there something you want to tell me?" she asked.

He scooted away from her, trying to decipher, in a flash, what she knew, and whether she was employing a reverse psychology tactic. She looked calm, so he relaxed against the pillow, certain he was safe. Now that she mentioned it, there *was* something he wanted off his chest. She was probably just craving some idle spousal chitchat. If he indulged her, perhaps afterward she would spoon him to sleep.

"I was thinking, there ought to be some form of mass psychotherapy. Something that could be dropped, for example, like nerve gas onto the unknowingly afflicted: paranoid schizophrenics, members of cults, church groups, that sort of thing . . ."

The moment he said it, he regretted it, but it was already out there, the church bit, stinking up the room and obviously not what she had wanted to hear. He backpedaled quickly. "I'm talking about the theme park," he said, gesturing to the newspaper she had discarded in favor of the Scriptures. "I'm concerned about the effect it could have on the stability of the town. If I don't mentally prepare my patients, several of whom have great *influence* over the town, not to mention people who are *not* my patients, but should be from what I have heard . . ."

Babe murmured a halfhearted response, but Chylak was lost in thoughts of his own. He was thinking of Immanuel Barrett, whom he had heard so much about from the mayor and Daulton. Barrett intrigued him. He seemed to embody the plight of the town: a man stuck between tenses, old world and new. Chylak had seen him once, parked outside the sanitarium in his truck. He wondered at first if the man was suicidal and was planning to gorge himself on carbon monoxide, then wait for the paramedics to find him. He'd heard such varying rumors about Barrett. Amazing how the man had so excelled at something (granted, baseball) that he'd had everyone eating out of the palm of his hand, worshipping the ground he walked on, and then poof— kicked the kudos to the curb and waltzed off to live alone in the woods. And why not? Just walk away from it all! Forget what people said! Let them worry about themselves for a change. People seemed desperate to mold Barrett into someone who would keep them on the map, their baseball hero, and thus inserted themselves into his affairs, in order to not face their own. What Chylak wouldn't give to analyze a real recluse! How enviable an existence.

"Good night, Kerwin," Babe said, turning off the light and rolling over so her back was to him.

Chylak stared at the wallpaper, allowing his eyes to adjust. Had he said that aloud? Had he said "envied," or "pitied"? He stared at Babe's back, certain he would hear about it at breakfast.

He focused on the wallpaper, compliments of the house's former owner. It looked like an advertisement for a forest: the kind of overamplified, pseudonatural decor that was popular of late, for reasons that defied him; perhaps it was meant to provide the illusion that one was surrounded by boundless flora and fauna instead of wall-to-wall synthetic carpeting. He found himself disappearing into the trees.

This wallpaper was exactly the kind of fad he suspected wouldn't last, along with the nation's fixation on John Travolta or the oh-so-subliminal Happy Meal. The world seemed to be teetering precariously on the cusp of a new decade—one Chylak dreaded would be full of quick fixes, an already visibly jarring transition from a subtle seventies of near techno retardation, natural fibers, and light feathery hair, to a more aggressive eighties of video games, *big* hair if Alice was any example, and cold synthesized sound. He made a game of it, attaching fads to trees in his faux forest, unable to fall asleep.

Charlie's Angels, who fought for justice with not a hot-rollered hair out of place, would undoubtedly become extinct. The new Iraqi president too, and perhaps Trivial Pursuit; the human brain couldn't retain trivia, let alone be *entertained* by it. Attention spans were growing shorter, computers more personalized. By the time Elliott was a man, the brain's functioning capacity could peter away to a mere five percent! And only people like Barrett, the physically fittest, would survive. It was a mere matter of evolution. Perhaps aging adults, all the Barrett wannabes out there, would become obsessed with physical fitness, while for children, contact with said adults would become increasingly irrelevant in favor of brain games and word processing. And if the result was an overstimulated, underachieving world, then by Freud, so be it! There were always anti-anxiety meds.

What *would* last, Chylak considered, shoving the sleeping Babe's Bible over onto her side of the bed so it didn't keep poking him, was people forcing their ideologies on each other. He thought about Iran, Vietnam, and Cambodia; the Soviets with an eye on Afghanistan. And, always a yin and a yang to the universe, picketing peace lovers too—people like Mother Teresa who had won the Nobel Peace Prize, thus scoring one for Babe's Bible Campers, which meant fewer points for Chylak's Heathens. Oil spills, nuke leaks, those would probably last. Anthrax, which, he had read, killed several people in some Soviet lab, might be a "laster" too. As would baseball, he supposed with a sigh, and with it fans and fanatics, tourists and teams, ballparks, theme parks, and Cooperstown, with or without them all.

He stared at the two-dimensional wilderness covering his walls, recalling the old adage about not seeing the forest for the trees. If only he could find a way to step back and examine himself, a lone tree in an increasingly dense forest. If he could understand what made some things endure, like healthy sex lives, while others fell by the cerebral wayside, he could be of real use to his new town. Perhaps he could start by finding a personal place within it, something more substantial than awkward exchanges with patients in public places. Such interactions seemed par for the course in psychiatry and in education: patients and children were unequipped to stomach the sight of doctors or teachers doing anything so base, so *human,* as purchasing toilet paper. Yes, he could learn to speak their language, that peculiar Cooperstonian dialect that left him so often in the dark. What was it Einstein had said? "You teach me baseball and I'll teach you relativity." He would visit the Baseball Library indeed!

Turning to kiss his snoozing spouse, Chylak realized it was Bobblehead Joe, and not Babe's Bible, that poked his side. He squeezed the ballplayer's head rather enthusiastically—he hoped not irreparably. Babe, so peaceful, her eyes beneath her pink transparent lids fluttering away into REM, was snoring. Chylak wondered if she dreamed heavenly dreams, dreams in which there was no room for heathens, agnostics, the non–sports fan, and the profoundly *un-American*. He dangled the figurine above her face, the bitty ballplayer's head bobbing back and forth like a manic pigeon, and counted backward from ten.

"You are getting *sleeepy*. You are back in Lebanon. You will cook meat. *Meeeat*—"

And with that, the good doctor somehow put *himself* to sleep, his mind drifting into a Freudian field day, a dream in which a hydrocephalic Joe Morgan, in a white lab coat, tossed Christ a prescription for a newly FDA-approved antipsychotic. "Hey, kid!" he said.

Meanwhile, down the hall, Alice's turntable skipped.

Sensible, logical, responsible, practical . . . clinical, oh intellectual, cynical . . . Who I am—Who I am—Who I am . . .

FIFTH INNING

This is who I am, dammit," Manny muttered. He sat alone in his truck outside the sanitarium, daring himself to enter. He knew the shrink was in. The shrink was *always* in. Half of the town had been to see him already, if what Mrs. Paquette said carried any weight, which it usually didn't. Why was he doing this to himself? They said you could tell Chylak anything, that his sessions were confidential. And that was important. Still, he wasn't going to let some damned witch doctor have his way with his mind. Mrs. Paquette sauntered by, her pink cosmetics case swinging from her arm. *Confidential?* Manny thought. A person you could tell anything to and they wouldn't tell anyone else? Not in this town.

He drove off toward the lake.

He thought about his sons, boys to whom he would probably never be given the chance to explain the hows and whys of being a man. Not because he hadn't figured them out himself. He was a warrior. He knew exactly what manhood entailed, the battles, the bullshit, the sacrifices.

Manny blamed himself for Chuck Daulton's death, for shocking Chuck to kingdom come with the news about his son's return. Few people knew that, however, and Manny sure as hell wasn't going to tell Terry Daulton. Few people also knew the truth behind Manny's "discharge" for a "mild psychotic break." He still didn't know whose touch the "psychotic" part was, but he blamed Amos. He hated him for it. He dealt with the consequences every day: people thinking he was a nut job. Still, it *was* clever, Fusselback covering his bases like that. It even led to speculation around town that Manny had gone AWOL from the army, which was even more insulting.

The truth was, Manny had never even been to 'Nam. His "enlistment" was Amos's idea. Amos and his cronies, who had dubbed Manny untrustworthy, Chuck included. The war provided them with a handy excuse to make him disappear, eliminating any urges he had to come clean and tell people why he *really* quit playing ball. No one outside of Amos and the others knew about that damned document he'd found them reading at the school so long ago. They made sure of that, threatening to throw him off the stone bridge and into the river, knowing he couldn't swim.

Manny had refused to play baseball after that. They let him stick around, but they made sure he kept his mouth shut for the next ten years. They made life as cushy for him and Ruby as could be. Until '67 when Manny could no longer keep up the facade and told them he didn't care anymore, that he was going to tell Ruby what had happened and earn his own way from then on. They banished him. What people thought was basic training at an obscure southern Fort Something-or-Other, followed by active duty, was, in truth, a sentence he had served alone, in the woods just miles from Cooperstown in Cheery Valley. He lived there from '67 to '71, lying low in a raggedy old pup tent. They said they'd take the house away from Ruby, tell her how he'd refused his shot at the big leagues, blackmailing them for cash and sucking their retirement savings dry. It was bullshit, but it seemed likely that Ruby would believe them; she had lost faith in him. She never forgave him for quitting baseball. And she wasn't alone.

Manny had tried to make the best of his exile, telling himself it was a rite of passage, man versus the land. He thought of himself as an Indian in one of Cooper's novels, or Natty Bumppo, establishing ties with Mother Nature that few men ever did. He got himself a part-time job pumping gas until Amos demanded that he quit before some Cooperstonian passing through on a Sunday drive saw him and grew suspicious. Amos gave him money for food, but Manny needed something more. He feared he'd go out of his mind with boredom. He got so sick of being dependent on them. So without telling anyone, even Coach Cartwright, he participated in French and Indian War reenactments for fun, figuring his costume was disguise enough if anyone he knew came by. He even taught himself how to swim. He started saving the money they gave him, subsiding on whatever fish he could catch, venison he could shoot, beef jerky or canned goods he could steal from unsuspecting hunters each fall, plus the occasional fruit basket compliments of Coach. The only discharge he got was from Ruby when he returned to Cooperstown. And who was she to teach their boys the world of men? Everything was so damn easy for her. She just loved that house the mayor and his men bought for her and had painted, free of charge, every year since. They looked in on her constantly while Manny was away, and he supposed he appreciated that.

He sighed—his sons would just have to learn things the hard way, like he had. He had lost joint custody of them, failing to show up for a court hearing. Ruby accused him of being an unfit parent, blaming the war. It was a war, all right, but an internal one, and damn her for not knowing the difference! If the woman you loved, your high school sweetheart, didn't know you, who the hell did?

Manny slammed his fist on the horn, warning a raccoon that had scampered into the middle of the road and stood staring at him, frozen. He knew that look. It was the look of the screwed. When he swerved the truck, the animal skittered back into the woods. "If you were smart you'd stay there!" he yelled, chucking the latest letter from Ruby's lawyer into the glove compartment and slamming it shut. Ruby had recently agreed to *consider* shared custody, "psychiatric evaluation pending." But no shrink was going to pick apart Manny's psyche like it was some kind of beached carrion, and anyway, Ruby was softening. He could tell. Just last week she had sent word that he could visit the boys on weekends come fall, under her supervision. Manny resented the term. Someone was always supervising him: one minute to be sure that he measured up, and the next that he didn't fuck up. He had willed himself more than once to see the shrink, but he never got past the parking lot. Sometimes he parked outside the doctor's house late at night, hoping Chylak would march out with his stethoscope, place it on his head, and be done with it. Screw that; Manny wasn't going to pass some lame mental-fitness test in order to be deemed father of the year. Besides, he was afraid. He was afraid that however much time he spent with his sons, with *anyone* for that matter, they still wouldn't really know him, or understand him. Who had ever tried to *understand* him?

He slowed as he reached the steep gravel drive that dipped toward the lake and his cabin, rolling down the window to snatch a tattered newspaper that poked out of his pummeled mailbox. Hit too often by careless winter plows, it leaned nearly parallel to the ground. He coasted down the driveway until he reached the shoreline, then turned off the engine and listened to some children frolicking at Ferret Springs, one of the town's public beaches. He carried the groceries from the back of the truck to his porch overlooking the lake. A family of tourists swam a few cabins down and he watched them for a minute, thinking perhaps he would take a dip after supper. He wouldn't swim in the river if he were paid to—he wouldn't go near it—but Lake Otsego was as cool and crisp and calm as it got.

A group of wealthy out-of-town culture coddlers were clamoring across the lake at the opera house. Cooperstown was expanding faster than Manny could blink. Souvenir shops were popping up as quick as weeds as far away as Fly Creek. There were vendors everywhere. They were even at the swimming holes, selling hot dogs and beach towels plugging the smug mugs of whatever ballplayer was the flavor of the day.

He sat in the pine Adirondack chair he had built for himself for his fortieth birthday and placed his feet on the railing, spitting tobacco over the side. He wondered what Daulton thought about all the expansion. Manny only subscribed to *The Journal* so he could clip out Daulton's byline, attach it to his dartboard, and give it a good beating when he was of a mind to. Daulton disappointed him, though it was mutual. It dated back some twenty years to that godforsaken day at the school. After Manny had read the document, and following the incident with the mayor and his men on the bridge, he'd ridden his bike like a bat out of hell to Raccoon Road. He wanted a minute to think before he went home and told his ma why he was such a mess. His T-shirt was ripped and one cleat was missing. Daulton was there, at the base of Lot's Tower, where they often camped. He was writing in his journal. Manny hadn't said a word; he couldn't, though he tried to later when visiting Daulton at home. He had planned to tell him everything, but Chuck answered the door and he froze. The last thing he wanted was another "meeting of the minds" on that damned bridge. That's what they had called it, Fusselback and his friends, like Manny had gone there of his own free will. He wouldn't go near that bridge now if he were paid to. Just the thought of it was enough to trigger flashbacks that would turn to vicious dreams come nightfall.

"Don't hurt him," Cartwright pleaded as Amos and Frank held the boy by his ankles, dangling him violently from the bridge and over the rushing river. "Swear it!" Amos yelled. "Swear you won't tell a soul!"

The flashbacks were getting worse. Twenty-two years without a good night's sleep was a hell of a long time. But he sure as shit didn't care, when all sleep brought him was nightmares. He wondered if the shrink could give him something for that. He wished he could talk to Ruby. Daulton was untrustworthy now. He was a reporter, and reporters were paid to pry. Manny had seen him coming out of the shrink's house once. God knows what Daulton told Chylak, what he actually *knew*. It was possible that Chuck had lied to them all! He had done so before. What if his dying man's urge to confess had extended beyond their secret "club"? What if he was putting them on, Manny and the mayor and Coach, and had, in truth, written Daulton a letter saying "Come home quickly, son!" Manny relaxed—Chuck didn't *know* he was dying until he actually did. He hadn't had time to send any letters.

He opened the newspaper, eyeing Daulton's latest article about the theme park. With the stick he used to clean mud from his boot treads, he poked a hole through it. The idea of Daulton covering the park made him uneasy. The idea of Daulton seeing a *shrink* made him sick. Manny had once placed great faith in Daulton. Daulton was the only one of his childhood pals who seemed like he stood a decent chance at one day getting out and doing things right. It was alarming to learn that the person you once felt held the most possibility was back at square one and in therapy. Was it that bad out there? Manny refused to believe a man had to be mad to make it. It made him feel more alone than he already did, as if any hope he had left for his future lay in the promise of Daulton, and if *his* foundation was rocked, they were both screwed.

Manny cracked open a beer, remembering how ticked off Daulton used to get when Manny began spending more time with Chuck than with him. Daulton started saying the oddest things, like, "Which one of us do you suppose is me?" Manny figured he was either being a smart-ass or was confused about the sudden shift in loyalties, and if it was the latter, Daulton had a right to be confused. Despite the bridge incident, Manny started hanging around Chuck, becoming like a second son. Chuck said they had big plans for him, that he and Amos had his best interests at heart. He wanted to believe them so badly.

After a while Daulton's behavior got weirder, got on Manny's nerves, so he ignored Daulton altogether with the same forced hostility he now summoned to ignore everyone else. He was perfectly content residing in the outfield, on the periphery of his former life. He got by just fine with no electricity or indoor plumbing. He was fit enough to paddle his canoe into town when supplies got low, but not low enough to merit use of his truck. His only companion was a Doberman pup with an ever-changing name, this week Smiling Stan, as in Stan Hack, because in his experience, it was best to keep one's loyalties loose. Being alone, being *forgotten,* wasn't so bad. It bought him time, gave him space. It made him invisible, and sometimes being invisible was damned revealing.

He rubbed a nickel across the Willie Mays scratch card tucked inside one of his grocery bags, erasing the ballplayer from head to toe while reflecting on his own day in the spotlight. Manny had played third base in high school during the fifties, when he was young and baseball still meant something to him. He had even gotten a scholarship to college. He had no intention of going, of course. Several scouts had their eyes on him and everyone suspected he would be signed. "You're my blue chip," is what Coach Cartwright used to say. "Play your cards right, and you could wind up in the bigs!" After a successful tryout, the Yanks wanted him. That would've been the best day of Manny's life, if the news hadn't come just days after he had sworn off the sport. "This is your ticket out!" Coach had yelled. It killed Manny to have to tell him no. He broke Cartwright's heart with three simple words— "I ain't goin'"—and it had never healed. Coach said Manny was making a huge mistake, one he'd regret until his dying day. He was right. And that was more or less the last thing Manny ever heard him say.

Manny missed his shot at college in the fall and spent the summer of '57 pumping gas while trying to figure out what to do with the rest of his godforsaken life. Chuck and the others decided for him. They paid for him to take night classes, bought him and Ruby a house, funded their wedding, and got eighteen-year-old Manny a job as bailiff at the county courthouse. Manny's first son, Aidan, was born in 1960. From '57 to '67 he played the part, being everything everyone wanted him to be— father, husband, Amos's lackey—except the thing he was best at being: a ballplayer. When Aidan was seven, he asked Manny to coach his Little League team. Manny said yes, foolishly. He didn't want to let the boy down. He stood on the field by the elementary school during that first practice and it all came rushing back. What everyone in town referred to as "the naked base-running incident": Manny running around Doubleday Field in his birthday suit in the middle of the '57 Hall of Fame Game. He couldn't hack it. He told Aidan, using words he hoped a seven-year-old would understand, that he couldn't coach. Then he screamed in rage and beat his chest like an ape right there in front of his son and his teammates. He scared the shit out of them, the kids that weren't laughing at him.

"I'll do anything!" the boy, the lion cub, screamed from the bridge. "I swear on my mother I will!"

Boy, did they take him up on that. Amos grew nervous when Manny refused to play ball, but that's what they wanted and Manny wasn't giving them everything, not after how they threatened him. He wasn't going to bust his ass to get to the Show just so they could suck the glory out of him when he got there, say he belonged to them. Everything he had ever believed about baseball, Cooperstown, and himself was lost upon reading that damned document. He was just a kid!

Manny was well versed in all the various opinions about him floating around town: that he was a hero, that he had run away, that he had never been wanted by the Yankees and couldn't stand the shame of it. That one pissed him off the most. He would have made it. He knew he would have! But they were right about the running. What they got wrong was what he had run from. He loved Ruby, even now, and his boys meant the world to him. He had simply been in the wrong place at the wrong damned time, too young and too stupid to do anything but flee. But he had come back, when the war, his war, was over, and had anyone noticed? Those who thought he'd gone AWOL had some nerve accusing him of being chicken shit when he lived day in and day out amid the presence of that which freaked him out the most. He would make his peace yet. And if things were contingent on making it from afar, so be it. He was fine biding his time, running in place. There was no need to measure the distance. Manny hadn't failed at anything; he hadn't even tried.

He poked a finger through the newspaper, Daulton's story, thinking he wasn't the only person who could stand to make peace with Cooperstown. Certain residents, and not just Daulton, had the annoying habit of wishing aloud that they could leave, like they were imprisoned here, cursed, that everything was just one big standoff between them and the village to see who could hold out and suffer the longest. What did they know about suffering? Most of them had entered this godforsaken, beautiful place of their own free will, same as him. Except Manny didn't take it for granted. He knew that the middle of nowhere had plenty to give.

He gazed at the lake, admiring the newly erected dock on which his old pup tent stood airing out. When Ruby sent word about joint custody, at least of Toby, since Aidan was now a young man, Manny took the tent out of storage as a reminder of how far he had come. He even slept in it one night, right there on the dock. He traced the numbers 1-9-5-7 absentmindedly with a stick in the dirt coating his porch railing, then poured beer over it and wiped it clean with his sleeve. He'd had a lot of time to think while living in that tent, lying beneath the stars; too much. There were only so many variations of shadow puppet a man could create.

After the Great Little League Freak-Out of '67, Manny had meant to come clean with Ruby and Aidan. Like a fool, he warned Chuck and Chuck told Amos. His "enlistment" thereafter was thus a vow of silence, a forced initiation into the old natives club. He didn't even put up a fight. Eventually, like a victim of Stockholm syndrome, he accepted it. He even began to like it. They became his new family, the mayor and his men. They banished him, but they never forgot him. They brought him supplies, mostly Coach, who was the best company anyway because he didn't lecture. He didn't talk much at all, in fact, and Manny didn't blame him. He knew he wasn't the only one who had been hit hard by that document. Every man was free to cope as best he knew how. If not, Manny thought, remembering Frank Paquette, there was always suicide. He had considered it once or twice himself while he was living in that tent, wandering around in the woods like some desperate scavenger, half-cocked. But he couldn't do that to his boys. Never.

Cartwright's trips to the woods to see him eventually tapered to a standstill and ceased altogether around the winter of '71. That was a particularly tough winter, even for a man like Manny, who was used to it by then and had built himself a fort. He had learned to survive with limited food and supplies and, hell, company even. He assumed it was too much for Coach to admit that the best company he had—the only person who didn't give a frog's ass if he wanted to talk—was the reason he stopped speaking in the first place. It was technically *still* Cartwright's duty to supervise him, to ensure that he kept his trap shut. But Coach trusted him. He always had because they were in the same boat, suckered in for the same damned ride, realizing only too late where it was leading them.

"I'll watch him!" Cartwright yelled. "Don't you drop him, Amos! On my soul, you can trust this kid."

Manny shivered, remembering how he'd come out of the woods when Cartwright's visits had ceased, realizing he could die there. It seemed hard to believe, but now he kind of missed that life, those woods. It was tough but he wanted it to be tough, he wanted it to hurt, because he felt like he deserved it; the more he suffered the more he evened the score with Ruby, easing her pain by replacing it with his own. And when the score was tied, he figured he had a right to come out of hiding and start over with a clean slate. He figured he could go back to Cooperstown and reclaim what was left of his life, his family. When his food ran out, it was motivate or vegetate, so he came out of hiding, discharged from "service" in '71. He followed Cartwright's lead and didn't say much to anyone. Amos's story that he had lost his marbles in the war took root and was scattered around town by old bird lady

Paquette. No one had second-guessed it, not even Ruby, and Manny wasn't sure he would ever forgive her for that. He had *wanted* someone to draw him out of his shell. The townsfolk were pleased to have him back at first, treating him like a war hero. Not Amos, but he came around, only because he was certain that Manny had been beaten. Manny had looked the part, all right: thin as a whip, scraggly beard, hair down to his shoulders, and a fierce look in his eye that could easily have been attributed to combat. The whole thing was so staged and absurd.

Manny had called Coach from a pay phone to warn him of his imminent return. Cartwright said nothing, but Manny could hear him breathing faster on the other end of the line. Then Amos scrambled to control his homecoming like it was some B movie with Manny as the lead, stumbling into town in the fatigues he'd picked up at an army-navy shop, carrying the bayonet he'd swiped during those war reenactments. He still had that bayonet. No one had questioned the dated weaponry. If he had been wearing a powdered wig or knickers, people still wouldn't have noticed, he was sure. The whole town was out that day, lining Main Street, cheering as Manny came marching in. There were yellow ribbons tied to the trees, which made him feel like an ass. He tried to walk down the street with his head held high, holding that bayonet over his shoulder and dragging his tent behind him like a kid with a security blanket, high-stepping his way back into their hearts.

It was too much for Ruby, imagining the "horrors" he had survived, and he refused to tell her otherwise. He stayed with Chuck, sleeping in Daulton's old room surrounded by evidence of the past: Daulton's Tom and Jerry comics and Chuck Berry posters. When Chuck got sick of waiting on him, Manny gathered whatever strength he had left to go home and face Ruby. He reentered society around '72, playing father to Aidan and reclaiming his job at the courthouse, acting the good civilian until his marriage fell apart a year later. Of course, he had gotten Ruby pregnant again in the interim. He had a habit of doing that, leaving her behind with a seed of the man he once was. He liked to think he'd left the best part of him with her and that by leaving he was sparing her more disappointment. But the truth was he couldn't handle it. He couldn't handle living in that tiny house with her and the secrets that drove them deeper into the marital grave. He retreated once more to the woods, permanently, to his family's old summer camp, the cabin on the lake where he now lived. And everything was fine until Chuck got sick and they learned what he had done.

Daulton returned to town then, on his high horse, still pissed at Manny for leaving him alone in a town he had never felt comfortable in. He wrote an article about Manny taking a literal crap on the courthouse. But in Manny's mind it was Daulton who had done the leaving. Manny had always been nearby. Seemed like Daulton never inquired about him either, at least according to Chuck, who wrote his son endless letters. Sometimes, Manny wished Daulton would put his sleuthing skills to the grindstone and start prying into him. If pressed enough, he was bound to split down the center like a watermelon, his loyalties loosening until he finally cracked. Every man had his breaking point. The suspense lay in guessing what his own would be.

Retired from his post as Joe Citizen, Manny had had plenty of time to wonder about that. He treated his newfound bachelorhood like a well-deserved vacation at first. He spent his days canoeing, or floating on his back in the cool water above the Sunken Islands, at the northern end of the lake. He drank beer, too much, while sitting around on his porch in a rocking chair like some old fart. Nights, he watched the sun set on the Glimmerglass, draped in an old bearskin he bought secondhand, intoxicated by the sounds of Wagner's *Die Walküre* drifting across the water from the opera house. He didn't know that music until he asked Mrs. Paquette what it was, and she asked Mrs. Nauss, her German neighbor. Eventually it became like his theme song. He listened to it while strutting around naked, beer in hand, dancing in the dark on the shoreline. He built bonfires and went skinny-dipping or night fishing for lake salmon and largemouth bass. During the day he wore camo fatigues, just to keep people guessing. He was getting tired of the act now, though, tired of people waiting for him to "snap out of it" and reclaim his old self, one that met their ideals. They made him and they broke him. Let them deal with the result.

Amos was still funding Manny's lifestyle, one of permanent retirement. The rest of the mayor's gang were dead aside from Coach, who didn't have a cent to his name, and Manny wouldn't take it from him if he did. He had no qualms about taking Amos's money, however. The deal was that if he kept his mouth shut and kept a low profile, Amos would keep the cash coming. Manny welcomed the arrangement, assuming the money was being drained from Fusselback's retirement fund. He didn't owe Amos shit.

He flicked a beer cap into the woods. It bounced with a twang off a rusted metal sap bucket tied to a sugar maple. He entered the cabin to put away the groceries before the flies got to them.

"Here boy, here Stan!" he said as the Doberman ran to greet him, paws on his chest like it wanted to slow dance. Manny scratched the dog behind its ears. He'd have been denied a fine companion like this if he had moved back in with Ruby, who was allergic. Everything would be easier once the divorce was finalized: no one nagging him, telling him to "open up." Nor would he have to listen to any more I-told-you-so's whenever he attempted to reconcile with Ruby and failed. They had been separated for ages, a seven-year swan song that suited them both because neither of them had the energy to move forward or to work out the past, even if their faults were bred from the same stock. They had grown up together in Cooperstown and were high school sweethearts. But now Ruby wanted to get on with her life, or so she said.

There was no way Manny could go back to living in that clapboard house on Elm the old farts had bought them as a wedding gift. Ruby didn't know that, of course. She had been all too pleased to remain in the dark over how the hell an eighteen-year-old kid was able to come up with a down payment on a house. Manny had never been proud of it. He was proud, however, of the way the boys helped Ruby maintain it, of how they were there for her when he wasn't. They would be all right. They had warriors' blood in them. Like him, they would eventually realize that the most important thing about being a man was earning the right to be left alone.

He gathered firewood from a pile on the side of his driveway; summer nights in Cooperstown could drop as low as forty degrees. He craved a hot meal, something spicy to make him sweat so that after-dinner swim would be that much sweeter.

Mrs. Paquette drove by in her pink Cadillac, honking, and he waved, then flipped her the bird once she had passed. Paquette was on his case lately to get in touch with Ruby. Manny didn't have a phone and wouldn't answer it if he did. Who needed one when that big-mouth trekked out at all hours of the day and night pushing grooming products on people? He used Mrs. Paquette's visits to his advantage, telling her just enough about himself to whet her appetite, to let her draw her own conclusions, ones she was bound to spread around town. He also used her to get information about Ruby. Paquette was like a carrier pigeon, delivering messages to and fro, too pea-brained to comprehend what they meant. She said the mayor was calling Ruby a lot lately; she seemed jealous. Amos had apparently tried to coax Ruby into making Aidan usher at the Hall of Fame Game, claiming it was all in the name of "town spirit." Manny knew it was an indirect appeal to him. You couldn't make Aidan do anything. It was all just a way for Amos to get him back in the game now that the theme park loomed near. He knew Fusselback. That man would be the first to break his own rules if it served him well. He would probably sell out his town as a last resort. His pride would be his downfall. He had some nerve asking for favors! Manny's exile was favor enough. "Just until you can keep it together," Amos had said, "until we figure out what to do." Now Amos was begging him to attend the induction ceremony, claiming there was safety in numbers. Manny suspected he was torn between wanting his estranged son, Johnny, to ride into town on his high horse and challenge him for his throne, and fearing Johnny's presence would threaten the empire he had so carefully constructed. Johnny was no better than his old man. He drank like a fish in high school, and probably still did. Paquette said he'd even hit on Ruby once, while Manny was away, writing her some "sympathy" letter. Johnny hadn't kept in touch much with his school friends. And he had long despised his father. He wanted that theme park bad. If he ever got wind of Amos's little secret, Cooperstown would go down hard. And Manny would go down with it. He wasn't sure yet if he would sink or float. All he knew was that he was tired of being the mayor's pit bull. Then again, if he went to the induction ceremony he might get a glimpse of Toby, who was seven now. It made him smile, the image of Toby approaching Mays for an autograph. When Manny was a kid, Hall of Fame Weekend was like a second Christmas, and he missed that sometimes. He never attended the games anymore, but last year he caught the induction ceremony, climbing a tree to the post office roof and perching there unnoticed to scour the crowd, strangers masked in formerly familiar faces. Surely he could do that again, watch it from afar, lest Daulton conjure up another desperate-for-news article about him: "Miracle Mays Draws Hermit Out of Hiding!"

He picked up an axe and began chopping wood furiously until he broke a sweat. No way. There was no way he was going to sacrifice himself, or his boys, in the name of "town spirit," a spirit he lost twenty-two years ago. Aidan was nineteen now and didn't give a damn about ushering ball games or anything else, from what Manny could tell. Paquette said he had gotten a job pumping gas, passing up college. Aidan had quit baseball too, after Manny's outburst on the Little League field. He had humiliated the kid.

"Shit," he said, mopping his brow with a bandanna. He was worrying about his boys and he'd promised himself he wouldn't do that. If there was one benefit to sticking around to raise your kids, it was to make sure they didn't end up like you: fucked. Ruby could handle it. Besides, Aidan hadn't wanted anything to do with him since he left the two of them with baby Toby. Aidan, at twelve years Toby's senior, had more or less played father to the boy. Manny hardly knew Toby, except by sight. He wasn't even sure if the kid knew he was his old man.

Recently he had gone to the gas station where Aidan worked just to get a look at him. Aidan looked so cocky, standing there in his new blue jumpsuit swinging a wrench like it was a pistol. He knew Aidan had seen him, though he sent a buddy over to fill up the truck. The damned place had no self-service—everything just one big perk to please tourists. Aidan had seen him, all right, that quick flash of father-son radar passing between them. Manny had been unable to get Aidan's expression out of his mind since: that bitterness, that knowing beyond his years. It was the look of the wounded, and Manny should know—it was inherited. It said the kid had been forced to give up life as he knew it, long before he was good and ready. Some kids got burdened with knowing things before they were old enough to know what those things really meant.

Manny slammed the axe into his chopping stump, scaring a flock of cedar waxwings nibbling berries in the brambles beneath his pines. They began to screech, fluttering beneath the canopy of leaves as though trapped. Manny stared up at the sun, blinded, and fell to his knees, crouching against the stump. He was trembling, holding the axe handle for balance, with one arm over his face, shading his eyes. He tried to will them away, the flashbacks. He tried to picture Toby's face, but he couldn't.

"Tell me if it's true!" the boy screamed, the blood rushing to his head. He was afraid he was going to vomit or, worse, shit himself. His cleats were starting to slip from his feet. He could fall headfirst into the river. He couldn't swim. He told them he couldn't swim! Then the crows came, hoards of them rushing from the bushes below the bridge like a blanket of blackness, shooting up from the riverbank like rockets, like cannonballs blasting into the sky. He

tried to focus on the sound of the birds, and the reflection of the sun on the water.

Manny shut his eyes, took several deep breaths, and stood, using the axe like a cane to support his rubbery legs. The blade came loose from the stump and he stumbled. "Fuck!" he yelled. He ought to sue those fuckers! He chucked a log deep into the woods, surprised that he still had his arm. He flexed it, winding it up and pitching another log, then another and another. Once he had thrown every log in the pile into the woods, he strolled, exhausted, down to the shore.

He stood on the dock and decided to stop by Ruby's place in the morning. Why not? He could just leave a note to see if Toby needed anything. Ruby was bound to be out. Paquette said some farmhand half-wit was courting her.

He kicked a rotting log into the water and sat on the dock he had built, foolishly thinking the boys might visit him. That Ruby would let them if there was something for them to do, perfect their dives or canoe, besides sitting around listening to his war stories, like he had any. He was sick of her treating him like some whack job apt to jump into imaginary foxholes at any moment. So he had done that once. *Twice* counting that one Thanksgiving in front of his in-laws, scaring everyone. The damned war reenactments hadn't helped with the flashbacks. A man could only play at so much violence before it caught up with him. Those outbursts are what broke them in the end, him and Ruby; that look in her eye one too many times; the knowledge that she loved him but feared him. Manny grew tired of living in a constant state of dread, knowing her fear would eventually win out.

He leaned toward the water, stirring algae with the axe handle and inhaling the clean green familiar scent. He stared at his reflection in the Glimmerglass, imagining the glacier that formed it. He looked old for forty, and tired. He wondered what his sons would look like at his age. He pictured them strolling down to the dock with their wives and his grandchildren in tow—the next generation with whom he stood a chance and who might not view him with caution, like he was just that fucked-up hermit on Lake Road who didn't give a damn about the future and who never looked back, because he did. Manny did look back, each year when the chaos of summer drew to a close. When the tourists petered out, replaced by endless autumn leaves falling in a certain pattern on his driveway. Or when he traced his fingers along the surface of the lake like this in the wintertime, before the ice set, recalling the smoothness of Ruby's skin. And especially when he gazed up toward the mountain, the Sleeping Lion he had dreamed of all those years while hiding himself away, the metaphorical embodiment of his pain, the giant he worked so hard to tame.

He looked at it now, admiring the subtle slope of the Lion's "paws" and the bold head that gave it its name. The beast inside him was asleep now. He was sure of that. No matter that he still wore camo, used a straight razor to keep his hair trimmed to an unfashionably low crew, or carried a rack of rifles on the roof of his truck year-round. When he looked back, quietly and to himself like this, Manny *knew* he had changed. And soon his boys would know it too. They would know there was a man behind the myth, a legitimate tale he simply wasn't at liberty to tell. But one that someone as innocent, as patient and attentive in their questioning as a child, as Toby, might come to understand if the desire was there. It wasn't too late for them. Manny wouldn't end up like Chuck, lying in the filth of his own guilt, on his deathbed, knowing that after all they'd been through, all he'd done, his biggest mistake was misleading his own son. And in that case Manny couldn't blame Daulton for returning. Who wouldn't want to know his father's demons?

He shook out the tent, folding it the way he'd learned to fold the flag in Cheery Valley. He thought of all those times he and Daulton had camped together at the base of Lot's Tower, an old stone structure that looked like a misplaced lighthouse stuck in the middle of the woods. Legend had it that Lot, a wealthy town forefather, had once locked his wife in that tower in order to carry on with his mistress. Every town had its Lot, Manny reckoned, and Cooperstown's owned everything from the street signs to the well water. If the theme park came, the state would own that, and that would be too much.

"You ever getting married?" Manny had asked Daulton on their last camping trip, after the graduation parties and the goodbyes, everyone assuming everyone else was getting out. They had been squatting around the fire—their pals Gene Newbeck and Perry Branson had passed out, and the Croughton brothers, Skip and Ron, had gone searching for more firewood. Manny and Daulton had laughed themselves blue, listening to Skip serenade his brother with Bobby Helms's "My Special Angel"—Ron cussing that he'd better quit it or he was getting a fat smooch from a hard fist. "Not if it kills me," had been Daulton's answer to the marriage question. He was referring to the legend that Lot's wife had since been buried within the tower walls. Legend also had it that he would become a great ballplayer and Daulton a famous writer. But then, legend had a lot of things.

"Don't drop me!" A little girl downstream squealed at a man carrying her into the cold lake, dangling her upside down by her slender ankles. The girl was laughing, all in good fun, but before Manny knew it, he was lying prostrate on the dock with his tent over his head, struggling to catch his breath. His heart was racing like a freight train and he told himself to "be still, be still and it will pass."

"Don't drop me! I'll do anything!" The boy was crying now. Then they took a vote—three to one—and reeled him slowly up toward the bridge, toward solid ground.

Manny pressed his fingers against the sides of his temples, drawing slow, deep breaths until his heart rate slowed. He considered charging through the rocky water to deck the man who had dangled the girl. But she was laughing now, floating peacefully on a blow-up dinosaur.

Manny dangled his feet over the edge of the dock, letting the cool water soothe his sunburnt flesh. He succumbed to a sudden desire to shout his name across the lake, just to hear it echo back, "Im-man-uel!" He wondered if the shrink knew how long a man could keep a secret before it turned to poison, churning away in his gut to a slow curdle, a vat of vicious yellow-bellied bile. He skipped a rock across the water to break his thoughts—regret was a dangerous place to dwell. Grabbing the axe, he vowed to one day cut that regret right out of himself, tell someone the truth, *his* version of Cooperstown's history. Perhaps his boys, who were bound to appreciate the irony, the beauty, the absurdity, and even—yes, even the shame of what it meant to be a hermit living just miles from the center of town.

He stood, water pooling at his feet, and picked up a rock. Holding the axe sideways across his shoulder, he rocked his hips, wiggling the handle to test his grip, then stared out deep into the horizon. Holding the rock at hip level, he tossed it into the air above the cool green Glimmerglass, and swung the axe blade flat against it as it fell—*whack!*

"Home run," he whispered.

SIXTH INNING

first base 1. Baseball.
a. *the first in counterclockwise order of the bases from home plate* . . .
2. get to first base, Informal.
a. *to succeed in the initial phase of a plan or undertaking* . . .
b. *to engage in petting that goes no further than kissing.*

—*WEBSTER'S NEW UNIVERSAL*
UNABRIDGED DICTIONARY, 1996

Dusty Paquette was proud to be a resident of "America's ideal village," almost as proud as she was to be a representative of America's ideal makeup company: Home-Run Cosmetics, an industry leader since '58. Like the company's founder, she believed in two powers, the power of self-confidence and the power of concealer, preferably one with an oil-free base. She, in fact, was the company founder.

She launched Home-Run, a door-to-door cosmetics service available strictly in Cooperstown, after her husband, Frank, died. It had always been her dream, and one he supported. Frank taught her to take pride in Cooperstown's history, and although she didn't know a baseball from a monkey wrench, she knew *plenty* about Cooperstown, especially its residents. It was an honor to be a prized citizen in a town so significant to American history. Dusty's ancestors had come over from France and had added a little something to American culture themselves: mascara. That's how the family lore had it anyway—cosmetics were second nature: show Dusty a blemish and she'd show you a toner that would have you looking as flawless as Audrey Hepburn in no time!

Frank was great at helping her dream up clever names for her products, but that's all it had been at first, a dream, until his funeral, when Dusty noticed that her skin looked sallow. Not "Oh God, my man's gone" sallow, but ashen like a woman pushing fifty-three years of age who had used discount beauty products for most of them. It seemed to her if your man was dead, you had every right to splurge on the good stuff. Whatever it took to make you feel fabulous enough to bear life without him or to catch a new man, if that was your mind-set. Since Dusty was a woman prone to chitchat, a door-to-door service seemed ideal. She created Home-Run, and now she was successful at seventy and her skin was vibrant as a rose, at least most of the time.

Home-Run was more of a distraction than anything. Dusty's real job was working part-time at the Hall of Heroes wax museum. But it was just so darn isolating—she didn't want to be around *wax* people. She wanted to be around fresh, pert living people in need of a good moisturizer; the more forthcoming those people were with their personal information, the better. Dusty considered herself the eyes and ears of Cooperstown, even if certain other people said she was the mouth. She *could* keep secrets, she simply chose not to. Secrets made life more interesting, especially life in a village. Collecting information about people, inspecting it for imperfections, then scattering it back around like so many precious seedlings—that was her specialty until the psychiatrist arrived to ruin it. What kind of doctor encouraged people to look *inside* themselves for answers instead of *outside,* where other people could hear them and offer suggestions? She had yet to have a proper sit-down-and-chat with that Chylak.

She sat in the breakfast nook of her home on River Street, chewing the end of the lip-liner pencil she used to scribble down names for new products. The view of the Susquehanna was inspiring. In fact, it was just this view that had led to the creation of the Dust Bowl, which Frank had taught her is what they call an underwatered ball field and which could hold three shades of foundation in one compact: ivory, bronze, and peach. Why a ball field needed watering was beyond Dusty. It wasn't like it was going to grow bigger, or retain a nice dewy glow. Doubleday Field belonged to everybody and therefore should be used for more than just baseball. She wanted to hold a ladies-only pep rally there—have each gal pitch her old unwanted cosmetics into the bonfire they would build on the pitcher's mound before offering themselves up eternally to the goddess of Home-Run. She was always coming up with clever promotional ideas like that; that one was shot down by the town council, who said if she set fire to the ball field they'd throw her in jail. You couldn't wear eyeshadow in prison. All she had wanted was an itty-bitty bonfire and to make a few sales! She debated targeting the mothers at the Little League games, but Little League meant children, children meant acne, and Dusty avoided both.

The Dust Bowl was bound to be her biggest seller yet, aside from Left-On Base, which acted as foundation during the day and emollient at night. Nothing said welcome to big-city tourists like a nice, rich emollient. Tourists were Dusty's best customers: all those baseball-loving men and boys dragging their poor womenfolk to the Hall of Fame. Those women deserved a little something special in the souvenir department—something with a drop of vitamin A and a trace of rose-scented talcum, for instance?

At the Hall of Fame Game this year, she planned to give away free blush samples that came in the Clutch Hitter, a pink plastic case useful for toting toiletries. She must remember to ask the mayor which teams were playing. Each year there were different teams, and a different famous somebody (last year it had been the president!) threw out the first pitch. Maybe she'd have Clutch Hitters designed to match both teams' uniforms. She smiled, reading the slogan on the back of a tube of RBI, Retinal-Based Injection serum, a serum she wasn't medically licensed to sell, but still.

Build confidence! Be seen!

Dusty knew how to build confidence, all right. She made it her business to build confidence in those around her too. She had a way with people, a certain Dusty kind of charm. And as for being seen? People could spot her a mile away—what with her claret-colored hair (claret was more sophisticated than red) and penchant for yelling "Yoo-hoo! I heard something about you!" She liked to think people skittered off when they saw her because she inspired in them a certain youthful enthusiasm. She prided herself on her youthful nature and her looks. Her complexion wasn't perfect. But why fuss over complexions when you had silken hair that had yet to turn gray at seventy? And so what if it was because of Home-Run Bleachers Claret Dye No. 7? She didn't care who knew it. Honesty was the key to sales.

Honesty and tradition!

Dusty knew all about tradition. She had been coiffing her hair in the same style for over fifty years now, thanks to the trusty iron crimper she had used since she was a girl. Old things lasted and new things bust up good after being used just once or twice. (New things were being made with nothing but a quick buck in mind by the cheapskates who made them.) Dusty used the best ingredients in her own products, and sometimes ingredients she borrowed from the wax museum, like paraffin sticks, which were used to mend broken limbs, and which, when melted down and doused with peppermint oil, created step three of the Home-Run Relief Pitcher manicure. Relief Pitcher was named for the little plastic vanity pitcher she jammed the wax into before affixing her smiling face to the label.

She patted her hair, tucking the curls inside the kerchief she wore whenever she had to rise early to make those sales, which meant less time for crimping.

Last night she had attended the Otsego County Film Festival to see *The Deerslayer,* based on one of Cooper's books. The original, not the German version Mada Nauss from up the lane loved, starring Bela Lugosi. She was curious, though, to see what kind of foundation they had used to make Lugosi look like an Indian. She was drawn to the gal who played Judith Hutter in the film she saw, and who managed to obtain a certain girlish glow despite being shrouded in a kerchief. The movie made her sad, however, because it reminded her of the remake she'd seen with Frank. Why were they always remaking things, like nothing was good enough the first time? That film had starred Rita Moreno (*no one* had skin like Rita). Last year they had done it again, created yet *another* version, a made-for-TV movie with Dusty's favorite part played by some dark-haired young beauty called Madeleine Stowe who needed a touch more rouge.

The phone rang and she went to answer it, pausing briefly to examine herself in the hallway mirror. Her new striped muumuu made her hips look wide. She considered slipping into a nice pink Laura Ashley frock, but the phone kept ringing, so she settled for blowing her wide-hipped self a kiss in the mirror—why not? She blew another. During that second kiss, however, she noticed a series of fine lines around her mouth, and leaned in closer to inspect them. "Hello?" she said into the telephone receiver, puckering her lips. She gasped as the lines stretched clear to her chins.

"Oh, my!"

"Dusty? Are you there? Are you all right?"

Dusty blushed beneath her Home-Run Brush Back Blush. It was the mayor, and she was certain he was finally going to ask her to dinner. She had no intention of letting it go further than that, of course. He could hold her hand but that was it. She lifted her face in the mirror, examining a canker on her upper lip. There would *definitely* be no kissing. She attributed the canker to having forgone Home-Run Triple Play, which acted as blush, eyeshadow, and lipstick, in favor of a discount gloss she had picked up at the drugstore. If you were cheap, you could just buy Double Play, but that meant no lipstick for you.

"You know me, I'm fine as silk," she cooed, and then inquired about which teams were playing at this year's game. She was surprised when the mayor said he'd get back to her on that. Dusty didn't like surprises. Not since the day she had found Frank hanging by his necktie in the garage. It was awful and it was her fault. He had looked right at her before he jumped off the ladder he'd been standing on and screamed as if he couldn't stand the sight of her.

Satisfied she would know what Amos the Fuss was up to before anyone else did, she put the phone down and fluffed her hair while the mayor prattled on. She stifled a brief urge to silence him with a smooch—the kind of obscene smacking sound people made in the movies. It had been years since Dusty had been kissed, over twenty. Frank had worked at the Hall of Fame as top security guard and, in the summertime, gave tours around town for those who wanted a taste of local lore. Cooperstown had plenty of that, and Frank had taught her that if you ever found it lacking, you made it up. He had used an old walking stick as a prompter, pointing out the sights, wearing what Dusty believed were called lederhosen, little pea-green hot pants, which he had bought off Mada Nauss's husband before he too died. Frank had no fashion sense whatsoever.

Dusty rested the phone on her shoulder, coating her canker, gently, with concealer.

She felt guilty about her interest in the mayor, even if that prune-faced old undertaker, Stanley Auffswich, said Amos had called her a yakker (which she didn't for one minute believe was a complimentary comparison between a curve ball and her sumptuous-for-seventy figure). She felt bad because Amos had been Frank's friend. Then again, Frank was dead and wouldn't know better. Nuzzling up to Amos would be like having a piece of Frank back to contend with. It *might* help her get over Frank. Amos was a cutie-pie. They were of the same stock, Frank and he, along with Chuck Daulton before he died of being so bossy, and daffy Duke Cartwright before he went clear off his rocker. Dusty was certain their little late-night powwows the year preceding Frank's death had less to do with plotting the preservation of the town, like they claimed, and more to do with drinking, playing poker, and crabbing about their wives. Frank was so melancholy, so secretive toward the end. She cursed herself for not seeing the signs. Depression overcame him like a rash from cheap deodorant, and darned if she wouldn't find out why before she met her own maker. Death made Dusty squirm. With no children, Frank gone, and all of her relatives back in France, she feared she'd eventually wind up a victim of Stanley Auffswich, and that undertaker had about as much skill with cosmetics as she had with a baseball bat! Blast him if he stuck a cheap wig on her like he'd done with poor bald Frank. Then again, it served Frank right for killing himself because he no longer found her attractive. At least *she* knew how to dress.

She thought about that night. She had been mad at Frank. He hadn't come to bed, so she went looking for him and heard a noise in the garage. He was in there, standing on a ladder. He screamed when he saw her, then jumped, hanging himself by that ugly Roy Rogers necktie. Her first thought was that they probably wouldn't make the matinee of *I Want to Live!* in the morning like he'd promised. Susan Hayward had such perfectly plucked brows. Then those fierce *furry* brows were bearing down on her, Frank's old moose head—he was dangling from the antlers. Dusty froze, fascinated by the way Frank's face turned a lovely violet, then a most disturbing blue, his body jerking like it wanted to dance. She gathered her senses and cut him down with a pair of toenail clippers, which took forever, but that was all she had on her and she couldn't think of what else to do. He flopped to the floor, his head bouncing on the cement, and she knew then that if he hadn't been dead before, he was now. She called Chuck. She was in shock and didn't want an ambulance to take away her Frank. She needed someone else to make that call. Someone Frank trusted who could be counted on to remain calm. But Chuck hadn't been calm at all; he'd held Frank, cradling him like a baby and screaming, "What did you do? Oh, God, what did you do?" Dusty assumed he meant *her*, that she'd killed her man. When the ambulance arrived, Chuck was more interested in the book Frank had been clutching than the fact that he was being taken away, forever.

"Uh-huh. And then what?" Dusty said, humoring the mayor while she inspected her nail polish for chips. Amos was going on and on about his ungrateful son, and Dusty withdrew whatever regrets she'd had about not having children. They were messy ingrates and Frank was child enough. It had taken her ages to sort through all the junk he had collected—ties, ticket stubs, autographs, and papers. What he couldn't stuff into drawers, closets, or beneath the bed, he crammed into any available nook or cranny at the Baseball Hall of Fame. Dusty had refused Honus's offer to let her reclaim Frank's things. It hurt too much to look at them, and she didn't have the heart to throw them out. This past spring, as a personal memorial she'd contributed a few more items to the museum: Frank's favorite blue socks, his Sinatra records, and the book he'd been clutching when he died. Chuck took it the day he died, and just a few months ago, Duke Cartwright returned it out of the blue.

She held the phone to her ear. The mayor had finally reached his point, the reason for his call: the historical guild. Dusty tried not to sound disappointed. Amos Fusselback wouldn't know a good woman if she walked up and slapped him in the face, which is exactly what his wife, Martha, had done before she skipped town. Dusty had been hiding in a thicket outside Reality Realty when it happened.

She asked Amos to be more specific. The historical guild could mean the Cooper Historical Guild, the Baseball Historical Association Guild, the Mohawk Valley Guild Society, the Farmers 'n' Merchants Historical Union Guild, or the Historical Social Association and Political Guild, a fancy alternative to "town council."

"The Leatherstocking Road 'n' Rail Historical Guild!" he barked.

There was that one too.

"I told you, Amos, I'm not interested! I'm too busy."

This was the third time he had requested her services this

summer. It was now July. He kept asking for favors, but he had yet to ask her *out*. She suspected these "favors" were his way of being flirtatious, but she wasn't having any of it until he learned to treat a lady proper and ask her to dinner. She was in no rush, however, until she had achieved a cankerless, line-free visage.

"But, we need a bookkeeper!"

"Get Angela Spitzer to do it!" Dusty snapped. Angela Spitzer was the mayor's secretary and, some suspected, his mistress (Dusty was the "some" who did the suspecting). She didn't see what was so enchanting about Spitzer, who had psoriasis of the scalp from washing her hair with Fabergé instead of Home-Run Foul Tip leave-on conditioner, which was also great for split ends. She knew about Spitzer's shoddy scalp because Mr. Peck, the pharmacist, told her. That, or she had rummaged through Spitzer's medicine cabinet during her last Christmas party, but still.

"I tried. She turned me down."

Dusty grinned—it served him right. She looked in the mirror. Perhaps she'd buy one of those cute Huk-a-Poo shirts that were all the rage of late. She pinched her cheeks to get the blood flowing, perhaps a little too hard. A tiny blood vessel burst below her eye, or was it a spider vein? "Oh, my!" It seemed to grow larger the longer she stared.

"You there?"

"Yes, I'm *here!* It's a nonprofit organization, Amos," she huffed, applying concealer to the blood vessel. "What do you need *books* for?"

"It makes things appear more professional."

"To who?"

"To whomever."

"Are you correcting me?"

Dusty didn't need grammar lessons from a man who had only ever read one book, his own diary. She put down the phone and curled her eyelashes while the mayor went on about the Railway Society's plan to have the old railroad behind the Farm 'n' Field repaired and incorporated into the sightseeing trolley line that toted tourists around town. She suspected he wanted it repaired for himself, not for tourists. She had learned from Mr. Gregory, the DA, that if Amos drove his golf cart, tipsy, into the lake one more time, that was it for the cart. That, or she had recently read it in Amos's diary when passing by his house, but still. The diary was just lying there on the porch, unchaperoned in that nasty old armchair. It was open to an old entry in which he mentioned reading William Cooper's diary, which was on display at the Fun-house, where he'd been searching for something (he didn't say what and Dusty dared not flip the page, lest it was marked). Apparently, the town founder had written, "The Poor Creatures think all is Safe if they setell on Land under my care . . . I find my Self in a Very Humble Situation seing so much is Expected from me." Dusty wondered if the pressure was becoming too much for Amos, running the town. She didn't know why he was so competitive with Cooper. Cooper was dead and both of them were terrible spellers.

She held her ground.

"I have to sell at least one hundred Triple Plays to meet my quota by the end of summer."

In truth, she refused to help Amos because folks from Oneonta had founded the Leatherstocking Road 'n' Rail Histor-ical Guild, and Oneontans stubbornly preferred Avon.

"It's a shame," Amos said. "We could use a girl like you."

Dusty tried not to be suckered in by the mayor appealing to her looks whenever he needed a favor. She said no a final time, hoping he would call back tomorrow. She hung up the phone and studied her face in the mirror. She pictured herself smiling away—her pearly-white teeth, her porcelain-smooth skin—when Amos called back to admit these little phone chats had a deeper meaning. She could see it now: the two of them dining at that cute little restaurant off Stage Coach Lane, Amos asking her to sit on his porch after supper, the stars lending a spectacular sheen to her skin, and the man in the moon smiling down at them with a giant pockmark on his cheek . . .

"Oh, my!" she gasped, touching her face. There was a mark on her left cheek, a blemish that was threatening to become more of a boil. It was red and raw-looking—the sort of blemish that even the Dugout (a blackhead remover shaped like a baseball bat, but with a hole in one end and flat like a spatula) would not be able to remove. She considered calling in sick to work, but she had promised Amos that she would get right on the new wax Mays mold that had been shipped in from the city for next month's induction ceremony. She dabbed powder on the blemish and grabbed her purse, remembering her motto: selling makeup is a good enough reason to go to people's houses and poke in their business, but wax pays the bills.

She walked up Lake Street, turned left on Pioneer, and headed toward Main, where the Hall of Heroes stood. If she kept to the right side of the street, she could see Amos's house without Amos seeing her. He sat on the porch, *drinking*. Lemonade, sure, but it wouldn't be when she told it to the waitresses at the Choke-Up Diner.

She unlocked the museum, flipping the CLOSED sign poised in Babe Ruth's hands to announce she was open for business. Dusty was the only person who worked in the lab before noon and generally for just a few hours. She had been a full-timer until the wax museum began losing money. The townsfolk said they didn't need to view life-size wax replicas of ballplayers when living players traveled through town each year, and the tourists weren't particularly moved by wax. Dusty could not imagine why. Wax was perfect. Why, the most mottled face in the world could be made pretty with some paraffin and a little foundation!

She winked at Ruth. The figures looked so real, like they might up and say "How d'you do?" at any moment. Her favorite was Lou Gehrig—two sets of dimples, *five* total if you counted the chin, which Dusty had accentuated with eyeliner. She was also proud of the Abbott and Costello "Who's on First?" exhibit. Abbott, with his dapper mustache, reminded her of Frank, and Costello, so stout and jolly with that cute little bow tie and bowler hat—why, she could just *squeeze* him! Sometimes, when she was feeling lonely, she *did*. All of the figures, thirty and counting, were life-size. They didn't make great conversationalists, but there were worse things than being surrounded by a room full of men who couldn't open their mouths to criticize.

She strolled through the museum, flicking on the lights room by room—the gift shop, the Baseball Blunders room—as she made her way to the lab where the cosmetic operations took place. She said hello to each figure as she passed, same as every morning, startled when she reached Joe DiMaggio and Marilyn Monroe, who were dressed for a night on the town. She had purchased a secondhand mink stole for Monroe, and had turned up Joltin' Joe's collar and loosened his tie, so he looked more naturally at ease. She couldn't place what was wrong with them at first—they looked more like they were dressed for a morning in, *after* a night on the town. Their clothes were rumpled and there was an imprint of a fingertip on Monroe's recently shellacked cheek. There was also a wallet-size photo of Honus Cronin in the pocket of DiMaggio's blazer. "That is it!" she snapped—having keys to the Hall of Fame meant having keys to the Hall of Heroes, and if Honus couldn't be trusted not to molest the heroes, he ought not have keys. She did pity him, though. Frank had liked him, not at first, but he eventually took him under his wing. "Starved for parental wisdom," is what Frank had said. Honus claimed to have no kin of his own, though Dusty knew his mama lived just miles away in Cheery Valley and invited him home each year for Thanksgiving. He had told her so himself. That, or she had read his mail at the post office, but still.

She donned her gloves and got to work.

Dusty was responsible for putting the finishing touches on the wax figures, the effects that made them so lifelike. The casts were special-ordered from a warehouse in New York City, but the real art was done on location to save cash. Dusty knew this because she used to give tours at the museum, a skill she had acquired from Frank. But ever since the budget cut last fall, she just handled the cosmetics. That was her specialty anyway, and she could not refuse when the museum agreed to let her test out some of her own products on the figures. Next to tourists, the Hall of Heroes was her best customer. Like she always said, "If it's good enough for paraffin, it's good enough for people!"

She decided to test the Dust Bowl on the Willie Mays cast. It stood there, naked and looking more like a tall, coffee-colored cocoon than a man. It was Amos's opinion that a nice wax Mays would draw more tourists into the museum, and Dusty agreed. People would pay for just about anything if you knew how to market it, and the key to good marketing was subtlety. For instance, you didn't tell the pasty-faced Ruby Barrett she needed Home-Run Foul Line facial toner. You told her she would not look so haggard, and be so resentful toward rumors all the time, if she used it. But that was the problem with Cooperstown: there was nothing *subtle* about it. Everywhere you looked, baseball, baseball, and more baseball!

She opened her compact and checked her eyeshadow, recalling the day Frank convinced her to move to Cooperstown. They had met in Vegas, where she was practicing to be a showgirl. She was quite a few years older than him, but he did not seem to mind. Over a drink they discovered that they both had French ancestry. Frank said French men made the best lovers, Dusty asked him to prove it, and the rest was history.

The longer she stared into the compact mirror, the smoother her skin became, and the younger she looked—aside, of course, from the ingrown eyebrow hair causing a welt on her forehead. "Nasty," she said, plucking the brow with the tweezers she had been using to insert Mays's glass eyes into his rubber sockets. The eyes were the most significant part of the molds. They made the figures look human, gave them eternal life, eternal youth. At least

baseball kept a person feeling young. Each summer in Cooperstown was just like the last. Time did not move forward, it slinked
to a standstill. Each year the game came around and with it a slew
of tourists, new customers; and a gal could pretend she was still
twenty-three and didn't have suspiciously large pores.

She checked her reflection in Mays's left eye. Is this what she
really looked like, how other people saw her, or did no one ever
see you like you saw yourself? She wondered if the mayor
thought she was pretty.

It was time for Mays's foundation. She examined a photo of
him; she always used photos as a guide to ensure that her work
looked authentic. He would need a warm base, cocoa colored,
and wide-set, smiling, sleepy eyes with a slight arch to the brows.
She wanted this figure to be perfect, so perfect that Mays himself
would say she was a genius, and Amos would say, "Nice work,
beautiful, now let's fall in love or go to dinner!"

Of course, there would be no dinner until all the hullabaloo
over the theme park subsided. It annoyed Dusty that, these days,
parks had to have themes. What happened to the parks of old,
when a couple could sit on a bench in the moonlight merely admiring each other without having to worry if they could afford
to buy cotton candy, which caused breakouts, or ride rides that
hindered circulation? She inspected the backs of her knees for
varicose veins. Frank would have hated a theme park in Cooperstown. Then again, it *would* mean more tourists, and more tourists
meant more customers. What said refreshment after a long day
of riding roller coasters better than Home-Run Sweet Spot
spearmint breath freshener? The "sweet spot," Frank had said,
was the fat part of the bat. It was also what he called her—

She blushed, placing her handkerchief over Mays's face. Some
things were too private even to remember.

Dusty was less concerned about the park than she was about
the people who *were* concerned with it. Amos, for instance,
didn't want the park as a matter of pride. He wanted a certain
cash flow, flowing in and out of Cooperstown, to be attributed

solely to its old-fashioned charm, *his* charm. He fancied himself a regular reincarnation of Abner Doubleday, and he may as well have been a wax reincarnation, because he had the waxy, hairy ear buildup to prove it; nothing, of course, that a pair of Home-Run Twin Killing tweezers couldn't take care of. "Twin killing" was apparently another name for a double play, which made sense because it was also good for tweezing nose hairs. It was the first product Dusty had named on her own after Frank died. Bitchy Bobby Reboulet said the reason it didn't sell well was because people didn't want to place sharp objects labeled "killing" up their noses.

There were other people wrapped up in the theme park, like Terrence Daulton. He just wanted something to write about, something that would give him an excuse to defy his roots and leave town once and for all. Writing about a baseball theme park was a far stretch from writing about baseball, and Dusty bet he liked it that way and liked it for foolish reasons. He had probably never even been a *real* writer, no matter what Chuck had said. As for his bosom buddy—*ex*-buddy—that reclusive Immanuel Barrett, who knew what he wanted? Certainly not the aftershave Dusty had offered him.

And as for Bobby, the lazy librarian, there would be plenty of time for being crotchety when she hit seventy. If that girl wasn't careful, her heart was going to dry up like unused mascara. She ought to go out with poor Honus.

And what about that psychiatrist? His wife so God-fearing she wouldn't even *try* a cucumber mask, just because it contained a smidge of alcohol? Something was going on in that house. Something Dusty was certain only a face-to-face, door-to-door visit would reveal.

She dabbed rouge on Mays's cheek. He looked good, proud to be in the Hall of Heroes. She began applying pink eyeshadow on his lids for an extra glow, until she remembered that Amos had said "nothing fancy." Who cared what Amos said until he said, "I'm taking you out!" She added some baby-blue shadow to accentuate the whites of Mays's eyes. She applied a thin coat of mascara to the ends of his lashes before affixing them to his face. She would shellac him later. All she had left to do now was the mouth, which she traced with plum-colored lip-liner, thinking about Frank.

His wake had been open-coffin. Auffswich had agreed to use Dusty's own special recipe for concealer to touch up his neck, which was badly bruised from the hanging. It still irked her that Auffswich buried Frank in those awful green shorty shorts when she had *said* to put him in trousers! His mouth had been wrong too; it had been pinker in life. Auffswich had not even *tried* to capture the correct tone of his complexion. He probably used Revlon. Then again, Dusty thought, looking into the wax man's vacant eyes, what did it matter when in the end skin sloughed off, unappreciated, once a body hit the ground? She wondered what it would be like to have dead skin, *really* dead, versus skin in need of a good exfoliation. Auffswich said hair and nails grow after death, a decent perk, but skin? She ran her fingers across her forehead, feeling for wrinkles. Her eyes began to tear and she dabbed at them with her hankie. What was the point of using cold cream if you just withered up like old bark in the end? Why keep up appearances when the man you loved was gone, and there was nothing left but you, a purse full of compact mirrors, and a room full of wax men? Sales, that's what.

Look good! Sell well!

She finished the mold, affixing a wig to Mays's head before spraying it with Home-Run High and Tight Hair Spray, and stepped back to admire her work. Perfect. This man would survive long after his namesake or his creator. He was so perfect that Dusty could not help herself. She stood on her tiptoes and pulled the figure toward her, the wax man towering over her four-foot-eight-inch frame. The lips were cool, smooth like Frank's had been as he lay in his coffin, the morning she said her final good-bye. She held the mannequin close, nuzzling the wig and struggling to recall the last thing Frank had ever said to her, which was, "You really ought to see a dermatologist." That, or "No one loves you like I do," but still.

C HYLAK CAUGHT MRS. PAQUETTE lingering outside his window during his weekly session with the mayor. The moment Fusselback left, he invited her in, hoping to enlighten her about a little thing called privacy. She won him over immediately with a free sample of aftershave, which smelled terrific, though he didn't need it smeared across his forehead. She said this was the best way to test products, for cheeks were too sensitive and chins too flabby. He asked her to sit. As the town busybody, Paquette was bound to shed valuable insight into his patients' lives. He had so few patients during the wintertime. They trickled in throughout the spring and early summer, and now that it was almost August, they seemed to arrive all at once—three of them together yesterday, in fact! Chylak had explained that therapy was more of a "one-at-a-time thing." There was no way he was tacking group sessions onto his schedule. It was difficult enough to deal with them one-on-one.

He felt lately like the traveling shyster in *The Music Man*. He knew it was wrong to build false hopes—to lead people into thinking he could actually *help* them. He felt guilty for, at times, eagerly anticipating the theme park because it made people desperate enough to seek his help and, more important, to *pay* for it. But Babe was pestering him to make a donation to the church, which apparently needed new pews, and soon school would begin. The children would need supplies and demand new clothes and improved allowances to match those of their newfound friends. Chylak feared that his patient load would decrease again come fall or, if there was no theme park, fizzle out completely. After Hall of Fame Weekend, the townsfolk might very well return to their former routines, and for once, he wasn't sure that routine was a good thing. Cooperstown seemed wary of progress, evidenced in the smallest details: the antique lampposts lining Main Street or the felt gingerbread men that hung, fading from brown to pink as the seasons changed, in the window of Skylark's Bakery. He was torn between wanting to *see* change, wanting his patients to genuinely improve, and wanting them to have full-fledged psychotic breaks over the park so he could remain employed.

Mrs. Paquette plopped down on the couch and removed a gold compact from her purse. She pinched her cheeks, inspected her gums, and began flapping her Cosmetic Sales Rep of the Year mouth. On and on she went about the benefits of nail buffers. She seemed self-conscious about her physical appearance in a way Chylak generally associated with prepubescents and hypochondriacs. He said he was pleased to officially make her acquaintance, and that yes, he would call her Dusty, and that no, he had not been avoiding her, he had simply been busy. He begged her pardon for nibbling Babe's braised-broccoli-on-a-bun—it was his lunch break—and encouraged her to chat away at will. If there was anything—anything about *anyone*—she wanted to tell him, he said, she could. Even about herself.

She chose the former.

First, she said, the mayor was estranged from his son not because he'd driven Johnny's mother away, but because Johnny had turned his back on Cooperstown and thus on his father. Did Chylak know Johnny Fusselback was the instigator behind the theme park? The mayor did *not* know, of course; no one did aside from Mrs. Paquette, apparently, who claimed to have her "sources." Chylak knew from a session with Daulton that those "sources" included sneaking peaks at the notes he'd tossed in his trash can whenever she stopped by *The Journal* to push hair gel on him.

Chylak glanced at the day planner in which he took notes during his sessions. It was well out of her reach. He listened patiently as Paquette explained that the mayor had a habit of drinking Geritol, sniffing liquid shoe polish, talking to himself, penning peculiar diary entries, and being bad with dates. Chylak wasn't sure if she meant dates as in time or the romantic kind, but he had hardly opened his mouth to ask when she began to rant about the mayor being afraid of change because he was afraid of *death,* which she said was easily remedied by an apricot face scrub (it gave the skin a youthful glow), and a woman who was clever with cleansing to tell him so.

Speaking of needing a woman: the *journalist.* According to Mrs. Paquette, Terry Daulton had no intention of staying in town, having professed so out loud in the dairy section of Save, America! That, or she'd overheard him saying so into a pay phone on Main Street. She wanted to know if Chylak suspected he had a lady friend back in the city. In her opinion, Daulton had *better* stick around, because Cooperstown was the only thing he had left of "family." All he needed was a good reason to stay, and if he was single, a certain grouchy librarian might be just that reason, if Paquette had anything to do with it (which for some reason she thought she did).

As for that librarian, where to begin? An exasperated Paquette knew where: somewhere between Ms. Reboulet's dire need for lipliner (her lips were apparently thinning prematurely) and all the time she spent reading, which caused crow's-feet. She said Reboulet had better find love wherever it was available, or before she knew it, she'd be old, wrinkled, childless, and alone at seventy.

Chylak waited for her to take a breath, impressed when she did not.

Bobby Reboulet, Paquette continued, was a moper, and moping meant not facing the possibility that a certain out-of-towner (say, an out-of-towner who had since *returned* to town?) might like her, which meant exploring that liking, which meant admitting she was a coward. Even though a concerned someone had offered to sell her perfume at a discount, to give her an extra confidence boost, Home-Run Perfect Game Patchouli being an aphrodisiac and on sale for seven dollars this month.

"Do you wanna buy some?" Mrs. Paquette asked Chylak.

He shook his head.

Next, there was "that hermit on East Lake Road." Immanuel Barrett could use a hygiene boost—did Chylak know he had no running water, and was a psychiatrist enough of a doctor to be able to say if that was sanitary? Barrett needed a friend, an *older* person to confide in. Someone with experience, she said, who could take his confidences and explain them all over town lest he be misunderstood.

Chylak longed to hear more about Barrett, to know if it was true that the man, whom he knew only by reputation, had once been a rather talented ballplayer. Paquette said yes, that was true, and that he would have gone pro were it not for some "mysterious idiotic epiphany" that sent him rushing off to war, ruining his future. She said he returned with the nerve to tell his wife—who needed a good firming eye gel, by the way—that he'd rather live in the woods with a dirty, matted little puppy in need of a hot bath and a good cream rinse than with her and his children.

When Paquette began inquiring about *his* personal life, Chylak excused himself and opened the window to get some air. Paquette rattled on about one thing or another, and Chylak could swear she briefly mentioned Babe. He took several deep breaths and stared out the window; he regretted having asked this whirling dervish of a woman inside. Now, he wanted her *outside* immediately.

Dusty stopped to catch her breath and flip through the doctor's day planner, wondering if Manny Barrett needed a brush for his puppy. The doctor had zoned out. Perhaps the aftershave was overpowering and he was too polite to say so; she hadn't quite nailed down the recipe. Chylak looked like he could use some moisturizer as well, and a decent manicure. His nails were chewed to the quick. He looked, in fact, unwell. Pity, because they were in the middle of a most fascinating conversation. It occurred to her that Frank would have liked Dr. Chylak. She decided to confide in him about her canker. She had asked another doctor about it recently, a young and thus inexperienced Dr. Jeffers, the resident dermatologist, who had ushered her, rather brusquely, down the hall to this very psych ward. A psychiatrist may be for the head, but the face was on the head, and this face was too old for cankers. There must be something else wrong with her.

Chylak returned to his desk, ventilated, and examined Paquette's upturned face. His own was rather flushed. He attributed his sudden bout of nausea to the aftershave and to breakfast—Babe's spicy tofu surprise was probably repeating on him. He patiently explained that, yes, he was a doctor who technically worked with *heads,* but that that did not really include *faces.* Mrs. Paquette seemed disappointed, so he professed to having seen such a blemish before. She then inquired about crow's-feet, vascular marks, hairiness, mammoth pores, and asymmetrical buttocks. Chylak suggested that perhaps she had more of a *condition* than a canker. Afraid she'd sign herself up for unnecessary surgeries, he wrote her a prescription for a low-dose tranquilizer. Goffman said that "social distance is typically great and often formally prescribed," so he prescribed that too.

Dusty asked what the tranquilizer was for. She could have sworn Chylak mumbled, "Think of it as vitamins for character flaws," but she could not always trust her hearing, because of her kerchief. She declined in favor of Home-Run vitamin supplements, which she was not legally licensed to sell, but still.

Chylak remembered that Babe had given him a Bible as a congratulations gift upon his graduation from medical school. He had browsed through it just once to please her and distinctly recalled one passage: *Every fool will be meddling.* Perhaps he now remembered it because he'd felt that *Babe* was meddling by inserting her ideologies into his moment of triumph. He recalled that Mrs. Paquette's own husband had committed suicide and wondered if the man had been chattered to death. He felt rather henpecked himself, Paquette having inquired about Babe during her ramblings. Or was it *Alice?* He had tuned out, mesmerized by the way his breath evaporated against the windowpane as fast as he expelled it. A blue jay was perched on the windowsill and flew

across the street where Elliott played on the lawn. He motioned
for the boy to cross the street and rescue him from the babbling
brook flooding his office with hearsay. But Elliott had simply
waved back, and then attempted a handstand.

Chylak considered charging this interloper seventy-five bucks
so their gossip session did not feel so unethical. But Paquette had
disappeared. He looked around the room. How long had he been
sitting there alone? He hoped he had not offended her with the
prescription. He wiped his forehead on his sleeve; the aftershave
combined with the rough polyester twill of his shirt was too
much in this heat.

He tilted back his chair, feet on the desk, trying to make sense of
Paquette's sudden departure. He retraced their conversation: the
mayor, Daulton, Ms. Reboulet . . . had she inquired about his *sex* life?

Perhaps he had dozed off. He rummaged in his drawer for a
fix, Freud's *A General Introduction to Psycho-Analysis,* that oldie but
goodie in which he had been reading about "slips of the tongue"
before a certain giant tongue slipped in and besieged him.

> *So we will probe no further into errors; but we may still take a fleet-*
> *ing glimpse over the breadth of this whole field . . .*

He underlined *field.*

> *. . . in the course of which we shall both meet with things already*
> *known and come upon the tracks of others that are new.*

He circled *new.*

> *In so doing, we will keep to the division into three groups made at the*
> *beginning of our study: slips of the tongue, with the coordinate forms*
> *of slips of the pen, misreading, mis-hearing;*

He glanced out the window to see Paquette, now sauntering
door-to-door. He half expected her to straddle a giant sable pow-

der brush and fly away. He removed his glasses, rubbed his eyes, and looked again. She was gone. Had he imagined her? Conjured her out of thin air? He scratched his head, and continued to read.

>   *. . . of forgetting with its subdivisions according to the object forgotten*
>   *(proper names, foreign words, resolutions, impressions);*

He had gotten the distinct impression from Paquette that she felt *he* needed to talk.

>   *. . . and of mislaying, mistaking, and losing objects.*

What had she said about Daulton? And what on earth had been plaguing Chuck? Chylak attempted once more to bury his head in his book.

>   *Mistakes, insofar as they concern us, are to be grouped partly under*
>   *the head of forgetting . . .*

"Dammit," he muttered, tossing the book aside, unable to concentrate. Suppose he *had* made a mistake by moving to Cooperstown? Perhaps that's not what annoyed Babe, so much as the fact that he had not run the decision by her first. Perhaps she sought in her God what she didn't get from him, a limitless ear and a certain amount of security. But they had been married for years. *Something* kept them going. If he knew what it was, he could nurture it.

His eyes wandered across his desk. There was a page missing from his day planner, the one containing his notes from the mayor's last session. Paquette must have snatched it while he was at the window escaping her relentless stream-of-consciousness assault. He tried to take the high road and place himself in her shoes—the orthopedic, open-toed sandals of a caustic, cosmetic dysmorphophobe—surprised to feel sympathetic. He had the distinct sense that his world had been turned upside down by that silly little woman during the course of a single lunch hour. He reached into his desk drawer for a bottle of Valium, popping a pill in his mouth. Babe was probably right. He was working too hard. He should go home right now and eat dinner with his family, engage in his own former routine, just do something "normal." And with that thought, Chylak wept.

Perhaps the aftershave smeared on his forehead had a lachrymal effect, but still.

SEVENTH-INNING STRETCH

I think they might have chosen a more suitable spot for their sports.
They are mistaking liberties for liberty, I fear.

—JAMES FENIMORE COOPER, *HOME AS FOUND*

The streets were bustling. The ratio of tourists to locals was overwhelming; over three hundred and fifty thousand visitors annually to Cooperstown, a quarter of whom seemed to arrive all at once at the beginning of August. People from across the country had journeyed to town during the hottest month of the year to shop, seek respite, and pay homage to the great Willie Mays, who was being inducted into the National Baseball Hall of Fame.

Cooperstown seemed, to Kerwin Chylak, to be quite a different town altogether in fact, one that had suddenly come alive with enthusiasm. He felt fortunate to witness the rousing of the beast from its slumber. Following a pitiful two morning appointments, he had fallen asleep at his desk, awakening at noon to the clang-clang of a marching band touting the local alma mater, Cooperstown's battle cry: *From the shores of Lake Otseeego . . .* The music revived him, beckoning him into the streets along with a craving for salami on rye. He temporarily sated his appetite with a loose pill he found in his pocket, then headed into town to treat himself to a hero.

Across the street Babe was watering the rose beds. He thought she might like to take a stroll. Her back was to him and she was singing to herself about a garden of dew-covered roses—*"He walks with me, and he talks with me, and he tells me I am His own."* She appeared so radiant, so angelic that it almost hurt to look at her. Chylak paused on the sidewalk, suddenly profoundly aware that he had neither walked nor talked with his wife in some time; that he was not her great love, and that it was in fact God—that old devil of a charmer—who was invoking her joy, the two of them tarrying merrily along in their magical Eden without him. He looked down to find he had stepped in dog excrement and wiped his foot on the grass, then one foot went in front of the other mismatched foot and the next thing he knew, like a magnet he was drawn toward the center of town. He strolled through the streets in the wake of the parade, a spring in his step, a colorful swish of baby-blue bell-bottomed pant legs, overcome by a sudden inexplicable joy all his own. He increased his pace to a jog.

On Main Street he was forced to slow down, carefully dodging bodies and booths of fresh pies. Baked treats were being sold on every corner, championed by boisterous matrons in embroidered aprons chirping, mixing, and mingling with tourists. Beneath the din of their passionate sales pitches, the faintest peck, peck, pecking about the theme park was audible. The local biddies had put their best powdered faces forward for the sake of tourists. Perhaps, thought Chylak, "the beast" was merely sleepwalking. Or was this a temporary retreat from hibernation, the opening act of a play that would inevitably result in a finale of mayhem?

The sweet scent of pastries seduced him further along: charred cinnamon and plump apples blending—a potent potpourri—with the aroma of aster, larkspur, hollyhock, lilac, and geraniums that the Ladies Auxiliary had stuffed into baskets that hung from the lampposts. He sampled a mocha Mays Muffin, enticed by the ambrosia, the atmosphere, pleased to for once experience the town from a solely primeval perspective. He sneezed, and when a tourist blessed him, he marveled at how people were always doing that, blessing each other, sanctifying mere acts of biology, and personal ones at that. A man ought to be able to expel a little pollen from his nose sans risk of being ushered straight into heaven.

Every lamppost, every flagpole and awning was strewn with red, white, and blue streamers, lending Main Street a celebratory feel, as though Cooperstown were an enormous gift, a big fat bottle of American spirit. At the lakefront a minicarnival appeared out of nowhere, nickel and dime rides for the kiddies and a casino for the adults. Everywhere, tiny tots consumed vast quantities of popcorn and cotton candy while clinging to their adult counterparts, their sticky-sweet paws bolstering that age-old bond between young and old. The tourists donned jerseys and caps boasting the names of their favorite ballplayers and teams; entire families dressed in matching outfits, like so many colorful species of patriot. Chylak devoured a swatch of cotton candy, suckling the sugar from his tongue, tainted blue. One, two, three patients sauntered by, each seemingly pleased to see him out and about on the town like a regular Joe.

He leaned against a lamppost and tapped his toes to the marching band's beat. There were so many people, thousands milling up and down the street, laughing and shouting and eager to spend. Everything seemed so vivid. He couldn't remember the last time he had felt so awake, so alive! The wind felt divine, the sun like a warm little kitty lapping at his face, and everyone, even the men, was absolutely striking. He closed his eyes and listened, lovingly, to the crowd. "Ummm," he cooed. "Ummm."

He headed toward the Hall of Fame, waving to passersby. The townsfolk were putting on quite a show, selling their wares, smiling smiles he hoped were sincere, and he suddenly remembered the last time he had felt like this. It was at the one ball game he had attended in his life, at Ebbet's Field on a trip to New York with his father, the only father-son field trip they had ever really had. His father, an immigrant from some long since abandoned Eastern European union, insisted that baseball contained the key to the American Dream; it was a riddle, and if a Polack, an I-talian, or a "colored" could solve it, it would better ensure their entrance into the Promised Land. Chylak had been unable to relate, content to be the first generation allowed to sit back and take it all for granted.

He remembered the forlorn look on his father's face when he compared the crowd to a pack of wild Hyaenidae, which he had learned about in science class. His father shook his head, waving an Oscar Mayer wiener toward the outfield, and said, "Pipe down and watch!" Chylak had tried, and what he saw remained a blur, for he had been more interested in listening than in watching the game. He imagined that he could hear the internal afflictions that plagued each player on the field: the first baseman with his demanding mistress threatening to call his wife; the pitcher unable to bear another pitch, wanting to go home and zone out in front of *The Jack Benny Program* so he didn't have to face the fact that he had gambled away the mortgage on his house; or the manager in the dugout, changing his mind about that divorce—he really did love his old lady.

But now!

Everywhere Chylak turned there were shops he hadn't noticed before, doors opening to welcome him in, a cool breeze busting through a blanket of humidity, and the sweet odor of apple pie! Inside the shops, apron-clad merchants stood at attention, sweeping popcorn, candy, receipts, and gift-wrapping remains from their floors, eager to aid him with comments like, "I wouldn't sell this to anyone else, but you look like a fellow who might appreciate it." Meanwhile, the insatiable tourists bartered and bargained, as pleased with their purchases as they were with the attention lavished upon them by the charming folk in this utterly charming town.

When Shane Gregory, the DA, walked by, Chylak took a risk and allowed himself to, for once, be part of the crowd. "What a bunch of kiss-asses, eh?" he quipped. The attorney smiled, shaking his head in agreement, the two of them sharing a wily wink, like proud parents of a newborn Cooperstown; Chylak was overcome by an inexplicable affection for this silly old bear of a town.

Children skipped rope in the middle of Main Street, which was lined with police barricades, the parade having passed. Teenagers strolled arm in arm, singing songs that seemed to accompany, rather than clash with, the crackling of an ancient gramophone, over which the National Pastime Orchestra played "If You Can't Make a Hit at the Ballgame, You Can't Make a Hit with Me." The music flowed through the corridors of the baseball museum, out the front entrance, and into the streets. Chylak felt giddy, like he had fallen asleep one wintry night in Indiana and awoke not in van Winkle's future, but back in time to a scrumptious summer day in a quaint little village in central New York State, one that, today, would surely have made old Willy-nilly Cooper and that fellow Abner Doubledeal (Doubledip?) proud.

He made his way toward the Hall of Fame, passing a bookshop where he took chance number two: waving to Ms. Reboulet, who stopped peering into the window long enough to gesture back with one questionable finger. At the wax museum, he paused to wipe his spectacles on his sleeve, for the figure in the window, a wax likeness of the eminent Mays, looked rather off-kilter. But before he could say why, he was caught up in the flow of the crowd, the other fish making their way to the shady steps of the baseball museum, where things bottlenecked to a halt, everyone eager to witness the induction ceremony and to hear Mays deliver his speech.

Every facet of his being, each opaque chunk in the Chylakian prism—doctor, husband, father, and self—suddenly made way for Chylak the child, who was back at that ball game with his dear old dad, and by God he would do it this time—he would pipe down and savor it! There was nothing in his psychiatric manuals that suggested spontaneity in small doses caused any harm.

He went into a shop and, on a whim, grabbed whatever appealed to him: souvenirs, caps, bobblehead ballplayers and bats, licorice-flavored lollipops shaped like baseballs, and white and dark chocolate molded methodically into itty-bitty pinstriped men. Where had it all been before, this business of baseball? The essence of the sport seemed to grow from the very trees! It tickled his senses. How had he not previously noticed that which lay smack beneath his bucconasal membrane, the old *tunica mucosa nasi?* The primal scent of the sport was now stuck in that groovy groove between snout and upper lip, the mysterious dimple the ancients had tastefully dabbed with perfumes to mask their stench or the stench of others, he couldn't recall which. He rubbed the tape on his nose, feeling as lucky as a dog able to scratch its own hindquarters—marvelous! Everything was so marvelous! He flexed his hand before his face, open and shut like a fleshy pink beak, admiring how gracefully his fingers moved, how warm his hand felt. He took in one final gulp of the sights, sounds, and smells of his town before worming his way through the crowd and into the baseball museum, where he began to come down.

Perhaps he drank too much coffee at breakfast. Perhaps that with the cotton candy and that capsule of imipramine, or whatever loose pill he had found in his pocket, on an otherwise empty stomach was to blame. He began to feel queasy. Outside, the townsfolk were smiling as though they hadn't a care in the world, and he began to suspect that beneath this sudden, surrealistic chipper veneer there was something forced, fake, and frenzied about the scene. He was thirsty, unbearably so. The change in temperature was unsettling. The air-conditioning was on full blast, another perk for the tourists. His skin tingled, the hair on his arms bristled uncomfortably, and he began to wonder whether it was possible to suffocate on feelings. What was happening? He feared the worst, that this was the sort of moment that seems pleasurable enough at the time but later manifests into some misdiagnosed neurosis.

DAULTON STOOD IN THE VIP section in front of the Hall of Fame, listening to the baseball commissioner introduce Mays. He wished the clapping would cease. He had a migraine, and there was hardly room enough in the crowd to breathe, let alone to usher around the gawky young photographer he'd brought along to help cover the ceremony. He tried to focus on the ribbons that barbershop-poled their way around the flag-poles in front of the museum. The heat was unbearable, bodies packed so compactly together that it was impossible to distin-guish one's limbs from another's; so many people, strangers, clinging together, morphing into one colossal fan chanting the mantra: *"Yay, Mays! Yay, Mays!"*

He wiped his brow, unsure if his stomach was in knots be-cause he stood so close to an icon, or because his was a time-sensitive mission. It wasn't just about work. It was a matter of personal duty. In his pocket was a baseball card that had be-longed to Chuck, his '51 Mays card. After the ceremony he planned to ask Mays to sign it in his father's absence. Yes he was here as a reporter, not a spectator. But Chuck would've loved this. He would interview Johnny, as promised, get the autograph, and then one final farewell before he left town: place the auto-graphed baseball card on Chuck's grave. Then he'd clear out the cottage and go.

Mays took the stage and Daulton clapped, robotic, along with the crowd, his moist palms smacking together like two dumb-founded fish. He was honoring one of the few men his fault-finding father had revered: Mays was saying, "I don't have any feeling right now, but tomorrow morning, when I wake up and I say to my wife, 'Was yesterday my day?' . . ."

Daulton wondered if Chuck was up there somewhere, watching the ceremony—if when a man died he got to see all the moments he would miss, moments in which he could have made his mark. Was Chuck up there, regretful that yesterday was his day? Was he frustrated that he couldn't control things below, like whether the mayor's shirt was buttoned, or if there were enough streamers wound around the museum? What if there was a transitory state be-tween life and death, a single hour in which people viewed an abridged slide show of their lives, images of the mistakes they'd made, or the events they'd miss but might have appreciated had they managed to stay alive? He imagined a beautiful goddess in a white peasant blouse pointing to a screen with her prompter and asking, "What about *this* one? Do you wish you had been there for *that?*"

Daulton realized he was staring at Bobby, who gazed into the window of the five-and-dime at the ass of a mannequin in a Yanks uniform. She seemed unaware of the ceremony, like she had strolled out of the library for a pack of smokes, oblivious to the fact that thousands of strangers stood virtually in her own backyard. He nodded his head and she returned the gesture with a hesitant wave.

It all seemed so familiar: Bobby standing there snapping her gum like she was sixteen; Honus scouring the crowd for trouble-makers, beside him the mayor and Johnny Fusselback, back home in Cooperstown for the first time in years. Even old Bumppo had come out of his cave to witness the ceremony. Manny was perched on the post office roof.

Daulton searched the Fusselbacks' faces for signs of discontent: two matching facades of steely reserve, each taking a hit for his team, disguising his pride. Exhibit number three, ladies and gentlemen: Estranged Father and Son. They were ignoring each other, Johnny shoving Amos aside to soak up the spotlight whenever he could. Daulton remembered this Cooperstown. Perhaps he had even missed it: tourists staring doe-eyed at the ballplayer, the townsfolk whoring themselves out for a buck, pushing baubles and baked goods—"Try my Ty Cobb Cakes! They're delicious! They're peach!"—and everyone waiting with bated breath for the ceremony to end so they could get their autographs, half of which, he suspected, would later be sold for a hundred bucks a pop.

He shoved the Mays card deep in his pocket, embarrassed now at the sentiment.

Mays was telling a story; someone once asked him where he wanted to go and Manhattan was the reply. "Growing old . . . power . . . react . . . understand me." When he paused, wiping his brow, the mayor blocked Johnny to hand Mays a bottle of soda, and then slipped something into his hand. Daulton raised his binoculars. What was it, a bottle opener? The mayor shook

Mays's hand, then made a gracious half bow and exited the stage while Mays continued his speech. As Fusselback brushed past him, Daulton noticed that the shoestring the old man generally wore around his neck was missing its peculiar pendant. He gestured for his photographer to shoot the mayor exiting the ceremony so early. Odd that Amos the Fuss, a stickler for routine, had abandoned the event he worked so hard year-round to execute without a glitch. The crowd was oblivious, however, now watching Duke Cartwright ride back and forth in front of the museum on his bike, honking his horn, like a circus bear trained to create what, if Daulton didn't know better, looked not unlike a distraction. Perhaps the mayor was drunk and Cartwright was covering for him. He told the photographer to stop snapping photos of the poor mayor's back as the old man toddled away.

When Mays was finished, Johnny took over, announcing that funding had arrived for a new wing of the Hall of Fame, which was to be dedicated to "our own local legend, without whom this ceremony was tough to execute this year, the dearly departed Charles Daulton!" Daulton fought an urge to flee the ceremony himself. To march onto the steps, grab the microphone, and tell the crowd that Johnny was full of shit. That he hardly knew Chuck. That Chuck was *his* father and that he had probably done his best but even so, he'd been a bully and a control freak and he'd refused to see his own son before he died. He crushed the baseball card in his pocket, desperate now to destroy something, anything, a balloon tied to a flagpole, Mays's perfection, or Chuck's reputation. The feeling was physical, like a skin he'd outgrown and was eager to shed. He looked at Johnny, the son returning for payback against his old man, and remembered why he was there: the theme park, the stunning cyclone that would ensue. Johnny, forcing his father's town to its knees; Cooperstown, overcome by a spontaneous combustion of wills; a stale old way of life reduced to a handful of meaningless ash; the remains of the father in the satisfied hands of the son.

A cloak was removed from the final tribute of the day. Beneath it, a wax statue, the perverse embodiment of—*Who the hell was it?* Daulton raised his binoculars. The figure had brightly rouged cheeks, pink frosted lips, and, instead of a baseball cap, wore a yellow kerchief on its head. He rubbed his eyes, afraid he was experiencing a fugue. He recalled asking Manny—the last time they'd talked, at the morgue, where he'd gone to identify Chuck's body—how, according to his combat expertise, it was possible for a grenade to explode without the person who pulled the pin getting hurt. He could not remember the answer, and realized now it was because there hadn't been one. Manny had blushed, tensed, and barked that he didn't want to talk about it. But Daulton had refused to back off. He kept asking about the war, pushing it, he knew, because every time he asked Manny about Vietnam his was not the typical, understandable, respectable vet's reaction. Manny acted *guilty*, like a child caught in a lie.

The winners of the annual J. G. Taylor Spink Award for baseball writing were being announced. The clapping was thunderous. The earth seemed to quake beneath him; Daulton got lost in the swarm, suddenly unable to distinguish himself from the surging crowd. What about this one, Chuck? he thought, disappointed, forgetting his interview, his autograph, and quickly elbowing his way out. Once on the other side of the street, he turned back to watch the crowd close in on the spot where he had stood just moments before, like beads of merciless mercury determined to pool. Some out-of-town reporter was now asking his questions. Some kid was getting his autograph.

He sat on the curb and pulled Chuck's crumpled Mays card from his pocket, angrily ripping it to shreds and tossing it toward the August blue sky. As it rained back down upon him like acid remorse—the agonizing awareness of his old man's afterlife slide show and disappointment in him—he looked up and yelled, "What about this one! Do you wish you had been here for *this?*"

◆ ◆ ◆

A MOS COULDN'T STAND another minute of sharing the stage with Johnny. The moment he departed the ceremony, however, he knew it wasn't a wise decision because things always fell apart when he wasn't around, evidenced by the wax atrocity Honus was now escorting away from the crowd. It was the Mays mold he'd asked Dusty to surprise the inductee with as a personal touch on behalf of the town. It didn't look a damned thing like Mays. It didn't even look like a *man*! Everything was perfect until that moment: the tribute to Hack Wilson, and Warren Giles's son Bill accepting the induction on his father's behalf. Then Commissioner Bowie Kuhn had introduced Mays, saying, "How do you embellish the unique! How do you paint the lily!" Followed by a gracious Mays taking the stage with, "Commissioner Kuhn, ladies and gentlemen, Hall of Famers, present and past. First I would like to introduce my family . . ."

The ballplayer had shared with the crowd how he'd lain in bed the night before wondering what kind of speech to write, pondering the importance of using his own words to describe his life. "How can you put it on paper, that's my theme. You cannot do it . . . They were years I have given you, you have given me back in many, many different ways. When I look at the kids out here, I say to myself, 'How can you put it on paper, how can you tell these young people what I did over twenty-two years' . . . I gave my life to baseball, you have to, no I wasn't shortchanged." Then Mays had said something that made Amos feel awkward standing there beside Johnny: "I say to you not with hate, forgive each and every one." He had felt a twinge of envy at the way Mays joked with his wife: "You can tell what a ham she is!" It made him miss Martha. He'd only ever wanted to make her proud, to do something that warranted writing a speech about his *own* life. He reached for the string that hung around his neck, feeling for the key, the anchor he'd been carrying for months, a good-luck charm turned sour. He'd been overcome today by a desperate need to purge himself, to pass the torch on to someone else. Or did he mean to seek forgiveness, and if so, from whom, Mays? Chuck? *Barrett?* He felt lighter when he let go of that key, lighter than he had in a long time, like a man who had been carrying a baton in a relay race he was breathless from running for years. Amos was the last runner, the last man standing. Not because he was the only one left worth his salt but because he had started the race. It was his fault. He just hoped, now, that he had not broken in that one simple gesture a twenty-two-year pact that now only he—a phony, a drunk, a sham of a mayor and a man—was able to break. Because he was the only one living who still cared. Barrett despised him, and Duke had taken the eternal Fifth. But no, Duke had saved him, diverting the crowd with his bicycle horn. He owed Duke one.

Amos removed his Hall of Fame pin from his vest, thinking about the inaugural five and about Frank, Duke, Chuck, and Manny. *They* were the real heroes of baseball, and no one would ever know it. Half of Amos's friends were dead, the other half weren't speaking to him, and anyone who fell in between, even his own son, could hardly look him in the eye. The last time he had felt so alone was the day Martha left. He had stood in front of Reality Realty, where she'd just given notice, begging her to stay. He'd looked the fool, down on his knees before her in the rain wearing his rubber boots and rain slicker. She had refused to look at him, climbing inside a sightseeing trolley and riding away. He had watched, silent, unable to distinguish the rain from his tears, aware that one single phrase, one sentence, might have kept her there just a little bit longer: I'm sorry, I love you. But he didn't have the courage to utter it. He was too proud.

He walked down Main Street, eager to get as far away from the ceremony as possible. "Dammit," he muttered, remembering that he had parked his golf cart in front of the museum. He walked up Pioneer Street, catching his breath at the top of the hill, and peered down toward the herd of tourists milling about on Main Street. He replayed Mays's speech in his head. Not today's, but one he'd heard Mays deliver on the radio some five years back, upon his induction into the Black Athletes Hall of

Fame: *"This award means a great deal to me . . . I had a lot of hardship that no one knows about . . . I've been told—you don't care about your people. But that's a lie. The suffering that I received in the last, I would say, twenty-three years, I couldn't talk about because it was inside of me . . . I had to hold it."*

He licked his lips and unbuttoned his shirt to let in some air. "Where are you going with that?" he growled when Honus rushed by with the tainted tribute, the wax Mays mannequin.

"The deputy mayor said to take it to your office."

"I don't want it in my office! Take it to the wax museum! That mold wasn't cheap. Maybe they can melt it down, reuse it, hell, I don't know."

"You all right, sir?"

"I'm fine," Amos snapped, yanking away the flag covering the mannequin. He gasped.

"It's pretty bad, huh?" Honus said.

Now that it was right in front of him, Amos saw that his tribute, this abomination of makeup and wax, was pretty damned *good* work, in fact. It was bonneted and lipsticked, crimped and coiffed, polished and perfumed. It was her—*Dusty.*

"Where are the reporters?" he asked, draping the figure once more with the flag.

Honus pointed toward Main Street.

"Daulton, is he with them?"

"I don't know, sir. I was just taking this to—"

"Never mind about that! Take it to the Hall of Heroes! I'll handle it from there."

He took one last peek under the flag. There was a yellow kerchief on the mannequin's head, covering a wig of red curls. He began to chuckle, holding on to the statue, and then on to Honus when the mannequin began to fall, his belly shaking and tears in his eyes. He wiped them away with the back of his hand.

"Where is she? Where's Mrs. Paquette?"

"She ran off, sir, as soon as this, uh, thing was unveiled. She was crying. I guess she didn't get the reaction she wanted. I can get her for you, if you want to have it out with her."

"No!" Amos yelled.

Honus looked hurt.

"I'll take it from here, son," Amos replied, patting him on the back. "You've done a good job."

Honus looked as though the world had just opened up and made him king. Amos watched him struggle to get a grip on the wax man and drag it back down the hill. When he was gone Amos headed down Church Street, chuckling as he imagined the look on Mays's face when he saw the tribute. Poor Dusty had for once exposed her own self.

He hoped the deputy mayor remembered to take Mays into the Hall of Fame for a photo shoot following the ceremony. They would be wondering where he was. Hopefully someone had the good sense to escort the ballplayer to the Omagotta Hotel for the ceremonial dinner afterward. "Shit," he muttered. Had *Johnny* seen the tribute? Of course he had! He was probably laughing himself blue at his father's expense.

Amos wiped sweat from his forehead. He smoothed what was left of his hair across the top of his head and sucked in his paunch. This was the most important night of his career, dammit, possibly his last official hoorah as mayor of Cooperstown. He stopped at a pay phone and called his office, telling his secretary to let people know he'd be at the Omagotta for dinner in twenty minutes. Then he entered the graveyard behind Christ Episcopal Church, succumbing to a foolish desire to talk to Frank.

The day hadn't been a total disaster. He'd spent the morning personally spit-shining the inductees' commemorative plaques to be hung in the Hall of Fame Gallery. He'd even had his picture taken with Mays. Amos the Fuss in his best seersucker suit, with his arm around the Say Hey Kid, who looked pretty dapper himself, a faint line of stubble visible on his upper lip, which made Amos feel less intimidated, since he hadn't bothered to shave. Mays kept forgetting his name, but no matter. Amos was honored to share the spotlight. Despite Dusty's blunder, he'd gotten through it all: every handshake, every speech, and every interview about that damned theme park.

He sat on a tomb and extracted a pen and his diary from his breast pocket.

> 5:00 pm. Common sense tells me not to write everything down, but there are things a man needs off his CHEST. I have not been involved in a support group since '67 (too many DUES) and in the past, I may not have been much of a leader. But, miracles happen. I met Willie Mays today: The man has SPUNK. I am thankful that my memory is good, but fear keeping it could mean having to SHARE it. There's a game I used to play with Johnny: Duck on a Rock. The first one to knock the SMALL rock off the LARGE rock with their own rock was the WINNER. I have a scar on my forehead (got hit with ROCK).

He taught Johnny that game when Johnny was little. It was a game about holding your own. And what good had come of it? What good had come of anything he had instilled in his son? Johnny had some nerve returning to Cooperstown on his high horse the moment the cameras were on. He'd ignored Amos all day, a polite nod perhaps, but that was it.

Amos dropped his diary and a newspaper clipping fell from it, the day's headlines from *The Journal:* "Bat's Out of the Bag! Mayor's Son Masterminds Theme Park!" He crumpled it into a ball and was about to chuck it at the tombstone in front of him when he noticed it was the grave of James Fenimore Cooper. Cooper's wife was buried next to him. His father, brother Isaac, and several other relations were there somewhere, too. Amos wiped the dirt from its marble surface, noting with some importance that he at sixty-five had outlived, in years, both Coopers, father and son.

He looked around for Frank's grave, trying to recall the last time he'd placed flowers on it or on Chuck's. Then he saw it, FRANCIS D. PAQUETTE, on the other side of the low iron fence that, even in death, separated the Coopers from everyone else. He bent over to retrieve his diary and realized that he'd been sitting on the tomb of Judge William Cooper himself. He sat back down, facing Frank, telling himself that the lump now forming in his throat sprang from thirst, sixty-five years of it. If he died right now, would anyone care? Sixty-five was hardly immortal. It was just old. He spat Geritol on the ground, thinking the Coopers, they were immortal. Chuck and Frank, the ordinary dead, were everlasting too. It was only the ordinary, living sons-of-bitches that went unappreciated. It wasn't fair. And if he died soon, and Johnny married and had a passel of brats all his own, he just hoped that when they asked about grandpa, Johnny had the sense to realize his father's life, Amos's history, wasn't open to interpretation. He could omit the drinking if he liked, and the part about Martha leaving, but he'd better not embellish Amos's faults.

He stared at Frank's grave, thinking about the '54 World Series, New York Giants versus Cleveland Indians. "Remember Game One, Frank?" he said. "Remember how Mays turned his back? He turned his back to the plate and caught Wertz's drive on a dead run in the deepest part of the park, and then spun like hell, making that perfect throw to the infield, holding the runner. I'm going to do that, Frank. I swear to you! I'm going to turn my back, gather my strength, and then bam! I'll throw that goddamned park right the hell out of town."

He took a swig of Geritol, gargling it in the back of his throat, and debated whether to tell Frank he was feeling sweet on his widow. That he knew he probably wasn't the best fellow for her, but that he would try. And that he knew he'd let Frank down. Instead, he tilted his head back, attempting to gargle while whistling "Say Hey," the Treniers' lyrical tribute to Mays.

"I remember that song. Though you're butcherin' the hell out of it."

Amos jumped, spilling Geritol down his chest. At first he thought it was Frank talking back to him, warning him to lay off his girl, or Judge Cooper beneath him, the dead rising from their graves to demand the latest score of the game, a game that, at last count, he was losing.

It was Johnny!

Amos suppressed a sudden desire to pat his son on the back, to draw him close with one bearish swipe the way he did when Johnny was small. The urge passed in favor of one to take a swipe *at* Johnny instead. "What are you doing here?" he growled, losing his balance and nearly falling off the tomb.

Johnny snorted and pointed to the newspaper clipping Amos had dropped on the ground. Everyone had read it by now anyway.

Amos eyed Frank's grave, thinking he was always the last to know when there was mutiny onboard, particularly when it was his own ship. He'd let Frank down, but Frank had let him down first. Chuck and Cartwright, they weren't any better. Amos had followed Duke once, spying on him as he delivered a fruit basket to Barrett in Cheery Valley back when they had sent him away. A goddamned fruit basket! None of them had ever taken him seriously. Traitors. All of them were traitors and his son was the worst. He knew Johnny was behind the theme park, the impending destruction of his town. He'd suspected it for a while. He just hadn't been able to prove it, not until Terry Daulton started poking around and proved it for him, meddling just like his old man. Amos glared at Johnny, seeing only an assemblyman with ambitions toward the Senate. Even if that meant forgetting his roots.

"I'd apologize," Johnny said, "but it is a free country."

"Used to be anyway," Amos snarled. "I suppose you came for the view?"

"Actually, I came to find you."

"Well, I ain't dead *yet*." Amos made a mental note to be buried down by the lake where there were fewer Coopers and he'd have a better view than Frank.

"I can see that. That old belly of yours is as pink and jiggly as a newborn's."

"What are you getting at?" Amos snapped, trying, unsuccessfully, to button his vest over his belly. "I may not be dead, but I haven't got all day either."

"Honus said I might find you here. I have a proposition for you."

Amos was about to chide, "I'll bet you do, you little bastard," but it seemed wise for the aged to remain civilized when on hallowed ground. If Johnny was making an effort, he supposed it wouldn't kill him to do the same.

"What did you think of the ceremony?"

"I thought it went well," Johnny said with a laugh, "aside from that stunt old wacky Paquette pulled—"

"That's enough now," said Amos, rising, his face red. He pointed to Frank's headstone. "That's her husband over there, and she's my friend!"

"Why doesn't that surprise me?"

"What's that supposed to mean?"

"Nothing, Amos. Relax. I didn't come here to fight."

"Why did you come?"

"I told you, I want to make you an offer."

"Hogwash. We're not budging an inch for that park. We don't want it! Why did you *really* come here today?" Amos couldn't help himself. He wanted to know and he wanted to hear it from Johnny. He felt betrayed. "What do you want out of all this? You only come here when it's convenient for you! You made it clear a long time ago that this was no longer your town."

Johnny laughed.

"It's nobody's town, old man. That's the *point*. If there were ever a town that belonged to everyone, it's this one. I've got a job to do is all. You of all people should understand that. And I'll tell you"—he waved his finger in Amos's face, his own impatience rising—"you can tell yourself and your little flock of visionless sheep whatever the hell you like. But the fact remains: the only thing that could prevent the park from coming is a miracle. And from what I hear, old man? You are fresh out."

Amos wanted to leap up and tackle Johnny, to throw him on the ground and beat some sense into him. But he was too tired. When had this happened? When had the roles reversed and respect flown out the window along with sobriety, spouses, and his son who now stood towering over him, saying in so many words, "Your time has come"? He could feel Johnny's eyes scrutinizing the stain on his shirt. He wanted to say that it was Geritol, not schnapps, if that's what Johnny was thinking. He wanted to say that as Johnny's father, it was his *right* to keep him in line, to warn him that as he grew older, he was in danger of becoming hard, bitter, and resentful just like his old man. He wanted to say that sometimes a little Jim Beam was the one true friend he had. He wanted to say he knew Johnny blamed him for Martha leaving, and that maybe Johnny should ask himself if he really wanted to be a politician, since he hated his politician father so much. He wanted to say that maybe, just *maybe,* they should heed Mays's advice, call it a draw and "forgive each and every one." That somewhere along the way Johnny had forced himself to enjoy all of this, to relish his power out of some stubborn need to prove something, just for spite. Spite that had turned to steely reserve, reserve to conviction and conviction to necessity. And that he knew from experience that necessity was blind. Instead, he mumbled, "We can still appeal," unsure whether it was audible, or true.

"It's too late for that. The park will be affiliated with the Hall of Fame. Saying no to the park would be suicide. To beat this you'd have to create quite a stink, convince people beyond all reasonable doubt that Cooperstown no longer gives a damn about baseball, and you know it. If you oppose the park you oppose the museum. You'll lose everything, and we both know you don't have it in you to take that risk. Frankly, neither does this town."

Amos wished he could curl up on Cooper's grave and just lie there, come what may. He poked a finger at Johnny's chest. "This town might surprise you," he said. He hoped it would.

Johnny shook his head and turned abruptly to exit the ceme-
tery.

Amos glanced at Frank's grave. "Did you hear that, Frank?"
he said, feeling defeated. "The town will have to sell itself to save
itself." As the wind rustled the leaves on the trees, he imagined it
to be Frank's response. Fight like hell, Frank seemed to whisper.
Play hardball.

"Wait!" Amos yelled.

"Now what?" Johnny said, turning around when he reached
the gate.

Amos marched toward him, his confidence growing with
every step.

"I have an idea. We'll *play* you for it! We'll go nine innings at
Doubleday Field. Whoever wins decides on the park!"

Johnny shook his head and exhaled, a response Amos interpreted to mean "You'll never change." Then he walked away
without a word.

Amos watched him go. He seemed to get smaller, younger,
the farther he walked—forty, thirty, ten . . . He watched until
Johnny was as tiny as a tot, a dot on the horizon, a brief flicker
of flame he had long ago squinted his eyes shut in the face of, in-
haled, then blown away like a wish, lost. He closed his eyes, imagining once more that the wind was Frank, now murmuring, "We
don't have a prayer."

"The hell we don't!" Amos said, and stomped, determined,
toward the church.

It was dark inside. The Gothic Revival decor lent the building
an ominous air. The church was empty. By now the townsfolk
had returned to their respective homes. The stores would soon
be closed. The tourists were probably heading back to their ho-
tels or to the carnival down by the lake. Mays and the committee,
the veterans and patrons, were eating their ceremonial supper,
Amos's supper, his last rite as mayor.

He walked down the aisle, appreciating the quiet and relieved
to escape the heat. One of the stained-glass windows was dedi-

cated to James Fenimore Cooper, who was warden at the church in 1851, the year he died. Amos read the dedication: "Faith is the substance of things hoped for, the evidence of things not seen." He toddled toward a pew and genuflected, unsure about proper Episcopalian etiquette. He then attempted the sign of the cross, touching his forehead, his nose, his right shoulder, and then his heart, like a confused catcher signaling, and slid into a pew. Cringing at the cacophonous crack of his knees amid such saintly silence, he knelt. Then Amos the Fuss—father, mayor, loser of time—bowed his head and prayed.

"Lord?" he said, glancing cautiously around, as though God were a hornet apt to sting him at any moment. "I've never been one for small talk. It doesn't interest me and I know some folks find that rude. But you seem like a busy fellow and I don't have time to talk about the weather with all that's going on, so I'll get straight to it. I just want Cooperstown to get what it deserves." He paused to clarify. "I mean that in a *good* way, Lord. Let no one pay for my sins but me. Do me this one teensy-weensy favor and keep that park *out*. Heck, Lord, it's what any good father would do." He stopped, tricked, almost, into repenting for bad parentage. "Fine! I'll throw out the bourbon and the Geritol. I'll even make amends with my boy if, for once, you let me *win*."

He stood, feeling optimistic as he strode toward the altar, touched by the Holy Spirit and then by the goblet of wine that had been left there unattended. He made an awkward curtsy in lieu of another genuflection, saying, "Lord, that was the *last* time, I swear." A statue of Christ, crucified, hung above the altar. Amos winked at it, and then threw in an amen for good measure. Using the backs of the pews for support, he made his way slowly back up the aisle, pausing to pick up a program that someone had dropped. "We Will Extol You" was the offertory hymn. Amos grinned, imagining his people cloaked in white robes like a flock of devoted angels praising him. He was confident that if the powers that be didn't come through, he could save Cooperstown himself.

Back on the street, he tossed the Geritol bottle behind a bush and buttoned his shirt out of respect, not for the dead or deified, but for the living and the taken for granted. There was one last thing to take care of, *sober,* before he went home.

CHYLAK STOOD ON THE third floor of the baseball museum, eyeing a 1939 World Series poster, Yanks versus Cincinnati Reds, on which Uncle Sam swung a bat looking maniacal around the eyebrows. He felt like a sleepwalker forcing himself half conscious into motion. He'd already covered two floors and had yet to feel the draw, the enlightenment—*Poof, you're awake! You're a good ole American boy!*—he had hoped to feel. Earlier, he'd been caught up in the flow of the crowd, sucked into the maze-like museum, and now he was in danger of becoming one of the oxygen-deprived automatons he'd seen lingering in shopping malls.

The next exhibit looked like a totem pole, a miniature object of worship with Babe, the Ruthian one, on top as a little deity. It confirmed his belief that sports, like religion, were best left unorganized. He apologized to a tourist whose shoulder he peered over to examine the next display, an excerpt from the *New York Evening Journal,* 1908: "Sentiment no longer figures in the sport, it is now only a battle of dollars." Now that was more like it. More like what he wanted to hear. He was glad too to see that the museum was sensible enough to display the full gamut of reactions to the fanaticism it bred. On one end of the spectrum, tokens, trophies, and statistics stating various triumphant feats. On the other, more sinister side, a cartoon from a 1934 edition of *The Chicago Defender,* depicting a black ballplayer peeking through a stadium fence; a "Notice to First Basemen," in which takers could work in the Treasury Department during the day, then practice ball at night, though "No Irish need apply"; a poster announcing the "Novelty and Sensation of the Day," female ballplayers, admission just shy of an insolent free by twenty-five cents; and, most affecting, a note chicken-scrawled to Hank Aaron on what looked like a piece of children's construction paper: "You must think people or dumb," "are" misspelled and its author referring to Aaron as an "old nigger." Beside it, in stark contrast, was a letter from JFK to Jackie Robinson, which Chylak noted, amused, was addressed care of Chock Full o'Nuts Company: "I have called for an end to all discrimination." Beside it was a death threat to Robinson from someone called "the travelers," with three pinheaded stick figures sketched below it.

Perhaps, Chylak thought, there was more to this business of baseball than initially met the psychoanalytic eye. He eyed JFK's letter, marveling that sports, like religion, could reach people, unite them in ways they were unable to unite themselves. He couldn't help but wish that *he* had the ability to bring people together under a common thread, to be part of a genuinely uninhibited communal spirit, misfired neurotransmitters and all. If only there were things he could say to his patients to make it all better, as Babe did for the children when presented with various psychosocial scrapes or badly bruised egos.

The next exhibit contained a book of poems written by various rabid ball fans, including one about Roberto Clemente, "the first Hispanic elected into the Hall of Fame," Chylak read. He had heard, somewhere, that Clemente was a bit of a hypochondriac. A placard said the man had died seven years ago in a tragic plane crash en route to aiding Nicaraguan earthquake victims. But according to the poem, he had been "body snatched by the Bermuda Triangle." It ended with the author hoping "those Martians realize they are claiming the rights to far and away the greatest right fielder of all time."

Martians indeed. Chylak amused himself with the idea that ball players were, in actuality, extraterrestrials who had come to earth to take the mickey out of people. He felt rather alien himself in this town. While doing his best to play credible counselor and heroic hubby, he'd forgotten how to be that fun-loving Joe. He tried to remember the last time he'd told a joke, read something other than dated psychology books, or helped someone as a friend, the mutual kind, versus the kind he billed for the time they shared. Perhaps this was his punishment: the bold move from Lebanon to la-la land had halted his evolution.

He squeezed past some tourists to view a poster of Max Patkin, "The Clown Prince of Baseball," a contortionist frozen in a two-dimensional world and making the best of it by entertaining himself. He looked, to Chylak, like an ape in a baseball uniform, the prototype of the early ballplayer, *Hominid sporticus.* Representative of the species Chylak was so determined to capture under his microscope until either he discovered the missing link—that spirit that would enable him to be caught off guard, to be caught up in the myth, the mirth, and the merriment—or his world turned upright again. *Cooperstown* had evolved since his arrival. Then again, its initial, larval possibilities—the hope and desire for change, despite a longing to remain the same—now seemed in danger of flying clear out the window with the rest of the cuckoo birds, back safe to the stagnant nest. If the amusement park came, he feared the town would evolve *backward.* And he would be partially to blame.

He reached into his pocket, extracting a lint-covered pill. The one he'd taken at noon had a delightful effect, so he popped this one in his mouth, assuming it was the same. He longed to feel that sensation, the warmth he'd felt on Main Street. But Patkin's face suddenly looked menacing. Chylak recalled something his secretary had once said about children fearing clowns because of the frowns visible beneath their smiles. A little girl was pushing her way, repeatedly, through a turnstile that once belonged to some ancient ballpark; the chunky clunking sound—*click, click*— over and over, was becoming unbearable.

Chylak walked briskly toward the men's room.

He splashed cold water on his face, then looked in the mirror and took several deep breaths. His chest felt funny, tight; that vividness, that hyperreality was back, but this time it didn't feel so good. He tried to focus on the tape above his nose, in search of his vanishing point: that spot on the Portrait of the Shrink as a

Young Man in which he could gain perspective, or disappear. He turned his head from side to side, embarrassed to be looking for physical evidence of change, improvement. Proof that there had been a Chylaktical eclipse since Lebanon. He waited his turn in line for a stall, watching people push back and forth through the swinging lavatory door, absorbing the exhibits, taking it all in and then letting it out: the waste that filled their systems while they filled their wasted minds.

He relieved himself, sipped water from the faucet, then made his way, slowly, toward the first and final floor. Easy now, he told himself. *Don't get wrapped up in the Rapture.*

He browsed the Presidential Pastime display: a collection of baseballs autographed by various presidents, including Taft, Hoover, and Carter. It was a nice sane look at American history. FDR's "Green Light Letter" to Kenesaw Landis was also there, a profound pep talk stating the importance of continuing the sport despite the war, to boost morale. Beside it was a placard that read, "William Howard Taft threw the first presidential pitch, to Walter Johnson, in 1910." Disappointed to learn baseball had been around that long, he recalled his vow to visit the Baseball Library. Perhaps research was the key to understanding the sport that these tourists, the townsfolk, and his patients seemed so ready to absorb, unable to pass it with some semblance of regularity.

As a child, Chylak assumed baseball arose, magically, that day with his father at Ebbet's Field. Things were like that for children: the assumption that no one had ever experienced what you had experienced until you shared it with another, a parent or a more mature friend, only to learn that they already *knew*. He fanned himself with a brochure, admiring a silver-plated Temple Cup, a mammoth trophy awarded to National League championship teams in the late 1800s that hung in the next display. It looked like a vase and reminded him of an article he'd read about the ancient Chinese, or was it the Spaniards? They placed their unwanted offspring, mere infants, in vases—vises—so their bones would develop deformed, then peddled them around as freakish roadside attractions.

Tourists began crowding the display. Chylak was suffocating. He heard a faint voice, crying for help. "Can you help me?" It was just a young man asking for directions to the Directory Room. He pointed vaguely down the hall between the Heart of Baseball exhibit and the No-Hitters display, then struggled to focus on the artifacts before him: thousands of objects, from bats to dissected ballpark bits, all acquired, donated, and incorporated into the insanity.

He fanned himself with a brochure. *What happened to the air-conditioning?* He looked around, wondering if anyone would mind if he snatched Satchel Paige's St. Louis Browns cap from a shadow box and used it to mop his brow. Yet the hat made him uncomfortable. It looked tight, too tight, like it was smothering the Styrofoam head beneath it. The letters embroidered across the front overlapped, the *S* winding its way, serpentine, around the others—*sssssssss! Sssssssss!*

Chylak struggled to focus on a photo of Eddie Gaedel, a midget in elf shoes emerging from a seven-foot birthday cake, beside a case full of Babe Ruth laxative gum.

"Oh God!" he said, clutching his stomach. He shoved aside a couple of tourists and leaned, with his head down toward his chest, against a display about the infiltration of baseball into popular culture, the more commercial side of the sport. One item was a box of Cornflakes depicting a bright-eyed ballplayer who seemed to beckon him, to invite him inside the glass case, whispering, "Fat free! Cholesterol free! Free me!"

Chylak removed his spectacles and peered in closer. Pressing his nose against the glass, he grew fascinated at how the moisture from his breath blurred his vision, then disappeared, as it had that day in his office when he'd gone to the window to escape from prattling Paquette. The man on the cereal box winked at him. "Psst, try some!" he whispered. "Try some, Chylak! It's good for you!"

The room went black.

Chylak, vertiginous, tried to focus on a chest protector worn by "The Prototypical Postwar Ump," a mannequin in the next exhibit. He wanted desperately to loosen the straps and let the poor fellow breathe. He pounded and pounded that chest protector until his faculties flew, like a pack of twittering birds scattered this way and that. He was mesmerized by a tiny gray ball bouncing on the bottom of a movie screen that hung on the wall; an old black-and-white baseball film. Up and down, up and down the ball went to the slow-cranked beat of carnival sound: Jack Northworth's famous ditty rewritten ("Take Me Out of the Ball Game!") just for him.

> *Kerwin Chylak was baseball mad . . .*
> *Had the fever and had it bad . . .*
> *Crackerjack . . .*
> *Get back . . .*
> *Don't win it's a shame . . .*
> *One, two, three strikes . . .*

And the doctor was out.

T HERE WAS NO ROOM to ride through the crowded streets, and Elliott was frustrated that Alice wouldn't wait for him. She walked her bike toward a lamppost, leaning it there and gesturing for him to do the same, then disappeared into a shop to buy Big League Chew, leaving him to watch the bikes.

A man selling ice cream gave directions to a lady with an accent who sounded like she was from somewhere far away. *Alien* was playing at the movie theater. Elliott wondered if Alice was old enough to sneak him in. Where was his dad? He stared at a boy standing in front of the quilt shop, wearing black pants with suspenders and a black hat, the kind a magician might wear. He didn't look like he belonged in Cooperstown.

"Don't stare, tardo," Alice said. She was back with a fat wad of pink gum peeking out of her mouth.

"What's wrong with him?"

"Nothing. He's just Amish."

Elliott watched the boy mount a wagon with horses attached to it; he was with an old man who was dressed similarly. Alice explained that being Amish meant you couldn't watch TV. She said the boy was probably from Lancaster, which sounded not unlike Lebanon, and Elliott began to cry. Alice rolled her eyes, then gave him the fakest hug ever, swearing everything would be all right once school began. "Don't ride in the road," she shouted, walking her bike toward a group of girls down the street who were calling her name. She forgot to give him some gum.

Elliott pushed his bike slowly down the street, regretting that he hadn't removed his helmet. That with his gym shorts, knee-highs, and the *WKRP in Cincinnati* T-shirt Joey had traded him for a photo of Alice in her bathing suit might not pass muster in Cooperstown. Today, all the other kids were wearing baseball shirts. He made his way to the Hall of Fame, searching the crowd that pooled at the entrance for his dad. "We're going to spend the *whooole* day together," his dad had said, "just the two of us!" When he attempted to enter the museum he was blocked by a large knee attached to a small man with a deep voice, the security guard he'd once seen in his father's waiting room.

"What do you think you're doing, little man?"

"My dad's in there," Elliott said. "He's waiting for me."

The guard asked to see his ticket and Elliott scrounged in his pocket, displaying two bright green Hulk dollars with which he hoped to buy his way inside. He offered them to the guard, along with a rock he'd found by the lake that was shaped like a jellybean.

The guard refused them both.

Elliott circled toward the back of the museum to try another entrance. That door was locked, so he sat on the steps. His father *had* to be in there! He would have to come out soon. They had to be home by six for dinner. He would appear any minute now, punch the guard in the nose, and buy Elliott some cotton candy.

Elliott waited an hour.

Children were gathering on the grass in front of the Baseball Library. He recognized some of them from church. Joey was there, with his friends from Little League. Elliott joined them, leaning his bike against a statue of a green man with a cane whose legs were crossed like he had to pee. The kids had gathered to watch a fight. Elliott didn't have a quarter, so he placed the jellybean rock into the hat that came around.

The fight featured two kids haggling over which was better, the Greatest American Hero or the Six-Million-Dollar Man. Being a Hulk man, Elliott had no preference. The opponents wrestled until the grass turned to mud, the statue watching over them like a referee. They shoved each other, pulling hair and throwing sloppy punches wherever they could get in a hit. The crowd loved it, egged them on, everyone squandering their meager allowances on bets as to who would win. An older boy stepped in to jerk one of the opponents out from under his feet, the old hook-the-knee trick, which was breaking the rules. The kid fell and the bully shouted, "Superheroes suck!"

There was a murmur in the crowd.

By the time Elliott realized a crime had been committed, the big kid was being tackled in a dog pile—fists flying, legs flailing about. He flung himself on top of the pile, pummeling any kid he could reach—whoever was next to him, a tourist, a neighbor, and then Joey, who was stealing Bobblehead Joe from his bicycle basket like an Indian giver. Elliott pulled and pulled until there was a sickening pop. Then someone shouted, "Run!" Joe's head flew from his hand and all hell broke loose, the minimutiny dispersed. A policeman marched toward them. The kids scattered in every direction. Elliott hopped on his bike and rode like the wind, glad now that he was wearing his helmet. His knee was scraped and he began to cry, because he'd been forced to flee without Bobblehead Joe's head.

The house was quiet. His mom was at church, and Alice was late. His father wasn't there either.

He went to his room and retrieved his baseball bat, trailing mud up the stairs, then down to his father's study. He stood on his dad's chair, the soft fart of the plastic Diazepam cushion not so funny today, and moved the snow dome, the one containing the town that was not Lebanon, to the center of the desk. The flakes inside swirled violently around and Elliott realized that it wasn't even snow, just stupid baby powder. He lifted the bat and swung down, like Captain Caveman, with all his might.

He swung for Lebanon . . .

He swung for Bobblehead Joe . . .

He swung for sandals with socks . . .

He swung for superheroes . . .

He swung for the out-of-place Amish . . .

He swung so hard that the plastic dome burst and the bat, smashing against the mahogany desk, broke clear down the middle, Mantle's signature now an illegible "Mi . . . Ma."

DUSTY SAT ON A stool in the Hall of Heroes cosmetics lab, wondering what to do. She had closed the museum the moment Honus delivered the awful mannequin. How had this happened? How had *she,* Dusty-who-knows-all Paquette, become fodder for *gossip?* That's what would come of it, hateful, hateful gossip.

She stood the wax Mays upright in a drainage basin in the middle of the floor while she scrounged in her purse for a match. She was afraid to use the blowtorch they were supposed to use, supervised, to melt the flesh off unwanted molds, so it could be recycled to touch up broken limbs. If only she had Frank's old silver lighter, which was probably somewhere in the Hall of Fame with the rest of his things. She'd been so anxious to erase any sign of him, to ease the pain when he died. He was quite a collector, and, if she'd been smart, she could've sold a few of his things and bought a plane ticket to Hawaii. She was ruined now!

They would probably hang her by her hot rollers from a flagpole in front of the Hall of Fame. She had made a real mess of Amos's ceremony, a mess he was not likely to forget. She touched her face, feeling for renegade peach fuzz that her tweezers might have missed. She dug around in her purse, disappointed to find an empty tube of Home-Run Chin Music Hair Remover. "You left me," she whispered to the photo of Frank glued to the back of her favorite compact. It was fake gold and gaudy as hell, but she loved it because he had given it to her. Checking her reflection in the little mirror, she said, "You left me because of this chin."

By now the verdict was in: she'd die a shriveled old unloved lizard lady who had finally gotten a taste of her own medicine. People would say she made a fool of herself. She would probably make the paper. Terry Daulton would print something nasty about her because of the time she told him he was aging poorly due to the cheap shaving cream he used. He would print it, and people would read it—people like Bobby Reboulet, who would laugh because Dusty had once gotten her fired. Bobby would tell other people, like Ruby Barrett, who would share it with her hermity ex-hubby, the two of them reuniting over Dusty's misfortune because she had suggested, only *suggested,* that their relationship was doomed from the start (Ruby didn't wax her bikini line). And Amos! He would never ask her to dinner now, or for any favors, or to share her unworthy cankerous company ever again.

Dusty wiped her nose, which was swollen from crying, bulbous and unsightly as a nose could be. She examined it in the compact, wiping a tear from her cheek and forcing a smile. The face staring back at her frowned; it looked old and pale. But the lashes were thick, and that was enough. She took a deep breath and tucked an unruly curl beneath her kerchief.

So she had given Mays breasts, so what? Worse things had happened, and they had happened to *her.* She was going to be a showgirl, for the love of Vegas, before she met Frank! She was going to be famous; the most beautiful gal in the world and everyone would say so! She was going to be so well loved that she wouldn't have to bother getting to know people, ferreting out their personal information as a means to get close to them, drilling uninvited into their secrets, the dirty little blackheads of their minds. If she were beautiful, they would come to her. They would *beg* for her company.

She removed the wig from the wax man, annoyed that Honus had left the mold near the window and it was already starting to soften. If she weren't going to melt it down and reuse it, she'd charge him for it. She pinched Mays's bicep, soft to the touch. She scrutinized the figure from head to toe, surprising herself with a genuine chuckle when she reached the face. So she had gotten a little carried away. She could see that! The eyeshadow, the rouge—maybe the fuchsia lipstick was too much? She had been so upset thinking about Frank when she made it, about the last time she saw him.

Remembering that frowns cause wrinkles, she forced herself to smile. She could apologize to Amos, maybe even a public apology to the town. She could write Mays a letter. Or write a letter to the newspaper, one of those editorial opinion letters telling people to lay off! Was she the only one who had a sense of humor anymore? She stared at the mannequin. The purplish hair, the fake lashes. But it *wasn't* a joke. *She* was the joke! She would just have to go out into the streets and hang her head in shame. And everybody would see that the hair on her crown was thinning.

"Ingrates," she said, stripping the wig off the figure. That's what they were, all of them. Who did they think had been holding them together all these years, and especially through the theme park hullabaloo? "*Me*, that's who!" she told the wax man. "Dusty Paquette!" *She* was the one who kept everything glued together, with concealer, wax, and a thin shellac of good gossip. And didn't that make things more interesting? Wasn't it her *job* to bring people to life? For years now she had generously dabbed the townsfolks' humdrum lives with a sweet, tell-all eau de toilette all her own, and had anyone thanked her for it?

She chewed on a perfectly polished ruby-red nail, debating whether to ring the psychiatrist. She'd been watching him, at first threatened upon realizing she was no longer the lone observer, the eyes and ears of the town, the potential scatterer of scandalous secrets. Chylak probably knew *all kinds* of interesting things about people. He probably knew things about her! But what if he said she was beyond help? What if he told Amos? Amos the Fuss was all she had left of fussy Frank in this world. He was probably at Angela Spitzer's house right now, drinking martinis and listening to Spitzer tee-hee at her expense.

"That's it, by God," she said, wiping her eyes. She yanked a blowtorch from a hook on the wall and slipped on a pair of plastic goggles. Throwing the windows open wide, she turned off the fire alarm and torched the wax man, fascinated as the synthetic skin slid from Mays's paraffin face. "I'm not perfect, dammit," she said, "and neither are you!" The statue's clothing caught fire. "Oh, dear!" she cried. She'd forgotten to strip it down and now the body was ruined. Watching it burn, she reached into her purse for a bottle of eyedrops, and threw that into the basin too, along with an eyebrow pencil. "Frank wasn't perfect either." She threw in a blush brush. "And God knows *Amos* has his faults!"

She dumped her purse upside down, shaking it hard and spilling the contents into the warm paraffin pulp that pooled in the tub at her feet. When the mold had melted down to reveal its wire frame, she waited for it to cool, then immersed her hands in the warm wax, kneading the mess. Paraffin was great for dry skin. If only she had some Home Run Heat peppermint ointment, which was great for calluses, arthritis, and soothing aches and pains. Even Home-Run Fungo antibacterial hand cream would do. "Fungo," Frank said, was a ball hit during practice, and it sounded close enough to fungus.

"Don't go anywhere," she told the wire man. "I just might have some in the freezer."

She stored peppermint oil in the freezer so it was cool and thick at the end of each workday, when she rubbed it on her sore hands. She loved the smell; it always triggered a memory of the day Frank proposed. He had blown a ridiculous bubble with his minty chewing gum and, too poor to offer a ring, told her, "Pop it if it's no, but kiss me, right through this bubble, if your answer is yes." He said that is how relationships are, sticky sometimes, but if she would have him he'd make it worth her while, and he had, until he didn't want her anymore.

Dusty began to cry. She stepped away from the freezer, forgetting the melted wax behind her, and stepped in the basin, slipping and skating backward as the Mays mold clamored to the ground. She held her breath, expecting to join it there any second. But before she had a moment to ponder whether warm wax would soothe a broken hip, an arm appeared around her waist, then two. She felt herself falling, and then landed with a thud against a big, soft belly. She looked down at the arms locked around her waist. They were strong arms, a little flabby, but still.

Twisting her head up and around, she faced her rescuer.

"Amos!"

"Shh," he said, brushing away a curl that had fallen across her face.

"Watch the canker," she meant to say. But for once, Dusty Paquette was struck utterly, gratefully, blissfully silent—

With a kiss.

"LISTEN."

Chylak opened his eyes.

"Listen. I got you, Doc. You took quite a spill!"

Chylak's head was on fire. He lifted it with the help of the guard. *Honus?* His secretary, that voice on the intercom, was unbearably loud. "Ladies and gentlemen, the museum is now closed. We hope you enjoyed your visit to the National Baseball Hall of Fame. Watch your step on the way out, and please come see us again!"

He sat up too quickly and then lay back down, dizzy. He felt like a woodpecker was pecking its way through the back of his skull. He looked around, expecting to be in his office on the couch or at home, in bed beside the biblical Babe. But there were people everywhere, paraphernalia, plaques, trophies, and bats. Was this *hell?*

A man in white offered him a paper cup filled with water.

"Thank God," he said, struggling once more to move.

He looked for Honus, but there was only the man in white with a number stenciled onto his shirt and a name above it.

"Mantle?"

"Yeah, right, I *wish!*" said the man. "I'm Ross Fatton, from New York. Fat-ton. It's pronounced like Patton or Manhattan, whichever. You hit your head pretty hard! The security guard is calling an ambulance."

Chylak sat up quickly, regretting it the moment a sledgehammer seemed to bust open his head. "No, please," he said. "I don't need an ambulance, really, I'm fine."

The man was a tourist, a friendly one, but Chylak wished he would go away, because he saw now, looking closer at the man's jersey, that he had misspelled the name Mantel on Elliott's bat. *Elliott!*

"I have to go!"

He tried to stand, but his knees gave out and the tourist pushed him gently back down.

"You don't understand! I have to go home!"

"Easy, Doc." Cronin was back. "We'll get you home just as soon as we get you checked out." He pulled Chylak out of the walkway with the help of the tourist. They leaned him against a display of baseball gloves, including one formerly belonging to Mays and famous for some '54 catch. A small crowd had gathered around. Chylak turned away, pressing his face against the cool glass display. The gloves looked worn, loved, and he had a sudden desire to smell them. He willed them to reach out and cradle his aching head. He slumped forward and his forehead squished against the glass. Eye to eye with his pug-nosed reflection, he stared at the tape between his eyes.

"You're lucky you didn't break your glasses, Doctor. *Doctor?* That's it, I'm calling you a doctor! The ambulance won't make it down Main Street in that crowd."

"No, really, I'm fine," Chylak protested. "It's the heat."

The crowd around him grew. He half expected someone to slap a cap on his head and stick a bat between his hands, wind him up and send him on his way. He felt awful. He had forgotten Elliott! His promise to take him to the museum. He was shaking despite the heat, and his mouth was dry, bitter with the aftertaste of whatever that last loose pill had been.

"Here you go," said another tourist, propping Maury Wills's hundred and fourth stolen base behind Chylak's back. Honus yelled at the tourist, making Chylak's headache worse. The crowd glared at the guard. "Fine. You might as well have these too, then," Honus huffed, offering Chylak a pair of sunglasses. "They'll help with that migraine you're bound to have. Just be careful, they belonged to Ty Cobb."

Chylak accepted the shades, grateful for a shield against the glaring fluorescent lights. It was all coming back to him: that poster of Uncle Sam, those awful eyebrows! That hat, the letters snaking their way around one another. And a clown? Or was it an *ape?* He had a sudden craving for cereal, Cornflakes. He had forgotten to eat lunch. Perhaps he'd had some kind of Hall of Fame–induced hypoglycemic attack. He felt the back of his head. There was a lump and his fingers were coated in blood.

"You kind of freaked, then passed out," Honus said. "You're not bleeding too bad."

Freaked? It was time to face the facts. He hadn't fainted from hunger. He'd had his first official anxiety attack, in a room full of strangers—the Great Moments Room, no less—in one of the most popular museums in the country, on the busiest day of the year, and, worst of all, in front of a *patient!* A tourist snapped his photo. He had become another object on display. It was comforting, however, to be the center of attention for once. He let them dote on him for a while—someone placed an ice pack on the back of his head—while he leaned against the case of gloves, trying to sort through what had happened.

He had been standing there, staring at that box of cereal and thinking about Mrs. Paquette, a comment she'd made during her impromptu visit to his office last month. She *had* been there! He had struggled with what to quote her, wanting to drown out her chatter. She'd dished out an entirely inconsumable-in-one-sitting casserole of opinions about every man, woman, and child in town. And before he had realized the act was familiar—this hiding the self behind the trials of everyone else—his own number was up. She had poked, pink polished fingernails jagged-end first, into *his* psyche! The bombardment was swift: a potent packet of psychoanalytic mishmash, a frenzied internal smashing together of synapses, citations, sex, vegetables, husbands (dead ones!), regrets, and theme parks, all spritzed with a fine layer of musk. He had felt himself floating, hovering above his desk, then heading toward the window for air. A newly hatched yellow lepidopterous lunatic speckled with gray matter flying far away from himself and his woes, toward a glimmering green diamond-shaped field. The world seemed so much bigger from up there, the world in which Paquette so tactfully proclaimed that his wife looked unhappy, that she needed something outside of her marriage to believe in, something other than her children, that could believe in her. Something she could *blame,* if need be, without being blamed in return. And Alice! Paquette claimed to have caught her "necking" with a boy behind the Farm 'n' Field. And Elliott? Poor Elliott! Paquette opined that he feigned affliction all over town because he needed someone to listen. "Listen" is what Cronin said. "Listen" is what they all said. And upon hearing that word, Chylak had drifted, that day, back down to his desk and now to the Hall of Fame floor, landing somewhere between regret and exasperation with a thud.

He did listen. He was *always* listening. Not paying attention was not the same thing! So what if he couldn't repeat everything he had ever heard? Who could? Who wanted to? That was the point of psychiatry! Protecting the self from itself! He listened and what he heard was that people, even his own flesh and blood, viewed him as a man willing to pocket their troubles, even if that meant hiding his own. He listened and he heard Babe say he didn't feel. He listened and he heard himself agree because sometimes, with his particular occupation, that was best. He worked on the fringe of the bell-shaped curve, beyond all standard deviations, where the real nitty-gritty oddities of reality lie. It got to him, dammit! But he listened and he felt, and sometimes he shut down as those infinite emotions too often amounted to an unbearable *one:* empathy. It was the one habit that despite his training, his cool, calm rationale, he had never been able to kick. And if he knew Elliott was at home, deeply disappointed, and that Alice was growing up too quickly before his eyes, he also knew that he would survive it, all of it, and Cooperstown would survive too. That park would come, and with it temporary trouble, even trauma, sure, but perhaps also a healthy burst of renewal. As sure as he knew all of that, he knew now that the woman who had vanished from his office that day in a puff of talcum powder and musk was simply lonely, unable to find a place within herself to shelve the information she so skillfully culled from those who were lonelier still, sacrificing herself as though it were her responsibility to clean it all up, to make it better, to explain it away when no one else could. Chylak had listened to Mrs. Paquette and he'd felt for her—oh, how he'd felt! Because, he realized, he was lonely too.

He hadn't *planned* to defy his own progression. Nor had he meant to withhold things from Babe! He hadn't expected Cooperstown to be like this, to have to contribute above a prescription or two. He had expected to sit back and smoke his pipe, playing rent-a-Freud and dreaming of early retirement. This town wasn't meant to be an escape, or an excuse, but a means to an *end.* "Nothing happens in a town like that." That's what his Lebanon colleague had said. And Chylak would be free. Free to disappear into the trees if that's what he wanted because in a town like that, no one would need him! He'd bought it hook, line, and sinker, like a sucker, and he'd believed it. No one would need him. *Until they all did.*

And by then, he had been reduced to a mere machine, an automatic filter built to sort the wheat from the whacko day in and day out with no regard for himself, to intake other people's afflictions, spew out diagnosis after diagnosis, and occasionally scrape himself clean of the emotional lint that was left over, lest he overheat. Lest he be held *responsible* for the residue that remained when they learned there was no cure for living.

Before the paramedics could make their way through the crowd that swarmed Main Street, Chylak was on his feet, feeling a bit better aside from his throbbing head. He was anxious to get home, assuring Honus and the rest of his captors that he'd probably just fainted from heatstroke.

He fled the museum before they could protest, passing through the Hall of Fame Gallery, where he paused to peruse the commemorative plaques of all those who had ever been inducted. The inaugural five were clumped together toward the front and he eyed each bronzed face, cautious and then accusatory, thinking, *You! You started this!*

Outside, the air was remarkably cooler, the sun having set. He turned for one final look at the museum. BIRTHPLACE OF BASEBALL etched into the brick facade. He felt like an ass. Like he'd just been spit out, rejected, an unwanted embryo from the all-American womb.

He trudged home, defeated.

The shops were closed, the empty streets strewn with garbage. He had missed dinner again and wondered what people were eating inside each home as he passed. Perhaps they were sitting around their dinner tables, families taking turns telling each other about their day, telling each other that everything was going to be all right, and meaning it. *Meaning* it. Or perhaps they knelt beside their beds in prayer, vowing to improve their minuscule selves amid a mind-boggling universe if only they could be

spared, and meaning that too. Perhaps they believed—an assurance that crossed the borders of science, sports, and religion—
that somewhere out there, some hero, god, doctor, ballplayer, or
regular fun-loving Joe was listening and believing in them; that if
enough people made the same request the odds were good that
one of them would get his wish; that something out there would
save them if they got tired of saving themselves, or tired of trying to save everyone else—if the sieve finally spilled.

He walked through Cooper Park, marveling—what a thing that
people could make up God! Why were some heroes everyone's heroes? What did they—Christ, Mays, or the Bionic Chunk—have
that everyone else craved? How was it that people who couldn't
agree on what to eat, where to live, what ideologies to instill in their
children, or even on what they meant to one another, find any
common ground when it came to what to *worship*? How was it possible when they refused to respect the discernible differences in
their own individual realities? The answer, he thought, was that
they had no choice. They had to agree on something, and that
something was that there had to be something worthier outside of
themselves, watching out for them lest they were screwed. Reality.
He sighed. People passed it around like a hot potato.

He looked down, having kicked a maverick cobblestone into
the street. Peering into the darkness, he wondered if on second
thought it was a baseball. But no, it was Bobblehead Joe's head.
He waited for a car to pass before retrieving it from the base of
the street sign, where it had stopped rolling. Chylak had never
been so happy to see an inanimate object in all his life. The head
was filthy and lay faceup, smiling up at him as though thrilled to
see him. "Looks like you've had a rough day too," he said, picking it up and brushing it off. It was less intimidating without its
base. He wondered what had happened to it, and to the street
sign that hung slumped from its hinges and leaned toward the
curb as though one street or the other, Church or Fair, were trying to escape. "Tourists," he said, shaking his head and assuming
one had backed into it.

A figure approached in the darkness, growing larger and larger as it neared, throwing its hands, exasperated, into the air.

"There you are! My goodness, Kerwin, you can't *imagine* how worried we've been! I called your office three times. They said you never returned from lunch!"

It was Babe, meeting him halfway down Fair Street.

He waited for her to berate him, to say he'd missed one dinner too many and that was it: she was taking the children back to Indiana in the morning and getting them a puppy. But she reached out to gently touch his head.

"Kerwin, you're *bleeding!*"

She led him slowly home, a place of warm beds and cold ice packs. The beautiful Babe, who didn't demand an explanation when he said he'd rather not talk about it until tomorrow, knowing better than anyone that on Planet Chylak, "tomorrow" was a synonym for "never."

"Lie down," she said, ushering him into the living room and onto the sofa, which sighed with a plasticky purr beneath his weight.

"Yes, but Elliott!" he said, struggling to stand. The frown beneath her smile implied that his paternal pity party was now officially over. She explained, rather curtly, that Elliott wasn't speaking to him. He had locked himself in his room and was refusing to come out, even, she said, for *The Muppet Show*. Chylak hopped up and headed toward the stairs, assuring her that he would handle it. The dizziness kept him from getting very far. He slinked toward the kitchen—he would talk to his son just as soon as he rinsed the awful aftertaste from his mouth, the bitter reminder of those regrettable pills. He splashed cold water on his face, downing several glasses of it, while listening for signs of life from upstairs, hoping to hear Elliott jumping joyfully on the bed. Silence.

Chylak took his glass to the living room, where Babe handed him some aspirin, then retreated, he assumed, to bed.

The Lawrence Welk Show was on. He sat back in his favorite pleather La-Z-Boy recliner, the one with the vibrating seat, allowing his muscles to relax. The soft palette of colors being emitted from the screen was comforting. He'd always liked Welk, whom he suspected to be on his last polka. The man looked so innocently out of place with his lavender suit and permagrin on the same screen where life could be summed up in *60 Minutes,* in a world of runaway shahs, rowdy sporting events, and space stations falling from skies. A woman in a royal-blue gown was singing before an orchestra of men in powder-blue suits, against a purple sunset backdrop. Myron Floren was on the accordion, expanding and compressing the instrument on cue to the wave of the conductor's wand. A floating bust appeared, the head of a beautiful brunette with hair feathered all the way around her head and a bodiless neck bedecked with dazzling diamonds.

Chylak willed himself to stay awake, fearing he'd once more disappear alone into the cramped forest and this time it would be inhabited by apes, clowns, and grinning gingham-clad Hotsy Totsy Boys singing about whip-poor-wills and rosebuds—"My Blue Heaven." He tried to imagine Babe's anticipated afterlife extravaganza, one of angelic floating feathered heads where handsome baritones stood before trellised gazebos, cooing, "Beautiful lady . . . open your heart" to the soothing strum of a harpsichord.

The program was interrupted by a commercial for mahogany marriage beds.

Chylak went to the kitchen to refill his glass, now with scotch, pausing briefly outside his study. The door was ajar and he pushed it slightly, peeked in, and then thought better of it— whatever work he had missed could wait.

He reached his recliner just as Welk's whip-poor-wills were singing "*America! America! God shed His grace on thee,*" everyone clapping as the melody faded into Welk's theme song, "*Make a wish, and a prayer, that all your dreeeams come true . . .*" Chylak wanted to snooze so badly, but there was Elliott to deal with, and he feared that if he fell asleep he would have terrible nightmares. What a day he'd had! What a careless combination of pills he had consumed. For that's what it was, he now realized, the pills he'd found in his pocket. He had devoured those dangerous little delicacies to numb himself to the guilt about the move. And that unidentifiable lint-covered gem he had popped into his mouth at noon—and, later, its less agreeable brother at the museum—was none other than a potent little ditty called methylene dioxymethamphetamine, or MDMA (which would later be called things like "ecstasy" and "illegal"). A sympathetic colleague back in Lebanon, the one who had recommended him for the Cooperstown job, had sent him a handful with a note that it was garnering a cult following in certain experimental sects of the psychiatric community that found it useful for treating patients with posttraumatic stress. That first hit— the wonderful wind, the warmth of his hands! It had been glorious. But the second pill, with his empty stomach and whatever else—Librium, lithium, or Valium—he had popped into his gob that morning had had an adverse effect to say the least. It saddened him to know the euphoria that overcame him on Main Street was merely a manic attack resulting in grandiose ideas, pressured speech, and—"Oh God!" he gasped—inappropriate sexual comments! He cringed, flashing back to a hazy moment in the Babes in Baseball room, in which he had commented on Ohioan "girl wonder" pitcher Alta Weiss's "rack" to a tourist.

Too exhausted to be embarrassed, he debated taking Ritalin for stimulation, lest he fall asleep and dream of frightful floating heads bedecked with diamonds, or, worse, *baseball* diamonds with creepy clowns aping around on them, force-feeding him (death by dry mouth!) a box of stale Cornflakes. The vibrating chair ceased to be soothing. He jiggled away in it, staring at the poster of Freud that hung on his study door. It looked as though someone had played pin-the-tail-on-the-psychiatrist on it. It was torn in several places and covered with gobs of duct tape. As the chair buzzed away furiously, Chylak felt suddenly like the lone inhabitant on a fragile planet in the midst of an earthquake. He shot up from the chair, stumbling—his leg asleep, his ass numb with vibration—and ran to his study.

"Good God!" he exclaimed, placing a hand over his mouth.

The room was a mess! Several books had been pulled from the shelves, including Josef Pieper's *Leisure: The Basis of Culture*, with its preface by T. S. Eliot, which he liked to think was so behind the tedious times that the copyright was written in Roman numerals. It lay faceup on the carpet, open to a page on which he'd once scrawled JUSTIFICATION OF LEISURE in chunky script. He picked it up.

> *The point and the justification of leisure are not that the functionary should function faultlessly and without a breakdown, but that the functionary should continue to be a man—and that means that he should not be wholly absorbed in the clear-cut milieu of his strictly limited function.*

Chylak's feet were wet. He assumed the worst: that he'd been overcome by his own strictly limited "function." But his pants were perfectly dry. A light powdery residue clung to his socks. He traced a tiny rivulet of water down the edge of his desk and onto the carpet, where it formed a pasty little puddle beneath him. The culprit was there on the floor: the paperweight the mayor had given him. The plastic snow dome was smashed to smithereens, the miniature Cooperstown inside it reduced to a mere handful of nubbins. Tiny white flecks soaked the carpet amid splinters of wood. He picked up a lilliputian house, cursing when he pricked his finger on a sharp shard of plastic. It was clear now who had made this mess and why Babe had left it for him.

Outside, the mayor's golf cart chugged along, sputtering to a standstill as the old man entered the Chylaks' driveway. Chylak looked out the window to see that Babe hadn't gone to bed; she sat on the front steps. Had she been waiting for him? "Shoot!" he muttered, wiping his hands on his pants and hoping she would cover for him, tell the mayor something, *anything* to make him go away. But Alice was there too, showing off for the mayor and her mom with a one-handed cartwheel. The adults laughed, and Chylak realized it was the first time he had heard Babe laugh out loud since they'd arrived in Cooperstown. He'd never heard the mayor laugh, but then again he discouraged chuckling in his sessions.

Fusselback was telling Babe about a plan he had, one that would include "everyone." Chylak headed for the front porch, but when he reached the screen door, he froze, hesitant to interrupt the moment—Babe was laughing so hard she was crying now, and the mayor clapped, as Alice attempted to jump with both feet through her arms, which she held in front of her knees like a hoop. "You try it, Mom!" she shouted. Chylak wasn't sure if he was stalling because he didn't want it to end, the laughter, because he felt his presence would ruin it, or because for a brief second there when the mayor said his plan included "everyone," he'd experienced a brief flicker of faith. Everything will be all right, he thought, meaning it.

He stepped out of the light, allowing himself a brief, heady instant in which he abandoned any urge to scrutinize, analyze, or rationalize, replacing it with pure, untainted, unmedicated feeling. He let himself become intoxicated by the fleeting, wonderfully unscientific sense that at that moment, that one small fragment of time in a vast chaotic cosmos, there wasn't a man or deity, alien or scientist, shaman, skeptic, ballplayer, or naysayer—including himself—who wasn't root, root, rooting for Cooperstown.

EIGHTH INNING

Perhaps no place of its size can boast of a finer collection of young women than this village, the salubrity of the climate appearing to favor the development of their forms and constitutions.

—JAMES FENIMORE COOPER,
THE CHRONICLES OF COOPERSTOWN

*L*ong Season, my ass," Bobby said, referring to the title of Jim Brosnan's book, which she placed on a shelf in the autobiography aisle. It had just been returned, dog-eared to death by the mailman. "Long *year* is more like it." She picked up a copy of Jackie Robinson's memoir, *I Never Had It Made,* which had been placed out of order beside it. Some people (like prying Paquette) might say it was a prime title for Bobby's own memoirs, should she ever have anything to write about.

She placed a pile of new returns on the wheel-away cart and made her rounds throughout the library.

It was revealing, the books people took out. What did the mailman know about long seasons, time stretching so thin you feared it would snap in your face? And did the sheriff honestly have nothing better to do than sit on his fat duff by his fireside reading *The Fireside Book of Baseball?* It had been infinitely more interesting to match books to their borrowers at the Town Library. But Bobby had lost that gig to this, her personal purgatory. The Baseball Library was a constant reminder that she was stuck here in Mudville, though she'd rather be around baseball books than no books at all. She read to escape, because she had no intention of actually going anywhere. Bobby was a professional piner. She saw no harm in being one place and wishing it was another. It was easier that way, and cheaper.

She shoved the books haphazardly onto the shelves, defying alphabet and card catalog in a hurry so she could celebrate ten minutes of tourist-free time with a smooth Virginia Slim. "You've come a long way, baby," said the ad on the back of the pack. Right, she thought, a lousy twelve blocks since high school. She considered lighting up inside, just to feel that youthful kick of rebellion that had long ago been replaced with less riveting sensations, like the dull satisfaction that came, at the end of the day, with hand-washing her delicates in the kitchen sink. Paquette, that old pickle, could be around any corner. She better not risk another job.

The streets were quiet, not a soul in sight aside from the statue of James Fenimore Cooper, which was just the way Bobby liked it. She waved to it as she did every day, flipping it off when it ignored her. The statue had become oxidized, its bronze sheen giving way to sickly chartreuse. Cooper sat and Bobby stood, staring at each other as though in a dare to see who would budge first. Cooper—his legs crossed, arm slung over his knees— looked like a man waiting for a bus, a ride out of town. Bobby felt sorry for herself for feeling sorry for a statue. But she couldn't help it; poor Cooper was destined to dwell forever, alone, on a patch of grass where his childhood home once stood.

"All right, you win," she said, looking away.

She *might* move if the right opportunity came along. She might even be inclined to ride the women's lib wave right out of town. It's not like she was getting any action here.

Duke Cartwright rode through the park, his bell-bottoms rubber-banded around his ankles so they wouldn't get caught in his bicycle spokes. Bobby used to do the same thing when she was a kid, riding all over town like a banshee with Honus and Johnny and the rest of those boys. She had been quite a tomboy.

Cartwright circled the statue while reciting his retired uniform numbers. "Four. Three. Five. Seven. Thirty-seven. Eight. Eight . . ."

Bobby said it with him, aloud and not for the first time. "Sixteen."

A group of tourists sauntered by, lost; nothing but the hospital and the elementary school lay in the direction they were headed. One of them took a picture of Duke, who had moved on to the Yankees. He reached the Yanks at the same time every day, three o'clock. Bobby wondered if Duke was content riding his bike all the time. She hadn't heard him speak above a grunt in years, except to shout stats or insults disguised as such. If one believed talk around town, it had something to do with having lost Manny, that old wife-abandoner, his star player once upon a time. Duke had lost his chance to relive a shot at the big time vicariously through him. His own moment in the sun had long ago been cut short by a torn rotator cuff. Duke's funk was apparently severe enough to have once merited electroshock, if you believed Mrs. Paquette, which Bobby didn't. She wondered, though: if it was true, had they zapped away the portion of his brain where happiness was stored? If so, she hoped they'd had heart enough to zap away whatever other portions might realize it was missing.

Cartwright was riding with one hand on the handlebars and the other holding a string attached to his mouth guard, as though to lead himself in the right direction. "Fifteen," he mumbled, referring to Thurman Munson, who had died recently in a plane crash. Fifteen had also been the year of Bobby's first kiss—and look how *that* turned out.

She poked her head quickly around the corner to be sure Honus wasn't lurking nearby, waiting to carry her books home for the umpteenth time since junior high. She was not in the mood for visitors today, especially him. She was spent, and it didn't help knowing the only reward she had to look forward to at the end of the day was watching TV alone in her duplex apartment on Susquehanna Avenue. Life was taut for Bobby; she had ceased to feel its pull. And who would when there was no *give?* She had long ago retired any assumptions that eventually there would be someone on the other end, tugging her close when she

needed it and cutting her some slack when she wanted that instead. She was skilled at self-persecution. It killed the time. She
could whittle away at her mind and *still* not reach her breaking
point. That was her curse. Still, she tempted it sometimes: the
point when enough is enough—when she was walking home at
night, peering into people's windows and making up stories
about them, the kind found in romance books. She thought
about how some people never learned to love, others were never
given the chance, and still others crapped on whatever chance
they were given. She was a crapper. She'd never found anything
close to matching her ideal—the one the books, the movies, and
the mothers pushed on young girls. People acted like it was okay
to sacrifice your whole life waiting for the One, only to find out
too late that the joke was on you: the books and films were full
of horseshit, and the mothers just pushing on you what they'd
been taught to swallow themselves. She had lost faith. Lost it and
replaced it with the solace that came at the end of the day with
knowing it didn't matter: few loves were truly for keeps. Pining
was not the same as waiting around. Pining protected you. She
would just as soon know that her past loves were her only loves
and that her demons, which she'd grown used to, belonged to her
and only her for always. She'd had lovers—mostly brief flings
with tourists, or casual romps in the sack with farmhands passing
through to practice on Doubleday Field. She'd also stayed celi-
bate for months at a time. She liked to flip-flop between the two
states. Lately, however, she'd gotten tired and just kind of
flopped, though everyone had accused her of flipping.

Bobby was sick to death of people talking about her behind
her back, sick too of the "battle of the sexes," people comment-
ing on the great divide that supposedly separated men and
women. To her, the greatest tragedy between them lay not in
their constantly counting their differences, but in their not cred-
iting their sameness. Not that she was an expert. It wasn't like
love had come looking for her, and she had no intention of hunting it down like some crazed she-wolf in heat. Even if it met her

halfway, at this point she just hoped she'd recognize it so she could tell it to take a hike.

Duke was on the Phillies now, Robin Roberts. "Thirty-six," he muttered.

Thirty-six was Bobby's exact age today. In truth, it was thirty-nine, but she would prance naked down Main Street on a pogo stick before admitting that. Forty was just around the corner, taunting her, and she had half a mind to give it a good, sharp slap in the face. Not even Dusty Do-Right knew her real age. Bobby couldn't stand Mrs. Paquette, who had a habit of speculating aloud as to whether she was a lesbian, a spinster, or a jezebel. It was 1979, for Farah Fawcett's sake! Bobby was none of the above. She was a heterosexual, born-again-virgin bachelorette in love with a dream: no secrets to ferret out, and no dark, syrupy past. Her life was downright suburban, if Cooperstown could be called a suburb, which it *couldn't*. The nearest city was approximately twenty miles away. The sign at the entrance to town said "Village of," and all life in a village got you was a microscopic view of a greater reality, one that seemed quaint upon first glimpse, but if you stepped inside—if you gave up your soul for a taste? It was a reality she was certain most people would pass up, if they knew what it was *really* like, here where the busybodies and the baseball boneheads lived.

"I was homecoming queen, for Donna Summer's sake!" she shouted at Cooper. Didn't anyone remember that photo of her and Johnny Fusselback riding tandem on his two-seater to the prom? It had made the front page of the frigging *Journal!* Lord knows what had happened to Johnny.

Johnny was a friend back when Bobby *had* friends. One day he just up and left in the wake of his mom. Martha Fusselback rode out of town on a sightseeing trolley all the way to Mileston while the entire town watched. There was nothing better to do, it having been a Sunday in the middle of fall. The mayor had gotten sloshed the previous night and left the motor running in their car. The vehicle died, as did Martha's love for her husband, and

Amos? He hadn't changed a bit. Bobby felt sorry for Mrs. Fusselback. What was the point of keeping on with a man who had to
get *drunk* to tell you how much he cared?

Extracting a stick of deodorant from her purse, she applied it
right there on the steps. It was hotter than Hades and the library
had limited air-conditioning. She could swear, sometimes, that
even her soul was beginning to smell. She stared at the statue,
wondering what kind of lover Cooper had been, and knew it was
definitely time to get back to work

"You're too old for me, you pervert!" she yelled to the statue.

Mrs. Paquette drove by in her pink Cadillac, stopping to chat
at Duke.

What the hell is *he* going to buy, Bobby thought, cold cream
to lube his bike chains? She wondered if pokey Paquette was still
going around telling people she needed lip-liner. What was the
point of explaining to *her*, or anyone else for that matter, that she
wasn't going to put a lot of energy into getting a date, just to
wake up one day ten years from now feeling dated? It was easier
on both ego and heart to pine for a man she could never have:
Dream Lover. That's what she called him. When she wanted him
to give her space, he did. And when she wanted him to hold her
tight, he did that too. He had only lately taken on a human form,
a face that morphed according to whim: a model from a magazine, the lead in a film, or the rebel from a romance novel, a
handsome stranger riding by on his white mustang to return a
particularly compelling book. That was her favorite fantasy. Of
course, there *were* no strangers in Cooperstown, aside from
tourists who didn't remain in town long enough for a person to
get to know them, which is why Bobby took her imagination
elsewhere. This week, for example, to Oneonta, where her mys-
tery man looked not unlike Don Mattingly, a young ballplayer
who had come up in the amateur draft to play for the Yanks'
farm team. He was good-looking, Don, and there was a humility
to him, a bashfulness that made you want to get close enough to
find out what made him so damned cute. Of course, Bobby had

no aspirations of busting up a relationship, and Don was taken, dating anyway. She would get by just fine with a dream. Dream Lover wasn't afraid to let her act out once in a while, to mix things up before they let each other down. What she *needed* was a little drama.

Bobby chewed a fingernail, debating whether to go back inside. "Screw it," she said. If anyone needed her, they could follow the smoke. There were surprisingly few visitors to the library this summer, considering the Fenimore Funhouse was closed for repairs. Word was that the mayor had lost the key, or was it that the roof had finally collapsed? The truth, undoubtedly, lay somewhere in between.

She sat on the steps and lit another Virginia Slim. Why quit smoking when you'd already missed your prime childbearing years? She didn't even *like* children. What was she supposed to have done, been like Ruby, marrying any old someone straight out of high school? Poor Ruby, raising those two kids alone on a teacher's salary, and Manny doing God knows what, alone in the woods with that dog. No thanks. Bobby was perfectly content playing the part of Miss Havisham's smarter sister: skipping the insincere marriage proposal altogether in favor of having her wedding cake and eating it too. People had called her a man hater for so long that she was beginning to believe it. Then again, look at the men around her. Look at Duke, or old Dr. Buckner! Buckner had to be a hundred years old by now, blind as a barn bat and *still* clinging to childish rituals, forcing tourists into his house to view his creepy old portraits. He hung a new painting in his foyer each decade. Last Bobby had heard it was Jose Cardenal, who had apparently missed a Cubs game five years back because he couldn't blink his eyes. They were stuck open, those eyes that Buckner now charged tourists a fat buck to behold. Obsessed, all of them were: give men a bat and a ball and they become boys in an instant.

Mrs. Paquette parked her Caddie and marched her plump pink self up the library steps. "I don't need any mascara and I'll be in when I'm good and ready," Bobby said by way of a greeting.

"Must be nice to have a job where you get such long breaks," Dusty said, giving Bobby her signature indiscreet once-over. "That's a fine pattern," she remarked, referring to Bobby's blouse. "The cut is a little low for your bust size, but the fabric is lovely."

"Thanks," said Bobby. "I think."

Paquette disappeared into the library in search of reference books that would inspire names for new products. Bobby blew a cloud of smoke in her wake. "Dragon lady," she muttered. She peered down the front of her blouse. It was *not* too low cut. It was a V-neck for Suzanne Somers's sake! Bobby resented the way, in a small town, people got shoved into molds they were not permitted to step out of, simply because there was no room. If you even thought about it, if you so much as changed your hairstyle or bought a new dress? You got a look from the likes of people like sourpuss Paquette. The reason Bobby had stopped associating with said people was that they had refused to let her grow up.

A handsome man—whom she guessed to be in his mid-forties and a tourist, because he was wearing a Cooperstown T-shirt— strolled by. She thought about calling out to him, humoring herself with a quickie in the stacks, but he was ogling her back, which took the fun out of it. It would be so much easier if the gods would pop down and stamp a "yes," "no," "worth it," or "doofus" on the heads of potential suitors. "God bless the self-evident doofus," she said, watching Cartwright cycle around and around.

She headed back inside and down to the stacks, avoiding Mrs. Paquette. Sometimes she hid from customers altogether in the Bullpen Theater, where she listened to old recordings of radio broadcasts featuring highlights of World Series games. She made the universal shush sign to two giggling girls poring over a picture book in the children's aisle. Baseball seemed to have something for everyone, she would give it that: fresh air, cute butts, and no time limits. The girls placed their hands dramatically over their mouths to keep from giggling more.

Bobby missed that phase sometimes: when there was nothing to do but sit around giggling with your girlfriends, giggling harder when it got you in trouble. That's what she needed: a female friend, someone she could tell her troubles to like she had done with Ruby in high school. She ran through a mental Rolodex of the women in town, searching for someone suitable. Ruby was chock full of children and dating somebody. Aside from obsessive gardening, Mrs. Coxey had plenty of time on her hands to hang out. But Bobby wasn't sure she wanted a confidant who grew giant green penises in her backyard, those phallic junipers peeking over Mrs. Coxey's hedgerows. And *she* was the one with issues? Joy Jennings, the elementary school art teacher, was sweet, but she was moving out west. And Paquette? Bobby had half a mind to befriend old meddlesome Myrtle, just to find out if she ever shut up. That new gal, Barbara Chylak, seemed nice, though nice in a way that Bobby feared would result in her being urged to pass out pamphlets to kingdom come. Why call yourself Babe and then act like such a goody-goody?

The library mascot—a stray cat Honus found at the Hall of Fame and delivered to her as some kind of primal offering—rubbed up against her leg.

"What are you doing in here?" she said, picking the cat up and scratching it behind the ears. When it scratched her back she dropped it and it scampered beneath a bookshelf. "You got me good this time, you little shit!" she said, heading back upstairs to the circulation desk to grab a Band-Aid from her purse. The cat followed, crying to be picked up or fed. Bobby marveled at how cats could be so soft and needy one minute, hurt you, and then act like nothing happened, wanting to cuddle some more. *That* was trust. Trust was the hard part of relationships. Getting to know someone was the easy part. The trouble was, once you knew whatever there was to know about someone, you wanted to know more, and eventually, you ran out of places to look. A girl could run out of *herself* if she wasn't careful. That was Bobby's fear. Wasn't it everyone's? It's why she never revealed herself to anyone. Dream Lover was safe that way. He could sit in silence with her for hours: a long Sunday drive, smoking butts in bed. He understood that silence wasn't lethal.

She scrounged in her purse, the old kit bag in which she packed her troubles, as the song went, or symbols of them anyway: cigarettes, stale makeup, an expired condom, and a pocket-size romance novel she'd bought off a rack at Save, America! She dumped the purse upside down in search of a Band-Aid. She was tempted to leave the mess; half the contents—gum wrappers, tampon wrappers, candy bar wrappers—were useless anyway. She stuck a Band-Aid over her wound and tossed the wrapper on the floor, wondering whether Paquette had the balls to report her for littering. The fact that that gave her a slight thrill was verification that something, somewhere between junior high school and tomorrow, had gone terribly wrong.

Stanley Auffswich marched up the steps and entered the building. The undertaker always marched, as though his daily contact with the dead, whatever secrets they expelled, gave him a confidence other people lacked. Bobby wondered what all he knew about death. She sorted through his returns: *The Killer Pitch, I'm Glad You Didn't Take It Personally,* Red Barber's *Walk in the Spirit,* and a book of baseball quotations. She smirked, imagining Auffswich sneaking downstairs at night to his embalming room, reading to cadavers. He mistook the smirk for a smile and eyed her with suspicion. Bobby was about to shout "Boo!" She had her reputation to think of. But it was Friday. Soon she'd be free for an entire weekend of pining—no harm in being friendly.

"What was your favorite saying?" she asked, opening the book of quotes to inspect the checkout card.

"It was anonymous," the undertaker said. "Confucius say: 'Baseball wrong—man with four balls cannot walk.'"

"Oh yeah?" she replied, realizing now that, according to the book's due date, it was in fact only *Thursday* and thus all friendly bets were off. "Well, man with *two* balls needs a calendar." She put out her hand for the late fine.

Outside, Cartwright honked away on his bike horn, having nearly been plowed over by Terry Daulton. Bobby and the undertaker watched through the windows as his sports car zipped toward Church Street.

Daulton had been the quiet boy in high school, the one no one doubted when he said he was going to grow up and be a writer. He was introspective but good-looking, with that black hair and those deep blue eyes. Bobby remembered him as the kid who read all the right books and listened to the cool music before everyone else did, like Coltrane. She sighed, nostalgic for those days, now that the King was dead, the Beatles kaput, and the rock of her day shattering, schizoid, into all sorts of confining categories—soft, hard, as though songs were eggs that would eventually expire. She wondered what kind of music Daulton liked now. Classical? Jazz? She didn't recall hearing if he'd ever married. Not that she was going to get her gauchos in a bunch over it. She'd caught him staring more than once during his little drive-bys. In high school, people had insisted that Daulton had a crush on her. Bobby rolled her eyes—too bad for him if he did. She removed the undertaker's last checkout card, stamping it: LATE RETURN.

I'D ASK WHAT YOU'RE doing, but if it requires a prescription, I don't want to know."

Chylak had hoped the librarian—who sat behind her desk with one hand under her blouse, groping her armpit—would laugh good-naturedly. She did not.

"Take those off if you plan to stay inside," she said, pointing with a stick of deodorant toward, he wasn't sure, his shoes or his pants, both of which were soaking wet. He had just come from feeding the ducks, gulls, and Canadian geese down by the lake and had fallen off the dock while attempting a heroic breadcrumb toss. His feet squished as he shifted his weight.

He did as he was told, kicking off his shoes and placing them outside on the steps, then returned to the desk.

"What can I do you for?" Bobby asked.

"Beg your pardon?"

Bobby stared at Chylak's hand, and he extracted it quickly upon realizing he was stroking the spine of a book of baseball quotations.

"Is there something you need?" she said slowly, enunciating each word as though he were a child with a learning impediment.

"I'm Kerwin Chylak," he said, extending a hand, which she didn't take. He put it in his pocket, feeling more awkward by the second. Maybe what they said about this woman was true. She was hardly the ice queen he had expected, but her demeanor was definitely cool. "I'm sort of new in town and—"

"I know who you are, Doctor," she said, motioning with a limp flick of her hand for him to get on with it.

"Good. Well, I'm pleased to meet you."

Another flick.

"All right, then. I want to learn more about Cooperstown, you know, to help myself acclimate. Do you have any books on the *origins* of baseball?" He realized it was a ridiculous question the moment it left his mouth. This was the Baseball Library. Then again, it was no more ridiculous than standing there, talking to a stranger in his socks, especially when she hopped up from her seat and motioned with a stick of deodorant for him to follow. She led him to several fat leather volumes in the history aisle.

"So, what's your take on the theme park?" he asked, using a tactic that generally induced small talk in town. She climbed a precariously placed ladder up a tall shelf and began tossing books down. Chylak stepped out of the way.

"Look, Doc," she said, "I'll get you your books, but the last thing I need is a shrink who needs to *talk*."

Chylak felt his face turn red and prepared for the rest of her lecture: libraries were quiet places, and she had other customers to attend to, et cetera. But her response caught him off guard.

"Actually, I changed my mind. Let's talk. What's wrong with me?"

"I, I," he stammered. "This isn't generally how I conduct sessions."

"I'm not asking you to put me on the couch. Just gimme your first impression. Humor me. Can't you tell, just by looking at a person, what their problem is?"

Chylak wished it were that easy. It would make writing prescriptions a breeze. He was certain that if this was a game, he was losing it.

"Uh . . . you're bored?"

She looked at him curiously.

"No, that's not it," he said, panicking, and wanting desperately now to guess right.

Mrs. Paquette toddled by and Chylak returned her wave.

"I got it!" he shouted. "You hate men!"

"Omigod! I can't believe you just said that! Who told you that?"

A man at a research table hissed, "Quiet!"

Chylak feared the librarian would poke him with the pencil she waved around as she spoke. He pointed, sheepishly, at Mrs. Paquette. Ms. Reboulet surprised him again with a laugh.

"I'm not good at guessing," he said.

"Relax, Doctor. Despite what you may have heard, I don't *hate* anyone." Bobby leaned toward him conspiratorially, whispering, "Sometimes? I just pretend to." She pointed toward Paquette with the pencil. "It keeps people guessing."

Chylak smiled. "Ah, so you're a pathological liar."

When Reboulet responded, "You asked about the park," he knew he had passed the test. She placed a finger over her lips and signaled, once more, for him to follow her, now to a table on which she laid out the books he requested. "It makes no difference to me if this town sells out to Walt Disney," she whispered. "And that's not confidential. You can tell whoever you want. Frankly, I don't see what the big deal is. I mean it's bound to bring more jobs."

"Progression," Chylak said. "The brain longs for it, then has to be medicated when it arrives. It's quite natural, really. Careful what you wish for and all that."

"You think too much, Doctor, I can tell," said Bobby, dropping a fat history volume on the table with a boom. "Too much thinking can kill a man." She waved the pencil in his face. "And that goes *double* for a woman." She leaned in conspiratorially once more. "You were right the first time, by the way."

Chylak looked at her.

She winked and waltzed off with her pushcart, disappearing behind an endless row of shelves.

"I *am* bored!" she yelled, and was shushed, now, by *all* of her customers.

Chylak speed-read as many books as he could before dinnertime, including one about town ball, a nineteenth-century game apparently traceable to Neanderthal times. The book jacket featured an illustration of an early man holding a bat and glove, which looked not unlike the fellow in Elliott's favorite cartoon, *Captain Caveman*. In fact, it looked not unlike Elliott himself probably had when he unleashed his wrath on his father's study. Chylak got lost in a daydream in which the townsfolk, large apes in pinstriped uniforms, jumped up and down Main Street, grunting and swinging bats while tourists threw peanuts at their heads. He sniggered and was shushed by two giggling girls.

He rejected one book, featuring an early American version of baseball, on the basis of its title alone—*One Old Cat*. He switched to a biography of Abner Doubleday, the man credited with inventing baseball in Cooperstown in 1839. The next book he scoured, however, implied that Doubleday had never even *been* to Cooperstown. It said he was a renowned Civil War general in the Union army, which sounded, for this all-American hero, both convenient and fishy. A book on the history of the National Hall of Fame Committee on Baseball Veterans provided more insights, but it wasn't what he was looking for. Perhaps this trip was a waste of time. Perhaps something about the physics of the sport was more his cup of tea. The librarian was nowhere in sight. "Shoot," he murmured, thumbing through a book on the history of Cooperstown, noting with interest that its early inhabitants had included a Mohawk man called Moses and that its original physician was one enviably entitled Dr. Powers. Another brief fantasy ensued, with Dr. Powers (who looked not unlike Chylak) in a leotard and cape, flying over Cooperstown and sprinkling its citizens with a hailstorm of lithium. Chylak read on, and was dismayed to learn that the very spot where his office stood, the sanitarium, was once favored by locals as a place to play ball before Doubleday Field was built.

He moaned and buried his head in the books, reading for an hour and a half until he couldn't take it anymore.

"You know, if you really want to learn about baseball, you should go to the Hall of Fame." The librarian was back and helped him carry his books to the circulation desk. She chewed her pencil in an apparent attempt to curb her nicotine habit. Chylak blushed at the mention of the museum, replying rather curtly that he had tried it already and found that it was definitely not for him.

She pushed the tempting book of baseball quotations dangerously close to him as she made room on the desk for his books, delivering her spiel about due dates, late fees, and the no-nos of dog-earing pages. *Must . . . not . . . succumb . . . Super Chylak,* he thought, eyeing the book. How he longed to snatch it right out of her nicotine-stained fingers and consume his quota of quotes! "I've got to go," he said, grabbing his books and heading out the door in his soggy socks. He donned his shoes and was halfway down the steps—*squish, squish*—when he remembered Elliott's book. "I almost forgot!" he shouted, poking his head back inside the library. "I promised to return this. Thanks, by the way, for your help!"

There was a unanimous "Shush!" from the readers inside.

"Thanks yourself," Bobby said, meaning for the doctor's diagnosis. He had already reached Church Street by the time she realized his mistake. "Wait!" she called, running down the steps and waving his book above her head.

Too late, he was gone.

She looked at the book, *The Last of the Mohicans,* annoyed, for she was fairly certain Cooper had jumbled up his natives. "You say Mohican, I say Mahican," she said, watching the doctor disappear behind the statue. Cartwright was still riding around and around it like a caged gerbil spinning in its wheel. Bobby watched him until she felt dizzy, wondering if it was true that Mohegan meant "wolf."

"Well, how do you like that?" she said. There was nothing more annoying than people returning books to the wrong damned library. It was poetic justice, she supposed. She'd been fired from Town Library for disrespecting its rules, and as part of her penance, she *still* had to deal with its returns. She sighed and looked at her watch. Hardly anyone came to the Baseball Library after five o'clock. What the hell? She opened the book. Reading would kill some time.

She sat on the steps and flipped, out of habit, toward the back cover to see who had taken the book out before the Chylak boy. It turned out he *hadn't* taken it out, his sister had, and it did seem as though she had gotten it from this library. "That's odd," Bobby said, trying to recall where she'd seen it before. She was about to march inside and blame the summer interns when she realized that Honus had stopped by a few weeks ago for a visit, claiming he had found an overdue book. She'd been so flustered by his hounding her for a date that she'd barely looked at it, but she'd smelled it, all right, and this was it—it stunk something awful. She'd been trying to shoo him out when a teenage girl approached the desk and Honus began chatting her up—she looked about twenty years too young for him. He'd tried to impress her with his knowledge of literature, which as far as Bobby knew consisted solely of *Sports Illustrated*. He didn't even know the Baseball Library didn't carry novels! She wished now that she'd asked the psychiatrist for his card. Maybe he took referrals. That is, if Honus wasn't already a patient. She wondered what Dr. Chylak would say about him. Whether Chylak had arrived in town, took one look around, and—*bam*—knew instantly who required his services. She pictured him with his medical bag in one hand, a bat in the other, ready to remedy (or club) whoever needed it, sauntering from door to door like Paquette, peddling psychology—just a spoonful of medicine to keep everything from tasting so damned bitter all the time.

The book was unusually light for such a standard volume. It had taken quite a beating over the years too. It smelled like mildew. She opened it at random to the middle, wondering what a person could get for a book of its vintage, a first edition. She took a deep breath and gasped, "My, my, my." There, in the center of the book, which wasn't exactly a *book,* but the hollowed-out remains of one, was an old piece of parchment paper, ripped in one corner and yellowed with age. It was a newspaper clipping, a legal declaration of some kind, and it had obviously been there for a while. It was stuck in place, melded to the text by mold and moisture. She carefully extracted it with her pencil.

"I'll be damned," she said, opening it and admiring the calligraphic font in which the document was printed. She looked around to be sure no one, primarily Paquette, was watching. The library was emptying out, and Cartwright was harmless, even if he *was* circling closer. In fact, he was making her nervous. She'd close up early, that's what she would do. Cook a TV dinner, catch *One Day at a Time,* and then flip through the book in case it contained any more little treasures, then return it to its proper home in the morning. It was hard to believe she had lost her job over smoking in Town Library, when her replacement there was *gutting* books, if that's who had done it. Then again, she wouldn't be surprised if it had been Honus. She inspected the checkout card to see who had taken it out before Alice Chylak.

"Chuck Daulton," she read, "in 1957!?" She calculated the dead man's late fee at ten cents per day to be $803. Pity there was no way to collect it personally. The library would probably just charge the cost of the book and that wouldn't go far toward all the work she needed done on her Toyota. Besides, Chuck was dead. She slipped the book into her purse. It would give her something to do tonight besides trying out Mrs. Paquette's free sample of

Home-Run Bag, her latest poorly marketed cold cream targeted at "handsome middle-aged women."

She went inside and grabbed her keys off the desk, eyeing a pile of new returns waiting to be put back on their shelves: *The Boys of Summer, The Suitors of Spring,* and *Nice Guys Finish Last.* She waited for a few remaining stragglers to leave, then let the cat out and locked the library doors.

Outside on the steps, she was alone once more with Cooper and Cartwright, who continued his rotary ride. The sun had set. She glanced from statue to cyclist and back, thinking that if this was her limbo, then these were her traveling companions. These were her men. She was grateful suddenly for their company; at least she could count on them to show up.

Daulton drove by again.

Bobby considered flagging him down to see if he wanted to grab a drink. But he would probably think she wanted something more. She had not said a word to him since he got back in town. She didn't know why. She just figured if he wanted to say hi, he knew where to find her. She had been more or less in the same place since he'd left. She opened her purse, glancing at the book and wondering whether the document inside it had belonged to Daulton's father. There were fines for butchering books. If the culprit was dead, was the next of kin responsible? Daulton probably had eight hundred bucks to spare. Dream Lover suddenly came to mind, morphing into Don Mattingly, then Terry Daulton. Bobby stared at Cooper, as though pleading, with her eyes, for the statue's permission to budge. It simply stared back.

"You know you want me, you big flirt!" she yelled at it.

Lighting her last cigarette, she had begun to descend the steps when Cartwright broke his vicious cycle and rode toward her. He gained speed suddenly, cutting across the grass. Bobby gasped and jumped back, wondering if he'd actually run her down. She had no idea, really, if he was dangerous.

"Mace is the key," he mumbled, or something to that effect, and Bobby quickened her pace, walking briskly across the grass and wishing the damned park lights weren't busted from boys pitching balls at them. She had the eerie sense that this man, whom she hadn't heard utter a coherent sentence in years, was more lucid than he let on. Was he trying to warn her or *scare* her? She ran toward the statue, ducking behind it to catch her breath. When she looked back Cartwright was gone.

Had he said *Mace?* She pulled her shawl around her shoulders, shivering despite the heat, and peered around the base of the statue. "Oh, my God!" she screamed.

Cartwright was there on the other side, off his bicycle now and standing stone still with his feet planted firmly on the ground, facing her. His silhouette seemed menacing—he was much taller than she'd imagined. She braced herself against the statue, holding her breath and closing her eyes, and when she looked back he was gone.

She exhaled, tucked her purse tight under her arm, and ran toward Church Street. Culling courage from the streetlights, she turned to see Cartwright, who was back on his bike, doing laps around the oval grass on which Cooper sat. Bobby stood in the middle of the street and watched him make his final loop. He mumbled his way down his list of numbers, and when he rode by her he had reached the Seattle Mariners. "None," he mumbled, and Bobby said it with him, same as every night, predictable as clockwork, the quiet streets, and the long walk home alone.

A CONFERENCE ON
THE MOUND

Baseball is a game, yes. It is also a business.
But what it most truly is, is disguised combat.

—Willie Mays

I don't catch fly balls, but I *will* make history!"
"You stole that line from Willie Mays!"
"Yeah, and you got it backwards!"

Amos banged his gavel, drowning out the crowd. He'd been leading the town meeting for over an hour, despite intense humidity and the nauseating flick of fluorescent lights—not to mention all the naysayers who were against him.

"Fine, I'm a thief," he conceded. "Now listen, people, I admit I screwed up that petition, but that was kid stuff. We need a *real* plan and I have just the—"

"Now, now. It's no one's *fault,*" said Dusty, even though she could name about five or six people in the room whose fault she thought it was; at least two of them had skin that didn't fare well under fluorescence, and if she weren't trying to change her ways in the name of newborn romancing, she would say so right now. Amos may not *realize* he was being romanced—she had refused to kiss him again after that day at the wax museum, on account of her canker—but he was. She moved her chair a little closer to his, offering him her best purple handkerchief, which he snatched and blew his nose into before handing it back. She had plans for his poor manners, which included teaching him how to ask a gal out on a proper date.

Babe Chylak suggested they pray.

Dr. Chylak said he had Valium if anyone needed it.

Dusty was shocked to see them both there, though Babe sat in the front row and her husband in the back, having arrived late at the meeting.

"We might as *well* pray," said Chief Bear. "This town is becoming a goddamned shrine!"

"Now wait a minute," interrupted Stanley Auffswich, who was prone to interrupting people because he generally kept company with cadavers and was rarely in danger of being interrupted himself. "I love baseball as much as the next guy, but I ain't prepared to get *religious* about it."

"You ain't prepared to get religious about anything, Stanley," Dusty piped in. "I *know* you buried my Frank in hot pants, even though I requested a suit!"

Auffswich replied that it was important to dress comfortably in the afterlife, to which Dusty called him a smart-ass, to which he called her a pancake-face.

"People, *please!*" Amos yelled, banging the gavel. The courthouse was sweltering. They weren't getting anywhere. Half the people did not want the theme park, half of them did, and half of *them* only wanted it if it was built in nearby Mileston. Those in Amos's camp believed the park was a threat to baseball itself, to tradition and Cooperstown's old-fashioned standards, which were part of its charm. They didn't want it crowded with too many tourists or tainted with loud, fast, ostentatious rides. Those in the opposite camp were more concerned with the jobs it would bring, the recreation it would provide for their kids, and whether it would have a good Tilt-a-Whirl ride.

"Where was I?" Amos asked Gil Jenchrist, the stenographer responsible for keeping minutes.

"'I'm a thief . . . I screwed up . . .'" Jenchrist read.

"I got it, thanks," Amos growled.

"Personally, I think this town could use a little modernizing. Why shouldn't our kids have a theme park?" said Ruby Barrett, who sat with her two boys near the back of the room. "I say build it anywhere you like."

"Technically, it's not *ours* to build," said Honus. "It's not, is it?" he asked the mayor before losing himself in the fantasy of a shiny new roller coaster being dedicated to him: the HonuSizer! The Moanin' Cronin!

"What do you think, Terry? You grew up here too," said Dicky Harring, the mailman.

Daulton shrugged. "I'm just here to take notes."

Dr. Chylak made a note of this, thinking Daulton was just there, *period.* Daulton had hardly said a word all night and had claimed, at their last session, that his fugues were getting worse.

Dusty suggested a vote.

"A vote would imply we have a decision to make, and the deal is already done. It's out of our hands! Why can't you people see that? The park is coming and I, for one, am buying *stock* in it," said Ruby.

"What happened to an appeal?" interrupted Mrs. Coxey, fresh from her garden and waving a hoe in the air. The room went quiet as everyone braced themselves in case her hand tremor sent the hoe flying.

"Appeals are for Girl Scouts. Ruby's right. It's out of our hands! We had a chance to petition, and we didn't get around to it. We had a chance to appeal and we didn't get around to that either, just like we had a chance to have a McDonald's in '75 and a decent beauty shop instead of all this door-to-door nonsense—"

"What's your point, Spitzer?" Dusty spat before reminding Angela Spitzer that she did not have the type of hair that fared well in humidity.

"Her point is we're not getter-arounders! That's why we have to charge people to come to us, which is why you might argue we *need* that park!" This from Joy Jennings, the art teacher who one or two people in the room reckoned *was* a getter-arounder, seeing how she was getting right around to moving to California.

"I heard your son is behind all this, Mr. Mayor, and that the park might even be called Fusselback's Field of Dreams, is that true?" one of the gals from the Ladies Auxiliary for the Beautification of Main Street asked.

"I'm not sure Albany will appreciate our interference," chimed another.

"I'll interference you!" Amos bellowed, rising abruptly from his seat when Dusty grabbed his arm.

"Look, there's nothing any of you could have done!" said Daulton finally. "I've done a lot of legwork on this. You people can't go on pretending you own everything in this town. You just live here. You can appeal all you like, but that park is coming." He looked nervously at Chylak, who offered a discreet thumbs-up.

"Don't listen to him; he's a reporter and he's not from here anymore!" said Mada Nauss, Dusty's German neighbor, who Dusty noticed had been batting her eyes all night at Honus and had clumpy lashes.

"*Journalist,*" Daulton corrected. "I prefer *journalist.*"

"Well, Mr. Big Shot Journalist, you live here too. Do *you* want it?" said Ruby, who was mad at Daulton in lieu of his former best friend, her husband, who wasn't around anymore to contend with.

"All right, that's enough, folks! Now, Terry is right. We have used up all of our legal options, but that doesn't mean . . ."

Chylak's thoughts trailed off after "legal options." He was afraid of hearing something he shouldn't and, worse, of agreeing with it. Something had come over him the night following his Hall of Fame freak-out. Something, he shuddered to think, with all the symptoms of community.

"Here's how the state sees it: more tourists equals more money. That's a fact. But Daulton is wrong about one thing. This *is* our town! We don't need an appeal! I have an idea, the best one I've had yet."

Amos realized, too late, that this was not the best approach for him to take. One person wanted to know if it was better than his idea about transferring the town sewage plant to the soccer field behind the junior high school. Another person wanted to know if it was better than his idea to dye the lake turquoise, which had caused one or two children in town to be dyed along with it. The truth was, Amos *did* have a plan, a good one, and if everyone just listened and cooperated, he could see it to fruition. It was not illegal, but it was unorthodox. And best of all, Johnny had agreed to it! Johnny had called him after their run-in at the churchyard and agreed to a game: Town versus State, for the removal or arrival of the theme park, depending on which team you bat for.

Amos searched the back of the room for Johnny's henchmen. If Johnny kept his promise, Amos would keep his. He silenced the crowd, then laid out his plan in full detail for the next half hour, followed by applause, protests, and umpteen questions. He was about to wrap up the meeting with a well-rehearsed "Now who will come to bat for the town?" when he lost his audience completely. The door opened, followed by a cool blast of wind, and everyone turned, row by row, seat by seat until they all faced the back of the building. There was a loud, collective inhalation and Amos, reaching for his chair in need of support, missed it entirely and fell to the floor. "Hallelujah," he said.

Manny Barrett was in the building.

B OBBY STOOD OUTSIDE THE courthouse, listening to the thunderous applause and wondering what she had missed. She had come outside for a smoke break and had passed Manny on his way in. Too shocked to speak, she nodded hello. She crushed out her smoke and continued reading quietly aloud to herself from her new treasure, the battered Cooper book. "'The shrieks of the wounded, and the yells of their murderers, grew less frequent, until, finally, the cries of horror were lost to their ear, or were drowned in the loud, long, and piercing whoops of the triumphant savages.'"

Mrs. Paquette exited the building.

"That lipstick is the wrong color for you, hon," she said.

"It was perfect when *you* sold it to me this morning, bitch," Bobby was about to say when she noticed Paquette dabbing her eyes with a tissue as though she'd been crying. Bobby suddenly regretted having come. She wiped the lipstick on the back of her hand. Maybe she was trying too hard. Maybe the doctor was right. Maybe her only affliction was too much time on her hands and no one to get naked with to fill it. She slipped the book in her purse before Paquette could inquire about it. "Hissss! Scram!" she said, and the startled old woman skittered off.

She flipped to the middle of the book to make sure the document was intact. She'd become rather attached to it, fantasizing about all the wicked things she could do with it. She'd even begun to doubt whether she wanted to hand it over. She'd scoffed at the mayor's plan. She had a *better* plan. No more excuses. She didn't necessarily think it would motivate her to move out of town, but that was the beauty of it: it would mix up the scenery a little, change Cooperstown, before she went bonkers out of boredom. She'd be doing everybody a favor. The theme park saga would be settled once and for all; then they could get on with their lives.

Some people stayed behind to chitchat or to give Amos donations for his Fenimore Funhouse Roof Fund, while others filed out of the courtroom. Bobby cocked her finger like a pistol, whispering "Gotcha" when her target approached. She wasn't sure exactly what she was going to say to him, nor did she know why she was so nervous about saying it, but it didn't matter. This was so exciting! She had been downright giddy since finding the book, and, if all went according to plan, in a matter of minutes she'd have a partner in crime. She'd kept herself captive for so long, like a dog winding its leash around the same old tree, choking its dumb self nearly to death. She'd martyred her best years for life in a town in which it was easy to avoid getting close to people, because everyone was so damned *close*.

She followed a discreet twenty paces behind, cursing him under her breath when he stopped to listen to the mayor arguing with somebody across the parking lot. She couldn't see whom, because she ducked behind a car so as not to be seen, but it sounded like there were several of them. She cursed again when she realized he'd parked all the way down Main Street by the Hall of Fame. Wanting to be sure they were alone before she made her move, she took the shortcut through the parking lot of Doubleday Field. She couldn't stop thinking about what she would say to him and was surprised when she felt a little tingle where it counts.

At the Hall of Fame, she ducked behind a bush at the base of a flagpole, careful not to burn the red, white, and blue ribbons wrapped around the pole with her cigarette. The museum looked like a half-opened gift. She had missed the induction ceremony, not that she cared. They could hold it in her backyard if they wanted to. At least it would be something *different*. She was going to sit back and enjoy the show, having found the means to go down in her own personal history as a martyr for change. What had the psychiatrist said about progression? *She* could handle it without medication. She would make the paper again, the front page! She'd go down as the gal who burst Cooperstown's baseball bubble.

She chewed her fingers, waiting for him, the one person she could turn to. The one person who she was certain would see things her way. "What the hell," she said, reapplying the lipstick she'd purchased from Paquette on the condition that that nosy Nancy wouldn't tell anyone she'd overheard Bobby telling tourists that the Baseball Library was closed, *permanently*, for repairs.

D AULTON STOOD IN THE back of the courthouse. He'd hoped to go unnoticed, which was impossible when his job was to notice everyone else. Perhaps he and Chylak, hell, even Mrs. Paquette, had more in common than he'd realized. He was surprised to see Manny at the courthouse. He wasn't surprised, however, that Manny showed up when the meeting was *over*. No one seemed to know why he was there, though there was plenty of speculation. True to form, Manny did not volunteer a reason. But he got himself an unearned standing ovation. It clearly made him uneasy. Apparently, he hadn't come to "rescue" them or whatever people expected. He had not made a peep, except to say hi to Ruby, who refused to acknowledge him, and Daulton had felt sorry for him, figuring Manny meant to inch his way back into her good graces. Daulton left during the applause.

He passed Mrs. Paquette on his way out of the courthouse. She was in the back of the room arguing with Honus, shaking a well-polished claw in his face and shouting, "You had no right!" Honus had a hangdog look to him and wasn't even trying to defend himself for whatever he had done, which Daulton figured was as petty as using Paquette for free hair tonic. That is, until she said, "That was *my* husband's. *Mine!*" The mayor had rushed to her aid, pulling her and Honus out of the courthouse. Daulton followed and heard him say, "Now, let's not ruin a fine plan with bickering! What's the problem?" Daulton walked away so he missed the rest of it, but when he looked back it seemed like Amos listened for all of a second before he grabbed Honus by the collar, shook him roughly, and then ran back into the courthouse, whisking a visibly perturbed Manny outside. The mayor patted a visibly upset Mrs. Paquette on the shoulder and then she left.

Now the mayor and Manny were arguing in the parking lot, with Honus standing sheepishly by. Daulton inched closer to hear what they were saying. The mayor cocked a fist in Manny's face and shouted, "It's now or never—we don't have a goddamned choice!" When the fight failed to result in fisticuffs, Daulton lost interest, along with several other onlookers who hadn't stuck around for cider and donuts after the meeting.

Daulton passed Manny's truck on his way to the Hall of Fame parking lot, where he'd left his Mustang. "Well, I'll be," he said, eyeing the license plate and then Manny, who was storming away from the mayor. It was the same truck he'd seen peeling away from Chylak's driveway, scaring the doctor's kids. The gun rack was full of rifles, and Daulton wondered if Manny ever actually used them and why he carried them around in the summertime. He didn't know the rules of hunting, however—maybe hunting season was year-round. There were shovels in the back of the truck and a bag of dirt. He pictured Manny planting a vegetable garden, struggling to subsist entirely on his own, or a flower garden full of black-eyed Susans and sweet Williams—his only company. Manny was heading quickly toward the truck, so Daulton took off down Main Street.

The streets were lined with cars. Everyone had attended the meeting, everyone but Johnny, of course. Daulton wondered if he was holed up at the swank Omagotta Hotel, sipping gin and feeling pleased with himself. Or was he feeling guilty? Johnny reminded him of Chuck, torn between town and state. Daulton was the one who had summoned him, asking for an interview. He had suggested that Johnny attend the induction ceremony. That's what that phone message was about, from the receptionist at *The Journal*—Johnny had agreed. He planned to run for Senate and was only too pleased to show his face, shake some hands, and have his photo taken with the legendary Willie Mays.

Daulton was glad, now, that he hadn't found a parking spot closer to the courthouse. The night air was rejuvenating. It felt good to stretch his legs. He had always liked the way the museum looked at night. There was something peaceful about it when it was closed. It just stood there, quiet, full of treasures and legends and specters of a sort. He smiled at the thought that Chuck might be haunting the Fenimore Funhouse right now, riffling through his papers or pounding on the door of his cottage, wondering when a new curator would arrive so he could boss him or her around.

The shops were all closed despite its being Saturday, generally the one night things stayed open late in Cooperstown. It was unorthodox for a town meeting to be held on a weekend, but people seemed to agree that with the park looming near, it constituted an emergency. Of course, Daulton suspected the Hall of Fame, which had never been closed during the week except once due to a fire, might be closed indefinitely. Part of him, the part that was still a local, still Chuck's obedient boy, felt guilty for having called Johnny. Johnny had confided his dream about incorporating the Hall of Fame into the theme park. That seemed a bit much, even to Daulton, who could not imagine Main Street without it. It was how tourists found their way around when they were lost, what everyone came to see. For the townsfolk, it represented stability. No matter what happened— whether theme parks, or fast-food chains, or souvenir shops swallowed them whole—Cooperstown's identity remained intact as long as it had its museum. He began to wonder if he was in over his head.

Something bigger than a theme park was brewing—he could feel it. And it wasn't just the mayor's cockamamie plan: A ball game? Daulton laughed—now, that was worth sticking around for! He'd decided to return to the city as soon as he came up with an original angle for his final theme park piece, including the interview with Johnny. He felt awkward about making the Fusselbacks, the father-son political battle of wills, the heart of his story. Then again, the mayor had hardly been cooperative. He had yet to let Daulton access Chuck's cottage. Daulton was definitely ready to clear it out. It was time to face the fact that he could postpone leaving as long as he liked, but that wouldn't bring Chuck back. The mayor had made so many excuses about being busy and about the stupid key. Doors were locked every damn day! That's why there were locksmiths, for Christ's sake. If worst came to worst, Daulton figured he could kick the door in. The game was set for next week. And he was looking forward to it. It wasn't the game he had *planned* to cover, but it was perfect for his Fusselback–theme park piece. Then he'd blow out of town and chalk it all up to one more summer in the Coop.

Bobby popped out from behind a bush, accidentally ashing

her cigarette on Daulton's shirt. Her hair was tangled up in streamers.

Daulton jumped back, startled, checking his chest for a burn mark. Forgetting himself, he reached to pick streamers from her hair. She smelled funky, *moldy*. He recalled Mrs. Paquette's prediction that that's what happened to women who went too long without sex.

"Here ya go!" Bobby said, handing him a parcel wrapped in brown paper like a freshly killed walleye, then marching briskly off.

"Wait a minute! What's this?" he asked, lunging to grab her gently by the elbow. He was flattered that she'd thought to give him a good-bye gift. Then he realized that not only did she not know he was *leaving*, she hadn't even bothered to say *hello* when he arrived. "What's this all about?" he repeated, suspicious now.

"It's a book," she said excitedly, watching him unwrap the parcel.

"I can see that, but why are you giving it to—"

Daulton felt his knees collapse. The next thing he knew, he was sitting on the steps in front of the museum. His suspicions turned to full-blown paranoia when he saw the cover. It was a book all right, and it *was* technically his. "Where did you get this?" he demanded, flipping it open to read the inscription: "DON'T READ THIS!!!"

"I don't understand." Daulton's head was spinning. It was *Chuck's* book! The one he'd given Daulton as a going-away present after Daulton graduated from high school. He wondered if this was some kind of sick joke. But it was Chuck's handwriting, all right. It was definitely the same book. And he had buried it! He looked at the museum, half expecting the ghost of Frank Paquette to saunter out and shout, "Surprise! Chuck's back!"

"I don't feel so good," he said, leaning forward with his head between his knees.

"Is it *yours?*" Bobby asked, sitting down beside him.

"My father's."

"Your name is in the inscription."

"He gave it to me."

"And? What did you *think* of it?"

Bobby seemed impatient. Daulton needed a minute to think, to figure out what answer she expected and, more important, what answer he wanted to give. If he said he'd buried it, would she think he was nuts? How the hell had she gotten it?

"I don't—I mean, I never read it." He was embarrassed to admit to a local librarian that he, who was born and bred in Cooperstown, had never read *The Last of the Mohicans*. "I've read all of Cooper's other books, though." Now he felt stupid, like a schoolboy trying to impress. Bobby looked disappointed. It was the same look Chuck used to give him whenever he didn't do something the way Chuck wanted it done, and he fought the urge to say, "What do you *want* me to think?" He looked at Bobby, who lit up a fresh smoke, wondering if she remembered graduation. It had rained so hard that the ceremony was held inside the school gymnasium. Daulton, Bobby, Johnny, Honus, and some others had gotten together beforehand to smoke in their cars—everyone but Manny, who stood in the rain playing watchdog in case any parents interrupted the festivities. Daulton had loaned Bobby his coat, which ticked off Honus. Her gown had been soaked, and when he went to wrap the coat around her she apologized, having burnt him with her cigarette.

Bobby didn't seem in the mood for reminiscing. And Daulton was starting to get that feeling again, the one where he steps into the shoes of the person he is talking to, *too far* in, until neither one of them comes out right. He stood and stepped away from her, stumbling down the steps. His head felt fuzzy and her cigarette was making him nauseous. He sniffed the air, wondering if it was actually pot—it reeked. Then he smelled the book. "Jesus!"

"I know."

"I buried this!" Daulton said, dangling the offensive book in front of Bobby like it was a mouse he'd just killed.

"Beg your pardon?"

"Chuck died last year. I could *swear* I buried this with him!"

He waited for her to say she knew Chuck died, but that she was sorry anyway, the way everyone else did. Instead, she reached toward him and placed a hand on his arm. Daulton flinched and she withdrew it as though she, too, had been burnt. He regretted having reacted that way, as if she were some wild man-eating cat. She looked so vulnerable chewing her fingernails and he felt a slight, sudden thrill at being close to her, the popular girl from high school, like Bobby was an exotic creature that people rarely approached, and one he was lucky enough to have stroke him with its soft, misunderstood paw.

"Why would you *bury* it unless you knew what was in it?" she asked.

"In it? The inscription said not to, read it, I mean."

"Do you always do what you're told?"

That pissed Daulton off. They weren't kids anymore. She wasn't above him, the pretty chick with all the boys vying for her attention. He didn't know how to answer her. The truth was, he *had* always done what he was told to do, until recently. Because every time he followed his own gut he screwed up. He remembered the Valium Dr. Chylak had prescribed, which he'd left in his car, wondering if they would be standing around long enough for it to kick in.

"I want to know where you got this!" he said, his patience petering. Maybe he hadn't buried it. Maybe he had left it behind in Chuck's cottage after the funeral. He was in shock. His dad had just died. People weren't in their right mind when they were grieving. He tried to think back. He'd been ushered away from the grave site by the mayor, who kept telling him to just leave and everything would be all right. Cartwright stole his honors, his last respect, by closing Chuck's coffin. Daulton looked once more at Bobby; he didn't really know her anymore. For all he knew, she might have grown up to be some kind of sicko. Dr. Chylak had said she wasn't a patient, but what else would he say? Had Chylak *lied?* Was Bobby lying to him now? He closed his eyes and placed his hand over his forehead like a compress. Maybe *he* was the sicko. It wouldn't be the first time he had considered that possibility.

"I didn't *steal* it, if that's what you mean," Bobby said, hurt. "It was returned to the Baseball Library where I happen to work." She hesitated, chewing her nails. "I got fired from the other one, in case you hadn't heard."

"I heard."

"I swear to Olivia Newton-John! That old two-face Paquette had better learn to—"

"Relax, it wasn't her. Chuck told me. In a letter."

Bobby opened her mouth but said nothing. It was a good mouth. Daulton didn't know anything about lip-liner, or whatever Mrs. Paquette said she required, but the lipstick looked all right. "Chuck wrote to me all the time about whatever was happening in town. I think it was his way of recording the history of the town, editing it just the way he liked it. I guess he thought you getting fired was news."

"Oh," Bobby said, disappointed. Daulton sensed he was batting two for two. "Well, you should read that book."

"I will." Daulton smiled. It was kind of nice talking to her. It had been a long time. His story could wait until morning. He cracked opened the book.

"Not *now,* nitwit!" Bobby shouted, snatching it back and yanking him out of the streetlight by the collar. She put her face close to his.

Daulton held his breath. Was she going to smack him or kiss him? He thought about asking her if she wanted to *split* the Valium, but she whispered in his ear, so softly that he could barely understand what she said. She didn't smell a bit like mildew now. More like menthol—fresh, minty, and warm. "Let's just say that things aren't quite what they appear to be in this town."

Daulton stepped back. She was so close, *too* close. The kind of close that made him forget who he was. He grabbed the book, possessive now of Chuck's gift, a message spewed straight from the grave. Maybe Chuck *wanted* him to read it. Maybe he had all along! Maybe this was a test, that part of Chuck's afterlife slide show when he gets to erase one small regret, one his son could help him undo. Maybe yesterday was *not* Daulton's day. Maybe it was tomorrow.

He began jogging toward his car.

"Not so fast," Bobby said, following behind and squeezing him tightly by the elbow. "We have to make a pact."

"What are you *talking* about?" he said, spinning to face her. His anger felt surprisingly good. Like he owned it. It was his goddamned book! What did she want with it? He didn't have to listen to her. He didn't have to listen to anyone. Something crazy was going on here and he had to get home and figure out what before he decided it was *him*.

"Promise not to tell anyone about what you read or this conversation until we have a chance to speak again. Deal?" That paw was back, soft and warm and reaching for him.

"What is this, junior high?" Daulton asked, relaxing again as he shook Bobby's hand.

"Feels like it, I know."

"Cross my heart and hope to die, that good enough?"

Bobby laughed, just a little, and then she said, "Good-bye for now," and walked away, disappearing just as quickly as she had arrived.

Daulton stood in front of the tranquil museum feeling suspiciously good—feeling not unlike his old self. He headed to his car, holding the book up to the moonlight and admiring it as though it were an old friend. He slid into the driver's seat and popped the book into the glove compartment, scouring the parking lot for witnesses, secretive for reasons he did not yet understand, feeling like a kid who'd been confided in above his means. He'd read the book tonight. He'd get it right this time. Chuck had to have known he eventually would. This was just one of Chuck's tests, some reverse-psychology tactic. But what did Bobby have to do with it and why was she being so damned weird? The old reporter's juices were flowing, the hound back on his trail. Daulton was certain the book was just another piece of the jigsaw puzzle, the story he was meant to piece together. The labyrinth from which he would finally make his way out.

He drove into the darkness toward Lake Street, his headlights off. Then he turned a quick left and headed toward West Lake Road, to Chuck's cottage, ready now to tackle its contents whether he was welcome there or not.

C HYLAK STRUGGLED TO SUPPRESS the feeling that overcame him at the town meeting, one that had shot straight from his brain through his bloodstream and landed in his gut like a lump of bad mutton. He feared another anxiety attack. He had something on his mind and was frustrated that his neurotransmitters were keeping it from the rest of him. Call it a hunch—the kind of primal warning flare he liked to think man had outgrown along with the appendix—but he was certain it had something to do with Chuck Daulton, their final session together. It was almost midnight. He walked home alone.

Babe had left the meeting early to relieve the babysitter. Apparently, she knew everything. She had told him so last night. Chylak had been lying in bed beside her, staring at the wallpaper and thinking about trees, how uncomplicated their existence was. "I *know*, Kerwin," she said. "I know why we moved." He had tried to shut her out, pretending she was crazy and then playing dumb. "We *had* to," she'd said. "You lost your job in Lebanon! Dr. Barker's wife told me so, *days* before we left." "That's ludicrous," Chylak had said, cursing Barker's nosy wife and telling Babe to get some sleep, to not listen to gossip. "Stop it!" was her response. "I want to talk about this! I *know* what the psych director told you. I know what the goddamned psych *board* said!" And it was her goddamning that broke him; that he had brought her, his biblical beauty, to this. "You should have told me," Babe cried. "I wouldn't have judged you then."

And at that moment it wasn't the goddamning that bothered

him as much as her choice of the word *then*. He could not get it out of his mind. It was the reason they had now switched roles, Chylak resenting Babe because *then* implied that *now* was too late, that he had fallen from grace in her eyes and it was no longer worth it to her to get her wings bent out of shape to save him.

The psychiatric board at the Lebanon Institute had unanimously agreed, preceded by a motion from Chylak's boss and instigated by his patients, that while he was "unarguably intelligent," "a nice enough fellow to golf with," he was "inept in the communications department." "Not so good with people," they said. "People" meaning patients, patients meaning a paycheck, and that paycheck being the key to all he and Babe had ever dreamed about: a house in the country, a quaint little town where the children would thrive on fresh air and wholesome ideals, not forced to develop too quickly ahead of their time. And that is what he had provided! *Technically*. The problem was it didn't feel so fantastic when it was forced on him. He fought the board's decision to no avail. "I'm a psychiatrist," he claimed. "We medicate, we don't communicate!" But they were adamant. Listening to patients was part of the job, and it wasn't acceptable to simply pop pills right into their gobs whenever one broke down in his presence.

He ought to warn the mayor against his own childish scheme. A ball game was irrational. And yet, it might actually be fun, if you were into that sort of thing. It might, for instance, be fun for *Chylak* as a psychosocial experiment. It wasn't often that a shrink had the chance, aside from group therapy, to see all of his patients working together for the common cause of finding their own cure. It was like his vision, his desire for some form of mass psychotherapy that could be dropped on people like nerve gas, except to calm them down.

He had worried about Daulton at the town meeting. The journalist had stood in the back of the room speaking as though reading from someone else's script. He had worried too that Mrs. Paquette was acting suspiciously less assertive. But what bothered him the most was the town recluse, Barrett, making an appearance like some ordinary Joe. He didn't know why it disappointed him, but it did. Even more disappointing was that he and Babe had not attended the meeting together: "I'm needed at home," she had said soon after he arrived, taking the car keys and leaving him to walk home. Chylak told her it must be nice to be so "needed." Regardless of whether anyone knew they needed *him,* he was the only person in town qualified to clean up the mess when the mayor's plan flopped, and his failure to be taken seriously left Cooperstown more vulnerable than it already was.

Chylak picked up his pace, realizing with regret that *he* needed Babe. He needed to know if she thought he was up to the task before him. Had she too judged him "inept"? He began to jog, dreading another meltdown, though he had scoured every one of his medical manuals and not one had suggested that his Hall of Fame horror show was anything more than an acute anxiety attack brought on by stress, drugs, an abrupt change in lifestyle, and sleep deprivation, which he blamed on a guilty conscience and too much sugary Tang. Of course, the pills hadn't helped. Last night Babe had made him promise to stop seeing patients at all hours of the day and night, not just for the sake of their marriage, but for himself. And she was right. He was settled now. He was no miracle worker! Nor was he the good country doc he had once longed to be. He was more of a mediocre twenty-four-hour hotline. He stopped dead in his tracks, feeling suddenly taken for granted.

There on the steps leading up to his home, at *midnight,* was a patient waiting for him. Chylak was about to announce his new policy about no sessions after hours, *especially* not at his house. But the look on the man's peaked face—that telltale frown beneath a forced grin—made him think twice.

"Doc?" Daulton asked, before leaning forward to upchuck on Chylak's lawn. "I saw my father tonight."

Chylak watched a dark truck roll down the street, then peel away.

He supposed he could make one exception. Daulton was not presently a patient, but more of a friend in need. Chylak told him to stay put and ran inside to get a cold compress and glass of water for Daulton, a cocktail for himself, and a low dose of tranquilizer for whoever needed it first. It was clear that this was going to be a long night, a long summer, and one that might yet prove his theory that psychosis bred freely in warm weather and under the pressure of organized sports. Tonight Chylak would be a friendly shoulder to lean on. But tomorrow? He was setting up more professional parameters: no home visits, no sessions after hours, no cocktail camaraderie, and absolutely no new patients, even if they came scuttling, desperate, out of the woodwork.

NINTH INNING

All foul lines are in fair territory.

—THE OFFICIAL RULES OF
MAJOR LEAGUE BASEBALL: 2.00 DEFINITION OF TERMS

I've been expecting you."

"Look, Doctor, it's not what you think."

The patient required no introduction. Nor, did Chylak suppose, would he be offering one. Pleased as he was to see the man, he suspected him to be the worst kind of patient: the kind that arrives smug at having already diagnosed himself. There was an urgency to this visit, however. It hung in the air thick as liverwurst.

He ran his eyes over his visitor, disappointed that the fellow was in fact *not* clad in animal hides but in parachute pants and a T-shirt. They had only met once before, during Chylak's first-ever stroll to the lake. He remembered it well. He was surprised to see so many landlocked seagulls lining the shore. They were a fine substitute for his Lebanon pigeons and waddled over to him, well trained in the area of demanding handouts. Chylak had leaned against a boulder, the base of a statue of a scantily clad fellow called *Indian Hunter,* and was tossing Babe's leftover lentils onto the grass, realizing too late that the wind carried them directly into this man's beached canoe. The guy was crouching on the grass with his boat, repairing a seat, and announced out of nowhere that he used to climb the *Indian Hunter* with a pal when he was young. Chylak suspected now that the friend Mr. Barrett spoke of that day was Daulton. He did not, then, get a chance to inquire, because Barrett barked, "Duck, motherfucker!" and flipped his canoe over his head, scrambled beneath it quick as a crab, and crouched in crash position. Chylak had jerked his head quickly, expecting some ferocious class of Catskill Mountain mallard to be after him. But it was just a seagull flying by, dropping an unpleasant, pulpy white surprise on his head. He wiped it off with his newspaper, and when he looked up, his rescuer was gone.

"Are you responsible?" Chylak now asked, aware these were potent words.

Barrett stared at the battered snow dome on his desk, which was held together by duct tape and glue. Chylak couldn't bear to throw it out after Elliott had had his way with it. It was the first genuine token of appreciation he had ever received from a patient. There were only two tiny landmarks left inside, the sanitarium and Doubleday Field. It seemed to make Barrett uncomfortable, a mini-Cooperstown held together by a flimsy sliver of tape. He stood suddenly and went for the door, apologized for having come, and said he had changed his mind. Yet he stood there with his hand on the doorknob, not moving in or out.

Chylak asked him to wait, suggesting that at moments of indecision, it was often useful to retrace one's steps, to recall what had motivated one to arrive at the point in question in the first place. "Please," he said. "Stay."

Barrett took a tentative step back into the office, though he refused to sit. He said he had been at the post office—his mailbox was useless and he often received important legal documents from his wife, which he did not read but did not want strewn around his driveway either, where certain nosy people might find them; hence a postbox in town. Inside his box were two pieces of mail, both hand delivered, which meant they were both urgent: a letter from his wife's lawyer about alimony, and a postcard from Terry Daulton, whom he described as "straight to the son-of-a-bitching point as always." On one side of the card was a photograph of the Sleeping Lion mountain and on the other just four simple words: I KNOW YOU KNOW.

When Chylak asked what those words meant, Barrett sighed,

succumbing to whatever had brought him there. He asked if he could sit in the chair across from Chylak's desk, or if it was necessary to lie on the couch.

"Please," Chylak said, gesturing toward the chair. "Tang?"

"I'll pass."

"How are you?"

"I'm not here to talk about me."

"Fine. Fruit leather?"

Chylak pushed a bowl of Babe's latest concoction toward his visitor. Barrett didn't strike him as much of a fruit eater, however. He looked more like the meat-and-potatoes type, and Chylak envied him his diet. He eyed Barrett cautiously, recalling Elliott's friend Joey's claim that the man was a cannibal. It was absurd, but on the off chance it was true, it would make a most *fascinating* case study. He watched closely to see how Barrett reacted to the fruit. "I understand you used to be quite a ballplayer," he said.

"That's what they tell me."

Chylak decided to test out his newly acquired knowledge on the history of baseball. "I understand the game is actually derivative of an *English* game called rounders?"

"I wouldn't say that out loud in this town. They'll hang you by your stethoscope."

"I don't actually use a—"

"Look," Barrett interrupted impatiently. "This is a one-time visit. No offense, Doctor, but I'm not one for small talk. I want to get this over with. I just want to explain a few things from my side. I'm sure you know what I mean. Just hear me out before you call the cops or slap a straitjacket on me."

"I'm not here to judge," said Chylak, disappointed when Barrett bit into a piece of fruit leather.

"Yes, but you have to listen, right? You're an intermediary? You're paid to be impartial."

Chylak was about to say he did not *have* to listen, particularly not for *free,* and that in case Barrett was wondering, he didn't take animal carcasses or pooka shells as payment.

But curiosity got the better of him, and he wasn't impartial to beef jerky, a packet of which poked its way, temptingly, out of Barrett's chest pocket. Barrett offered him a stick and he devoured it slowly, savoring each morsel while he figured out how best to handle yet another unorthodox session. He was already breaking his no new patients rule, and what about his promise to Babe? Last night they had made a dinner date, the romantic sort sans children, so they could talk. He could call her, of course. Better yet, it would just take a sec to run across the street. But he had the distinct sense that, regardless of whether Barrett realized it, he *was* there to talk about himself, and that if he didn't listen now, no one would ever be given the chance to do so again.

"This is confidential, right? You can't tell anyone what goes on in this room." Barrett seemed to be telling, as opposed to asking, him.

"Yes, that's right," Chylak conceded, wondering if he should call in a witness. Barrett had been in combat. There were rumors that he was psychotic and perhaps even dangerous. But Chylak knew the hermit's visit had something to do with what had happened to Daulton the previous night, and likely involved the theme park. *Everything* did. The state had begun laying plans for it. There was talk of its being built near the entrance to town, so it would be the first thing tourists saw when they arrived. The blueprints hung in the window of Johnny Fusselback's district office for all to see, at least until someone spray-painted "Fascists!" across the window.

Chylak sized up his patient for signs of aggression. Despite the size of Barrett's biceps, he looked too tired to use them. Besides, there was an oddly civilized odor to him, which made him less threatening. Chylak recognized it immediately.

"Home-Run Setup Man Musk Number Three?"

Barrett tried to suppress a grin and said no, that it was Home-Run Perfect Game Patchouli; Mrs. Paquette had doused him for refusing to buy it.

The ice was broken.

Chylak drew the shades, lit his pipe, and gave his usual spiel: aside from some exceptions—if Barrett had *harmed* anyone, for example, he would have to tell the authorities—their conversation was strictly confidential, and there was no fee for initial consultations. This wasn't true, but he feared his usual rate of seventy-five bucks an hour would send Barrett, who had no known source of income, running back out the door. The jerky was payment enough. He leaned back in his chair with his feet on the desk, prepared, almost, to enjoy this session, the company of this mysterious man whose issues seemed so intertwined with those of so many others whom he had come to know, their internal afflictions twisted together like sinews of the same enviably carnivorous beast.

From the moment Barrett opened his mouth to explain the reasons behind his visit, it was as though a dam had broken, releasing a river of pent-up emotions. A torrent of torment that ran for *three* hours.

"I changed my mind," Chylak said when Barrett was done. "I'm going to have to charge you." Not because the session had run over, or because Barrett refused to become a regular patient and was therefore taking advantage of a freebie, but because Chylak was totally ticked. He had missed dinner with Babe for this? The sheer futility of it all! The absurdity that such a trivial thing was at the root of Barrett's troubles, wreaking havoc on so many willing lives. Posttraumatic stress or not, "Vietnam" did not hold a candle to what Barrett considered the great trauma of his youth. Combat had not caused his stress. *Cooperstown* had! Cooperstown, which he feared was *not* the true birthplace of baseball.

"Your problem is stupid," Chylak heard himself say.

"Beg your pardon?"

Barrett tensed, blood rushing to bulge from the veins in his muscular neck. His jaw was clenched, and he looked as though he might spring across the desk at any moment and tear poor Chylak to pieces.

Chylak panicked. Had he said that *aloud?* Don't judge, he told himself, stay on the sidelines. He backtracked, quickly. "*Utrama is- tuvid.* It's, uh, Latin, for . . . *stress.* You exhibit several classic symp- toms of posttraumatic stress disorder. It's quite fascinating, really, now that I know your background."

He knew better than to say that while he was listening to said background, for the first time in his professional career he des- perately wished he could share patient confidences. The entire time Barrett was speaking, Chylak had fought the urge to place his hands over his ears, squint his eyes, and sing, "*Lalalalalaaa!*" like Elliott did when told something he did not want to hear (re- cently, Chylak's excuse for forgetting to take him to the Hall of Fame). It was all such nonsense! Some dubious document claim- ing Cooperstown had once banned baseball from being played in its streets. He began to buckle and blamed Barrett, retrieving *Psy- chology for the Fighting Man: What You Should Know About Yourself and Others,* copyright a delectable 1943, from his desk drawer. Flip- ping through it, he neglected his vow to lay off the quotes, not to mention that he was about to expose himself once more as an impostor in front of a patient. "Here we go," he said, having found a passage he hoped would spare him from a lack of pa- tience with patients. "Anger is infectious and can spread from one person to another through personal contact." Chylak felt as though an invisible corset, that snug, smothering chest protector, had been loosened.

Barrett *was* angry. He was a near mountain of anger that years of neglecting therapy had, fortunately, not morphed into a vio- lent volcano of wrath. Chylak was about to tell him so when he spotted a paragraph suggesting that anger spreads "when the be- holder is sympathetic." He may be "the beholder," but he was *not* sympathetic. Nor was there danger of anything spreading, least of all anger, since it was all he could do not to chuckle out loud. He scanned the book, pleased that Barrett had no clue this wasn't generally how therapy worked: a perk of his being a hermit. "The sympathetic beholder . . . blah, blah, blah . . . who is 'able to put

himself in the angry man's shoes, when the injured person is
"one of us."'"

Chylak got lost in thought. Was he now *one* of them? He read
slowly to himself. "Anger shared, controlled, and directed to the
single purpose of destroying the enemy is a powerful force for
survival and victory." He smiled, imagining himself in a pinstriped uniform, waving a bat above his head in victory stance
while his patients chanted: "Chylak, champion of the people!
Thought leader! Demon slayer! All-around regular—"

"Doc, are you with me?" Barrett asked. "You're freaking me
out."

Chylak realized he was staring at Barrett's camouflage pants. It
was the pattern, that mesmeric forest again. It made him think of
The Deer Hunter—or was it *The Deerslayer?* Barrett reminded him of
the character played by Christopher Walken, singing *just too good to
be true* in one scene, then running a bullet through his cranium in
the next, playing a foolish, continuous game of roulette, knowing
that in the end he would lose. That the odds were against him.
There was no rewriting history, particularly buried history. In Barrett's case, *literally* buried. Someone would question it eventually—
he thought about Babe. Someone always did.

"Right, sorry. Here you are," he said, scratching a note on
Selma Wellmix Sanitarium stationery and folding it into a little
funnel. "For the lawyers." He then sprinkled the MDMA samples
left over from his Hall of Fame fiasco inside the funnel and
handed it to Barrett. "And *these* are for you. They're not for
everyone," he warned. "I'm not even certain they're FDA-
approved. But a colleague whom I trust completely recommended them for stress."

He winked at Barrett and walked him to the door.

IT WAS DARK OUT when Manny left the sanitarium. He had
trouble finding his truck in the parking lot, until he spotted the
golf cart parked beside it with a brightly colored beach umbrella

poking out the back. The mayor was asleep in the cart, or passed out. Manny wasn't sure. He shook him.

"It's not my fault!" Amos yelled, waking with a start.

"Relax, Amos. You were dreaming."

The mayor looked around, relieved, and then resumed his sourpuss scowl. "I wish," he said.

Manny looked away, uncomfortable. He wasn't sure if it was the glare of the lights or if Fusselback's eyes were actually tearing.

"It was more of a nightmare. I feel like I'm living in one," Amos said, gesturing with arms open wide as if to encompass the town. He hesitated, inhaling slowly before he looked Manny straight in the eyes and said, "I'm afraid it's worse than we thought."

"*We?*"

Manny stepped toward Amos, fighting an urge to shove the old man out of his cart, just throw him on the ground and pummel him. But the mayor was in a bad state. His shirt was half off, and his breath reeked.

"Have you been *drinking?*"

Dammit! Now he felt sorry for the man. He was about to ask how things could possibly get any worse—they had unburied their own excrement like a pack of wild mutts, opened old wounds, and for what? Just to roll in it all over again, for old time's sake? But he said nothing, whispering to the lion within to stay quiet, to be like Coach Cartwright.

"Now, I know you don't want to hear this, but it's important." Amos placed a hand on Manny's arm.

Manny brushed it off violently.

"You're obsessed, Amos!" He poked the mayor in the chest with one finger. "That's your problem! I told you last night like I told you twelve years ago: I'm through. Kaput! Do you understand that? I've paid my fucking dues."

"Just listen to me, Immanuel. Ten minutes, that's all I'm asking."

Manny crossed his arms over his chest, shaking his head.

Relieved he was not about to be hit, Amos began speaking quickly.

"All right. Now, I know things got kind of crazy at Chuck's place last night, but we have to stick together. We have to see this through, more now than ever and you *know* it. I don't think Auff-swich stole the book because I spoke to him this afternoon, and I don't guess it was Honus's fault either."

"That's a first."

"What do you mean?"

"You're partial to blaming others."

"Just listen to me, dammit! Now, I questioned Dusty too."

"Paquette? How could you be so damned stupid?" Manny said.

"Relax! She doesn't suspect a thing. You were there after the meeting when Honus told her he found it. I just asked her where she got it in the first place. She has quite a memory, that gal."

"I ain't got all night."

"Fine. I always suspected that Chuck gave the document to Frank. I'll bet he slipped it to him one night at the Pit Stop after I left. Those bastards, I never did trust them when they were drink—"

"Gimme a break," Manny said.

The mayor's eyes were bloodshot, and it looked like he had puked on his shirt.

"Dammit," Manny said with a sigh. Now he felt sorry for *both* of them. The mayor was barely sober enough to stand, let alone get to the son-of-a-bitching point. "Amos," he said, gentler now.

The mayor turned away, embarrassed. "Don't! I don't want to hear it."

Manny spat chewing tobacco on the pavement. He didn't want to hear it either. He was worn out by too much human contact for one day. He should get in his truck, head for the woods, and hibernate forever. Store up all that godforsaken human contact, break it down into unwanted fiber, and pass it once and for all while he slept, completely unfazed. He opened the door to his truck, pausing to unwrap the paper funnel Chylak had given him containing the peculiar pills. It was some kind of makeshift psychiatric evaluation on which the shrink had written "Passed."

"Wait," Amos said, grabbing Manny's arm.

"Get off of me, old man!" Manny barked, waving the paper in Amos's face. "I don't need you anymore! You see this?" He climbed into the truck and revved the engine.

Amos stuck a fist inside the window before Manny could roll it all the way up.

"I *know* where it is!" Amos said.

Manny paused, his foot on the brake. The mayor's hand was turning purple, trapped in the window. He thought about driving off, ripping it clean from its socket and taking it home to mount beside his dartboard like a trophy, a reminder that he didn't belong to *anyone* anymore. But he wanted to know. He wanted to know so badly that he savored it, the anticipation. He could sit there all night waiting for that hand to turn black. Quiet, boy, he thought, closing his eyes and taking a long, deep breath. *Stay cool.* He willed himself to turn off the engine and unroll the window to release the mayor's hand.

Amos eyed him with caution, rubbing his fist and stepping back away from the truck as Manny climbed out and faced him, like soldiers on opposing sides of a war, the last men standing: enemies forced to decide in a matter of seconds whether to hug each other or shoot.

"Now that's better," Amos said. "Just hear me out. Dusty never opened the book. She said she couldn't stand the sight of it because it was what Frank was holding when he died. And Chuck told us the rest, you remember, before he died. She called him the night Frank croaked and he took it from Frank. He never goddamned destroyed it, that liar. I know he told us that in the hospital, but I guess I didn't want to believe it. Until it turned up at his funeral. And Daulton buried it with him."

"But, he *didn't.*"

"You were there! You saw!"

"Yeah, and I was there last night too and I didn't see *shit.*"

"Well, someone obviously went back for it! I don't know when, but I know *who*."

Manny stared at him, waiting.

"Duke," Amos said.

"Now I *know* you're sloshed." Manny wished he had stayed in the truck and slammed on the gas. He pointed a finger just inches from Amos's nose. "Don't you goddamn blame him, do you hear me?" He was surprised by the conviction with which he said it. Those old loyalties were tightening again.

Amos stepped back too quickly, falling against the side of his cart. His knees went slack and he slumped, defeated, to the ground. Manny despised himself for every step he took toward the old man, for propping him up and setting him back on his feet. "Take it easy, Amos," he said. Why was he letting himself get sucked into this bullshit again? He wanted it to end, right now, all twenty-two years of it. "I don't want this anymore. I can't—"

"I know that, boy," Amos said, allowing himself to be propped upright. "I don't want it anymore either."

Manny wanted to believe him. If he didn't know better, he would even say Amos looked sorry. He leaned the mayor against the golf cart, limp as a rag doll.

"This is your deal, Amos. *Yours*. It was from the start."

But it was Manny's fault too and he knew it. It was his fault for being young, naïve, and stupid enough, once upon a time, to think legends counted for crap in the real world, which was as jaded and tired and mean as they come.

"What do you want from me now? You know where that book is. Town Library! Honus said so last night. You swore you were gonna get it out of there and leave me out of this!"

"I did, I mean I tried," said Amos. "I searched all night. I'm telling you it wasn't there! But then I realized something. We misunderstood Honus."

Manny's mind was racing. He thought back to the previous night, trying to piece it all together. "What do you *mean*? What do you mean you returned it?" Amos had shouted, shaking Honus by the shoulders. Manny had stood by his side, yelling for him to quit it because people were filing out of the courthouse, and were beginning to stare.

Manny had convinced himself for so long that he would be ready for this moment if it ever arrived, knowing one day it would, and now wishing it would hurry up, just explode regardless of the casualties, even if he was among them. "What . . . did . . . Honus . . . *do* . . . with it, Amos?" he asked, prolonging each word as he grabbed the drunken old man by the collar.

Amos was too tired to be scared. "It *is* in the library," he said, so quietly that Manny had to lean in close and inhale his boozy breath to hear. The mayor's head hung down so his chin was nearly touching his chest.

Manny shook him again, violently, shouting, "Don't you pass out on me!" He knew Amos, who was in dire need of a cold shower and a hot cup of coffee, would have to walk home or sleep in the parking lot, unable to risk the loss of his cart or his reputation with a DWI, particularly with all the press in town for Hall of Fame Weekend. For both their sakes he should offer him a ride, force him into the truck, take him to Chuck's cottage, and lock him in there like a badly behaved puppy—rub his face in the scene of the crime until he realized the error of his ways. But he couldn't. He couldn't move. He was frozen, rendered as speechless as Cartwright, when Amos lifted his head and whispered, "The *Baseball* Library."

"Jesus."

"I told you it was worse than we thought," Amos drawled, taking a swig of bourbon.

Manny caught him before he fell, dragging him to the truck. He opened the back and pushed him inside. Amos passed out cold, his head landing with a thud on a half-empty bag of soil. Manny slammed the tail shut, then went around to the driver's seat and climbed in. He eyed the doctor's evaluation on the seat beside him, shoved it into the glove compartment with the letters from Ruby's lawyers, and peeled out of the parking lot.

He flew down River Street, panicking when he passed the stone bridge. *"Don't! Don't drop me!"* the boy inside him, the lion cub, screamed. He made a sharp left onto Lake Street, nearly driving the truck, himself, and the mayor straight into the lake. He didn't know where he was going. He had to think fast. Maybe he should swing by *The Journal* to see if Daulton was working late. He could surprise him—apologize—but where to begin? Their relationship was over now, permanently damaged, and he couldn't blame Daulton. The only person he could blame was himself. Then he remembered the old man passed out in the back of his truck and decided he'd rather blame him. He could confide in Daulton just like he used to. Tell him everything, the whole story from the beginning! Daulton would print it up in the paper, and then it would be over. He would be free. The lion would sleep. But Daulton had printed that cruel piece about him crapping on the courthouse steps. Maybe he should just crack Daulton over the head with a rifle butt, to buy himself time while he figured out what to do. The mayor was out of it. It was up to him now. If Daulton got wind of what was in that book, he was bound to do some digging on his own. Manny would sit back and wait. Let the enemy come to him. This was personal now, all the way around.

He slammed on the brakes, turning a sharp left toward Main Street, then drove to Cooper Park. If Daulton stuck around and started snooping, the trail would eventually lead here, to the Baseball Library. At least if what Amos said was true. And there was no telling what Bobby knew. Worse, what she would *do* if she realized what she had in her hands. Bobby epitomized the self-professed cage dwellers Manny despised. He couldn't let her do it. He couldn't let her take them all down.

He glanced in the back of his truck, realizing now which side he was on: the wrong side, but perhaps that's where he had always been, where he belonged. He couldn't let all of this, his past, be for nothing. He had sacrificed too much. He never meant to hurt Ruby, or Coach either. And he didn't think it was possible that Coach had ever meant to hurt him. Cartwright wasn't a liar. He wasn't a thief. Manny just hoped Daulton wasn't stupid enough to fall for whatever crazy ideas Bobby got if she found that book, to use his own people to get ahead. Daulton was sitting on a career maker now. If he sniffed around enough, he was liable to scoop one of the greatest tell-alls in American sports history: Cooperstown was a cool myth based on hot air.

Manny relaxed, lifting his foot off the gas as the truck purred to a standstill in front of the Baseball Library. It was closed. It was late. He tried to remember where Bobby lived, laughing loud enough to make the mayor stir, because what was he going to do, *kill* her? Burn down the library? He reached out the window to finger the straps holding the rifles on the roof of his truck. He eyed the snoozing mayor and knew there was only one option left. He hated to admit it, but it might even be fun. He could do it. He could sacrifice himself one last time. He'd do Amos one last favor. But he'd do it on behalf of Coach, Chuck, and his boys, and for the innocent boy he'd once been. He revved the engine and backed up away from the building. Then sped out of the park down Main Street toward East Lake Road.

Daulton was through with baseball stories. He had said as much himself. Even Chuck had said it—Daulton did not have the balls for it. He was too damned timid to even conduct a proper interview. And he sure as hell didn't have the stomach for combat! Surely, somewhere deep inside, he was still his father's son. Manny just hoped that meant he knew where his own loyalties ought to lie. Daulton called him names behind his back: Bumppo, an alienated, ungovernable squatter in a world that increasingly belonged to everyone else. But the truth was, Manny had lived his entire life according to other people's rules, in a hell all his own.

"Let him go!" Cartwright shouted. "He's a helluva ballplayer! Just let him go and if I'm wrong, you won't hear another word from me again!"

Manny pulled into his driveway, thinking that if Daulton broke the story he would break the dam. Then maybe Manny—

unlike certain other folks in town who longed to get out—would finally be let back in. He sat in the truck, facing the lake, the sound of the idling engine calming his nerves. He peered through the windshield at his mountain, his Sleeping Lion. "Time to wake up, old boy," he said, stepping out of the cab and into the crisp evening air.

He removed the rifles from the roof of his truck one by one and laid them on the ground. Then he dragged the mayor from the back of the vehicle and laid him beside them. He loaded a rifle and aimed it at the unconscious man, cocking the trigger. Then he lifted the weapon quickly away, sending a silent shot over the water toward the mountain. "Pow," he said, with a smile.

The battle had begun.

EXTRA INNING: TEN

It's like you came to a controversy and a ball game breaks out.
—MATT KEOUGH

Chylak had fallen asleep and was dreaming about umpires. With only a vague sense of what umpires *looked* like, his subconscious took certain liberties. His ump was garbed in a straitjacket of bedsheets depicting scenes from *Battlestar Galactica;* on his head he wore a baseball cap with a sprig of turnip leaf behind one ear like a plume. He read from a stone tablet, some newfangled version of the Ten Commandments, while Chylak urgently explained that he didn't have time for all that: he had to get inside the room labeled HEAVE (or was it HEAVEN?—it was difficult to tell from the ostentatious script), because he was due to meet Babe inside for supper in ten minutes.

He rubbed his eyes and looked around the room. He was in his office. A glance at the clock revealed it had been a rather long nap. He stretched life back into his limbs, reaching for the citrus-flavored bicarbonate, Mello Yello, that sat on his desk. Alice had assured him that it was tastier than Tang. He glanced at the list he now blamed for having knocked the consciousness right out of him: Ford C. Frick's *The 10 Commandments of Umpiring,* which the mayor had swiped from a thirty-year-old copy of *Baseball Digest* he had found at the Baseball Library. He loaned it to Chylak "in case we need an extra ump for the game."

Chylak had been firm, explaining that he preferred to watch the Town versus State game, having never played baseball himself and not being at all the dexterous type. But the mayor said that was what umpires did: they watched. Chylak promised to think about it, and the more he did so, the more certain he was that his initial prognosis was correct: it was a terrible idea. The mayor's entire *plan* was terrible: Cooperstown playing the state of New York to see who got their way with the theme park? Then again, some good old-fashioned exercise might be the key to releasing the aggression building up to a precarious boil on both sides of the conflict.

He flipped through the book in case the mayor quizzed him on it later. At least he could say he had tried. The very notion of commandments gave him the uneasy sense that he was slowly being sucked into a hazardous cult. Commandment number one said, "Keep your eye on the ball," proving his theory that baseball wasn't a game for people with astigmatism. Commandment number two was a goodie, "Keep all your personalities out of your work." Chylak was certain he could do that, though he couldn't say the same for some of his patients. Commandment three said, "Avoid sarcasm. Don't insist on the last word." Babe said he was prone to sarcasm, but as a rule he avoided having the last word. There was too much pressure in it. He was, however, guilty of part of commandment four, "Never charge a player." After all, he had charged half of Team Cooperstown. Or did Frick mean to charge like a bull?

He skipped down to number five, "Hear only the things you should hear—be deaf to others." He was certain he could handle that one, as well as keep his temper, watch his language, and, under the right circumstances, take pride in his work, in accordance with the next three commandments. Number nine began with the suggestion "Review your work," which he would rather *not* do, followed by "You will find, if you are honest, that 90% of the trouble is traceable to loafing."

Chylak removed his feet from his desk and wiped away the spittle that had congealed in one corner of his mouth during his nap—no loafing here. In fact, he had taken a rather vigorous stroll downtown at lunchtime. There was no place to buy lunch, however. Main Street had looked like an abandoned movie lot—

not a soul in sight, aside from tourists who wandered zombie-like, as confounded as him. Several of them demanded to know why everything was closed on a Saturday. They were, of course, unaware that the townsfolk were preparing for a shoot-'em-out against the state the following morning at Doubleday Field.

Why was it that whenever Chylak left his office lately, Cooperstown seemed to change? He'd come here to escape that sort of thing. The physical village was as fickle as its inhabitants. One minute there were full-on fanatical fetes and the next the town was asleep. The shops were abandoned, the signs in their windows stating SORRY, CLOSED INDEFINITELY. One or two of them even took the message into slightly more hostile territory: BEAT IT! said the sign at the entrance to the bakery. Chylak hadn't even been able to find a newspaper. The natives, it seemed, were restless. Every one of them sucked into the mayor's plan, from his patients to the gingerbread men that hung in the bakery window, newly endowed with red cinnamon-dot tongues affixed to their mouths in a way that implied they were protruding at passersby. He wondered how much money the town would lose by closing down for an entire Saturday. The implication was clear: Cooperstown was at war with itself.

When he passed by the Hall of Heroes at lunchtime, Mrs. Paquette had rushed out, nearly knocking him over and claiming she had no time to chat, which was unsettling too. She had an armful of odd baseball uniforms, pink, though it was hard for the visually impaired Chylak to say. She ran toward the mayor's house, dropping one in her haste, and he retrieved it, realizing her frenzy had sprung from the fact that the word *Cooperstown,* stenciled on the back of the uniforms, was misspelled. COPERSTOWN, it read, and Chylak wondered whether that was a more suitable name for the team.

The rest of the townsfolk seemed to have disappeared altogether. He had rapped his knuckles on the bookshop window, seeing a light on, hoping to find someone who could tell him where everyone was. The game was not until tomorrow. He was answered with a tactic he knew well: the drawing of blinds. On his way back to the hospital, a tourist asked him how to find Fair Street. Pleased to be of some use—for the opportunity to play genuine local—he had let the man walk with him. When that question was followed by another, "Why is it called *Fair* Street; is it a baseball reference?" Chylak took Mrs. Paquette's lead and improvised, inventing his own little chunk of Chylakian lore right there on the spot: the street was named after Cooperstown's former, and very well loved, psychiatrist, one Dr. Finnius Fair, who was overcome with dementia paralytica from syphilis in 1862, and had been irreplaceable until recently. The tourist replied in a rather uppity tone that in *his* town of Hershey, Pennsylvania, everything was named for chocolate. Chylak considered shoving him off the sidewalk and was glad, now, in light of Frick's "Keep your temper" commandment, that he had not. Still, it was the first time he had felt an inherent desire to stick up for his town.

He looked out the window at the street sign standing on the corner just yards from his house: FAIR. It was a word he felt should be plucked from the English language altogether. He was tired of people abusing it, of children and wives and patients complaining that life was "unfair." He opened his *Webster's New Universal Unabridged Dictionary,* a transitional tool while he weaned himself, and Elliott, off psychology books, and looked up the word.

> *free from bias, dishonesty, or injustice . . . neither excellent, nor poor; moderately or tolerably good.*

A flip through his etymology guide said "fair" was derivative of some Latin-French mishmash: the selling of animals at market, religious fetes, and the most common use of the word, which did not bear repeating. He marveled at the efficiency of it all. That with this one little word a person could obtain a pet, religion, and justice. "Moderately good" was one thing, he thought, but—as he eyed the ghastly game uniform that had been left on his couch compliments of the mayor—"tolerably good" was something altogether different.

He packed up his briefcase, hoping to grab a quick bite with Babe, to explain a few things from his side, and to talk her into seeing the new Peter Sellers film, *Being There*. It was a slow week at work, with no signs of its improving. Half of his patients had phoned that morning to reschedule their sessions, though none of them had bothered to say for when. Chylak, once more, panicked at the thought that his Cooperstown career could end.

It was a thought that came too soon.

There, out the window, was what, upon first glance, he assumed to be a picket line. Perhaps the mayor had altered his plan and the town was on strike, though none of the folks lined up outside the sanitarium were carrying those nitpicky little picket signs. They were shouting, however, people in jerseys and caps still sporting price tags, which made them look not unlike—

"*Tourists?*"

He stepped into the waiting room.

"What the hell is going on?" he said, despite having just commended himself on passing Frick's commandment number seven: "Watch your language." His secretary, Mrs. Gibs, appeared to be gone, though it was impossible to say for sure, as the waiting room was packed full of bodies vying for seats, magazines, and Tang.

"The spare filter is empty," said a fellow in a Pete Rose T-shirt.

A befuddled Chylak offered him the remainder of his Mello Yello. A Japanese fellow in a Sadaharu Oh Yomiuri Giants jersey rolled his eyes and said Cooperstown was "overrated."

Who *were* these people? What on earth did they want? What were the odds that so many people could be simultaneously lost? Chylak held up a finger to shush the crowd. "Just a sec," he said, then ran back into his office and locked the door.

He pinched himself. Good, he was awake. There was the Frick list right where he had left it. His intercom, apropos of his daily napping ritual, was turned off. He had forgotten to plug the phone cord back in its jack. He plunked down onto the couch, struggling to come up with an explanation, or a solution, to the phenomenon that awaited him in the other room. He was about to call Mrs. Gibs at home and scold her for a rather unprofessional early departure. But there she was outside now, shouting at people to form a line and take a number. "The doctor will see you shortly!"

A *number?* How many of them were there? Chylak glanced at the door and thought better of it, then climbed out the window, landing on the grass with a thud. He lost a shoe in the process and looked at his feet—the other shoe felt strangely snug.

"What *is* this?" he asked, picking up his shoe and escorting Mrs. Gibs by the elbow brusquely across the street to his house, where yet another crowd milled.

"It's a bedroom slipper."

That wasn't what Chylak meant, but he saw that he indeed held a slipper and that his other, snugger shoe was a penny loafer.

"I just assumed you were one of those eccentrics."

Chylak wasn't listening. He hopped over to a woman waving a piece of paper in the air as though she had just won the lottery. He snatched it out of her hands, gasping when he read it. "Eighty-seven? Eighty-seven people?"

Mrs. Gibs confessed she had been forced to give out numbers because it was "difficult to say who is next."

"*Next?*" Chylak asked, to which she explained that yes, what did you know? He had had so many cancellations that week and then all of a sudden, just look at all these patients!

"*Patients?!*" Chylak shouted, less out of anger than because it was difficult to hear above the din of the crowd. A radio was blasting Melissa Manchester's "Don't Cry Out Loud." Upon closer examination, he saw it was the "ghetto blaster" he bought Alice as part of her enjoy-your-new-school bribery package before they had moved. He had not seen it since the Walkman entered their lives, enslaving his daughter. People were singing along to the music, picnicking as they waited on his lawn.

"These are not *patients!*" he shouted. "They're, they're—"

He was about to say "tourists" when one rather tiny day-tripper looked at him with such longing—that same puppy-dog face Elliott used when trying to convince someone he would die of schizophrenia if he didn't get his way. The child looked so helpless, so hopeful.

"You're number ninety-one!" Mrs. Gibs said cheerily to a young man in an Oakland jersey.

Ninety-one? Ninety-one people there to see *him?* Chylak took a moment to gather his thoughts. Downtown was closed and it was the busiest weekend of the year. Perhaps this was some kind of epidemic, which he was not qualified to handle. If he wasn't good with people one-on-one, he *certainly* wasn't good with oodles of them! These people had come to see a game. They expected to shop and to hit the museums! They had come so far; weary pilgrims having at last reached their mecca only to find it was closed for repairs.

He gasped as Mrs. Gibs scribbled "105" on the palm of a girl with an I ♥ GEORGE BRETT tank top. "I ran out of paper," she said, turning the radio toward the street so more people could hear it—*Don't cry out loud. Just keep it inside and learn how to hide your feelings.*

Babe came out of the house wearing a wide-legged peach pantsuit and nearly tripped over the radio. Chylak's jaw dropped when he saw that she was carrying a sandwich tray. "You had the veggie delight?" she said to one tourist in a voice that implied not only was this not her *first* round with the tray, but she was enjoying catering to these people! Alice followed behind with a pitcher of lemonade and a stack of plastic cups.

Chylak opened his mouth to assure them that he had nothing to do with this scheduling crisis, and that he couldn't possibly be home in time for dinner, *ever.* But nothing came out.

"I tried to wake you," Mrs. Gibs said as Babe led him toward the steps, urging him to sit. His legs felt flimsy, and it was difficult to keep hopping about on one foot. "But you looked so tired. And I was sure I could handle it. They have nowhere to go, the poor dears. Just look at them! One or two at first seemed all right."

"One or *two?*"

"Oh dear," she murmured in a guilty little voice.

The line went all the way to the end of the block.

"They do seem to be multiplying, don't they?" Mrs. Gibs said.

"I'm sorry about this," Chylak told Babe. "I swear I don't know how—"

"It's fine," she said. "Here!"

Chylak bit into a sandwich, wondering what to say to her, how he could possibly handle this wild bunch of—

"Turkey?" He looked up at her, shocked.

"What can I say? I ran out of barley burgers."

"But you hate meat!"

"I don't hate it. I just don't think it's healthy. And I had to give them *something.* Some of them have been here for over an hour! We tried calling you. Alice even went round to knock on your window. You were out cold. You really ought to pace yourself better, Kerwin."

Pace himself? Did she think this was all in a workday?

Alice handed him some lemonade. "This is neato, Dad!" she said.

Chylak looked from his wife to his daughter to his secretary and back.

"But you *hate* meat," was all he could think to say.

"And *youuu* love it," Babe chirped, giving him a proud peck on the cheek as though he were finally about to embark on something worthy of Almighty praise. She gestured for him to hurry up and finish eating so he could get to work. Alice and Mrs. Gibs both complied with a thumbs-up. Then the three of them returned to their self-appointed roles of caterer, beverage girl, and ticket taker.

Chylak slipped on his bedroom slipper and shuffled across the street, glancing back twice with a hangdog expression to see if he might be let off the hook. Did they actually expect him to *help* these people? He stepped on a STAR-EYED FOR STARGELL button and then bit into a second sandwich.

Baloney!

A MOS TRIED ON HIS uniform for the third time. Dusty had ordered the wrong size and, flattering as that was, he was going to have a hell of a time catching in it. He unbuckled his mask and removed his mitt, one used by Yogi Berra during Don Larsen's perfect game in '56, the year before Amos's life went sour. He had "borrowed" it from the Hall of Fame, hoping it would bring him good luck. He hummed Fred Fisher's "I Can't Get to First Base Without You," a song cowritten for Lou Gehrig with Gehrig's wife, while thinking about Dusty.

He had talked her into playing first base, thinking it was unlikely that anyone on the state team would be able to run very far; they were bound to be a bunch of stodgy old politicians, which was why he had decided to make himself catcher. He had to be part of the game. If necessary, he would get himself a pinch runner, and a pinch hitter, and a pinch Geritol-sipper if things got too tough. Amos had been stone-cold sober since his slip the other night. He hardly remembered confronting Barrett, drunk, in the hospital parking lot. He had spent the night on Manny's couch. Dr. Chylak had heard about it and had upped his sessions to twice weekly. The doc had also donated a container of Tang to the sobriety cause. Now, if Amos's knees would just hold up, he was sure he could crouch comfortably behind home plate for as long as was necessary, and as clean as a church warden. He was certain the game would be won by Cooperstown on passion alone.

He squatted, stretching the uniform to see if the legs would allow for a little more give. It was a one-piece number, which made it difficult to stretch one's legs without ripping one's seat, if one was hefty. Not to mention the dilemma of *relieving* oneself in a hurry. The color, however, was eye-catching. Orange zest,

Dusty called it. Amos had left the uniform ordering to her, it all being so last-minute, and she had once again taken his suggestion to be creative too far, convincing the laundress at the jail to loan her prison uniforms. Cooperstown was short on criminals, so there were plenty to spare. The few it did have would be let out for the game tomorrow to sit in the bleachers, on three conditions: that they were not to pickpocket unsuspecting tourists, that they cheer loudly for Team Cooperstown, and that they paint their faces orange in accordance with the colors of the home team. The game was at two o'clock tomorrow—Amos's plan, his brilliant idea. Johnny's one condition was that if Cooperstown lost, Amos would step down as mayor. Amos had complied, certain that wouldn't be necessary. Johnny hadn't offered an explanation as to *why* he was giving the townsfolk this chance, aside from wanting to play fair.

Amos was proud of his team, of the way his people had eventually rallied around him at the town meeting. Manny's presence had inspired them, which is exactly what he had hoped for. He just didn't think Manny would actually show up. And once he got their attention away from Barrett and back onto him, they took a vote. The majority of the townsfolk were pro game. Suddenly people were volunteering to pitch in, and some even to *pitch*. Mrs. Coxey had won that role, despite her hand tremor, for she'd played softball in her youth and claimed to be quite good. "What the hell," Amos had said, enthusiastically doling out field positions to whoever seemed the most sincere. The game would not require skill so much as chutzpah. Whether it was on the field or in the stands, everyone was doing his or her part. It was going to be a sensation, a real spectacle! Cooperstown's residents were born and bred in the heart of baseball. And on the off chance they lost, Amos had come to terms, that night in the parking lot, with the fact that his job here was nearly done. With Manny back in the picture, whoever had that document could be bullied into handing it over and keeping it mum.

Part two of Amos's plan was to ask Dusty out on a date. He'd promised to take her to dinner after they won. He even gave some thought to asking her to travel with him in the fall, maybe take a vacation to someplace exotic. The Poconos, perhaps.

He looked up from his porch to see the state's team parading down Main Street, fresh from batting practice at Doubleday Field. Each team was allowed two practices before the big game, but Johnny had set strict rules that they were not to interact before then. Now Amos knew why. His heart sank. There wasn't an old, pudgy, stodgy politician among them! These were trim young bucks, and he recognized more than one of them from the Yankees' local farm team. Johnny, that son-of-a-bitching cheater! He had probably promised them tax cuts, or free year-round passes to the unspeakable theme park.

"Play fair, my keester!" Amos shouted, waving his catcher's mask at them. He sank into his armchair; it would take too long to reschedule the game. All of the tourists, the *reporters* were in town. He consoled himself with the idea that Team Coopers-town could win on sheer adrenaline. Like Dusty said, they had more inspiring uniforms. If only they had Manny.

Amos sighed and went inside to practice his speech, the one he would give on the steps of the Hall of Fame after his victory, the same steps where, forty years ago, baseball's first commis-sioner, Judge Kenesaw Mountain Landis, stood saying, "I should like to dedicate this museum to all America." Remembering that day gave Amos a sense of empowerment. However, it was noth-ing compared to the thrill he had felt upon phoning the owners of the two major-league teams that were scheduled to play the thirty-seventh annual Hall of Fame Game—the Texas Rangers and the San Diego Padres. "Boys?" he had said. "We don't need you this year. Cooperstown has got its bases covered." Normally, the Hall of Fame Game took place the day after the induction ceremony, but with that out of the way, Amos had time to pre-pare for his own game, and there wasn't much time.

Dusty said his speech needed editing, along with his diary. He meant to ask how she knew so much about his diary, but she was so perceptive she could probably read his mind. With Martha, he always had to explain himself, which was difficult to do when he had one interpretation and bourbon had another. Martha didn't understand the importance of recording one's thoughts. She wasn't like James Fenimore Cooper's wife, who people said had encouraged him to write. Amos wouldn't need a diary after tomorrow anyway. His victory was bound to stir up interest in publishing his memoirs.

He reached, out of habit, for the key that once hung from his neck, recalling Mays's speech at the induction ceremony: "How can you put it on paper, that's my theme. You cannot do it . . . how can you tell these young people what I did over twenty-two years . . . I gave my life . . ."

With the Baseball Library closed for the day, Amos was able to search for the book containing the document in peace. He had finagled the keys from Bobby, unable to tell whether she knew why he needed them. His mission, his search, was unsuccessful, but it wouldn't matter after tomorrow. Tomorrow would prove who loved baseball the most and who got to say how and where it should be enshrined, which wasn't through some damned amusement park. He thought back to the other night, to awakening hungover at Manny's cabin. Manny hadn't said a word. Maybe Amos couldn't count on Manny for shit anymore, or Duke, but Chuck and Frank would be there in spirit. The past would soon be erased by Amos's triumph, all transgressions absolved.

He got to work on his speech, thinking the godforsaken document had waited twenty-two years. It could wait one more night. He read aloud with bravado, "To me, home plate represents birth, childhood, a place one longs to return to, *safe*. And first base is the teenage years—not too far from home, but far enough." Maybe he would grab the nearest kid, put his arm around him, and tousle his hair for effect.

"Second base," he continued, clearing his throat and struggling to make out Dusty's edits, which were scrawled in red lip liner, "second base is like adulthood: you're in the base path, waiting to make your move, to take off running as soon as you get the chance." He would pause there, maybe even look at Johnny, depending on how Johnny handled being a loser. "Third base," he continued, "is the descent into ripe old age . . ."

Amos put down his notes, annoyed at the direction in which Dusty's edits were taking his speech. There was nothing ripe about being old! It was downright rotten, in fact—people assuming you had lost your wits and couldn't handle things as efficiently as you used to. Besides, if home plate was birth in paragraph one and its opposite in paragraph three, that was like saying you were stillborn. What was the point of running yourself silly around the bases of life just to end up back where you started? He crumpled his notes, determined to make something up on the spot, in the heat of victory.

"Grab his ankle, Amos! His shoe's comin' off! It ain't worth it—we don't want blood on our hands."

Amos stared at a photograph of him and his boys, trying not to think about that day with Manny on the bridge. He jumped when the frame was knocked facedown by wind banging his shutters. He closed the window, praying the weather would hold and the game would not be rained out.

He held the picture in his hands, remembering well the day it was taken. It was the summer of '39, the summer of the baseball centennial when he got to meet Ty Cobb. In it, Amos, Frank, Chuck, and Duke stood on the stone bridge, smiling, with their arms around one another like they were on top of the world. Amos shuddered, recalling how Frank had nearly busted his neck jumping off the bridge and into the Susquehanna. He said it was a good thing he had not died, or Dusty would not forgive him for not taking her to see *Gone with the Wind*. Then Duke had asked, "What do you boys make of that Stotz fellow in Pennsylvania? You hear about this new Little League for the kiddies? I think it's just dandy! Get it, 'cause they're *little?*" From there, the conversation had run from the World's Fair to the war in Europe to Lou

Gehrig getting his uniform number retired, and somewhere in the middle the four of them stood on that bridge without a care in the world, Chuck smiling from ear to ear; it was the day his son was born. Over and over he sang that Bing Crosby song—*"Go fly a kite and you'll imagine you're a king. 'Cause you've got your world on a piece of string!"* Duke knocked his fedora off and into the river. Frank volunteered to go after it, swinging like Tarzan from the rope they had tied to a tree on the riverbank. He was laughing as he flew through the air, teasing Duke, who had finally gotten to cop a feel of those new nylon stockings all the ladies were wearing.

Amos shivered, turning the photograph facedown on the table. He remembered how Frank had stood waist-deep in the cold river, his lips blue as a ghoul's, saying, "Couldn't you just *die* here? Couldn't you just hang around in Cooperstown forever?" Amos wished he could go back there right now. He wished he could return to a time before his paradise was overcome with weeds. Before Frank died, before the once outspoken Duke stopped speaking, and before they banished Manny to the woods. Back to when Chuck's heart was strong and his reporter son was just an infant, a harmless babe. What Amos wouldn't give to have them all back together again for tomorrow's game: the last of the Mohicans alive and ready for one final inning! Chuck would have written him a great victory speech, and Frank would have made a real fine pitcher. Amos just hoped he could get Duke off his bike and onto the outfield long enough to play center field.

He decided to keep it simple, to open his speech with, "Ted Williams said 'they invented the all-star game for Willie Mays,'" and let the press take it from there. Let them fill in the blanks about how he was an all-star mayor while he rode the momentum to glory. Someone would likely suggest naming a new wing of the Hall of Fame after him.

He removed his "Coperstown" cap and tried on his mask once more. Eyes closed, he willed away the tension that had been building throughout the summer in his shoulders and neck, grateful for the future, for a day when people would finally pay tribute to him.

Amos opened his eyes to see the case of bourbon he planned to donate to the Venerable Veterans Powwow glaring at him. It occurred to him that Cooperstown *had* to win tomorrow or he would look like a damned fool. He fought the urge to crack open a bottle. Grabbing the photograph, he looked them straight in the eyes—Frank, Chuck, Duke, and his young self—as though to cull from them strength, approval, the assurance that he was doing the right thing. And that he had done so from the start. They had all spent so much time trying to outdo one another. People didn't understand it. But it had only ever made him want to better himself. Maybe he *was* trying to prove something, but he would be damned if he would outdo a heart attack and a hanging to do it. A little sportsmanship was all that was required, that and some good old-fashioned wiles. Like Cobb, he would throw right and bat left. He could do anything. He might be second to Judge Cooper, to Abner Doubleday, and even to the man he should have been, but history would pardon him. Of that he was certain.

He took out his diary and penned his last entry as a loser.

> 11:37 pm. I awoke at five this morning to hear a mourning dove sing—COO COO. The seasons are changing. I resurrected the ginkgo tree in front of the Hall of Fame. People said it was DEAD. The Bible says, "This is the day the Lord has made." So be it.

There was a loud thud on the porch.

Amos went to explore. There was no one there, the streets were empty, but a large box had been dumped in front of his door. Inside it was Rawling's usual donation of balls for the expected big game, plus scorecards for the fans. He picked up a handful of Cooperstown pendants "compliments of the Hall of Fame."

"Honus?" he said, looking around. The pendants must be an

apology for the other night, for Honus messing with the whereabouts of that book. Amos smiled. He could always make room for new boys.

Much of what was in the box was dirty, covered in rubbing mud that had been shipped from New Jersey to dull the shine of the game balls according to major-league standards, as was traditional. The bag containing the mud had busted open, which seemed like a portent, and Amos began to doubt himself and his team. But then Duke rode by on his bike, tooting his horn three times, a gesture Amos interpreted to mean, "Let's give 'em hell!"

T HE GAME GOT OFF to a slow start. Fortunately, there were plenty of distractions, such as Cooperstown High's perky cheerleaders and enthusiastic marching band. Cooperstown took the lead in the second inning: 2–0—one earned run and one unearned. By the third inning, they were ahead by three.

Mrs. Coxey's weak grip was an asset when it came to throwing her assortment of off-speed pitches. She got several of State's sluggers to chase junk on the outside corner. She also threw a couple in the dirt and shook off a peeved Amos twice. He had failed to heed Chylak's warning that he might suffer from delirium tremens due to going cold turkey off booze, so it took a while for the two of them to get their signs straight. Cooperstown carried a 4–0 lead into the fourth before State finally broke through. With a runner on second and one out, State's third baseman, Johnny Fusselback, lined a one-one pitch to right, breaking up Coxey's shutout. By the top of the fifth it was 4–1, Cooperstown.

Daulton zoned out during the sixth inning. He wished he had sat in the press box with the rest of the reporters. Sister Sledge was giving him a headache. Every time Cooperstown was up, "We Are Family" came blasting throughout the park, a tactic borrowed from the Pittsburgh Pirates and meant to intimidate State with a show of solidarity. The bleachers—front row, right field near the exit in case he chickened out and decided to leave early—were cramped. The stands held ten thousand people and were packed, which wasn't unusual for a Hall of Fame Game, but the difference this year was that Cooperstown's residents were in full swing, and this was no Hall of Fame Game. Still, some people were calling it the Game of the Year. There was the usual handful of celebrities in town who had stayed on despite the cancellation of the regular game. Daulton spotted the guy from *Mork & Mindy,* and behind him sat a young comedian, Billy somebody whom he recognized from *Soap* and a fleeting TV show he had caught last fall: *I'm a Celebrity '78.* It was an absurd premise: real-life celebrities struggling to survive in the Australian wild, including Joan Rivers, William Shatner, and Loretta Swit. Crystal, that was the actor's name! Daulton turned around and asked him to stop kicking the back of his seat. The man apologized and then began singing along with Sister Sledge in a thick Long Island accent.

Daulton looked over at the press box, which was surprisingly full. Several reporters from nearby towns had turned up expecting the usual major-league goodwill spectacle and stuck around once they got wind of the political battle that had replaced it. Word had spread across the county, then across the state, attracting journalists from all walks of life. He even noticed a few from out of state. In Daulton's opinion, the draw of the game was the feel-good angle: "Underdog Coop's Coup Against State!" Or, "Small Town Goes to Bat Against State's Big Balls!" At least that would be the spin if he had a mind to write that type of story, which he didn't. It wasn't the game he was excited to write about anymore, or the Fusselback family saga. There was a much bigger story out there waiting to break. Besides, headlines like that implied Cooperstown was a winner. Even if they won the game, Daulton knew better. His angle was groundbreaking.

He reached inside his knapsack, feeling around for the book Bobby had given him. It seemed fitting that Cooperstown would be the catalyst to finally break his ties with baseball. He felt exhilarated, nervous, and a touch duplicitous, knowing the document at the heart of his story was right there in his bag in a ballpark full of unsuspecting spectators. He closed his eyes, drowning out the crowd, imagining that he could cull Chuck's strength through its pages. It gave him confidence. He'd found a way to please both father and son. Of course, he would have to destroy everything Chuck had ever believed in to do it.

He scoured the crowd, trying to erase the image of Chuck in the outfield shaking his fist. He wondered if Cooper senior had ever warned *his* son not to poke around in his affairs, and if he had, had Cooper junior listened? Bobby had said that when she was working at Town Library, she took a fancy to Cooper's *Home as Found,* a satire about his father's town. Daulton had never heard of it but thought it ballsy of him. Screw it, he decided, eyeing the knapsack. Didn't people know if you told a kid not to do something, he would do it the moment you turned your back? He consoled himself with the promise that if there *were* an afterlife, he would explain his intentions to Chuck when he got there. How he had thought it through a hundred times and the result was always the same: he didn't have a choice. He had to open the Pandora's box he now suspected had helped kill his father. *The Journal* was paying him to reveal facts, to expose truths. History had done a three-sixty, was all—it was time to rebuild civilization as Cooperstown knew it. The process was inevitable: what goes around comes around.

State was coming to the plate in the top of the seventh, trailing 2–4. Mrs. Coxey struck out Johnny, which elicited an unsportsmanlike "Wahoo!" from his father; the mayor jumped up from his crouch so quickly that he split his uniform right down the backside.

Daulton spaced out for a while as he sketched out his story in his mind. When the gal beside him jumped, he turned his head toward the parking lot, where there was a loud ruckus—the *Apocalypse Now* soundtrack, Wagner's *Ride of the Valkyries* blasting from a dark pickup truck that screeched to a halt, nearly running down a hot dog vendor. Its driver was laying the fear of God into his horn, shouting at tourists, "Get out of the way! Get out of the way, incoming!" The gun rack on the roof of the truck was strapped full of bats.

"What's going on?" Daulton asked the woman on his right, who shrugged and motioned to the scoreboard. It was the eighth inning: 5–3. Cooperstown was ahead until Al Moroni, one of Johnny's henchmen and a State batter, hit one out of the park. Mrs. Paquette was playing first, right there where she could get in on all of the action. Bobby played second. Daulton had tried to talk her out of it. It seemed like Bobby derived some kind of sick pleasure from playing for the home team, knowing that she would be partly responsible for its demise come morning when his story broke. He thought about *Uncle Charlie,* the stone giant stored at the Farm Stead, and of how Frank Paquette used to bastardize local lore to get more bang from the tourists' bucks. What if the document was a *hoax?*

Duke Cartwright rode his bike onto the outfield and was chased by two State players who cursed him for tearing it. They were yelled at by Honus, Cooperstown's shortstop security guard. A group of rough-looking, bare-chested men with orange paint all over their faces were in the bleachers, hooting and hollering for Cooperstown to win. Daulton scanned the field with his binoculars, following Cartwright, whom he had not seen this animated in years. The old man rode around the field waving his fist in the air as though in triumph, shouting toward third base. Daulton zoomed in on third and dropped the binoculars, knocking over his soft drink—*What the hell was Manny doing there?*

He reached for the knapsack to make sure the book wasn't wet. "Shit. Shit," he said, waving a vendor over, wishing he could buy something stronger than Coke and that Chylak was there to give it to him with a handful of tranquilizers in a Tupperware cup. "You seen the doc?" he asked Shane Gregory, who sat beside him. The DA shrugged.

Manny was going to *play?* Part of Daulton, the part still

rooted in the past, was delighted—now *this* would make a great story! But the rest of him felt sick. What if Cooperstown *won?* How could he bring the town to its knees the day after victory, the day after Manny was back among the living? The townspeople would hate him. He regretted not having run his plan by Chylak first. Maybe it was irrational. Maybe he was being paranoid again. He knew Chylak didn't believe him, at first, about seeing Chuck. How he went to break into the cottage the other night to gather Chuck's stuff. But he *had* seen Chuck! Not the living, breathing Chuck, of course, but he had seen his body.

He closed his eyes and took a deep breath. He felt like he was unraveling, faster and faster ever since Bobby had given him the book. "Do what you think is right," she had said. "No pressure." Why did no pressure suddenly feel a hell of a lot like *pressure?*

It was tied going into the ninth. Daulton feared he was having one of his fugues. Things had been foggy since that night. The tranquilizers Chylak gave him weren't cutting it anymore, as if he were immune to them, to anything that could help him keep his head straight. He closed his eyes, thinking back to the town meeting, how he'd run into Bobby afterward at the baseball museum. He went to the cottage after she gave him the book, the last gift Chuck had ever given him. He felt determined to open the cottage and claim the rest of Chuck's things. They might be junk, but they were *his* junk now.

The undertaker was at bat. He swung.

"Foul!" yelled the ump.

Daulton recalled the foul odor that had infused the air as he approached the cottage. The door was open. Someone had beaten it down, beaten him there. He could see them creeping around. The mayor, Manny, and Honus, of all people, were poking around on Chuck's property in the middle of the night, property on which he was buried, and property the mayor had continuously claimed was "inaccessible" until summer's end. Daulton had crouched silently behind an elm tree, watching as they slinked about in the moonlight, shovels in hand, like bandits—*grave* robbers! He watched those bastards and did nothing as they unburied his dad. The cottage had been ransacked. Chuck's baseball cards and research papers were strewn about, boxes and boxes of papers. And that's when Daulton made up his mind. It wasn't the desire to make something of himself, to piss off or please Chuck, or to please Bobby, who had smelled so nice and vowed to stick by him whatever the cost. That's not what drove the story he wanted to break. It was because he had looked at the mess they had made in his childhood home and knew, immediately, that they hadn't found what they were looking for. Because he had it. The book.

That night, Manny kept saying, "This ain't right! This just ain't right!" Amos was upset, shaking Honus by the shoulders and shouting, "What did you mean? You said you *returned* it, what did you mean?" Honus apologized over and over, confused, telling them he meant he had returned the book to the library, *not* to Chuck's grave. He kept blubbering, "I thought it was Frank's! I thought we were digging for worms! You said we were goin' night fishing!" Daulton would have felt sorry for him, but Honus had a shovel in his hand, too. He couldn't see Chuck's body from where he crouched, just the mayor and Manny digging faster and faster like Honus's confession meant nothing. Then he saw the tombstone. DAULTON, it read. And he was glad that he had what they wanted, gladder still for the irrational idea that opening Chuck's coffin would release the tension between them, all that remained unsaid. He felt his father's presence, Chuck changing teams, finally on his son's side. Daulton could almost hear him, lying there pissed off in that cold coffin, whispering, "Now. *Now* you can read it. I trust you, son!"

He glanced at the field and opened his notebook. Chuck wanted a baseball writer for a son, and now he was going to get one.

It was the top of the tenth: 5–5. As Mrs. Coxey grew tired, her pitches began to straighten and State took advantage, turning three singles into the go-ahead run, 6–5. After a brief visit from

Amos, she regained her composure, setting down the next three batters, and kept Cooperstown within striking distance.

Daulton nodded to Dicky Harring, the mailman, who was chatting up the gal who ran the movie theater. They were having a grand old time, oblivious to the fact that the game was now tied. He held the knapsack on his lap, stroking it like a cat, trying to recall the last time he had seen this many Cooperstonians drawn together in one place of their own accord. Then he remembered Chuck's funeral. Seemed like everyone in town had turned up, not to mourn but to celebrate Chuck, as he would've wanted. And on both occasions, then and now, Daulton thought, looking around at all the familiar faces—at the folks he had grown up with, been schooled by, played with, or dated, cheering on their team—every one of them looked as if there were no place else they would rather be.

The bottom of the tenth found Manny, the living legend, on deck, looking formidable. The townsfolk went wild, cheering as he wound his weighted bat faster and faster. He knocked off the donut, strode to the plate, and dug in. He watched the first pitch zip by.

"St-eee-rike!"

Manny casually knocked the dirt from his cleats and awaited the next pitch. He swung, cracking the ball far and wide.

"Foul! Strike two," yelled the ump.

Manny was behind in the count 0–2, which disappointed Daulton despite his desire to remain objective. Bumppo hadn't picked up a bat for over twenty years! He prepared himself for the possibility that watching Manny play ball would be like watching a champion racehorse you once rooted for now reduced to plowing fields.

There was a loud *pop!*

Manny knocked one over the pitcher's head, the ball soaring like a rocket, a beautiful white bird. There was a collective inhalation from the crowd as heads turned, row by row; a wave of anticipation and the ball flew straight toward the top of the wall.

Daulton gasped simultaneously with the crowd, struggling to remember what team he was for—*no team*. It wasn't easy when the ball bounced high off the top of the wall, briefly hanging there before it disappeared over the other side.

"Yes!" he said, jumping out of his seat along with every man, woman, and child around him. He felt a friendly slap on the back and cheered, along with Cooperstown's fans, turning toward the dugout to wave to Bobby, who was staring at him like he'd lost his mind. He sat down quickly, embarrassed, and gathered his composure as Manny ran the bases all the way home and the crowd went ape-shit. Then there was a loud *boom,* a crack like a shot from a cannon, and suddenly what seemed like a hundred blackbirds were flying from the roof of the grandstands over the field to the wall, staining the sky dark in their wake. The next thing Daulton knew Manny was screaming. He was on his knees on home plate, shouting, "Don't do it! Don't drop me! I can't swim!"

There was nervous tittering from the crowd. Daulton waited for Manny to stand and then looked at the sky, expecting lightning to strike down the birds, tiny black carcasses raining onto the field, littering the stands with the empty popcorn containers and half-drunk soda pop. "Do you know what happened?" he asked the gal next to him. "Was that thunder?" If it rained, the game could be postponed, and he wasn't sure he had the guts to sit through it again. But the sky was clear, blue as can be. He cocked his ear to listen again for the boom that had brought Manny to his knees, and was met with stone silence.

The crowd grew hushed, everyone on the edge of their seats, concerned as Ruby ran out onto the field with her hand over her mouth. "Immanuel!" she yelled. "Manny!" She fell to her knees beside home plate, cradling her ex as though he were one of her kids, and then she led him slowly off the field. She was whispering in Manny's ear, something Daulton desperately wished he could hear. "It's all right now!" she yelled. "It's all right, everybody! Show's over!"

The thunder boomed again.

Daulton jumped, startled, and turned toward the parking lot. "For God's sake," he said, relieved. It was just the mayor's golf cart, driven by one of his deputies, backfiring.

Ruby escorted a dazed Manny to the dugout, their arms locked. She sat him down between Bobby and the mayor, and then started smacking him across the head with her purse. Over and over she hit him, screaming, until Bobby pulled her off.

"What is this, the friggin' Keystone Kops?" someone behind Daulton said. He watched as the Cooperstown teammates shoved a recovered Manny from the dugout for a curtain call. The crowd cheered like he was a long lost prisoner of war, a beloved hero, who had finally made his way home.

Daulton looked at the press box, wondering if he could go through with it. He wondered what the other reporters were going to write. The big-league game they had been sent to cover had turned out to be more of a small-time comedy of errors, but none of them seemed to mind. Like the fans, they were enjoying themselves. And from where he sat, it looked like they, too, were rooting for Cooperstown.

After retiring the first two batters in the top of the eleventh, Mrs. Coxey's luck ran dry. Dave Wilbutt, a State slugger, hit a towering, Ruthian shot to dead center, giving State a one-run lead heading into the home half of the inning.

Daulton flinched, pegged in the back of the neck by a peanut. A guy behind him was shouting for the ump to get his glasses fixed because the ball Bobby had just hit had *not* been foul. He watched Bobby swing and took her cue, putting on his best game face. He would do it. He would write the best piece he had ever written. He would tell all, just like he had promised her he would. When people, when *Johnny,* got wind of the beauty in his knapsack, there was bound to be controversy. Cooperstown would become the butt of its own joke. It's the right thing to do, he assured himself, watching Bobby strike out, and the right thing wasn't personal.

He peered through his binoculars at home plate. Amos was pulling Elliott Chylak onto the field, the kid dragging his feet the whole way. The crowd loved it, however. The kid was pinch-hitting for the mayor, who had agreed to come out of the game for the sake of his team—he was shaking too badly to play. The boy tried to run off the field and the crowd ate it up as if everything, his apprehension and Manny's collapse, was all part of the show. Daulton was relieved to see Dr. Chylak was there too, crouching on the sidelines and shouting for Elliott to go ahead and hit the ball. Chylak removed the baseball cap he was wearing—LITHIUM CARBONATE was embroidered across the rim, a gift from a peddling drug rep. Then he tossed it to the boy, yelling, "Hey, kid!" His son grinned from ear to ear.

Daulton gestured for his photographer to take a picture—if he didn't follow protocol people would get suspicious, and it was a great shot. He jotted down more notes for his story, filling a page, then another and another. Chief Bear offered him some popcorn and he felt guilty taking it, wondering if Cooperstown realized how vulnerable it was; the man it depended on to protect it was sitting right there by the knapsack, completely unaware of what was in it.

Elliott bunted and made it to first. Cartwright had groomed the base paths to ensure that Cooperstown's bunts had a better chance of rolling fair. He was back with the bike, rounding the perimeter of the field and shouting, "Bonus baby! Bonus baby!" Some State players ran after him, followed by the prisoners Amos had bribed to sit in the bleachers; they hopped over the barrier and onto the field, now chased by Chief Bear, who accidentally elbowed Daulton in the head as he leapt off the bench. He was shouting for them to make a choice. "Back to your seats or back to your cells!" Daulton chuckled, enjoying the spectacle along with the crowd. He raised his binoculars for a better look and the world went black. A large man loomed above him in the glare of the sun. "Chuck," he whispered, dropping his specs.

Someone laughed. People were staring as if they were waiting for him to make a decision. They were chanting his name, louder and louder, cheering him on like they wanted him to do something. Suddenly there were men on both sides of him, pulling him from his seat, and he panicked, desperate for someone to tell him just exactly what the hell he was being designated to do! The man blocking his view was Mr. Peck, the pharmacist. "You're wanted down there," he said, taking Daulton by the elbow, the DA on the other side of him, pulling him toward the field.

"What?" Daulton lost his grip on the knapsack. "Are you *crazy?*" He wondered if they'd discovered what he and Bobby were up to and if they were taking him behind the stadium to beat him senseless. But Peck motioned toward home plate.

"Oh, no. No, no, no, no!" Daulton yelled, his feet making skid marks as he was dragged across the grass. "You've gotta be kidding me! I don't even know how to play!"

"Terry! Terry!" people were shouting, and at first it did not compute: they were shouting his first name. It had been so long since he had been called anything but Daulton, and it felt pretty damned good.

"Come on," said Mr. Peck. "You're the pinch-hitter!"

"This is insane!"

"We need a warm body and right now Coxey doesn't qualify. Let's move!"

Before Daulton could protest, he was pushed toward the dugout.

"Here's our man!" Amos said. Bobby was beside him. Daulton couldn't tell if the look on her face was one of horror or relief. She looked surprised and then surprised *him* by giving him the okay sign. *What* was okay? What the hell did she mean? Daulton began to sweat. "This ain't right," he said, pleading with his eyes for her to help, to make them stop. They held him down and forced him into a bright orange uniform.

"Don't be such a stick-in-the-mud," Bobby said, pinching his ass.

Before he knew it, Daulton was on the field. He looked at the crowd, then at the scoreboard. The game had run into extra innings, the eleventh, and he feared it was never going to end. The score was 7–6, State: two outs. He was Cooperstown's last best shot, and the irony hadn't escaped him. He considered turning around to punch the mayor, who was now yelling, "Buck up, boy! We need you!" It reminded him of that day at the morgue— Amos shaking Chuck. "Do it for Cooperstown!" Amos yelled, and Daulton held his breath, hoping he wouldn't say it, but he did.

"Do it for Chuck!"

Daulton stood like a dazed rabbit beneath the lights. It seemed as if the entire universe were awaiting his next move. The pressure was unreal. He looked back at Bobby, who held his knapsack—she had gone after it. "Thank God," he said. Then he looked at Manny, in the dugout beside her, and could swear old Bumppo tipped his cap, ever so slightly. Whether it was an illusion, a trick of the lights, or a trick of his mind didn't matter. Not then. Not anymore. It was enough.

"Gimme a goddamned bat," Daulton said.

Until the moment he stepped up to the plate, he wasn't sure if he wanted the bat to smash the lens of the cameraman following his every move from the side of the field or to knock himself unconscious so he could wake up back in Manhattan tomorrow morning and the whole thing—this game, the book, Chuck's death—would all just be a bad dream. He stood on the plate and swung a few times to get the feel of it, just as Manny had. The bat was lighter than he had expected it to be. He looked out at right field, recalling the numerous times that he had stood on this same field as a kid, doing his best to throw decent pitches so Manny could better his swing. What he wouldn't give to be Manny right now. The golden boy. The favorite son.

A round white bullet hurtled toward him, growing bigger and bigger the closer it got; Daulton willed it to hit him. "Faster," he said through gritted teeth. "End this. End this!" He swung, his knees bent and nearly locked together. His back straight and tilted forward. His shoulders set. Elbows up and locked, head turned—everything for once perfectly aligned and then—*bam!*

He hit the ball down the right field line and ran toward first, about to touch the base when the ump shouted, "Foul!" He had bitten his lip when he swung and wiped the back of his hand across his mouth, inspecting it for blood. Then the bullet was back and he swung again, determined now to get it right. He hit a pop foul that was caught by Johnny at third and the ump yelled, "Yooooou're out!"

Daulton didn't hear State's victory cheers, nor did he hear the Cooperstown crowd booing as Johnny led his team around the field; they picked Johnny up and carried him on their shoulders, lapping the perimeter. He didn't hear his own teammates either, shouting for him not to sweat it, that it was a good game. All he heard was that *bam,* that shot over and over in his mind. And when he reached the dugout he looked at them—Manny, Bobby and Chylak, who sat beside his son—and the expression on his face said that he wasn't sorry. And that he wouldn't trade a hundred home runs nor one single sensational story for the feeling that came over him the moment he realized that great smacking sound, that great big *bam* back into place, was coming from him; it wasn't the sound of him cracking up, scattered into pieces like a jumbled-up jigsaw puzzle. It was solid. It was Terry Daulton. Cooperstown had lost, but its prodigal son was back home to give it another swing.

EXTRA INNING: ELEVEN

Eve stole first and Adam second,
St. Peter umpired the game.
Rebecca went to the well with a pitcher,
And Ruth in the field won fame.
Goliath was struck out by David,
A base hit on Abel was made by Cain.
The Prodigal Son made one home run,
And Brother Noah gave out checks for rain.

—ARTHUR LONGBRAKE

Poor Amos." Dusty debated whether to stop by his house after work, fearing she would find him as she had found Frank, hanging from the rafters by his necktie. Then she realized that not only did Amos not wear ties, she would be lucky if she could get him to button his shirts. No matter. There was plenty of time for that sort of thing. She knew Amos well enough to know that he probably did not want to talk anyway. Of course, getting people to talk was her specialty.

Ever since they had shared that kiss at the Hall of Heroes, she had felt shy around Amos. They had both been single for so long and were stubborn and set in their ways. But she feared now that if she didn't make a bold move, that old prune Angela Spitzer would. She wished she had changed out of her purple polka-dotted caftan and into that new dress she had bought upon the recommendation of a woman's magazine that said Japanese designers were going to be the next big thing.

She reached toward the canker on her lip, withdrawing her

hand immediately upon recalling her vow, earlier that day, to Dr. Chylak not to give in to any urges for reassurance about her looks. "No more mirrors for a while," he had said. It was some kind of experimental therapy exercise he said he needed her help with. She just *knew* that man would see the light eventually and ask for her help! He said it would also be helpful if when the Funhouse reopened for business, she would examine herself in its wacky distortion mirrors every day for a week. Dusty didn't need some malicious magic mirror making her look short-limbed and bloated, but she had agreed anyway because she wanted the job: Chylak's secretary had quit, complaining the patient load was too much. "Way, *way* too much," were her exact words to Dusty, who had called her up and interrogated her the moment she heard.

Having decided to quit the wax museum, Dusty pounced on the opportunity to fill Mrs. Gibs's shoes. Chylak agreed to give her a trial run, as long as she understood that anything she saw or heard in his office was strictly confidential. He did not say anything about reading his notes, however, so Dusty figured she could Xerox them to read in the privacy of her own "office" later.

She removed the GIT! sign she had hung from Babe Ruth's neck while trying to repair Team "Coperstown"'s uniforms. Amos was upset about the misspelling until she told him "Coperstown" was French and thus made them seem cultured. He said not to wear herself out so much anymore, making statues and such for him. She was hurt until he said, "I want you *all* to myself." This was her last day at the wax museum, but there was no way she was going to quit selling makeup, so if he wanted her, he was going to have to share her with Home-Run. Dr. Chylak's notes were bound to provide great insight into her customers, like a handy little marketing survey.

She walked through the Hall of Heroes one last time, saying good-bye to the statues that had been as good and as loyal to her as family since Frank died. "See ya, Joe, see ya, Marilyn," she said.

She pulled the mink wrap tight around Monroe's shoulders and touched the mannequin's cheek. "Now you stick with Joe, honey, or else things aren't gonna turn out so good for you. And Joe? You treat her right!" She slipped a lipstick in Monroe's purse. "That's a good color for you, doll." Then she pinched Costello's cheek. "You be good to Abbott!"

She hit the lights and, wiping a tear from her eye, paused at the entrance to her Hall of Heroes to smooth a wrinkle in Babe Ruth's shirt. "Now, don't you cry too, my baby, Babe," she said, hugging the wax man. He was her first, so she took extra time with him, making sure every hair on his head was in place, admiring her handiwork, which had stood the test of time. She blew him a kiss. "One for the road, big boy," she said, then locked the door and walked to Amos's house.

The mayor was on his porch, sipping, Dusty was pleased to see, chamomile tea—and tea it would be when she told it to the gals at the Choke-Up Diner. He looked so sad it broke her heart. He had a swollen ankle, which was elevated on the porch rail. It was wrapped in gauze and reminded Dusty of a television program she'd seen about mummies, which were chock full of preservatives so the body inside looked perfect for always and ever.

Without saying a word, she extracted a tube of Home-Run Heat from her purse and sat down beside Amos, pointing to his ankle as if to say "May I?" and then massaging the peppermint oil into his leg. He closed his eyes, and it felt strange at first, touching a man like that after so long. He still wore his uniform, having slept in it. It was past suppertime the day after the game.

Amos opened his eyes and grabbed her wrist, holding on so tightly that she feared he was still miffed about the Mays mold. But he looked her in the eyes and it was a tender look. Dusty held her breath, closed her eyes, and puckered up.

"Frank did not kill himself," Amos said.

"What?" Dusty said with one eye open but her lips still puckered.

"It wasn't suicide."

Dusty squeezed the tube of peppermint oil so hard it began to spurt all over Amos's ankle. When she wiped it off with her hankie, he howled in pain.

"Oh, Amos," she said, her eyes beginning to tear. It took all of her strength not to pluck a compact from her purse and check if her mascara was running. "Let's not talk about that." She didn't need to relive the moment she realized she was repulsive. She could see Frank so clearly, that terrified look on his face before he jumped.

"You need to hear this. It's important."

Amos leaned in close, taking her hands in his. "I would have told you. I *should* have told you months ago. Chuck told me before he died, but I didn't want to believe him. I wasn't sure until recently, and I didn't know that you and I would—I'm sorry. I messed up." He hung his head, ashamed, and Dusty squeezed his hands, which were warm and softer than she expected. Numerous thoughts ran through her head, thoughts about chafed skin, taking things slow, how it didn't matter what had happened to Frank because he was gone and he wasn't coming back, and they were here and might as well make the best of it while they still had the time. But she just listened.

"Frank had something of mine," Amos said. "Technically it was Chuck's, but that doesn't matter. He hid it in your garage. I guess he went to get it that night and just . . . well, you know what happened. The ladder must've slipped out from under him. You had those awful moose antlers mounted there and Frank was wearing that big ole necktie."

Dusty put a finger on Amos's lips. "Shhh," she whispered. Her heart was beating fast. *She* was the one who had found Frank! No one could tell the story better than she could. She reviewed that dreaded night twenty-two years ago, sharing the memory with Amos.

Frank had disappeared in the middle of her telling him a most delicious story about how she had discovered that Mada, the

German gal next door, was really a brunette. Frank was acting funny, real absentminded all day. She was upset that he wasn't listening, so she pouted for a while, then indulged in her nightly beauty ritual—brushing her hair, squeezing lemon juice on her elbows, and taking her time out of spite. She meant to show Frank there would be no "whoopee," as he liked to call it, if he was going to walk out in the middle of good gossip. She took her time. When he didn't come to bed, she grew concerned. It was too late for one of his evening strolls. She heard a noise in the garage and went to inspect.

The lights were off, so she grabbed a flashlight from a hook on the wall and shone it upward, assuming there was a squirrel in the rafters. And then that horrible headless beast was glaring down at her. The stuffed moose head Frank had bought at a pawnshop years before. She screamed, and that's when he saw her. Frank shone his own light down to where she stood on the cold cement floor in her fuzzy pink slippers and new black hooded kimono, with oatmeal slathered all over her face. Then he screamed twice as loud as she had and jumped.

Each time Dusty replayed it in her mind the memory grew fuzzier. Did he fall or did he jump? Did he fall or did he jump? Maybe he had turned too quickly. She could see him looking at her even now. Every night before she went to bed she was haunted by that look of terror, or was it surprise? She had waited for what seemed like an eternity for Frank to hit the ground, and then the worst part came: he jerked back up like a yo-yo, just a little bit, then dangled there, peaked and then purple, his head rolling forward with a moan. His body went limp and he swung there, hanging by that tacky Roy Rogers tie.

The more she thought about it, Dusty realized that Frank was afraid, but not because she was hideous and he would have to spend the rest of his life lying in bed beside her ugly face. She had *scared* him! Her bedtime look was not her best, but it was what made her look so radiant throughout the day. In the back of her mind—behind the doubts and insecurities, questions and rumors, several of which she had started herself—she had always suspected that if Frank really *had* killed himself, he would have left a note about it. He was a man of contradictions: messy but organized, adventurous but rarely spontaneous, selfish sometimes but never when it came to other people, never when it came to her. He could not keep a room clean, but he could list every artifact in the Hall of Fame off the top of his head and every baseball player who had ever done anything worth remembering, and he never once forgot to buy flowers on her birthday.

Dusty let go of Amos's hand to dry her eyes.

"You see what I mean?" he said. He offered his sleeve, which normally would have repulsed her, but right now it seemed kind of sweet.

Dusty let him wipe away the tears. She had always been ashamed of the truth, not about how or why Frank died but that she had contributed to the rumors; suicide sounded more mysterious than a man being clumsy and accidentally hanging himself like a fool. That or she did not want to believe it had anything to do with her, that he had left her for a more flawless world. Or that she had done nothing but stare, waiting for him to turn blue before she thought to call for help.

"I told you Chuck took the book Frank was holding."

"I know," Amos said. He had learned that from Chuck too, before he died. "That's what Frank was looking for when he fell."

If that was true, Dusty was glad Frank had found it. She was so mad at Honus the night after the town meeting when she learned he'd taken it from the Hall of Fame. She liked to think that whatever it was about, Frank took its story with him, reading material for his eternal journey. That's why she hid it in the museum when Duke gave it to her several months ago: she wanted it to be with Frank, with his spirit in a place where forever was just another stat.

She sighed. Frank, dead over a lousy book. "What's *wrong* with you boys?" She looked at Amos. They were her boys now, both of them. She would take good care of Amos for Frank.

"I'm all right," she told Amos when he reached to wipe a fresh tear from her eye. She went inside his house to find something with which to blow her nose before he could offer his sleeve for that too, and to get him an ice pack. When she returned, Amos's eyes were closed. She panicked, thinking he'd had a heart attack and now she would have to romance Duke Cartwright, which would be like trying to curl eyelashes with a granny fork. She waved a hand in front of Amos's mouth to see if he was still breathing and he opened it, pretending to chomp at her fingers. "Ruff!" he growled, and Dusty giggled. He took her wrist again, gently now. She held her breath, applying the ice to his ankle, doing her part to remove the sting of the previous day's events. She felt certain that if Frank were watching, he would approve. After he punched Amos's lights out, but still. Frank was gone, accident or not, and she had a sumptuous-for-seventy figure that would spoil if she didn't put it to use.

"Did you speak to Johnny?" she asked, never having imagined in her wildest fantasies that she'd be sitting here with Amos the Fuss inquiring about his personal life because she actually *cared,* or that he'd have kissed her that day in the wax museum, or that afterward they'd be able to cherish the memory of Frank together. She anticipated his response, thinking that maybe, if you told all your secrets, all your dirty little white lies, you wouldn't care so much about what other people were concealing. You wouldn't need to because you yourself had nothing to hide.

"Yeah, I spoke to him. He approached me after the game."

"And?" Dusty prompted, pinching Amos's arm. "What did he *say?*"

Amos sighed. "He accused Duke of letting the grass on the field overgrow to slow down State's ground balls."

Dusty placed a hand on his shoulder and squeezed.

"And he gave me these," Amos said, opening her palm and sprinkling two tiny trinkets in it.

"What on earth are they for?" she asked, examining the little plastic duck and rock. The expression on her face made Amos laugh.

"They're to do with a game we used to play. I'll tell you about it later." He pulled her toward him. "You look real pretty tonight."

"I do, don't I?" Dusty said, surprising herself, even more when she allowed herself to be pulled down onto Amos's lap. She hadn't looked in a mirror all day, but she felt it somehow. She *felt* pretty. So pretty that she didn't stop to think, to warn him about her canker or that she hadn't waxed her chins. She leaned toward him and planted a kiss on his forehead, then one on his cheek, his ear, and then on the tip of his nose.

"You're a tease," Amos said, squeezing her bottom.

She slapped him playfully, giggling like a schoolgirl.

Amos lifted her chin and this time Dusty gave in completely, planting a kiss right smack on his lips. They were a little chafed, and his breath was sour, but no matter: Home-Run Whiff breath freshener would take care of that. She extracted some from her purse—a squirt for her, a squirt for him—then kissed him again. They had all the time in the world to better themselves, together.

"What're you going to do now?" she asked. "I guess that theme park will be here before we know it."

Amos looked weary.

"You did the best you could," Dusty said. "Everybody knows it, no matter what they're saying."

"What're they saying?" he growled.

"Never mind about that. I'm not one to spread rumors."

Amos cocked an eyebrow.

"Fine! Stanley Auffswich said you're stubborn as an old goose and should've talked to Johnny from the get-go, and Dicky Harring told Mr. Peck that if you were smart you would run yourself right out of town. But mostly people don't care. Most folks are just glad it's over and they can finally get on with their lives."

"And what do you think?"

"I think you gave it a real good fight."

"Did I?" Amos said. "Because I can't help thinking if I had only had a better plan. If I had acted sooner, taken it to the courts or talked to Johnny like Stanley said . . . just *talked* to him, you know?" He shook his head, frowning. "I could've at least found some decent players for our team!"

"Hey," Dusty said, jabbing him in the belly with a sharp nail. "I was part of that team, mister, and I say we did just fine."

"It was something, wasn't it, Barrett at bat?" Amos said with a grin.

Dusty simply nodded. It was *something* all right, but she would stay mum, because the memory seemed to brighten Amos's mood. He held her closer.

"I didn't tell anyone this," he said, "but I promised Johnny that if we lost, I'd retire."

"Oh, Amos! Why'd you go and do a foolish thing like that?"

"I'm sixty-five, Dusty! And damned tired."

"Too tired to take a girl to dinner?" she asked.

Amos stood up, smiling, and picked her right up along with him. He set her on her feet.

"I'm thinking about renting a Winnebago come fall," he said, stretching. "Might be nice to get a change of scenery for a while. Take a little vacation. If you know anyone, I mean, who needs the same."

"I might," she said, batting her lashes and glad for once that she hadn't worn fakes.

"I might even sell my house. I don't want to live across the street from a bar anymore. This place is in a real good location, though, right in the middle of town. It might make a nice beauty salon, if you know anyone who's in the market for one."

"I do," Dusty said, smiling coyly. She pulled him gently by the collar, her fingers curled to say come hither as she led him slowly inside.

"What about dinner?" Amos said, grinning mischievously.

"I don't know about you, but *I'm* on a diet," she said, kicking the screen door closed.

She didn't hesitate for a second. Perhaps just one *tiny* second, while she wondered what people would say if she spent the whole night there. Heck, she thought, giggling. Let them talk among themselves.

B OBBY WATCHED DAULTON LUG the last box from his office and pile it in the back of his car. She asked for what seemed like the hundredth time if he needed any help.

"Nope," he said, "that's it. I travel light."

He smiled when he said it, but it ticked her off. What was she hoping he'd say? "There's plenty of room on this pony for two"?

It was the day after the big game, the day when the world was supposed to change, when she was supposed to wake up to a cup of hot coffee and the newspaper, those glorious headlines. Daulton's story was supposed to bring some *real* excitement to town, or launch her into a new world where no one knew her well enough to say they knew her when. "I can't convince you to stay, can I?" she asked, biting a fingernail, then spitting it out right there in front of him; there was no point in keeping up pretenses if the man was leaving. She felt foolish for having dressed up, for wearing a prairie skirt instead of jeans. Normally, *nothing* came between Bobby and her Calvins. She wiped lipstick from her mouth with the paper in which she'd been reading Daulton's article about the game. It was a story that had made its mark, though not the mark they had planned.

"Nope," he said again. "I have to do this; you understand."

When he placed a hand ever so hesitantly on her shoulder, Bobby knew she couldn't blame him even if she didn't really understand. She knew the moment she turned that book over to Daulton that she was taking a risk, that his were not necessarily more capable hands. At the game, he stood there swinging that bat and, afterward, smiling even though he had cost them a win.

He looked like a kid, and that made her feel young again, and full of possibility too. She knew as soon as Manny hit that homer that Daulton wouldn't go through with it, their plan. She saw him jump out of his seat and cheer. He had begun to look an awful lot like Dream Lover.

She watched him close up his office, thinking it odd that for a writer, he was a man of few words. Words were everything to Bobby—she spent nearly every day surrounded by thousands and thousands of them. But for him it was all about body language. He had a new spring in his step. He was clearly excited to be leaving. He looked like a wild colt new on its legs, eagerly anticipating how it was going to get through the rest of its life once it broke from the pack.

For Bobby, the excitement, the possibility of change had been enough. She had forgotten what that felt like, having goals, a concrete plan. It was clear now that the decision not to go public with the document they had found was one Daulton needed to make on his own and as a Cooperstonian, not a reporter. The home team didn't lose yesterday, Bobby thought, not completely. Cooperstown had won over even its most stubborn residents. In fact, it would never know what had almost hit it.

A sportswriter, who Daulton explained was from *The Boston Globe,* exited the courthouse and crossed the parking lot toward them—he was there to pay a fine for parking on Mrs. Coxey's front lawn; he had run over one of her junipers. Bobby pictured the three of them standing there laughing at his mishap, like the chummy roommates on *Three's Company,* the men complimenting her on her white peasant blouse and her giggling, "Oh please, you guys, stop!" Maybe the sportswriter would take off to do some swinging at the Regal Beagle while she and Daulton hopped into his car like a couple of teenagers up for a ride, up for anything. Bobby shaking her feathered mane in the wind like they did on those shampoo commercials: *Don't hate me because I'm beautiful!*

Her fantasy was cut short when the writer asked for a minute alone with Daulton. Bobby leaned against the trunk of his convertible, watching the sun set on the town, as the men walked away.

"Thanks, though, for the offer," Daulton said a moment later as he shook the man's hand. He gestured to Bobby, hands outstretched, that he had to get going. He opened the door to his car and was about to climb inside when the sportswriter yelled, "You know where to find me if you change your mind!" They watched him walk to his car. There were juniper berries squished all over it. Bobby didn't ask Daulton what the guy meant; she already had an idea. He had been taken with Daulton's story, his feel-good angle on the game, and had offered to get him an interview with *The Globe*. Everyone had read the story, all those big-city journalists in town. It was a front-page feature in *The Journal*. People praised the personal angle—Daulton coming to terms with the memory of his dad. It made the game seem like more than just a game. It made people who had missed it feel like they were there, or wish they had been with their own dads. It didn't seem to matter that Cooperstown lost, and that the ending was bittersweet. Daulton was right: everyone loved an underdog tale. Mrs. Paquette said he'd even gotten a call from an editor at *The New York Times* who had previously rejected his work, saying they should discuss his career if he returned to the city. And *The Journal* offered him a column, "At Home in Cooperstown," which would include covering the annual Hall of Fame Game, profiling inductees, and anything else he saw fit to print from the birthplace of baseball. There was even talk of shooting for syndication—sharing a dose of local flavor for a pastime that included *all* Americans. It was everything Chuck had ever wanted for his son, and, in a way, what Daulton wanted too. But he passed up the opportunity with a humble no thanks, and Bobby didn't ask why. She didn't have to. The answer was the same one she gave her employer that morning when she handed in her keys to the Baseball Library. He needed a change. His beat, whatever it was, was still out there, waiting.

"At least let me help with the cottage," Bobby said, hitching her skirt up and climbing into the Mustang before Daulton could say no thanks to her, too. He got behind the wheel and revved the motor. Bobby looked in the side mirror and fixed her hair. What the hell, she thought, pulling the pins from her bun and letting her luscious locks fly loose in the wind as they drove down Main Street.

At the intersection on Chestnut, Daulton fiddled with the radio dial while they waited for the light to change, tuning it until he found a song he liked. They caught the tail end of Neil Diamond and Barbra Streisand whining about who did or didn't bring whom flowers anymore. Bobby smiled, thinking she had her answer about the kind of music Daulton liked. He had grown up to be a romantic. Who knew? He sang along, not the least bit timid—*"Well, you'd think I could learn how to tell you good-bye . . ."*

Bobby turned away, saddened by the lyrics. "Pull over at the pharmacy," she said. "I want to pick up some smokes." She was stalling and she knew it. She didn't want him to drive her home and leave her to sit there all alone, facing the fact that she'd been stalling for so long that she had gotten herself plumb stuck. She knew why she'd never left Cooperstown: codependency. She and the town butted heads repeatedly, but at least they could both count on the other to be there in the morning.

As they drove toward the drugstore, they passed the art gallery where a portrait of the induction trio hung in the window; Joy Jennings had sketched it as a good-bye gift to the townsfolk before she moved west. A similar sketch of Willie Mays was propped in the bookshop window beside his biography, which a bright red and white sign stated one could win via raffle. Bobby tried to remember the last time she'd seen something advertised in Cooperstown that she might actually want to *buy*. What if you were a Ping-Pong player or a polo fan, for Dionne Warwick's sake?

At the pharmacy, she took her time flipping through magazines and then bought a pack of smokes, a cheap lip-gloss that would make Mrs. Paquette cringe, and some gum. When she returned to the car, she had to climb over Daulton because his was the only door that wasn't rusted shut, and there was no way she was straddling her own door in a prairie skirt.

He blushed, saying, "You smell good," and Bobby paused half perched on his lap, sliding against his smooth leather vest and then onto the seat. She looked him in the eyes. Daulton looked away and Bobby felt her face burning. "Sorry," he said, "that was a stupid thing to say." Then he started the car and headed back up Main, turning right on Chestnut toward the lake.

Bobby lit a cigarette as they drove toward the cottage in silence. She *could* make Daulton feel better for ruining the moment by telling him that, sadly enough, "You smell good" was the sweetest, most honest thing a man had said to her in years. But the truth was, it *was* a stupid thing to say. Bobby was back. Terry Daulton was too soft for her, a find-your-inner-peace type of guy, and she had promised herself a good old-fashioned tortured fellow! Besides, how could she pine over him if he stuck around, fading out her fantasies with his ever-present face?

They flew up West Lake Road until they reached the Fenimore Funhouse, where Chuck's place stood, a small stone cottage on the periphery of vast green grounds. Bobby offered to help Daulton grab the last of his father's stuff, but Daulton didn't move. He just sat there, hesitant to enter. It looked like no one had been inside the cottage in ages. Both it and the Funhouse looked terribly neglected. Weeds had taken over the flower beds lining the walk to the museum, and the cottage door was busted right off its hinges. From where Bobby sat it looked like a pigsty inside.

"Rats!" she yelled, pointing to the doorway. They watched two fat rodents skitter out of the cottage.

Daulton fumbled around in the glove compartment. "I have pepper spray, or Mace or something, in here. When I moved to the city, Chuck insisted I carry it around." He smiled at the memory, but Bobby eyed him suspiciously. "What?" he said, uncapping the spray and testing it with a quick squirt onto the ground,

"*I* didn't bust the door down, if that's what you're thinking!" He tossed the empty spray back in the glove compartment and slammed it shut, but it wouldn't latch.

"You don't look surprised to see it like this," Bobby said. "This was your *home*."

"I know, and it breaks my heart. But the mayor wouldn't give me the key! I guess I didn't need it. I found it like this, I swear. The night you gave me the book . . ."

Bobby wasn't listening. She was staring at the open glove compartment, at the bottle of Mace that had rolled out and into her lap. She was thinking about the photo that had run in *The Journal* following the induction ceremony, of the mayor handing Willie Mays an object people were still speculating about. She remembered what Cartwright had said that night at the library when she thought he was chasing her. He *was* trying to tell her something. But it wasn't a warning. He hadn't said, "Mace is the key."

"*Mays* has it!" she said. "Willie Mays has the *key!*" She turned to face Daulton, who had disappeared, having lost his audience. He was walking around to the back of the cottage to pay his last respects, a final good-bye at Chuck's grave. Bobby decided to give him a moment alone and stayed put, surveying the state of the house and the museum. A large wooden door lay on the ground beside the driveway. She tilted her head sideways to read the sign nailed to it: CURATOR NEEDED.

She wondered if it was difficult for Daulton to leave his poor dead father all alone in Cooperstown, especially when his mother was buried all the way across town behind Christ Episcopal with James Fenimore Cooper, his wife, and everybody else. How odd for husband and wife to be buried separately. Everyone knew the Daultons had had a good marriage. Then again, what was more sensible than taking one last stab at independence before the good earth swallowed you whole? If there was an Other Side, everybody probably met up there again anyway. Everybody who had ever lived and died, and if a girl couldn't find someone to couple up with then? She was *really* a spinster, or a jezebel, if she played the whole great white field. Bobby was midway through a fantasy lip-lock with Elvis when Daulton returned.

They sat for a minute in silence.

Bobby hadn't sat in silence with a real man for a long time. It was more awkward than she had imagined it would be. She stared at him and he stared back, just like in junior high. She wondered if he was debating whether or not to kiss her, and if there was any point since he was leaving town. Then she realized he might just be having one of those fits, or whatever he had. He had some kind of condition, Mrs. Paquette had told Ruby, who told Bobby. An identity crisis spun out of control, sprung from feeling like Chuck had long ago chosen Manny over him. It didn't help that Chuck had refused to see him before he died. Ruby said Mrs. Paquette thought he'd always been kind of lost, that a motherless boy couldn't tolerate such a controlling mother hen of a dad. But Chuck wasn't so bad. He was about the only person Bobby had ever met that truly loved his job.

She looked again at the sign on the fallen door. *Why not?* Britain had gotten its first female prime minister, and something had finally killed Sid Vicious—anything was possible. She didn't know squat about funhouses, but she knew plenty about James Fenimore Cooper, his books anyway, and being around his novels was a hell of a lot better than being around *baseball* books.

Daulton exited the cottage with a stack of boxes and a few loose items, which Bobby helped him arrange in the backseat. A tattered old teddy bear and some Tom and Jerry comics were among them. He climbed in beside her and she placed a hand gently on his arm. Daulton froze, the key half inserted in the ignition. They stayed like that for a second, watching barn swallows flit back and forth from the museum to the cottage roof. A rat ran inside, past the daffodils that lined the walk. Bobby looked at Daulton, wondering if she would have done things any differently if she had kept the book, taken matters into her own hands.

When they reached her apartment, she climbed out of the car and leaned down to hug Daulton, who protested, opening his door to get out.

"Please," she said, her hand on the door. "Stay put."

Daulton slid back down in his seat. "I hate good-byes," he said.

"Me too," said Bobby. "It's why I never go anywhere."

She leaned down to kiss him on the cheek and he blushed, hugging her, hesitantly at first and then tighter when she squeezed back.

"Nice car, by the way," she said, slapping the side of his vehicle like it was a horse about to gallop off.

"Thanks," Daulton said, smiling. "I might come back, you know, for a visit. Not that you're holding your breath."

She nodded and returned the smile. And when he was halfway down Susquehanna Avenue, she exhaled the breath she had been holding from the moment she slapped the car, to avoid feeling that flutter in her heart upon noting the brand—*a handsome stranger riding by on his white mustang to return a particularly compelling book.*

"For the love of Streisand!" she said, one hand over her heart.

Inside, she kicked off her clogs, slipped out of her prairie skirt and into her favorite faded Calvin Klein jeans, then mixed a martini and lay back on the couch. Don Mattingly had been at the game. Bobby had seen him with his fiancée. Kim Sexton, Mrs. Paquette said her name was, and wasn't that just peaches for her? Why was everyone called *Babe* and *Sex*ton, and names that got you somewhere, got you *someone,* instead of plain old Roberta, a name that implied its owner was destined to linger between genders, not adapting well to either? Bobby closed her eyes. Dream Lover appeared, his face blurred. She would lie there with him, her ever-changing ideal of a man, in silence for as long as it took. Not because someone would eventually replace him, someone real, but because she could. She always *had* been a piner. Pining took patience. And what better place to sit back and wait for something to happen than Cooperstown? This town was chock full of surprises if a girl knew where to look.

She opened her eyes and reached for the phone, dialing the mayor.

"Hello?"

"I heard you need a new curator."

MANNY SAT IN THE dugout, staring at the field. The ballpark was empty now, aside from its groundskeeper, Cartwright, and the soda cans, popcorn, and peanut shells littered throughout the stands. He traced the path of his homer across the pitcher's mound and over the wall, past the ballpark and above the rooftops of Cooperstown, unable to envision anything beyond.

Tonight he was having supper at Ruby's. He'd even worn a tie and a new pair of Wrangler blue jeans, freshly pressed thanks to Mrs. Paquette, who had stopped by that afternoon to douse him with musk. For once, he obliged her. He had driven into town too early, nervous he supposed, and it was nice to have some time alone on Doubleday Field.

Ruby and the boys had been at the game. Manny could swear he had even heard Ruby yell "Go get 'em, Immanuel!" when he was on deck, but it was hard to say. It had all happened so fast. He'd flatly refused Amos's offer to play third following the town meeting, Amos having suckered him into attending by saying it concerned the future of the town, and thus his boys' futures. Even though all those people to whom he never gave the time of day had applauded him when he entered the courthouse. It was later, that night in the sanitarium parking lot with Amos, when he'd gone to the Baseball Library and thought about burning it down. That's when he changed his mind. Some stubborn sliver of hope suggested there was an easier option: that if he played ball, his boys would finally be able to see him do the one thing he was good at. It didn't turn out so hot, but at least he had hit a homer. He imagined Ruby running onto the field after he lost his shit, that damned golf cart backfiring and all those birds shooting through the sky, turning it black like that day at the bridge when he thought he was going to die. All he could think about then was whether crows were scavengers that fed on dead mammals.

He didn't feel much about those old birds now, however. He had the shrink's evaluation in his pocket and planned to present it to Ruby tonight. She had rescued him at the game; the least he could do was accept her invitation for supper. Maybe he was a freak, he thought, smiling, but he was a freak who had belted one right out of the ballpark.

Ruby had come up to him after the game, the boys in tow. Toby clung to her, as if afraid she would leave him too. Aidan just stood there shuffling his feet, eyeing Manny with that cocky look, pretending not to care. But at least it was a different kind of look than the one Manny saw at the gas station; this one said that whatever they had to say to each other, they would say it, eventually. There was not hope in it, per se. It was more dignified than that. It was will. Aidan was as stubborn as he was, but he would come around eventually, at least for a shouting match, and that was a start. Ruby's boy toy had been with them, though he was smart enough to wait by the car.

Manny stared into the empty grandstands, replaying his postgame conversation with his ex in his mind.

"I was thinking," he told Ruby, "maybe I could stop by this weekend, you know—help you clear those gutters." Ruby thought it over, chewing a strand of her hair like she had done since high school, whenever she wasn't sure how she felt about a thing. It was accompanied by an ache in the pit of Manny's gut that he hadn't expected to feel or to miss.

"Yeah, all right," she said, eyeing her beau, who stood by her car, chatting up a Cooperstown High cheerleader, and then, "On second thought, let's make it tomorrow. If you have time." Manny had the time.

"Will he be there?" he said, nodding at her boy toy, a young minor leaguer whom he had noticed playing for State.

Ruby snorted, "What do you care?"

"What do you see in him?" Manny asked. He hated the idea of her one day marrying the jerk-off now batting air balls like a clown for the giggling cheerleader. He hated the idea of any man, come to think of it, raising his kids, any man but him.

Ruby shrugged. "Oh, I don't know," she said. "He's there?"

"I'm here!" Manny said. "We could try again, you know."

"You already struck out twice, Immanuel, and you know the rules: that means you're out."

"It's three strikes and you're out."

"Yeah? Well, the third one is liable to be across your head!"

Manny looked away.

"That was a joke," Ruby said, softening.

He smiled, brushing the hair from her mouth. "Ruby?"

"Don't," she said, pulling away and glancing at her boyfriend. She pulled Toby closer. The child was staring at Manny, fascinated. Ruby changed the subject, gesturing toward Aidan, who stood by the car with her boyfriend and was smoking a cigarette. "The boys are so far apart in age, some people don't believe they had the same father."

"Have," Manny corrected her. "They have the same father." He gestured with a scowl toward Aidan and the half-wit. "And it's a good thing, because I don't want them smoking. You tell your friend there to quit pushing cancer sticks on my son."

"Aidan buys them himself. He's a man now, in case you hadn't noticed. It's too late to school him."

"The hell it is!"

Manny started walking toward Aidan and the asshole ballplayer, thinking how nice it would feel to deck the bastard.

"Don't," Ruby repeated, grabbing his arm.

Manny looked at Toby, who looked scared, like a kitten about to be ripped from its mama too soon. He shrugged Ruby's hand off and stayed put, only because he knew now the only thing that could ever truly break him would be to see that look, that fear he used to see in Ruby's eyes, in the eyes of his younger son. There was still a chance for him and Toby, a chance to be there for him before he too became a man.

"I never wanted to hurt you, Rube," Manny said, staring out at the field.

"I know that," she whispered, placing her hand on his shoulder, which got her boyfriend's attention. He started over toward them, but Ruby held her hand up for him to let well enough alone. "Look, I gotta go."

Manny watched her take his son by the hand and walk away, Toby turning back to look over his shoulder at his dad. He didn't look frightened then. He looked curious as hell. Manny didn't know what the future held for him and Ruby, but if he knew one thing, it was that he wanted to know his boys. He ran after them, grabbing Ruby around the waist and leaning her back, planting a long, smooth kiss right on her lips in front of the ballplayer and his sons.

"How do you like them friggin' baseballs?" he shouted at Ruby's fellow, right before the guy charged over and decked him in the mouth.

It was worth it, Manny thought with a snigger, even though it was followed by another jab that knocked him flat on his backside. Because the look on Aidan's face at that moment had definitely been a smirk. And a smirk was close enough to a smile. Coach Cartwright had witnessed it too; he stood on the edge of the field, facing the parking lot, and if Manny didn't know better, he could swear he had heard Coach chuckle.

He wondered if Cartwright missed coaching. If he had the courage to call him over right now, he'd ask him, and maybe tell him that he knew he had disappointed him. That he remembered that day on the bridge, Coach vowing that if they let him go he wouldn't cause any trouble, because he was going to play ball. And that if he didn't, that was the last word they would hear from him on that, or anything else. Manny had broken his vow. He didn't play. But Coach kept his.

It was all over now. The lion was asleep. It was the first time Manny had thought about that day without a flashback, without falling to his knees and crying out. But history was cyclical. He knew that much. He would let the beast hibernate for a while and find some peace, get some sleep in the interim. And if he was lucky, he'd be dead the next time it came around. Unless a man's number only came up once, if he proved he wanted something badly enough that he was willing to sacrifice everything he had for it.

Daulton drove through the parking lot on his way out of town, tooting his horn.

Manny put up a hand, not waving but holding it there like an Indian greeting a friend, as he watched Daulton's car fade to a white dot.

Daulton had surprised him, showing up at his cabin late the night after the game. "Nice play," was his greeting as he stepped out of his car, and Manny knew he meant the panic attack, not the homer. He joined Manny, uninvited, on the porch, wanting to know what had made him decide to play. Manny responded that he owed someone a favor and left it at that. He meant Chuck, among others. Manny wished he'd defied Chuck's orders sooner and called Daulton home quickly so he could say good-bye to his old man, and to tell him everything, his story and the secrets he'd been dying to tell. He supposed Chuck was the reason Daulton had allowed *himself* to play in the game: he felt he owed Chuck one too. Manny wasn't going to pretend to understand what Daulton's debt was. That was between father and son. But Daulton knew everything now.

Almost.

That night after the game he'd brought the book to Manny's place. They'd stayed up late arguing, then, as their trust grew, comparing stories, trying to piece the history of the book, the document, back together, and tying up loose ends. They'd built a campfire down by the lake near Manny's barn, and that turned to reminiscing, and drinking beers like they used to do. Then they burned the book, perhaps on a whim, perhaps because they were drunk, or perhaps because neither one of them had any use for it anymore. Manny said if Daulton had any more questions, as a friend, not a reporter, to call him when he got settled wherever he was going. It seemed like the appropriate thing to say to a man who had once been his best friend. Particularly since they had performed a sort of black mass ritual together, burning the book in the fire. "You don't have a phone, Bumppo!" Daulton had teased, and Manny replied with a smirk that said that was the point. Then Daulton said, "Well, there's always postcards."

I know you know.

Of course Manny had known. He'd *always* known. He also knew that Daulton had been asked to interview at a big Boston paper and had refused, and he knew it wasn't because Daulton hated baseball, or reporting, or Cooperstown, but because it would have pleased his father, and sometimes there was only so much pleasing a man could do. Chuck had died, thereby abandoning all claims to how his son ran his life, and Daulton understood now that he wasn't the only one Chuck left behind. There were other people who had depended on him: Amos, Cartwright, and Manny. He'd left, sticking them with a burden he alone had unearthed by poking around in the past. A burden that was too big for one man, too big for any of them, to bear. Manny figured the real heroes in the story were the tourists. They came with the preconception that Cooperstown was some kind of mythical place. And when they arrived, they saw regular folks just like themselves with jobs to do, bills to pay, cars to fix, kids to rear, and all those ordinary, everyday things. But they kept coming, year after year after year. Like they owed it something. Like they knew Cooperstown would dissolve right before their eyes if they didn't. It was *why* they came: to keep the past, the myths and the legends, alive.

That night by the campfire, Manny had given Daulton a watered-down version of exactly what that past, those myths for Cooperstown really were, letting him ingest the facts of his father's tale one at a time. It was important to him that Daulton understand that Chuck would have welcomed him back with open arms if things had been different. He was simply afraid his son would stay, and he couldn't risk that. Mostly because he had higher aspirations for Daulton and did *not* want him to follow in his footsteps, to make the same mistakes he had made. Chuck

knew Daulton would bring the book back with him, bring everything he owned, and plant himself right there in the past instead
of pursuing a promising future. Daulton didn't need to know
that the shock of his return had killed Chuck. Manny would take
the blame for that.

Manny stared, mesmerized by the rich green grass on the ball
field, marveling at how easy it was to release his story once he
started, to tell the shrink and then Daulton what he'd never been
able to tell his own wife. He had lost everything because of his
silence, and it hadn't protected him like they said it would. It
hadn't protected Chuck, Frank, or Coach, who stood now in the
rain on the pitcher's mound with his face upturned to catch the
drops. It looked like a pretty good way to spend an evening, and
Manny imagined himself running onto the field to join him,
shouting, "Hey, Coach, I'm back! I'm ready to play!" He admired
Cartwright's strength; he'd come out virtually unscathed. As if
keeping his mouth shut had enabled him to store up energy,
strength to put to use at a later date, when it was needed most.
Manny wondered when that would be. He thought about that
day, in the summer of '57, when it all began.

He had walked in on them—Amos, Coach, Frank, and
Chuck—arguing in Cartwright's office at the school. Coach had
access to the gym during the summertime because he also
coached Little League and they used the gym for calisthenics to
warm up the kids. The team uniforms had arrived that day and
the kids were excited, convincing Coach to let them wear them at
practice. As Coach's assistant, Manny had worn one too.

He was cleaning out the gym, helping Coach like he always
did after practice. He had every right to be there, in Coach's office, where he went for a moment of privacy, standing in the dark
because it was cool and quiet and it gave him a moment to think
about how he'd propose to Ruby the second he got to the Show.
He figured he would get down on one knee like they did in the
pictures. And if she said it was too soon, he would wait for her,
and he hoped she would wait for him. Then he would get those

guys, the quartet that sang on the library steps, to serenade her with Sinatra's "All the Way."

Coach had entered the dark office then with his pals and they were arguing. Curious, and not wanting to get in trouble, Manny just stood there, frozen in the corner of the room behind the door, planning to slip out as soon as they left. They didn't turn on the light, which made him more curious. Coach got a flashlight from his desk and gave it to Frank, and Chuck handed Frank a piece of paper, which he said to read fast. Frank was standing in the doorway like he didn't want to enter, then Amos barked for him to hurry up. And behind the door was Manny, who could see everything through the crack. He held his breath and read over Frank's shoulder, feeling like he was undercover, like Joe Friday from *Dragnet*. The next thing he knew the light was shining through the crack and someone flung the door open. He stood there, gripping that bag of balls like it was the last thing he would ever touch that was right in this world. He had read the whole document, twice, not understanding at first what it meant. He just knew it was wrong. Because it said Cooperstown had once forbidden baseball, and if it was right, he wasn't who he thought he was, because Cooperstown wasn't what it claimed to be and he was its favorite son, its golden boy. Then they turned on him all at once like a pack of vultures, Amos shouting, "What the hell is going on here? What did you see?"

Manny had run out of the room, followed by Amos, who grabbed him and dragged him, kicking and screaming, to the parking lot, where the others helped throw him in the back of Coach's truck. "Now hold on," Cartwright said. "Let's think about this!"

"Drive!" Amos yelled, and he did. Coach drove to the river, a spot tucked deep in the woods.

Manny was ushered, blindfolded, onto the old stone bridge. They held him by his ankles over the side. Amos threatened to drown him, to strap the cinder blocks in the back of Coach's truck to his limbs and toss him into the raging river below if he told a soul about what he'd read. He wouldn't, Manny swore he wouldn't, and by then he was crying. Coach was shouting, telling them he had a great shot at being signed by the Yanks, so they stopped. Manny was a ballplayer and he was from Cooperstown. He wasn't going to tell.

They didn't drown him. They didn't even beat him up. They opted for the next best thing: they took him under their wings. They said they had "saved" him, and that it was his turn to save them back, to make it to the bigs and credit his town when he got there, for giving him his start. But it was a lie, everything Manny ever knew seemed like a lie and so he refused. Then the bribes started coming. They bought him a house. And at first it seemed like a pretty good deal when all he had to do in exchange was keep his mouth shut. Except he was forced to grow up too fast, two decades in one summer just to catch up with them, the only company he would have for a very long time. But he did it. He became one of them. He learned to live with his decision, to swallow the lies for "the cause" because it meant he was part of a team.

The rain had stopped. Manny watched Cartwright smooth a patch of mud near first base. He wondered if Coach remembered things the same way. Did Cartwright remember the look on Chuck's face, that combination of dread and delight, as he stood on that bridge in the dark telling them how he had found the document? They had tied Manny up at that point and he knelt on the bridge, the sharp gravel cutting through his pants. They seemed to forget him, lost in Chuck's words.

Chuck said he'd been reading one of James Fenimore Cooper's books on his lunch break. The Funhouse, a stone mansion built in the thirties, stood on a plot of land near the lake where Cooper's home once was. It was transferred from owner to owner, along with many Cooper artifacts, until it became a museum. Mock-ups of Cooper's old furniture and other more genuine memorabilia were displayed throughout its numerous rooms. The state historical society turned it into a sort of half museum, half freak show to attract more tourists. The artifacts remained, but distortion mirrors were installed, plus a high-tech sound system with speakers in every room, through which Chuck's voice acted as Cooper's. Tourists could get a taste of local lore and have some fun with it too. There was even an interactive room for kids and a portrait room where paintings of all the Coopers hung. Chuck hated what they did to the place, but the taped tours allowed him free time to poke through the archives in the ballroom, where Cooper's actual house once stood. The ballroom was off-limits to tourists and a total mess. It was located in a wing of the museum on which the roof had begun to collapse. The town council was desperate to get funding to repair it discreetly so that the state historical society, which was responsible for the property, wouldn't close it down. The townsfolk feared they would lose a landmark that was as much a part of their identity as the Hall of Fame. Amos took donations, he was *still* taking them, and the roof had yet to be fixed, but neither had anyone caught on. The ballroom became a place to stash artifacts that hadn't yet been appraised or that were too damaged to display.

It was a slow day at the museum, so Chuck said he extended his lunch break, starting at the back of the room and picking his way casually toward the front, searching for something new to show off to tourists. He loved nothing more than presenting the past in his own original way. And that was the problem. He came across a box of papers—notes Cooper had taken while researching one of his novels, a satire of his father's town. The papers were in terrible shape. He didn't want to damage them further because technically, they belonged to the state historical society, and since that organization controlled the property, it was also responsible for his cottage. He left most of the stuff as he'd found it, but there was one box in particular that piqued his interest, because of what was written on the label: HOME AS FOUND. The papers inside it were dated in and around 1838, the year before, as legend had it, Abner Doubleday invented baseball. They were Cooper's notes for the one novel of his that Chuck had never read. He said he'd heard of it, but that it wasn't something he came across often, not like *The Deer Slayer* or *The Last of the Mohicans*. He described the notes as barely legible, scrawls yellowed by time. But they were quite a find for him personally. He grew excited at the possibility of having them restored, maybe opening a new wing of the Funhouse, and returning it to the serious shrine it had once been. He discovered an old newspaper clipping that Cooper had used in his research. It had been there for over a hundred years, no one suspecting a thing. The bottom was smudged, one line barely legible. Chuck's excitement was quickly extinguished when he read it and realized what it meant for Cooperstown. In Cooper's world baseball was still new, kid stuff. In Chuck's world it was the law. Cooperstonians took their history seriously, so seriously that they had begun to believe their own myths.

Chuck showed the paper to Amos, who called a meeting at the school, the one Manny interrupted, which they hysterically continued on the bridge. Amos told Chuck to destroy the paper or he would ensure that Chuck lost his job. Chuck was faced with a tough decision: break a hot story or protect his livelihood and people? He would never do anything to put a black mark on his town. But, as a historian, how could he ignore such a find? Once Amos had yelled himself hoarse, Chuck complied, vowing to go straight home and destroy the document. And he did. Or so they thought.

The next day, Amos stormed the Funhouse, ransacking the ballroom with Frank and a hesitant Cartwright, just to be safe. They took every box of paper left inside it down to the lake and set them on fire. It had nearly killed Chuck to watch. Then Amos went to the Baseball Library and destroyed any hard copies and any microfiche he could find of the *Otsego Herald* in and around 1816. It was the *Herald* in which the dreaded words had appeared: Cooperstown had initially banned the sport it claimed to have birthed.

Years later, when Chuck was in the hospital, he confessed the rest of his tale. He could no longer take the guilt. He was afraid he would die, and wanted to die knowing he had done right by his town. He never destroyed the document. He clung to it instead. He gave the newspaper clipping to Frank, his main confidant, to hide tucked inside a copy of *The Last of the Mohicans,* which he gutted and carved up into a makeshift box. "Just a few days," he told an apparently nervous Frank, "until I figure things out," and Frank hid it in his garage. But days turned into weeks, and it was too much for old Frank.

Frank went to retrieve it one night, perhaps planning to confess or turn it over to Amos, not knowing he wouldn't have to bother because it would be the last night of his life. Chuck was the first to arrive on the scene when he died. Mrs. Paquette called him, in shock, before she called an ambulance. He took the book she had pried from Frank's hands. She had removed it when she tried to lift him off the floor to wrap his arms around her one last time. And Chuck gave it to the one person he trusted most in the world: his obedient son. Perhaps he figured that as long as it remained in the hands of a Cooperstonian who was moving far away, it was safe. That way, he wouldn't have to choose between present and past, between destroying history and preserving the future of his town. He just picked the wrong Cooperstonian. Or perhaps not, Manny thought now, considering Daulton had just forfeited the opportunity of a lifetime by not printing a story that someone, someday would inevitably print.

Amos was livid when he learned Frank had hidden the document for Chuck. He'd never really trusted Chuck, or his journalistic offspring. Manny suspected that he probably didn't even trust himself. *None* of them could know what they would have done in Chuck's shoes, if they had been the ones to find it. Manny had had plenty of time to wonder about that over the years when he was off warring with himself in Cheery Valley. There came a point when he was forced to admit he didn't care anymore. Whatever happened, it was better than living a lie.

It was stupid, he thought now, watching Cartwright ride his bike through the mud he had just raked. The news of Daulton's imminent return resulted in Chuck having a massive coronary. And Amos broke down: "Chuck *always* takes the easy way out!" He was lost. Under different circumstances, Chuck would have loved to see his son. But he knew Daulton, which meant he knew Daulton would come back and stay, for good if he was needed.

It killed Manny not to be able to tell Daulton that until the night after the game, when they burned the book. He had to make a choice of his own then: tell Daulton the reason Chuck didn't want him to come back or go on pretending. He chose the former, assuring Daulton that if he had it to do all over again, he would *still* call, only next time he would say "Hurry home!" He consoled himself with the idea that he'd stood in for Daulton that day as Chuck's surrogate son. Chuck had pulled him close to the bed, the others gathered around, whispering, "Bury it. Bury the book!" They promised they would, that they'd get it back somehow without involving his son and bury it once and for all. But they didn't have to.

Daulton buried it for them.

They had all watched, at Chuck's funeral, with bated breath as the prodigal son laid the book on his father's chest, closed the coffin, then sprinkled it with the soil of Chuck's beloved Cooperstown. Daulton gestured for Auffswich's crew to lower the coffin into the ground, and it had all been so convenient, poetic really, until someone went back for the book.

Amos suspected Cartwright, who had stopped Auffswich, requesting one last private moment with Chuck before the coffin was lowered into the ground. Because it was Coach who had returned the book to Mrs. Paquette. Who knew what made him do it? A last-minute whim, or had his silence been masking resentment all along? Duke, after all, was a descendant of the late great Alexander Cartwright, "the Father of Modern Baseball," whose legend (and relatives) throughout history had given Abner Doubleday's a run for its money. Cartwright said he wanted to bury a baseball with Chuck, in case he got bored on the Other Side and met someone with whom he could have a catch. But there was no baseball in that coffin when they dug it up recently, nor had there been the book. Amos was right. Perhaps Cartwright reasoned that Mrs. Paquette had a big mouth, and thus would eventually leak what was in it, thereby chalking one up for his ancestor. Or perhaps Coach thought if the document was made public, it would release them all at last from their self-made prisons. That's what Manny liked to believe. Coach had baseball in his blood, more than any of them, and he was the best of them, the smartest. Because if you couldn't trust yourself to keep a secret, what was more sensible than refusing to speak? Frank had snapped his neck, Chuck had a heart attack, Manny lost his wife, and Amos lost his. Amos also lost his son, his sobriety, and dove straight into denial. He had been there so long that he had begun to believe his own bullshit. But Cartwright? All he had to do was sit back and enjoy the rain.

Manny stood, stretching life back into his limbs as he surveyed the field. He pictured it packed once more. A full house provided distractions, so many people that you did not have to be noticed if you didn't want to be. He didn't mind playing that part, not anymore. He was drawn to it, his role in this crazy old town. Baseball was the only thing he had ever excelled at, marriage being the second until he had messed that up by going off to fight all the wrong battles. He had never really stopped fighting. But at the game—the crowd chanting his name, Ruby running out to rescue him—he'd come as close as he was ever going to get to his childhood dream. And last night, he had slept like a baby. He was too old to play ball now. There wasn't room in Cooperstown for too many people with dreams bigger than its borders. The river, the lake, and the field—everything contained in this one tiny capsule, an invisible snow dome preserving a more easily digestible reality. That's what the tourists loved.

Manny glanced at his watch; still an hour to kill before dinner. Debating whether to pick up a gift, some flowers for Ruby, he opened his wallet for a quick cash count. Inside was an old, yellowed piece of newspaper poking its way out from behind a photo of his kids. He thought about himself and Daulton when they were young, and then the two of them burning that book, burning old bridges. Daulton had done the honors, tossing *The Last of the Mohicans* into the pyre. That's when he'd asked Manny what Chuck's final words, that second order he'd shouted, had been. Manny made them up right there on the spot, the words he figured Daulton wanted so badly to hear: that he was proud of his son and for Manny to be sure to tell him that when he called back. Then Manny threw in the truth, because Chuck's had been a great exit line: "If I die, never, under any circumstances, let anyone touch my '51 Mays card."

Manny extracted the paper from his wallet, unfolding it carefully and grinning from ear to ear. It was the document, those words printed in the *Herald,* which they had come to dread.

He had fooled them all.

He glanced at his watch and decided there was only one gift he had time to deal with.

He got in his truck and drove to the Selma Wellmix Sanitarium, reflecting on Daulton's version of his own role in the events: how Bobby had given him the book after Honus returned it to the wrong library; how he'd decided not to go public with what was in it; and what had led him to give it to Manny—the two of them, together, destroying it. But Daulton had left out one thing. Because there was one thing that even that top-notch reporter had missed: Manny had removed the document from the book before it hit the fire. He told himself he had gotten used to having it around, taunting him, lingering out there in the outfield, able to call him out at any time. But it was more than that. It seemed kind of like it would be tempting fate to destroy it now, like his number really *could* come up again before he was dead. Like as long as that paper existed, it wouldn't bring what was left of his world to its knees. And now he knew the perfect place to hide it. In the hands of the one person in town who was objective enough to not be sucked in by its spell, and rational enough to get some damned help if he ever was. A person to whom a man could tell anything—reveal the worst, most vulnerable, tender, or pathetic parts of himself—and it would never come back to haunt him. It couldn't. That was the deal.

He had paid for it.

EXTRA INNING: TWELVE

Consider the entire structure of myth, superstition, and faith, and especially storytelling, that makes such deception possible. That's genius, that's the closest we'll ever get to divinity. Now you'll excuse me. I need to do some work in my study.

—KEN KALFUS,
THE COMMISSARIAT OF ENLIGHTENMENT

We have a waiting room," Chylak said, gesturing for the man poking his head through the window to come around through the door.

"Sorry," said Manny, "I didn't want to be seen."

He thanked the doctor for his evaluation, revealing his hopes that Ruby and the judge would now allow him joint custody of Toby. Chylak said to take his time, to get himself some normal clothes, put an extra coat of polyurethane on his dock, and get his mind straight before sharing it with his kids. He wanted Manny to tell Ruby the truth about why he had left her and how he was too ashamed to go back. Manny wasn't sure he could do that without feeling like more of a jackass than he already did. Knowing Ruby, it would only piss her off more, and they were finally on speaking terms. Of course, now that they were getting divorced.

"Mello Yello?" Chylak asked.

"I just stopped by to say thanks." Manny paused before handing Chylak the paper he had pulled from his wallet, which he had wrapped in the front page of *The Journal* featuring a photo of the doctor's son pinch-hitting for the mayor at the game. He was surprised at how difficult it was to let go. "And to give you this. I guess you could say it's a little token of appreciation, from Cooperstown."

Chylak was visibly moved and began unwrapping it immediately like a kid at Christmas.

"Don't," Manny said. "I mean if you don't mind, could you wait till I leave?"

Manny wasn't afraid he'd change his mind. He just didn't want to see it, that torch once it was passed. It was the embodiment of all he'd lost, all he'd forfeited—a lousy piece of paper, the meaningless words of a group of stuffy old trustees. He shook Chylak's hand and headed for the door, pausing for a moment in afterthought.

Chylak rolled his eyes, shaking his head. "I know, I know!" he said, putting both hands in the air above his head. "Whatever it is, I won't tell a soul. I'm just the 'intermediary.'" He winked two fingers on each hand—air quotes—which seemed to give him more pleasure than Manny recalled ever having seen the gesture give. Chylak grinned and Manny was certain that his secret was safe. If not, he thought, reaching into his pocket to feel the MDMA tablets Chylak had given him ("I'm not even certain they're FDA-approved"), there was always blackmail. If the rumors were true, and they generally were in Cooperstown, Chylak couldn't afford to lose another job.

Manny left the hospital and drove toward Ruby's, slowing when he passed through the parking lot of Doubleday Field. Cartwright rode his bike across the field, pulling up beside Manny's truck. Manny waited for him to move out of the road, but his old coach hopped off his bike and approached the window. "How much you want for it?" he asked.

Manny's jaw dropped. He wondered if Coach somehow knew what he and Daulton had done, if he had followed Daulton to the cabin after the game and watched them burn the book. Did Coach see him remove the document? But Cartwright was looking at him like he was crazy. "For the truck!" Coach said. "How much?"

Then Manny remembered that Ruby had given Coach his old bicycle eight years ago, one he was still riding, when she couldn't make payments on her car and Coach had loaned her his truck. It was an odd request, but he supposed he owed Cartwright that much for looking out for his family. He took the registration out of the glove compartment, wondering what to say next. "I let you down"? And what would Coach say, "I did it first"?

"It's yours," Manny said, handing Cartwright the registration. "I guess we're even now. You can keep the bike." The old man took it and tucked it in his pocket, then looked Manny straight in the eye, holding him there like that, like he was unwinding, in that one long, serious stare, twenty-two years of unspoken regrets, and then he said, "I'll come around for the vehicle next week. Nice shiner, by the way." He rode off through the parking lot, shouting, "Hey, batter-batter!" scaring a group of kids.

"I'll be damned," Manny said, watching Cartwright nearly break his neck trying to pop a wheelie. The kids were laughing now, and one handed Cartwright a buck. He pocketed it and pedaled away—Cooperstown still had one or two secrets left to keep.

Manny had fifteen minutes to kill before supper. He was nervous about seeing Ruby. He drove toward the lake, hoping to quell his nerves. The Glimmerglass sparkled like a field of diamonds. He stopped right there in the middle of Lake Street, looking out over the water toward his mountain. The Sleeping Lion rose up from the north end of the lake and somewhere behind it to the east was Cheery Valley, where Manny had squatted, a veritable Bumppo, for years. It was difficult to gauge its breadth now that the sun had set. Perhaps it was the moonlight, the shadows reflecting on the water. But that mountain looked like more of a hill really, just a little thing poking its way above the horizon. Something a really big man could squash with one fist if he felt like it or climb right over it. Or, Manny thought with a smile as he headed toward Ruby's, take a bat and whack the hell out of it until it split into pieces, plenty to go around.

◆ ◆ ◆

CHYLAK WAS AT HIS desk, feet up, bouncing a baseball off the wall. He marveled at having chosen as the target of his profession the impenetrably gelatinous enigma that is the human brain. What if what they said was true, that psychiatrists became psychiatrists in order to dissect their own psyches? It seemed like a plausible theory, considering his behavior of late. But if he had issues, that didn't leave much hope for his patients. *Or did it?* How had he expected to bat for both teams?

He flinched, having vowed against baseball analogies along with psych text citations. He had learned from Mrs. Paquette, among others, that improvisation had a more natural ring to it. One could argue that there was an aerodynamic element to flying by the seat of one's pants, which made it sort of scientific. His new policy included listening more and regurgitating dated data less. He would always be a prodder into origins, but helping people figure out *why* they needed answers now seemed more important. Answers to things like who had started something, who should take the blame, who left the toilet seat up or the top off the toothpaste; or why people drank too much, hurt themselves, became recluses, or relocated families that did not want to be relocated. The question of who was responsible versus the fact that everyone was cursed as the sole carrier of a different perspective. If you asked yourself these questions enough, he thought, you began playing both parts: responsibility to self and responsibility to others, whose ideas of your responsibility to them didn't often mesh with your own. How much easier it would be if a man could simply state, "My actions bear no explanation, I am simply an ass!" Or "Why should I explain myself to you, who are asinine?" One person's sensory motor apparatus interpreted things this way and another's that. "You're real. I'm real"—*where to go from there?* The only thing that was real, he decided, was what you told yourself. Everything else was open to interpretation. It was only fair.

He looked at the brand-new snow dome that sat on his desk, which Elliott had bought off a vendor with his allowance at the game, as an apology for having mutilated the old one. This one had little baseballs inside instead of "snow" and featured an old-fashioned Cooperstown, one stuck in the fifties. Chylak was certain one of the tiny buildings inside it was the psych ward, just a little nub on a hill overlooking the river. Peering inside that little dome, it seemed to him that the town—a cow pasture–turned–baseball diamond in the heart of it—was literally built *around* baseball.

He had given Elliott a baseball cap at the game—Team Lithium Carbonate. Elliott looked so pleased with himself wearing it. Chylak supposed that children were better equipped than adults to adjust to versions of things.

He had apologized to Elliott for forgetting to take him to the Hall of Fame, and in turn, forgave the boy for pummeling his study. He assured Elliott that when one struggled to adapt too quickly to a new environment without first letting go of the old, such behavior was inevitable, even natural, though he should not make a habit of it. He didn't mention his own Hall of Fame hissy fit, of course. He was too ashamed.

Elliott said he didn't trust Joey Olsen after what had happened to Bobblehead Joe. He had even refused Joey's generous offer of a replacement, Bobblehead Johnny Bench. He wanted his *own* bobblehead, he said, a new one, a New York player now that he was "from the Coop." Sweeter words had never found their way into Chylak's ears. Chylak assured him they would get one, together, at the Hall of Fame. It was clever, Elliott warning Joey that he was just getting over a highly contagious "adjustment disorder" and to watch it if he wanted to stay friends. Chylak was pleased to hear Joey had passed the test in responding, "That's cool, I guess."

Chylak had slept through three-quarters of the ball game, having pulled a brutal all-nighter the evening before with umpteen complimentary consultations for the tourists who had besieged his office and lawn. Had he charged them each his regular rate, he could have saved a little something toward an early retirement. But he wasn't thinking about that. He was thinking how pleased he was that he had made it to the game in time to see his son standing in for the mayor. "You were like the Incredible Husk out there today, sport!" he said to Elliott after the game, removing his cap and mussing his hair. Elliott had rolled his eyes. "It's the *Hulk,* Dad," he said, giving Chylak a sympathy hug. Then he announced that he had decided to give Cooperstown a second chance because, in the poignant words of Alice, "How bad can it *suck*?"

Mr. Barrett had just left Chylak's office. In his opinion, the hermit had a better shot at improving his communication skills than the entire lot of his patients combined. Barrett alone had come forward to release himself from himself. And now, Chylak was again smack-dab in the middle of the *moment*. He suspected now that one's arrival at such was largely self-propelled, whether one allowed oneself a brief heightened sense of the now, or returned intentionally to recapture a moment past and beat it into submission before it got away again. It seemed less about the moment than the awareness of such, and the fight to remain in it, alert, if only to prove that every witness counts.

Taking his cue from the mayor, he made a list of his moments: meeting Babe and savoring every sweet minute of her soft-spoken biblical spiel; the births of his children; witnessing, through the windows of a neighboring house in Lebanon, the individual reactions, room by room, of a family following its matriarch's wake; the day after his own father died, when he opened the shutters to curse at the world for continuing and was met by a series of cumulus clouds so exquisite that he could only be grateful; and at age seven, a young Chylak harassing a friend who owed him a nickel, calling an unspoken truce when the kid's dog was hit by a car, knowing he'd never ask for that nickel again, because he had lost the right, the world had become bigger than him. He supposed these highlights were ingrained in his noggin because they were all occasions in which he'd been forced to analyze himself, to gauge his reaction to the world to be certain they were in sync. Or perhaps it was simply the desire to retrace his steps back to a time that once seemed significant or sweet. Or these were all just random imprints burned into his brain, an inherent system of self-hypnosis: you will remember *this* but not *this*. And what a remarkable pattern they formed! Babe would probably say that the majority of his Moments had a theme: atonement.

Regardless of the events, bad and good, that occurred to bring Chylak to *this* moment, he quite consciously cherished the gift he had just been given—Barrett's document. The trust it took, or the testicles, depending on which side of the glass you drank from. It was, in fact, his most precious moment since arriving in Cooperstown, and he was proud to say that it had caught him only *slightly* off guard.

Barrett had stopped by not for another blowout session or to retract what he'd confided earlier that month, a tactic first-timers often used: "Never mind, I didn't kill anyone, Doc," or "I was kidding about the voices." He stopped by to say thanks and to give Chylak a gift, this well-worn piece of newspaper, the itch in Cooperstown's baseball bonnet that had been unraveling its collective consciousness long before—thank heavens—he had arrived. The first resolution in the new Chylakian order of handling patients would be to remind himself whenever necessary: "None of this is *my* fault."

He remembered what Barrett had said during his initial visit following the night of the town meeting, how he and the others had hidden this once legal, and now rather asinine, ordinance revealing that Cooperstown was perhaps *not* the birthplace of baseball, because it had initially barred the sport from its streets. In other words, Cooperstown was no fan, not at first anyway. Cooperstown struck Chylak as being a mother who'd once abandoned her infant, only to return years later, seeking forgiveness, urging everyone to "pretend this never happened." He pictured them, the mayor, Honus, and Barrett, unearthing Chuck Daulton's grave in the middle of the night. The mayor swilling Geritol, perhaps singing some ancient barroom dirge while the baffled security guard dug, and Barrett struggled with wanting to do what was right and wanting to be a part of a community again. They were looking for a book, Barrett said, containing the paper now in Chylak's hands. An ordinance penned by the old village trustees, presided over by one Isaac Cooper, Judge William Cooper's lesser-known son.

The only thing that had kept Chylak's mirth in check upon Barrett's revelation was that he had already heard this story before, from Daulton, a journalist who for once had witnessed the entirety of a situation he was determined to scoop and which involved the exhumation of his father. Daulton was right that night he had appeared peaked and puking on Chylak's steps: he *had* seen Chuck. His remains, at least, and he'd witnessed, with horror, the men who claimed to respect his father in life disrespecting him in death. Daulton, the poor traumatized, depersonalized son of a gun, so afraid he'd lose his mind.

The mayor had apparently considered exposing the ordinance as a desperate last resort, a metaphorical group suicide to keep the theme park out—Cooperstown chewing off its own paw in order to send the message, "Go away! We banished baseball! We don't deserve a whole theme park full of it! Forgive us! We're phonies! Psychosomatics! It was a placebo sort of thing!" For who would build a baseball temple on such unhallowed ground? The plan was short-lived and incomplete. They could have lost everything, the Hall of Fame, the Baseball Library—and soon they learned they had never even had a choice: the park was coming, the book was gone, and by then nobody wanted it out there where it could cause more harm than good. But Cartwright had swiped it and given it to Mrs. Paquette, who had enshrined it in the museum with her dead husband's things. Honus found it and returned it to a library at which it did not belong, to the librarian his heart belonged to, just to prove *he* belonged. And Ms. Reboulet exposed it, giving it to Daulton, who struggled with it. He turned it over to the hermit and they burned it, unbeknownst to Daulton without its precious creamy filling. Barrett gave that part to Chylak, who felt dizzy now trying to piece it all together. He recalled an old nursery rhyme from one of Elliott's books, one he felt, in this case, ought to be entitled "The House That Ruth Built":

> *This is the house that Ruth built.*
> *This is the ball that lay in the house.*
> *This is the rag, about the ball, which lay in the book that consumed them all.*
> *This is the mute who stole the book to give to the gal obsessed with looks,*
> *To leave with a crook who loved a gal who worshipped books,*
> *Who tried to exploit it with a reporter for whom it was fodder for a good yarn*
> *Who enlisted the hermit with the great arm to burn near the barn.*
> *Except for the rag hid in the bag:*
> *A gift for the doc, new on the block*
> *Who saved the ball*
> *For them all,*
> *For who would think*
> *To ask the shrink?*

Chylak was pleased with himself for managing to stay largely on the periphery of all this nonsense, when he realized that wasn't true. The book he had returned to the library for Elliott, one that had been in his own home under his very own spectacles unobserved, and the book in question were one and the same: *The Last of the Mohicans.* He had, in fact, returned it to the library *himself.* It was not as though a person could be expected to smell hysteria! Still, he would have preferred knowing that he was in the presence of it, lest some higher power somewhere out there now be laughing hysterically at *him.*

So he had served his purpose after all—who knew he'd been breaking some age-old pact by returning that book, that he had been such an important player in such a cockamamie, though significant, chain of events? He had passed the torch to the librarian, thereby causing the mayor and his men to make one last madcap dash for the document, Amos desperate to lock away his secret and any more that might come oozing out of Chuck

Daulton's museum and cottage, the key to which had not been lost, but handed over to one totally trustworthy, though unsuspecting, Mr. Willie Mays.

Chylak remembered now what had been plaguing Chuck Daulton during his final days: there *was* a possession that had troubled him! One might even say it had possessed him. He had defied the mayor's orders and never burned Cooper's papers. Amos's ransacking of the Funhouse ballroom had been for naught. Chylak pitied the mayor, though he admired the ferocity with which Fusselback had tried to protect both his pact and his pack, unaware that the unsympathetic-to-Cooperstown's-cause librarian was already on the trail, scooping the journalist, who was finally free to take off running the moment the story broke.

The whole thing reminded him of those odd wooden dolls Alice kept in her room, which opened endlessly, one tucked inside the other until there was just the tiniest little embryo, a concept that had always disturbed him, yet he fell for it every time, opening them over and over to the very last one, as though there would eventually be a different result, a surprise. He hated being tricked by so obvious, so redundant a conceit.

The ordinance was the cause of a heart attack, a hanging, a questionable speech impediment, an unfruitful "enlistment," and an unquestionable penchant for alcohol. It had affected so many lives, and he couldn't help but feel that if he had only arrived on the scene sooner, he could have stopped it, the eruption, instead of arriving in the Moment in hindsight once more. But that was his role, where his skills really lay: someone had to be the one to piece everyone else back together once they cracked. There was no "rescuing" people who had no idea they required rescuing. Unfortunately, one had to wait for them to fall. He rubbed the tape on his glasses, certain that he wouldn't have been any more licensed to repair things had he arrived sooner. For once, Kerwin Chylak was right on time.

Barrett and Daulton had had their way with the book one last time, an obsessive last rite, burning it in a sort of funeral pyre behind the hermit's cabin. They had watched *The Last of the Mohicans* disintegrate in silence, not, Barrett said, because the moment was profound, or because he and Daulton hadn't spoken in so long that they had no clue where to start, but because too much had already been said without anyone really hearing it.

Chylak thought about Babe—how badly he wanted to tell her this story! How Barrett had pulled one final trick from his "Cooperstown" cap, removing the ordinance from the book before it burned. He gave the book jacket to Daulton, however, as a keepsake, a reminder of having shed his former skin.

Chylak had listened to Barrett describe what it was like to lay his hands on the object that had plagued him for so long. The release he had felt upon burning that book. And Chylak had asked him *why* he had then kept the document, thinking a direct approach to the epidemic that plagued his new town was best summed up by one of its own. Barrett merely replied that he had gotten used to it the way you got used to a wart, or a callus on your heel: the next thing you knew you were rubbing it smooth out of habit, accepting it as a part of you until it wasn't so monstrous anymore.

Chylak glanced at his copy of *Psycho-Cybernetics: A New Way to Get More Living Out of Life,* by Maxwell Maltz, MD—fighting the urge to open it, just one quote, an appetizer. He knew what Barrett meant. A man grew accustomed to his faults, and when given a choice to eradicate them was hesitant to let them go.

Daulton had bid Chylak good-bye before he left town. He promised to write if Chylak promised not to tell anyone where he wound up, at least not until he had a chance to establish a career on his own terms away from the pressure of his father's memory and those who so doggedly kept it alive. Chylak had surprised himself, trading Daulton for his confidences. "I didn't move to Cooperstown for a change of scenery," he said, thinking that since Daulton was no longer his patient, he could afford to have him as a friend. He confessed that he hadn't consciously been seeking a bucolic haven in which to play good country doc. "I was fired," he said, "from my last job." Fired in Lebanon for not being "people oriented," for lacking "interpersonal skills." Fired once more, *dismissed* by Babe for keeping the news from her until it was too late for her to say "I told you so," or even "What can I do to help?" He had been worried about finances, about his reputation, and, most of all, that Babe would leave him: that she would forget she had chosen him too. He had, in effect, chickened out and flown to "the Coop," and by the time he was ready to talk, as was always the case with Babe, she already knew. That damnable Dr. Barker, his Lebanon replacement, had told his wife, who had questioned Babe. Babe had known all along: the cold looks, the silent treatment, penance in the form of relentless vegetables when she knew damn well he loved her pot roast. He wasn't sure about the blatant bedtime Bible-reading. She had pretty much always done that. He just hadn't noticed, or wanted to. These were all messages he had missed, ones his neurotransmitters had let fall by the wayside, a volley from one synapse to another until—*kerplunk*—they fell into a gray-matter void. And had he not dropped the ball, he would have realized Babe's message all along was simply this: "Tell me. I already know, but you owe it to me to hear it from you."

Not being "people oriented" and his wife being a "people," Chylak had lost his confidence when he lost his job, his patients, and the trust of the people he loved. He became a self-fulfilling prophecy with a little help from the Lebanon Institute, the psych board giving him that final push. And Babe had saved them— telling the children that Daddy had been given a great new opportunity, making the best of things like she always did. Going along with it. And Chylak, with everyone saved, had had nothing left to do, no role to play, and thus had found it easier to retreat into his books, relying on the wisdom of men who had gone before him and who probably knew better. The advice he doled out was out of context and out of date in order to distance him from reality, so the sting of being incompetent wouldn't be so painful, should his new patients feel the same as the old.

But here he was now, he thought, carefully unfolding Barrett's document, orienting himself to people, able to see that he needed this job, that he needed them as much as they needed him.

He laid the crumpled old clipping from the *Otsego Herald* on his desk, smoothing it out. It was dated a delicious June 6, 1816, this culprit that lay under the heading VILLAGE ORDINANCES, circled in black ink.

> *Be it ordained, That the several ordinances heretofore passed, relating to swine running at large in the streets of the village of Cooperstown . . .*

"I swear to Freud," Chylak said, scanning the remainder of the document, "if this turns out to have all been about *pork*." He continued.

> *Be it ordained by the Trustees of the village of Cooperstown, That from and after the passing of this ordinance, no swine be permitted or suffered to run at large in any street or alley in this village.—And that the owner of any swine, that shall be found running at large in any street or alley in this village, shall, for each and every offence, forfeit and pay two dollars and fifty cents, for each and every swine so found running at large . . .*

Chylak was about to give up on the dreaded document. It read more like one of Elliott's Dr. Seuss tales than any newspaper he had ever read. He was about to give up on the whole lot of them, in fact, Barrett included, until he read the last line.

> *Be it ordained, That no person shall play at Ball . . . in this village, under a penalty of one dollar, for each and every offence.*

Bingo! The bit between "ball" and "in this village" was so smudged that he couldn't decipher it completely, but he got the gist of it, as had all those who had read it before him: Cooperstown, home of baseball, had initially tried to prevent the sport from tainting its virgin borders. And for all intents and purposes, one could argue it was doing so again with the theme park. Only now, Cooperstown was dependent on baseball for its very existence.

During Chylak's trip to the Baseball Library he had skimmed a book that suggested, to he who did the math, that Abner Doubleday may have never even set foot in Cooperstown. Another implied that baseball originated much closer to the city. Much of the Doubleday evidence, it seemed, had reportedly been destroyed in a fire in 1916, and Doubleday's own diary apparently never mentioned it, which was odd in light of the mayor's diary, which documented every absurd thing he had ever done. Another text suggested that there were, in fact, *two* Abner Doubledays, and Chylak considered that the man might have had a split personality. The real kicker, however, was a tome on one Alexander *Cartwright*, an engineer-turned-Hall-of-Famer and acclaimed "Father of Modern Baseball," a founding member of the first organized ball club and the man who sanctified the sport's rules— the first officially documented game of which was in 1846: Cartwright's Knickerbocker Base Ball Club versus the New York Baseball Club, played in *New Jersey,* no less. Cartwright, whom Barrett had claimed was an ancestor of Cooperstown's very own Duke! Barrett said that Alexander Cartwright's relatives had challenged the commission that dubbed Doubleday baseball's daddy, and Chylak wondered if Duke was challenging it still, and if *that* is why he had stolen the document. He envisioned himself as the hero that got Cooperstown's longtime mute to at last open his gob and sing out that Coo, Coo, Cooperstown was not what it claimed to be.

Barrett said he was unable to play ball once he realized that everything he had ever believed in was up for question. But he had never been able to stop loving the game, and sometimes stood on his dock late at night batting stones with branches into the lake, imagining it a baseball diamond, and imagining that the tourists hooting and hollering downstream were cheering for him, and that the music that wafted across the water from the opera house came from the speakers of some major-league ball-park, a song played only for him.

As for the mayor, Chylak had told Amos, during their last session, to continue putting his thoughts to paper, to fill the pages of his diary lest he forget his own Moments. He consoled Fusselback with the suggestion that perhaps, one day, even *that* document might be of some worth. After all, Amos the Fuss had witnessed the evolution of Cooperstown through decades of glory and gloom, and now that the theme park was on its way, commercialism could very well consume the town as he knew it, for better or for worse. And no one outside its borders would ever know that Cooperstown was the bear that had almost chewed off its own foot in order to free itself. In the interim, Chylak thought, relieved, its residents had faced their own personal histories: not bad for a day's work, even if it had taken him all summer to see it, to *listen*.

His new secretary flew into the room, not being much of a knocker.

"Come in," he said facetiously, tucking the ordinance quickly into a drawer, having learned the hard way during Mrs. Paquette's first week on the job that she inquired about *everything*.

"You have a new patient!" she said.

Chylak looked at his appointment book—completely clear. He had cleared it intentionally to spend more time with his family.

"What's wrong with him?" he asked, hopeful that if it didn't constitute an emergency, he could reschedule and escape unscathed.

"Ask *her* yourself," said Mrs. Paquette, smiling her up-to-no-good smile and ushering the patient in.

Babe.

Chylak's wife plunked down on the couch across from him. "Ooh, it's quite cozy in here, isn't it?" she said, looking around the room. "You ought to have this couch re-covered, however. I can feel the springs in my tush."

Chylak was stumped. It occurred to him that he had never invited Babe to see his new office, nor had she ever asked to come, nor had he ever heard her use the word *tush*.

"Do you remember when we got this couch?" she asked with a smile.

"I do," he said. It was their first couch in their very first home in Lebanon. They bought it just before Alice was born. He stared at Babe, trying to figure out what was different about her. The hair? It looked more *buoyant* somehow.

"Are you wearing makeup?" he asked, shocked.

She smiled again and Chylak decided now was as good a time as any to test his newly developed interpersonal skills and ask his wife something that had been on his mind since they first arrived in town.

"Babe?"

"Kerwin?"

"What do you make of idolatry?"

Babe frowned and sat up, reaching across his desk to rattle the snow dome. Chylak snuck a quick peak at her bosom, which had for so long been cloaked beneath neck-high nighties and burdensome Bible Camp tees.

"What kind of question is that?" she asked, shaking the snow dome violently.

Chylak treaded carefully.

"What I meant was: are you *for* it, or *against* it?"

"*What?*"

"Hero worship!"

"Kerwin, really," she said with a sigh, her expression shifting from amused to relieved to confused to suspicious. "Everything isn't a contest. You *know* I believe. The Lord is my hero . . ."

Chylak cringed.

"Next to you, of course," she said, returning the snow dome to its rightful place and looking at him in the manner in which a mother examines a child whose temperature needs taking. "Are you feeling all right?"

Chylak nodded, afraid to speak.

"I mean, what do you *think?*" Babe continued. "That I've been making it up all along, my beliefs, just to spite you? Is *that* what you think?"

"Of course not," he said. "Well, I had hoped—"

"Kerwin!"

"Sorry!" He decided to keep mum about his theory that scrupulosity was an obsessive trait.

Babe softened, saying, "Well, hope to yourself, please." She turned the snow dome upside down, shaking it upright again.

Chylak was mesmerized by the way the flakes swirled madly around, then floated gracefully one by one like minuscule feathers, or dandruff, back to the bottom again. He decided to take it home to his study, where (he hoped) it would be manhandled less. "I didn't mean *you*," he said. "I just meant people."

"I know that," said Babe. "But what about you? Don't you believe in anything?"

Chylak had never really thought about it. He supposed he believed in the Hippocratic oath, and in those who challenged the FDA. He definitely believed in the research being done on a drug called Xanax, which might prove useful for mania. He believed in progress, in people, in the CAT scan, sedatives, and science, and he believed in his marriage, though he was at a loss as to how to say all this to his wife.

She drummed her fingers on the desktop, waiting.

"You know," he fumbled, "I read a theory that—"

"No, Kerwin, *you*. Right now: do you as a person believe?"

John Wayne had recently died, and in a way, Chylak had worshipped *him*. If that's what she meant. If they were playing name your idol. He hoped they weren't, for if his was an actor, then her Almighty Defender would undoubtedly win. Was this a game of my hero's better than yours?

"I suppose," he said, looking his wife straight in the eyes so she didn't get the wrong idea and whisk him off to church. "On *my* terms."

"Man's terms," Babe sighed.

"Well, you may not have noticed lately, but technically I am a *man*."

"That's nothing," he expected her to say, watching for a sign, a huff of breath, or, worse, for her to start mouthing a prayer for him. But her face was calm. And Chylak watched her alter her diagnosis right there and then, now content with the notion not that he was being a pain in the ass, but that he did not actually *know* better.

"Fair enough," she said before he could defend himself. She rose and straightened her skirt. "Dinner. Six o'clock. Me and you." She gave the snow dome one last rattle, kissed him, and left.

"Hold the fort, Dusty, my dear!" Chylak announced into the intercom once Babe was out of earshot. "*I* have a dinner date."

Mrs. Paquette made a high-pitched whoop and barged into the room, hosing him down with Home-Run Perfect Game Patchouli. "It's an aphrodisiac!" she said with a wink, and Chylak blushed.

Alone once more, he felt tempted to let out a little whoop himself. *Next* to him, Babe had said, He was her hero. Chylak hadn't been asking her to choose, and he knew it was a lie, that she was only trying to soothe him, but he would take it. He would take it and run with it—*he* was still her main squeeze.

He listened to be sure Mrs. Paquette was immersed in a phone call in the other room, knowing it was probably about him, then looked up toward the ceiling, toward Him, and succumbed to a tactic his children used whenever one had outwitted the other. Holding his hand in front of his face with his thumb on his nose and the remainder of his fingers upright in the air like the keys of a trumpet, he sang, "*Na-na-na-na-naaaa-na!*" wiggling his fingers. He touched his lips to savor Babe's kiss, feeling a slight stickiness there. He licked his fingers. Home-Run Batters Faced Boysenberry Lipstick. Babe's makeup, her bouncy new perm—Mrs. Paquette knew no bounds, and for once, Chylak thanked heaven that Babe had made a little sacrifice just for him.

Mrs. Paquette was cackling away in the other room and Chylak realized what it was that he liked about her: she didn't give up on anyone. She pried and she tried and she meddled and she occasionally mucked things up. But she always meant well. She did her best to draw people closer together, closer to her, to crack them open like a barrel of nuts so she wasn't left stranded alone and vulnerable in a world that was often too big to tackle alone.

He retrieved the ordinance from his drawer, accidentally getting Babe's lipstick on it and wiping it away carefully with a tissue. "Shit," he said, having wiped harder than he intended to and thus removing not only the lipstick but whatever had been smudged across the latter part of the document, which now read:

> *Be it ordained, That no person shall play at Ball in Second or West street, in this village, under a penalty of one dollar, for each and every offence.*

"Oops," he said, grabbing the phone to call Barrett and give him the good news, and then remembering the man had no phone. Then he began to wonder if it *was* good news after all: if this was simply a standard ordinance suggesting that baseball not be played in the streets, and only in *two* streets at that, probably to keep windows from being smashed, was it wise to mention that to people just coming down from twenty-two years of hysterics over it? Chylak thought not. This would be his little secret. It would kill them, some of them perhaps quite literally, to know they had tortured themselves for naught. Besides, it had proved rather fruitful for them to sweat it out. A nice little cleansing, as Mrs. Paquette would say.

Chylak looked around the room, smiling when he spotted, on the top of his bookshelf, the *Oxford NIV Scofield Study Bible* Babe had given him on the day they met. Babe had no idea he had kept it, but he had for sentimental reasons. He stood on his chair and retrieved it, blowing dust from its cover, pleased to find the bookmark she'd slipped inside it that wintry day at the bus stop—her phone number scrawled on it. On the other side was a poem entitled "Footprints," across a golden beach that, he imagined, enhanced to the preposterous proportions of his bedroom wallpaper, could actually be quite soothing. The poem was about a man miffed at the Almighty, feeling he'd been let down at the moments in his life when he most needed saving, proved by the fact that there was just one set of footprints in the sand representing his life's journey during his most difficult times. Times when perhaps his divine idol ought to have been there, walking alongside him. But the man is mistaken: the Lord had simply picked him up and slung him over his shoulder, the lone set of footprints thus belonging to *Him.*

Chylak looked at his feet, thinking it was a nice sentiment but would be nicer still if there was a lone footprint due to the man having worn the wrong shoes (perhaps one of them was a flimsy bedroom slipper) and thus hopping along, doing his best on his own, aside from an occasional slip. He flipped through the book in search of a fitting place to store the document—what better place to hide it than in a book that wouldn't likely be manhandled by him, or anyone else who entered this room, often enough to merit alarm?

He skimmed a story about a man called Lot who offered up his virgin daughters in order to save his guests from being sodomized—damned if he did, damned if he didn't, not unlike poor Cooperstown. He stopped at 2 Samuel upon seeing the line *I am the son of an alien.* Perhaps there was more to this Bible busi-ness than he had previously assumed. He wondered if the pre-quel, 1 Samuel, delved further into the extraterrestrial bit, and then read on about David and a man called (what else?) Abner in a fight for a coveted kingdom: *The battle that day was very fierce, and Abner and the men of Israel were defeated by David's men.* At one point Abner cried, *Don't you realize that this will end in bitterness?* and at an-other he posed a question to David through his messengers: *Whose land is it?* A jealous rival murdered him; the king wept at his tomb and *all the people wept also.*

Compelled, Chylak flipped through the rest of the book, amused to find a chapter entitled Ruth, and shocked to find one called Amos. He was searching for a Daulton or a Barrett when he came across a bit in Isaiah about an Immanuel: *Before the boy knows enough to reject the wrong and choose the right, the land of the two kings you dread will be laid to waste.*

Satisfied with having baby-stepped his way through Babe's Big Book, he tucked it into a drawer beside *Going Crazy*. If there was a God and what they said about Him was true, He likely knew a thing or two about internal conflicts and therefore would surely forgive one small moment of weakness. Chylak browsed through *Going Crazy* to learn that "therapy" derived from *therepeia* (to serve). Then he found what he was looking for, a page dog-eared as evidence of his last fix. He scrolled to a section called "How Radical Therapy Can Help People: The Radical Thera-pist." Then he locked the door, drew the shades, and lay back on his couch.

> *The person who wishes to help people through a medium which [he] calls therapy (or problem-solving, or crisis-intervention or whatever) needs to be liberated from as many of the mystifying aspects of life in Amerika as possible. . . . The therapist must try to discover the ways in which [he] is mystified. [He] must be in touch with [his] own ex-perience and feelings and reject the interpretations of that experience made by others. The radical therapist must as much as possible reject living as a therapist.*

He closed his eyes and lay there for a spell before returning to his desk. He dropped *Going Crazy* in the drawer beside the Bible, now housing "his" document. Let the Good Word and the rational one duke it out on their own. *He* had a date for dinner: Chylak and Babe, man and wife, supping on roast beet loaf with lamb gravy, all part of their new Cooperstown Compromise. One he hoped would soon come to include a meatier diet for him and silent prayers from Babe at bedtime, preferably ones that didn't include him in the context of "people en route to hell."

He was looking forward to hearing about Babe's day when he got home, and all the days hence, to their worshipping each other's company for a change. And afterward, when it was his turn to recount his day, he would tell Babe he had read that ole Bible of hers, and that while the glorious gates of heaven hadn't sucked him miraculously in, he could see how it at least made for decent toilet reading. For instance, had she read the bit about *aliens?*

HOME

This is the last pure place where Americans dream. This is the last great arena, the last green arena, where everybody can learn the lessons of life.

—Marcus Giamatti

There was nothing so welcoming to changelings as New York State in fall. It was late October. The tourists and the media were long gone and Cooperstown was now prime leaf-watching country: sugar, red, and silver maples, oak and beech—an entire palette of colors that Kerwin Chylak had never before seen. It was good, this country living. He and Babe were learning to negotiate. They had even discussed the possibility of moving closer to the lake, or to the outskirts of town, where they could have a small chunk of land for the kids to enjoy. He had just driven through a quaint township called Hartlick, thinking perhaps *it* would be nice—an easy commute into Cooperstown for work—until he saw the sign stating FORMERLY NEW JERUSALEM. They might be negotiating, but, formerly or not, he wasn't ready to go *that* far.

He drove to Cooperstown's new theme park, Fielders' Dream, which the press had dubbed "the formative gemstone of the future of baseball." It was targeted at kids, those who wanted some good clean fun as well as those determined to one day grow up to become serious ballplayers. Chylak and Babe were not the only ones who had worked out a compromise: the park was built on the outskirts of town. Chylak was pleased for the townsfolk, though to him it seemed rather like the baseball disease was merely spreading itself beyond its host. Johnny and his henchmen had met with Amos and his cronies. Together, they had agreed to merge past traditions with a modern sensibility. The theme park was chock full of ball fields to be used for Little League camps, drawing children from across the nation. It also boasted plenty of batting cages for anyone who wanted to try out their swing, and ever-changing exhibits geared toward all ages that managed to compliment, not threaten, those found at the Hall of Fame. The baseball museum remained where it had stood for decades, on Main Street. Part of the park was equipped with carnival games and a few spectacular rides. It wouldn't be completed until the following summer, but it was open for tours: a sneak peek for those who wanted to bring their children or to feel like a kid for a day.

Chylak pulled up to the entrance and waved to his kids, who ran through the gates. Alice worked at the park part-time on weekends, selling hot dogs at one of the numerous concession stands. Sometimes, if she wasn't busy, she let Elliott and his school chums—he had several and the friendship bracelets to prove it—use the batting cages for free. Chylak thought, watching his children exit that source of so much anguish and amusement, that perhaps it did not matter *where* baseball had originated. It clearly belonged here, on the fringe of the bat-shaped curve that was Cooperstown, with the people who had committed themselves to upholding its legend.

His children knew everything by now, the reasons behind the move, everything but the details of his baseball breakdown, of course. In hindsight—a place from which Chylak hoped to finally break his sublet—he felt it would have been easier if he had been up front at the start, certainly easier on Babe. She was so patient, so supportive while he explained to the kids that he had not won the coveted Cooperstown post in a drawing at the Lebanon Psychiatric Institute, nor had the town's desperate residents read about him in *Psychiatry Yesterday* and sent fan mail begging him to come save them. A sympathetic colleague who had interned in Cooperstown, and who knew of his situation, had simply taken pity on him, recommending him to the director of the Selma Wellmix Sanitarium—the same colleague who loaned him the questionable MDMA tablets, which he now realized had been intended solely for *him*. That colleague had recommended Cooperstown as the perfect place to get away, to make a new start. A quiet place "without a lot of drama." Chylak laughed, recalling that conversation. Cooperstown was quiet, all right, but in its own rather boisterous way. And it had not taken him long to realize, within the confines of this Eden upstate, that he had come to escape from none other than himself. But by then it was too late: he had taken his wife and children hostage. He, a psychiatrist whose job it was to merely dole out meds, found himself playing psychologist, father, husband, and friend and *liking* it. He suspected now that his colleague had known exactly what the position would entail. And it pleased him to think that meant he had also known that Chylak was up to it.

Alice and Elliott climbed into the car and began chattering away, Alice snitching that Elliott had broken a bat, and Elliott tattling that Alice, who wouldn't let him move his seat back, had been "sucking face" with a boy behind the batting cages. Chylak cringed and was about to inquire about this further when he saw a familiar face. He told the kids to wait in the car and walked toward the security booth.

Honus stepped out and asked to see his identification. Chylak smiled, annoyed when he realized Honus was serious. It was good to see him working again. Honus had spent the month of September in a terrible funk, which Chylak walked him through with thrice-weekly sessions. He had been fired from the Hall of Fame for replacing a display of a red silk ribbon embroidered CREIGHTON 1860, honoring player Jim Creighton, with a pink polyester ribbon that read CRONIN 1979. Chylak suspected that on some subconscious level Honus wanted to get fired, to break free from Frank Paquette's overpowering shadow. Honus was racked with guilt at first, because he'd done what he swore he'd never do: favor the park over the Hall of Fame. But Chylak convinced him that getting paid more was not necessarily the same as selling out. Now, if only he could convince Honus that the fact Amos had called him "son" recently didn't mean the man was going to let him move in with him and Mrs. Paquette-Fusselback. That happy couple lived in Dusty's old house on River Street, having turned the former mayor's place into a beauty salon, which townsfolk and tourists alike seemed to appreciate. As a favor to Chylak, the Fusselbacks had invited Honus to Sunday brunch, Chylak hoping to demonstrate that in the absence of family, friendship was often a close second. Honus was his new pet project, his reformable narcissist who he was determined would not spend the rest of his life alone inside his own head. Cronin may never come *out* of his head, but someone would care enough to join him there, eventually—Chylak thought about Babe—for someone always did. Honus did not have to wait long, however, for Mrs. Paquette-Fusselback had invited a charming neighbor to the brunch as well, one Mada Nauss, the German widow, to whom Honus had taken an instant liking. *Too* much of a liking, considering the woman was twice his age and Chylak would now have to wean him off mother figures again.

A new wing of the Hall of Fame was being erected, dedicated to the memory of Frank Paquette. The ribbon-cutting ceremony was set for spring, and Chylak was taking Alice and Elliott. That was the biggest news of late. Though what hit the town hard was the controversial news about Willie Mays being asked by the baseball commissioner to distance himself from major-league baseball by stepping down as goodwill ambassador to the Mets if he took a post as a hotel casino greeter for Bally Manufacturing Corporation. Mays took the casino gig and gave up his position, though that hardly meant he had not "chosen" baseball. He had been inducted. He was immortal now. Chylak had read about it in *The New York Times,* along with an article about a new television network called ESPN, which he was horrified to learn would be devoted solely to sports. He had been browsing the paper in search of Terry Daulton's piece on the history of baseball in the

Dominican Republic. Daulton had become what Chylak thought of as a grounded nomad: a travel writer–sportswriter whose beat was the *history* of baseball worldwide, ever his father's son and now a respected journalist. The last Chylak had heard, Daulton was researching a piece he hoped to write on an LA high school team, Crenshaw, and a kid called Huckleberry (or was it Strawberry?), who he said had tremendous talent reminiscent of a young Manny Barrett.

Chylak said good-bye to Honus and returned to the car. The amusement park gates were as close to baseball as he ever wanted to get again, aside of course from living in Cooperstown. The Fusslebutts, as Elliott called them, giggling hysterically, pulled up in a large Winnebago: Amos and Dusty were about to embark on an "exotic" trip to the Poconos. They gave Honus the key to their love nest so he could water Dusty's plants while they were gone. Amos had retired his longtime post as mayor earlier that month, and rumor had it (according to his new wife, of course) that *Johnny* might take his place. He was among several candidates up for the post since losing the Senate race. Amos and his son still weren't speaking, though there was talk of a play-off for dibs on the furniture in Amos's office, some silly game, Chylak had heard, involving a duck and a rock. And that was all the evidence Chylak needed to stay put. He could not leave Cooperstown alone with itself. Granted, no one would rule it with more chutzpah than another Fusselback. But he'd better stick around just in case. They might need him. It was like he had told Elliott at bedtime not so long ago: "I'm talking about the *individual* at a pivotal moment in history. You never know who that individual is going to be."

Chylak was glad Daulton had escaped for a while, knowing he would eventually find a home base and accept the fact that he'd be compromising with his father's ideals for the rest of his days, like any son who admired his dad, so he might as well sit back and learn to live with it. Chylak also knew that Ms. Reboulet, with permission from the state, had turned Chuck Daulton's old cottage, where she now lived, into a bed-and-breakfast to house minor leaguers in town for various exhibition games at Double-day Field. Manny Barrett had surprised everyone by donating a large sum of money to the cause, money that only Chylak knew the source of: the ex-mayor's Fenimore Funhouse Roof Fund. For years, Amos had been skimming cash off the top of the donations he solicited to repair the museum's roof, using them to care for his pet hermit, Barrett.

As the new curator of the newly repaired Fenimore Funhouse, Bobby Reboulet was a busy woman, though not so busy that she didn't have time for romance. She had become quite a serial dater in fact, her affections devoted strictly to ballplayers passing through town—no strings attached. Her outlook had improved, as had her complexion, according to Mrs. Paquette-Fusselback, who kept her b&b supplied with Home-Run toiletries for the guests. Chylak also knew that Manny had recently taken his younger son to the hospital for a badly bruised buttocks, the boy having misjudged the distance to the water during an attempted cannonball off his dad's dock, and that Ruby, who had become friendly with Babe, had broken up with her ballplayer beau and was considering inviting her ex over for Thanksgiving.

Chylak knew these things because he had their confidences, all of them. He was the new keeper of Cooperstown's secrets, including those it kept from itself. All that had been revealed to him had been done so under the Hippocratic oath: "What I may see or hear in the course of the treatment or even outside of the treatment in regard to the life of men . . . I will keep to myself." He was well aware that the coveted role of hero—therapist, ballplayer, or God—was cyclical, always changing, that there would always be room for one more Incredible Hunk. It was just a question of who steered the course in the interim, of who grabbed hold of the Moment.

Duke Cartwright exited the park in his new truck, which had been repainted orange zest by the Little League team he now coached. The back was filled with baseballs, and sitting on top of them like a cocky young king on a mountain of white gold was

Aidan Barrett, his new assistant coach. Manny was now groundskeeper of Doubleday Field. That pickup truck that often idled outside Chylak's office and sometimes his house, the one now belonging to Cartwright, had of course been Barrett's. Sometimes, Chylak still saw Manny out there, sitting silently in his Jeep with the engine running. He knew that when Barrett was ready he would come farther out of his shell. Perhaps all the way, to unwind the damage he had done to himself. He imagined himself leading Barrett triumphantly across the old stone bridge above the Susquehanna where his troubles began. Or was it possible that he'd misdiagnosed the man? Perhaps Barrett had made his peace and only sat parked in his pickup spying because he was curious about Chylak the way Chylak was once curious about him. They were on opposite ends of the microscope, flip-flopping between examiner and examined, or communicator and incommunicado, each wondering about life on the other end of the spectrum. The other side of the forest.

Cartwright pulled up alongside Chylak's car, tagging the windshield, and said something that sounded not unlike "earned run." Alice thought it sounded more like "eardrum"; Cartwright had apparently been lobbed in the head earlier by one of Elliott's more enthusiastic balls. Chylak admired Cartwright, partly because he seemed to be a man uniquely capable of working out his inner kinks on his own and because he had nobly sacrificed his claim as heir to the throne of "the Father of Modern Baseball" for his town. Chylak expected, however, that the question of who invented baseball and where and when would be cyclical. There would always be another theory, some ancient artifact unearthed in a basement, a doozy written in a long-forgotten diary, an illuminating prize poking its head out of a forgotten past, just to keep people guessing.

"What's this, Dad?" Elliott asked, extracting a book from the glove compartment as Chylak pulled out into the road. It was a leftover from his former addiction, *Psycho-Cybernetics: A New Way to Get More Living Out of Life,* by Maxwell Maltz, MD. Wanting to test his "sobriety," the latest stage in the evolution of a Chylak, he asked Alice to read from it aloud.

Elliott insisted that he could handle it, having just turned ten. Chylak had given him stationery for his birthday, so he could write to his friends in Lebanon about life in "the Coop," which had become a term of endearment. The stationery was monogrammed not with "Selma Wellmix Sanitarium" but with, as requested, "Super Elliott," and included a photo of him: the one Daulton's photographer took at the now notorious game. Elliott read.

> *We marvel at the awesomeness of interceptor missiles which can compute in a flash the point of interception of another missile and "be there" at the correct instant to make contact.*
>
> *Yet, are we not witnessing something just as wonderful each time we see a center fielder catch a fly ball? In order to compute where the ball will fall, or where the "point of interception" will be, he must take into account the speed of the ball, its curvature of fall, its direction, windage . . .*

Elliott paused to ask what "windage" meant. They had reached downtown Cooperstown and Chylak said to look it up in the dictionary when they got home. The boy skimmed down the page, reading with his finger poised as a prompter to get him through "the biggies."

> *He must make these computations so fast that he will be able to "take off" at the crack of a bat. Next, he must compute just how fast he must run, and in what direction in order to arrive at the point of interception at the same time the ball does. The center fielder doesn't even think about this. His built-in goal-striving mechanism computes it for him from data which he feeds it through his eyes and ears. The computer in his brain takes this information, compares it with stored data (memories of other success and failures in catching fly balls). All necessary computations are made in a flash and orders are issued to his leg muscles—and he "just runs."*

"I don't get it," Elliott said, tossing the book down by his feet and turning on the radio. He made puking sounds at Donna Summer who was *lookin' for some hot stuff baby this evenin'*.

"Gimme that," Alice said, reaching from the backseat for the radio knob and turning it rapidly—*They're gonna have to introduce conscription. They're gonna have to take away my prescription* . . .

Chylak turned the volume down. Perhaps it was the crisp autumn air, but he was feeling inspired. "Before we get home, I want to tell you something," he said. Alice crossed her arms over her chest and rolled up the window. Elliott blew a bubble, which popped all over his chin. Chylak interpreted both gestures as grounds to go ahead. "I just wanted to say—well, you're really very incisive little people and—"

"*Daaad,*" Alice said.

Elliott asked how to spell "incisive," which merited another eye-rolling from Alice, who cranked the radio volume up once more—*Careers, careers, careers* . . .

Chylak turned the radio off. He did not need some latent pubescent punks beating him over the head with reminders about prescriptions and vocations. He'd had enough of both all summer. "I just want you both to realize that sometimes people forget one another, even parents. The brain has all sorts of erratic neurotransmitters that—"

"*Daaad,*" they sang in unison.

Chylak blurted it out. "All right! The reason I forgot Elliott at the Hall of Fame that day was not because I don't love him, *both* of you. It was because I was, I had a . . ." He paused, eyeing Alice in the rearview mirror and wishing she would assert her misplaced adolescent authority right about now and turn up the radio again before he embarrassed himself completely. "I had an anxiety attack!"

There, he had said it.

He held his breath and looked in the mirror at his daughter, who was now braiding her hair and yawning, then at his son in the seat next to him, who was casually picking his nose.

"*Pleeease,* darling," Elliott said in his best Paul Lynde voice, which made Alice laugh. "I have those all the time—yayayaya."

"All right, then," said Chylak, patting his son's hand and smiling, tentatively, at Alice in the rearview mirror. "Well . . . we're going to work on that. *Together.*"

"Dad?" Elliott asked.

"Yes, son?"

One child's somewhat undivided attention was better than none. "Did you know there's a disease named after a baseball player?"

"No," said Chylak, though he wasn't surprised. Upon questioning Elliott further, he realized what the boy meant and explained that no, Lou Gehrig's Disease could *not* be contracted from playing baseball, that it was perfectly fine for Elliott to try out for Little League come spring, and that it was technically called amyotrophic lateral sclerosis and thus was more of a *nerve* thing.

As they drove down Fair Street, Alice was back at the radio dial, singing into an annoyed Elliott's ear. Elliott pulled her hair and Chylak threatened to have the radio removed from the car altogether. His son slumped in his seat and his daughter in hers, pouting until Chylak—not wanting to bring Babe home this duo of downers when tonight they were celebrating her new role as director of the church choir—did his best to stumble through the lyrics for their amusement. Eventually, they joined him, singing louder and louder as they reached home.

"*We could steal time! Just for one daaay. We can be heroooes—*"

"Dad, watch out!" Alice yelled as they pulled into the driveway.

Chylak parked the car and stepped out, crouching to inspect the cause of the crunch beneath the tires. He picked up the remains of his secondary snow dome—an unnamed naughty someone who had been told he could play with it, carefully, inside, whenever he liked had apparently taken it *outside,* and its milky, wet remains now dripped down Chylak's arm.

"I'll be in my study," he said, after a long, slow, deep breath, "if anyone needs me."

ACKNOWLEDGMENTS

With heartfelt thanks and utmost gratitude to . . .

My extraordinary agent Amy Williams for her sage counsel, friendship, and continuous faith in her "ADD client"; and my gifted editor, Brett Valley, for taking a chance, telling it like it is, and bringing the characters of *Cooperstown* to life. The Touchstone team: publisher Mark Gompertz, editor in chief Trish Todd, art director Cherlynne Li, publicist Shida Carr, senior production editor Lisa Healy, senior VP and general counsel Elisa Rivlin, the special sales and marketing folks, and for first-rate copyediting, Jane Elias. The irreplaceable Jennifer Gilchrist for early line-edits and umpteen adventures over the years that are bound to inspire more stories.

Various baseball aficionados, particularly Scott Ross, for a better than "bobblehead good" fact-checking job and for helping to authenticate the game scene; Jeffrey Weaver, for periodic research input and for schooling me so long ago in the sport; Mat Blumenthal, for his prompt responses to various research questions; and Kevin Guilfoile, to whom I'm grateful for an early read and insight into the editing process. Ted Spencer, curator and VP of the National Baseball Hall of Fame and Museum, for patiently answering questions about the museum and providing (along with Tom Shieber, curator of new media) me with copies of Abner Graves's letters to the *Akron Beacon Journal* and A. G. Spalding; Glen Perrone at the Clark Estates, for information about the Hall of Fame; Brian Schreckinger, Hall of Fame research intern, for sending me, free of charge, a transcript of Willie Mays's induction speech; Freddy Berowski, Hall of Fame Library research associate, for clarifying certain facts about the Mills Commission and Willie Mays; and Sean Holtz, webmaster of the Baseball Almanac family of sites, for input on Arthur Longbrake.

Cooperstown connoisseurs: Hugh MacDougall, secretary/treasurer of the James Fenimore Cooper Society, for valuable insight on the history of the town, the *Otsego Herald* ordinance, and for the copy of Cooper's *Home as Found,* which I shall cherish; Peter Elkan, my go-to nature guy for input on all things wild; Adam Hurtubise, for confirmation about selected C-town geography and lore, fond reminiscing, and an early read; and Kay Pierro, for confirming the Council Rock myth is probably just that.

Thanks, too, to Ron Swart for key input on U.S. Army enlistment during the Vietnam War. My peeps: Richard Harris and Rebecca Grove, for early reads; Raoul Bhavnani, Amy Ziff, Anton Anikst, and Jennifer Gibson, for constant support and encouragement. Also to Gibby and my other ex-roomie Rohini Runganadhan, for letting me burn the midnight oil in the living room without a single complaint, and for occasionally feeding me snacks. "The Cootches": Amy again, Molly Stern, and Susan Hobson, who have helped turn a mysterious men's sport into a wonderful women's playground.

My former and exceptional day-job editors, Sandy Fernandez at *The Washington Post* and B. J. Sigesmund at *Us Weekly,* for their understanding and encouragement when I had to bury my head deep in the book; Judy Eberhardt, for her friendship and film expertise; and the admirable Alison Bond, who taught me much of what I know about publishing.

My beloved family: my incomparable sister Danielle Elkan, for suggestions on certain characters and street names, and for making childhood in "the Coop" adventurous, hilarious, and imaginative enough to inspire me to grow up and still worship make-believe; my über-keen dad, Eugene Pilek, for valuable and entertaining insight into the world of psychiatry, and for living the motto *"Can you imagine?"* which has been nothing short of inspiring; my always encouraging mom, Beverly Cutting-Pilek, for her immeasurable support, and for fact-checking "the big book"; and to both parents for never once saying I couldn't, or suggesting I seek Plan B. And Greg Swart, my personal touchstone, for his limitless patience, support, and enthusiasm, including occasional aesthetic advice like "Why don't you turn the overhead [light] off when you write? It looks so much better."

I would also like to acknowledge that I took certain liberties regarding the history, landmarks, and geography of Cooperstown and its neighboring towns in the name of what I hope is amusing fiction, as well as with the National Baseball Hall of Fame, a not-for-profit educational trust, including the timing of the Hall of Fame Game and Weekend; the location of the induction ceremony, for dramatic purposes; and certain exhibits that existed in 1979, but had not yet been incorporated into the museum. I drew early inspiration for some Hall of Fame exhibits from the *Baseball As America* tour and tie-in book *Baseball As America: Seeing Ourselves Through Our National Game* (National Geographic, 2002), and those found at the National Baseball Hall of Fame. I'd like to credit writers whose important works provided me with inspiration and valuable background information on Cooperstown, particularly Alan Taylor's *William Cooper's Town: Power and Persuasion on the Frontier of the Early American Republic* (Knopf, 1995), in which I stumbled upon the old map of Cooperstown, William Cooper's "diary" excerpt, certain information about the town's founder and early inhabitants, and the *Otsego Herald* ordinance, indeed a real document, but of little significance at the time. Also regarding the document, James Fenimore Cooper's *Home As Found: A Novel of Social Criticism and Observation* (and a shout-out to *The Last of the Mohicans*). Authors of the various texts cited throughout the Chylak chapters. And last, for insight into Cooper's Bumppo character, the late Nick Alicino's *Character Development in Natty Bumppo,* penned, according to the James Fenimore Cooper Society, for a course at SUNY Oneonta in, coincidentally, 1979.

1.   At the end of the prologue, we are told that Frank "can't stand miss-
     ing history." What history do you believe he is referring to? In what
     sense would he have been missing out?

2.   In the beginning of the book, Chylak has a different opinion about
     the residents of Cooperstown than he does at the end. How do you
     think his opinion changes? What about his outlook, as a psychiatrist,
     on patients?

3.   Discuss the father-son relationships among the residents of Coopers-
     town. Do you see any similarities between these relationships?

4.   Discuss the themes that appear throughout the book—for example,
     communication, the fine line between history and myth, and faith ver-
     sus fanaticism. What other themes are present?

5.   Considering that the town of Cooperstown relies heavily on baseball
     history and attractions for its economic growth, discuss why some res-
     idents in the novel are so against the construction of a baseball theme
     park. Do you agree or disagree with their point of view?

6.   Frank tells the tourists that Cooperstown is "a town built upon myths."
     Manny is described similarly. Discuss the parallels between Manny and
     Cooperstown. How is he representative of Cooperstown's plight?

7.   Pilek tells us that Frank considers Amos and his other pals to be "their
     own inaugural club, the real McCoys, the last of the Mohicans." In
     what way are they representative of a dying breed?

8. In what way is Dusty's self-image satirical, in light of the way society sometimes views women? Is gossip a vehicle for her own self-exploration? Or does she hide behind it?

9. Were the contents of the dreaded document what you expected? Were there any previous passages that may have hinted at what it contained? How destructive could its contents have been for Cooperstown? Knowing what was in it, would you say the actions people took to keep it secret benefited the town or caused more harm than good?

10. If you were in Manny's situation, having gone through all he went through and knowing the secret he knew, would your reaction have been similar? Do you think his departure from baseball was logical?

11. Discuss Daulton's inability to publish what was revealed in the document. If placed in a similar situation, would you have published it?

12. Were you disappointed that Bobby did not end up with Daulton? How were her experiences, despite her hopes, liberating in the end?

13. What do you make of Manny giving the document to Chylak? Why do you believe he preferred to preserve it by passing it along to the town psychiatrist instead of burning it that night with Daulton?

14. Would you say the story's ending is a happy one? Discuss the resolutions that are made at the end of the novel.